CARVER'S QUEST

Nick Rennison is a writer, editor and bookseller. His books include *Sherlock Holmes: An Unauthorised Biography*, *Robin Hood: Myth, History, Culture*, *The Bloomsbury Good Reading Guide* and *100 Must-Read Historical Novels*. He is a regular reviewer of historical fiction for both *The Sunday Times* and *BBC History Magazine*.

CARVER'S QUEST

NICK RENNISON

CORVUS

Published in trade paperback in Great Britain in 2013 by Corvus,
an imprint of Atlantic Books Ltd.

10 9 8 7 6 5 4 3 2 1

A CIP catalogue record for this book is available from the British Library.

Trade paperback ISBN: 978 1 84887 179 3
E-book ISBN: 978 1 78239 036 7

Printed in Great Britain by MPG Printgroup, UK

To my sister Cindy

PART ONE

LONDON

CHAPTER ONE

rouched over the shallow bath of chemicals in his dark room, Adam Carver watched an image begin to appear on the photographic plate resting in it. Slowly, out of the darkness, the ghostly outlines of buildings in a London street emerged. Walls and tiled roofs, silvery grey on the plate, swam into view through the liquid in the tray. Adam gave a brief sigh of pleasure as the picture took shape. It was interrupted by a sudden irruption of light into the small room as the door was thrown open.

'What is it, Quint? I'm busy. And shut that blasted door. The light will spoil the photograph.'

'Some'un to see you.'

'Who is it?'

'A lady.'

'A lady would scarcely call on me here in Doughty Street, Quint. Not alone.'

'Well, maybe she's a lady, maybe she ain't. But she's here. She's in the sitting room.'

Still bent over the photographic equipment, Adam looked over his shoulder. He watched impatiently as Quint closed the door of the dark room, returning it to its usual crepuscular gloom. He heard Quint's footsteps retreating along the passageway. Adam wondered who could possibly be waiting for him in the sitting room. No lady he knew would risk her reputation by visiting a single gentleman in his rooms. And those few women of his acquaintance who were not ladies knew better than to come calling upon him at home. There was but one way to find out, of course. Whoever she was, it was the height of impoliteness to leave her waiting alone.

However, Adam was annoyed to be disturbed. His work had been going so well. In the course of the morning, he had brought three views of London streets from the darkness into the light. If ever he had cause to question what he was doing, a successful session in the dark room was enough to quell his doubts. He was recording the city for posterity, for a future that Londoners in this thirty-third year of Victoria's reign could not imagine. If Macaulay's New Zealander, sitting on the broken arches of Westminster Bridge, were ever truly to gaze out over the ruins of London, then he would have a guide to what had once been. Adam's photographs and those of other pioneers he knew would survive to show the visitor what had been lost. Some friends – Professor Fields for one – had chastised him for deserting archaeology and the classical world for this new pastime of photographing the city's architecture but Adam knew he was, in his own way, still serving the same end. He was assisting the archaeologists of the future. Had the technology existed in the past, what would Fields not give for photographs of Periclean Athens or the Rome of the Caesars?

There was, though, no help for it. He would have to leave his labours and look to learn what this woman wanted. He took the plate from the bath and placed it carefully on the workbench, which ran along one side of the room. He removed the long white frock coat he had taken to wearing to protect his everyday clothing from the chemicals he used, donned the jacket he had been wearing earlier and exited the dark room.

Quint was loitering at the far end of the passageway where the door to the sitting room opened. He pointed a stubby forefinger through the door and mouthed, 'In there,' as if he thought that Adam might have temporarily forgotten where his own sitting room was.

Adam walked through the door with Quint close on his heels. He was both delighted and disconcerted to find that the lady waiting there unchaperoned was a beautiful young woman. A very beautiful young woman. Seated on the only chair in the room that was not covered with old newspapers and magazines, everything about her invited admiring attention. Her auburn hair, which looked unfashionably natural, was long and lustrous and nearly hid the small pillbox hat that was perched in it. Her milky pale complexion clearly owed nothing to powder or cosmetics. Her greenish-blue eyes danced and sparkled with life. Cosmo Jardine, the Pre-Raphaelite painter Adam had known since his schooldays in Shrewsbury, would have had no hesitation in describing her as 'a stunner'.

Faced by her charms, Adam was suddenly conscious of the bachelor disarray in which he lived, of the piles of books strewn around the room and the papers scattered everywhere. He drew his finger through dust that was lying thickly on the table in the centre of the room. To his slight embarrassment, he noticed that his finger was stained with the chemicals he had just been using.

'The place is filthy, Quint. I'm embarrassed that our visitor should see us amidst such squalor.'

Adam bowed slightly towards the woman as he spoke. She acknowledged him with an almost coquettish tilt of her head.

'Well, I ain't got neither the time nor the inclination to be prancing around with a feather duster,' Quint said. 'If you're planning on getting finicky about a bit of dirt, we'd best get a maid.' With that, he turned and walked out of the room.

Adam looked again at the young woman, smiled and shrugged his shoulders. 'Quint,' he said, 'is a temperamental soul. We were both members of an expedition to Macedonia in sixty-seven. We sailed home from Salonika together and he has been with me ever since. I would call him my valet except that, as you see, he has few of the attributes usually associated with a manservant.' Adam smiled again. 'Of course, I have few of the attributes usually associated with a master. So we are well matched.'

'Mr Quint was politesse itself when he showed me to the room, Mr Carver. I can have no complaints on that score.' The woman was perfectly self-possessed and seemed amused rather than upset by the disorder surrounding her. 'And I am not such a dainty housekeeper myself that I am likely to worry over a bit of dust. I have something to discuss with you important enough to make a little domestic disorder seem a trifle in comparison.'

Her English was perfect but Adam noticed that she spoke with just the smallest hint of a foreign accent.

'I am at a loss to know what this business might be, madam.' Adam remained politely puzzled. 'I might wish it were otherwise but I am obliged to confess that I have not had the pleasure of meeting you until now.'

'No, we have not met. But, nonetheless, I know something of you, Mr Carver.'

'Indeed – and what is it that you know? Something that shows me to advantage, I trust?'

'I know that your name is Adam Brunel Carver. That your father was Charles Carver, the railway baron.'

Adam started slightly at the mention of the name. Even now, more than four years after he had watched his father's coffin being lowered into the ground at Kensal Green Cemetery, he disliked reminders of the death. Did the woman, he wondered, know the circumstances in which Charles Carver had departed this world? He doubted it. So few people did. Two of his father's colleagues had made it their business to keep the details from gaining any wider circulation, and burial at Kensal Green would have been impossible had they not succeeded. But it was unlikely this auburn-haired beauty knew anything of that. Indeed, Adam found it difficult to hazard a guess how she knew anything of the Carvers at all. Or why she had arrived at his rooms here in Doughty Street.

'I know that you were obliged to leave Cambridge when your father died,' his visitor continued, 'and that you travelled with Professor Burton Fields in European Turkey. And with Mr Quint, it seems. That you published a book when you returned called *Travels in Ancient Macedon* which made you quite the literary lion.'

Adam had recovered his poise. He laughed. 'The small celebrity I won when my book appeared has lasted little longer than the money the publisher paid me. If I were ever a lion, I have lost my roar these last few months.'

'There are still many people who admire your book very much.'

'Yourself amongst them, I hope, Miss…?' Adam left the question mark over his visitor's name hanging in the air, but the attempt to discover her identity was unsuccessful. She simply ignored it.

'Indeed, I admire your book so much, Mr Carver, that I have put my reputation at risk of compromise by coming here to tell you so myself.'

'I can assure you that no one will know of your visit save myself and Quint. Now, I am the soul of discretion and Quint can keep a secret even in his cups. So your reputation is as safe as the gold in the Bank of England.'

'I am grateful for your assurance, sir.' The woman, sitting demurely amidst the chaos, spoke quietly and apparently seriously, but Adam could not help but notice a hint of half-hidden irony in her voice. 'I thought long and hard before I decided to visit you. I know that perhaps I should have left my card first or come with a chaperone. Or acted in almost any way other than that in which I *have* acted. But I was *so* determined to see you.'

Adam was sensible of the suggestion of play-acting, even insincerity, in his visitor's manner but it was not every day that a beautiful woman expressed determination to see him. He decided that he was happy enough to ignore any doubts he might have about the reasons for her arrival on his doorstep.

'I am sure that your reasons for acting as you have done are important enough to outweigh any minor transgressions of etiquette, madam.'

'You are right. I *do* have important reasons for coming. But, before I vouchsafe them to you, I must tell you something of myself.'

Not a moment before time, Adam thought to himself but he said nothing.

'My name is Emily Maitland. I am not a native of London. Indeed, I have not spent time here since I was a small girl. My mother and I have been abroad for many years. We have made our home in a number of places. Constantinople. Athens. Rhodes. For the last three years we have lived in Salonika. A city which, of course, you know.'

'An unusual city in which to make your home, Miss Maitland.'

Adam was surprised. He recalled the harbour at Salonika and the houses rising gradually from the water up the steep slopes to the castle on the summit. He remembered the white walls of the city and the long stone fingers of the minarets pointing heavenwards. From a distance it was a beautiful sight, but it was also an unhealthy spot with a reputation for malaria. Why would a young woman and her mother choose to live there? Salonika, he remembered, had its small English community, mainly merchants and traders, but he could not believe that it included many women living on their own.

'There are reasons for our choice of Salonika,' Emily said, sensing his surprise, although she made no attempt to reveal what they were. 'We travelled to London in the spring of this year. A distant relative of my father had died and we were beneficiaries in his will. We needed to visit the lawyers to make the proper arrangements to receive our legacy.'

The young woman paused and looked up at Adam. He smiled and made a gesture that he hoped would be interpreted as an encouragement to go on.

'However, I need not trouble you with the details of our family affairs,' she continued. Adam found himself very nearly agreeing with his visitor but he bit his tongue. 'I must hurry on to the point in my story when it will become clear why I have called upon you in so unconventional a fashion.'

Miss Maitland moved her hand across the front of her dress, as if brushing from it a fragment of lint she had just noticed.

'When your expedition arrived in Salonika in the summer of sixty-seven, my mother and I had only just become residents of the city ourselves. We were staying in a hotel by the waterfront. We saw you land from the Constantinople steamer. As you disembarked we could see you were English. We decided that—'

Adam was never to know what Miss Maitland and her mother

had decided. Her words were interrupted by the most terrific uproar from the direction of the dark room. The sound was as if a shell had exploded in a glass factory. As the noise ceased, Adam and his visitor looked at one another in shocked surprise. He was the first to recover composure.

'If you will excuse me for just a moment, I will endeavour to discover what Quint is doing.' He bowed himself out of the room, leaving the woman sitting amidst the disordered books and papers. 'And why he is making that infernal racket as he is doing it,' he added to himself as he left.

He was gone just long enough to learn that Quint, his *amour propre* injured by the remarks about dirt and dust, had been cleaning the equipment in the dark room when several of the glass plates had – of their own volition, according to Quint – crashed to the floor. Lingering only briefly to curse his servant for his clumsiness, Adam made haste to return to the sitting room and his guest.

'I must apologise for Quint. A bull in a china...'

His words dried up as he realised he was addressing an empty room. There was no one sitting in the chair. Emily Maitland was gone.

CHAPTER TWO

The following day found Adam sitting in the Marco Polo Club, listening to Mr Moorhouse talk about whatever subjects flitted briefly through his butterfly mind. The Marco Polo, established in the early 1800s by a group of army officers who had served in India and travelled in the rest of Asia, was not the best-known of London's gentlemen's clubs but it was, its members felt, the most agreeable and, in its own particular way, the most prestigious. Only those who had, at some time in their lives, travelled extensively beyond the comforts of civilisation were allowed membership in the Marco Polo: a little *dilettante* journeying through France or Italy was insufficient qualification for admission. Adam himself had been hard pressed to convince the membership committee that his travels in the mountains of Macedonia had been dangerous and discomforting enough to allow the doors of the Marco Polo to be opened to him. Only the support of the club's secretary, Baxendale, a man who had spent two winters in the 1850s sharing an igloo with a family of Eskimos in northern Canada and was thus able to speak authoritatively on the subjects of danger and discomfort, provided Adam with an entrée. Baxendale had enjoyed *Travels in Ancient Macedon* and let it be known that he believed its author would be a worthy addition to the club's membership roll. Within days of the secretary expressing his opinion, Adam was admitted to the Marco Polo. In the thirteen months since his admission, he had grown to love the club and had spent many happy days in its Pall Mall premises.

Mr Moorhouse, Adam's conversational partner on this particular day, was the oldest member of the club. Many decades before, when Lord Byron had set a fashion for discontented young men of fortune to journey abroad in search of experiences unavailable in England, the 25-year-old Mr Moorhouse had set sail for the Middle East. Landing at the ancient port of Sidon, he had travelled on to Damascus and then set off through the wilds of the Syrian desert, accompanied only by a supposedly faithful Arab servant named Ibrahim. Eighty miles into their journey, Ibrahim had handed Mr Moorhouse over to a Bedouin chieftain in return for two camels and a dozen goatskins filled with water. The Bedouin, delighted to gain a young and handsome Frankish servant for so low a price, had immediately set Mr Moorhouse to work on a series of humiliating, indeed disgusting, tasks about his encampment. It had cost the British consul in Damascus three weeks of negotiation and ten more camels to arrange his countryman's release.

By the time he was free and able to sail home, Mr Moorhouse had been cured permanently of any further desire to leave his native land. Now, more than fifty years after his Levantine adventure, he rarely set foot outside London. He sat for hours in the smoking room of the Marco Polo, puffing contentedly on a succession of foul-smelling cigars and indulging in amiably inconsequential conversation with anyone prepared to join him at his table. Adam found him a curiously relaxing companion.

'Clever fellow, that Boucicault,' Mr Moorhouse remarked out of the blue, after several minutes of silence. 'Saw that play of his, *After Dark*, at the Princess's a couple of seasons ago. Did you see it?'

Adam said he had not had the pleasure.

'Damned great train comes thundering across the stage halfway through it.' Mr Moorhouse made vague, waving motions with his hands to indicate the size of the train. 'Man lying bound to the tracks. Engine getting closer and closer. Train whistle going like billy-o. Terribly exciting. Thought I was going to have conniptions.'

Adam said he was sorry he had missed it.

'Train didn't hit him, though. God knows how. Think I must

have looked away for a second and next thing you know, the man's up and free. Never did work out how the blazes they did it.'

Mr Moorhouse fell silent again, as if he was still struggling to understand the logistical details of the sensational scenes he had seen two years earlier. Adam returned to his own thoughts, many of which circled around the attractive figure of the young woman who had called at Doughty Street the previous day. Who had she really been? Was her name really Emily Maitland? And what had been her purpose in flouting convention so flagrantly by visiting him in his rooms? Although his vanity had been tickled by her claim to be an admirer of his book, he was not sure he believed her. Nor was he sure he believed her interrupted tale of watching the Fields expedition arrive at Salonika's waterfront. The professor, he remembered, had gone out of his way to ensure that they had arrived without fanfare. It was unlikely that she and her mother could have learned their names or that they were English. And why would she knock on his door three years later in order to inform him of the fact that she had seen him in Salonika? It made no sense. He was at a loss to imagine *any* reason for her visit. And, once she was there, why had she left so suddenly and without a word of explanation? Quint's noisy destruction of the plates in the dark room had been a shock, but surely not sufficient to scare a young woman into flight. Certainly not one who seemed so self-possessed as Miss Maitland. Adam was faced with plenty of questions but few answers. After a minute, his companion broke in upon his thoughts.

'By the way, Carver. Almost forgot to tell you. Fellow was in here asking after you last night. Asking if you'd be at the memorial dinner for Speke on Thursday. Told him I thought you would be. Hope you don't mind.'

'Fellow, Mr Moorhouse? What sort of fellow?'

Mr Moorhouse seemed taken aback by the question. 'Tallish chap. Balding.' The old man quickly exhausted his powers of description. 'Don't recall much more about him, to be honest... except, now I come to think of it, he did have a scar you couldn't help noticing. Above his eye. Like a crescent moon. Here.'

Moorhouse pointed to his own brow. 'Sorry, old chap. Hope I haven't committed a faux pas of any kind.'

* * * * *

With Adam at the Marco Polo, Quint Devlin was alone in the rooms in Doughty Street. He had seated himself in the best chair in the sitting room and was busily engaged in packing his favourite pipe with the villainously smelling tobacco he favoured. His intention was to spend the next hour doing nothing more strenuous than inhaling and exhaling it.

Quint had gained his present name one day in 1828, when he was but a month old. Perhaps he had had some other name bestowed upon him before he was discovered, wrapped in a blanket and lying on the steps of the St Nicholas Hospital for Young Foundlings in Ely Place, but if he had, it had been lost. The Reverend Malachi Merridew, spiritual director of St Nicholas, who had been presented with four other orphaned infants that week decided that, as the fifth, this one should be named 'Quintus'. The 'Devlin', more prosaically, had come from the blanket in which the baby had been found. On the blanket was a label which read: 'The property of Devlin's Boarding House, Ardee Street, Dublin'. So it was as Quintus Devlin that the Reverend Merridew presented this particular foundling to the world. The foundling no sooner reached an age when he could speak than he decided that a two-syllable Christian name was simply too cumbersome. Quintus became Quint and had remained so for forty years.

During those forty years, Quint's life had had both its ups and its downs. Downs had included a short spell working the treadmill at the Coldbath Fields House of Correction, after a misunderstanding with another man involving the ownership of a horse; and an even shorter spell spent soldiering in one of the least illustrious regiments of the British Army. Quint had found being a soldier a tiresome business and had deserted after only a month. Luckily, he had taken the precaution of enlisting under a false name. Even more luckily, the name he had chosen had been 'John Smith' and he had decided, quite rightly, that the chances of the army catching up with a deserting John Smith were so negligible that they could be dismissed from his mind. Two days after leaving his barracks in Aldershot without the necessary permission, Quint had been back in familiar haunts in the Borough, renewing his acquaintance with London street life.

If anyone had questioned him, as he sat blowing plumes of smoke in the direction of the bookshelves, he would have acknowledged that his association with Adam Carver represented a very definite up. He might also have acknowledged that the association was an unlikely one. However, Quint was a firm believer in fate. Fate, he thought, had to be behind the events which had brought master and man together. It had surely been fate that had led Quint to join the Fields expedition to European Turkey in the first place. What else would have led him to pick up the discarded copy of a morning newspaper in a Southwark pub? He was not usually a great reader. What else but fate would have drawn his eyes to the advertisement that invited men of stout heart and strong body, interested in shaking the dust of England from their feet, to present themselves at an office in the Marylebone Road at nine on the following morning, where they would learn of certain plans that might prove to their advantage? Money, it was clearly suggested, might be offered to those who possessed the qualities the advertisers sought. Quint had been intrigued. He was unsure whether or not he had a stout heart but he did have a strong body. He was also enduring one of his periodic spells of pennilessness. His creditors, of whom there were several, had begun to insist on payment. One of them, familiarly known as Black Ben, had let it be known that broken bones might well follow failure to cough up. Cash, or the opportunity to leave London – or both – seemed an appealing prospect to Quint. On the principle of 'Nothing ventured, nothing gained', he had decided to turn up at the Marylebone office at the appointed time and see what game the advertisers were playing.

A queue of men who had read the advertisement had already formed outside the office of Mr William Perry, the agent Professor

Fields had appointed to recruit half a dozen dogsbodies for his expedition. Quint was there to join it. While every other man waiting in the line looked like a disgruntled clerk or unemployed shop assistant, he was the only one who could be vaguely described as belonging to the labouring classes. The distinction was a decisive one.

'The gentleman I represent is looking for men of stout heart,' Mr Perry had said, 'men who are unafraid of hard physical labour in the blazing summer sun of distant lands. Not pasty-faced hobblede-hoys who spend their days behind a draper's counter in Holborn.'

In Quint, Mr Perry thought he had found the ideal candidate. He was taken on. The rest of the supplicants were sent packing. The agent was not the first to make the mistaken assumption that Quint's air of surly obstreperousness was only a mask hiding ster-ling qualities beneath it. And so fate decreed that, within a few weeks, together with Professor Fields and Adam Carver, Quint was one of those who shook the dust of England from their feet. Black Ben and the other irritations of London life were left behind as they sailed for Salonika.

Equally surely, Quint had thought, it was fate that dictated that he was on hand to rescue Adam in an alleyway in Salonika when the young man was confronted by four unfriendly Turks demand-ing any piastres he had about his person. Adam, who had boxed for his college only a few months earlier, succeeded in knocking two of his assailants to the ground, but weight of numbers began to tell. He was facing a beating from the other two when Quint provi-dentially turned the corner into the muddy backstreet. The Turks were significantly heavier than the Englishmen, but Quint had ear-lier decided, soon after the party had reached Salonika, never to walk anywhere in the city without a billy stick to hand. The billy stick, especially when wielded with enthusiasm, changed the odds in the fight in favour of the visitors. The Turks were swiftly ren-dered unconscious. Adam's piastres remained in his pocket. He and Quint, who had hitherto taken little notice of one another, now formed an alliance. Months later, in the mountains south of the city,

Adam had been able to return the compliment. Quint had tumbled from his mule and into a fast-flowing river. He would have been swept halfway to the Thermaic Gulf had Adam not hauled him from the waters. The unlikely partnership between the two men was strengthened. Quint came to be seen by others in the party as Adam's man.

When the expedition returned to London, Adam had suggested that he had a vacancy for a manservant and that Quint might be just the person to fill it. Quint, behaving as if he would be bestowing a favour on Adam if he accepted the post, had agreed. Adam duly availed himself of the money that John Murray had advanced for the privilege of publishing *Travels in Ancient Macedon*, and man and master had moved into the rooms in Doughty Street. They had been there for nearly two years and the arrangement seemed to suit them both.

None of this past history crossed Quint's mind as he smoked his pipefuls of noxious tobacco. At such times as this, he had a capacity for tranquil existence in the present moment that would have been the envy of an oriental sage. For nearly an hour, he was troubled by nothing more than the need to tamp down or refill his pipe at regular intervals. As midday arrived, however, and he listened to the sound of the mantle clock striking the hours, he became aware that something was wanting to complete his happiness. A smoke, he thought, was nothing without a drink. It was time to make his way towards the Lion and Lamb. Quint walked from the sitting room to the small side room which was exclusively his domain. He picked up the blue serge jacket that was lying on the bed and put it on. Thrusting his dowsed pipe into one of the pockets, he left the room and headed for the stairs that led from the first-floor flat to the ground floor.

As he began to descend those stairs to the hallway, he saw that someone was standing in the ill-lit passage. To his dismay, he realised that it was Mrs Gaffery. Mrs Gaffery, courtesy of her late husband's will, was the owner of 65 Doughty Street. Unfortunately, ownership of the property was all that Mr Gaffery, a solicitor with a small practice in Chancery Lane, had been able to leave his wife. Unwise investment in an Australian gold mine which, on closer inspection, had proved to contain very little gold, had eaten up all his other worldly goods. After his death, his relict had no means of support at all. She had been obliged to let the upstairs rooms of her property to paying tenants while she continued to live on the ground floor. She had been forced to become a landlady. It was not a situation that either Mrs Gaffery or many of her tenants enjoyed.

Mrs Gaffery's loss had occurred many years earlier yet her already formidable appearance continued to be made even more tremendous by the mourning clothes of black crape and bombazine which she still wore. Unkind rumours suggested that, during his lifetime, Mr Gaffery had been a severe disappointment to his wife. His last will and testament had certainly been so. However, now that he had long been a member of the great majority, his faults had been forgotten. It seemed that Mrs Gaffery, like the queen, was determined to advertise her status as a widow until she followed him to the grave herself. Now, black and unmistakeably threatening, she stood in Quint's path.

'Women,' she said. 'I won't have them.'

Quint's method of dealing with Mrs Gaffery was the same one he employed to deal with any social superior likely to trouble him. He feigned idiocy. If he had been able to feign cheery idiocy, he would have done so on the grounds that it was more likely to produce the results he wanted. However, Quint being Quint, he was obliged to feign surly idiocy. Over the years he had found that even surly idiocy was remarkably effective in persuading people in any kind of authority that he wasn't worth questioning or bothering any further. Faced with an apparently furious landlady, wagging her forefinger in his direction, he simply grunted and stared fixedly at the wainscoting. The storm, he knew, would eventually pass over his head.

'Not in my house. Not under my roof. Flibbertigibbets flaunting their shamelessness. They have fewer morals than a pack of Pawnee Indians, the lot of them.'

Quint continued to gaze floorwards. He had been puzzled by

Mrs Gaffery's opening remark but he had now worked out that it was the visit of the mysterious young lady that had disturbed her sense of propriety. He could think of nothing useful to say so he remained silent. Mrs Gaffery's outrage continued to erupt around his ears. Quint waited for it to pass and eventually sensed that it was reaching its conclusion.

'... and you can tell your master that from me. Tell him there shall be no more women coming calling upon him at all hours of the day. Or he shall hear more from me. Much more. You tell him that, Quint. Do you understand me, man?'

Quint grunted again. Taking the grunt as an indication that her words had hit home, Mrs Gaffery turned and retired to her lair. Quint, grateful that his ordeal had been a short one, continued on his interrupted journey towards a pint of India Pale Ale.

* * * * *

Standing under the portico of the British Museum, Adam looked towards Great Russell Street and the traffic passing down it. It was a few minutes after ten on a Wednesday morning and, behind him, the doors of the museum, which welcomed members of the public only on alternate weekdays, had just opened. He was waiting for Professor Fields, who had despatched a letter to say that he was coming up to town from Cambridge that morning. 'There is an Attic vase from the bequest of Sir Charles Tankerville that has been newly put on display,' the professor had written, 'and I am particularly eager to see it. You would also find it of interest and I propose that you should meet me at the entrance to the museum prompt at ten.'

The letter was, Adam thought, typical of Fields's somewhat peremptory style of correspondence. There was no suggestion that the young man might have other plans which might conflict with the professor's. He had been summoned to appear and appear he must. The fact that Fields himself was not in evidence prompt at ten was not unexpected. The professor was also given to issuing strict instructions for behaviour and comportment which he then failed to follow himself.

Adam pulled out his watch on its silver Albert chain from his waistcoat pocket. It was nearly ten past ten. He glanced idly at the small stream of visitors climbing the steps to the entrance of the museum and then looked towards Great Russell Street once more. He felt a small surge of affection as he picked out the sturdy figure of the professor turning into the grounds of the museum and heading in his direction. Fields could be difficult and argumentative and irritating, it was true, but he had become an important person in Adam's life. Thomas Burton Fields had been a senior master at Shrewsbury School, and was already a legendary figure when Adam had arrived as a timid thirteen-year-old boy from his prep school. Fields had seen something in him, had encouraged his burgeoning love for Greek and Latin and for the long-vanished civilisations of the Mediterranean. When Fields had left Shrewsbury to accept a professorship at Cambridge, Adam had been lost but he had followed his mentor to the university only a year later. The death of his father and the consequent change in his financial fortunes had ruined his hopes of a life in academe, but Fields had been on hand to rescue him. Although Adam had found it necessary to go down from Cambridge without taking his degree, the professor had arranged for him to join him on his expedition to European Turkey. In many ways, Thomas Burton Fields had been a second father to him.

'We must make our way to the Tankerville Vase immediately,' the professor said, as he strode up the steps. He made no attempt at a formal greeting and spoke as if it was Adam's fault that they had not been able to enter the museum the moment it opened. 'Doubtless there will be hordes of gawking visitors in front of it already.'

Adam thought it unlikely that an Attic vase would draw the crowds Fields was anticipating.

'Should we not first take a side turning into the Elgin Gallery?' he asked teasingly, knowing what the answer would be.

'Those marble statues are much overrated,' the professor said dismissively. 'I would exchange all of them for the finest examples of Athenian red-figure wares.'

'Or the Phigalian Saloon? The bas-reliefs from the Temple of Apollo are much admired.'

'They are even worse than the works Elgin prised off the Parthenon. No – we are here to see the Tankerville Vase.'

As Adam had anticipated, there was nobody in front of the case that held the vase. Both men bent double to peer more closely at the decoration.

'It is unmistakeably a depiction of the Centauromachy,' the professor said. 'The same subject that appears on some of the sculptures you mentioned earlier but a purer, more authentic rendition of it. I had read that this was so but I wished to see for myself.'

They continued to examine the tiny figures on the pottery.

'This must be Peirithoos, the king of the Lapiths. Yes, the lettering makes it clear.'

'And these are the drunken centaurs,' Adam remarked, pointing to the half-men and half-horses reeling across the vase's bulging middle.

'An illustration of the dangers of inebriation.'

'Never allow a centaur more drink than it can hold,' the young man said.

'A lesson that Peirithoos learned to his cost.' Fields straightened and stood up. 'I am pleased to have seen this but I cannot linger over it as long as I would like. I have another appointment.'

Adam, directed so autocratically to meet his mentor, could not help feeling exasperated that the professor was hastening away so swiftly.

'I had hoped to have longer to speak with you, sir.'

'Of course you did, my boy. But it was not to be. You have seen the Tankerville Vase and that must suffice.'

'You will not be able to dine with me tonight?'

Fields waved a hand, as if to suggest that the very idea of dinner was ludicrous. 'I must return to college.'

The two men made their way back through the museum towards the entrance.

'I believe that I *shall* make a diversion here and see the Phigalian

Marbles,' Adam said, as they reached a door to another gallery. 'So we must go our separate ways.'

He held out his hand and Fields took it. 'We will see one another again soon, Adam. Of that I am certain.'

Several inches shorter than his one-time pupil, the professor looked up at Adam's face as if scanning it for signs of continued irritation. He let go of his hand and smoothed the thinning hair on the top of his head. Then he turned abruptly and marched briskly in the direction of the door to the outside world. Adam watched him go, his annoyance slowly fading, and then turned to enter the gallery on his right. He would see how the battle between the Centaurs and the Lapiths appeared in marble.

CHAPTER THREE

On the evening of the Speke dinner, held to commemorate the achievements of the late African explorer and member of the Marco Polo, Adam asked the cabman to drop him at one end of Pall Mall. It was a fine night and he wanted, however briefly, to take the air. As he strolled up the street towards the entrance to the club, he was in a cheerful mood. The world in general, and London in particular, seemed to be filled with the promise of pleasure and enjoyment. Entering the door to the Marco Polo, with its mosaic portrait of the Venetian traveller above the portico, Adam was immediately aware of the hurly-burly of what had become, in a few brief years, one of the busiest events in the club's social calendar.

As he paused just inside the threshold of the main room and looked around, he caught sight of himself in a large, extravagantly framed mirror that hung on a wall to his right. His spirits still high, he liked what he saw. Tall and well built, he filled out the evening dress he was wearing. His black hair shone with the macassar oil he had applied earlier. He looked, he decided, exactly as a fashionable young man in the greatest metropolis on earth should look. He turned to face a room of men all dressed like himself. Of all ages, from fresh-faced youth to bewhiskered maturity, the members of the Marco Polo seemed to Adam, in his elevated mood, a happy band of brothers. He was inspired by a feeling of collegiate attachment to them all. Here, he thought, were some of the most enterprising men of the day. The kind of men whose spirit made the country great. Here were men who had ventured into the furthest corners of the known and unknown world. Here were men whose travels around the globe made his own journeys in Turkey in Europe seem small beer in comparison.

Filled with the glow of comradeship and admiration, he moved further into the room. Instantly, he was caught up in the crush. In a moment he had, it seemed, lost his own power of volition and was obliged to surrender to the movements of the crowd, which pitched him back and forth across the room from one group of people to another. Around him swirled the curious fragments of a dozen conversations. To his left, a peppery little man was squinting upwards at the much taller man by his side and spluttering with indignation.

'Damn Landseer and his wretched lions. I've seen real lions in Africa and those beasts in Trafalgar Square are all wrong.'

'Bit of artistic licence, old man,' his companion suggested.

'Damn his artistic licence. If a man's going to sculpt a lion, it should bloody well look like a lion, if you ask me.' The peppery little man looked furious that the artist hadn't taken the trouble to ask him.

To Adam's right, a red-faced man kept saying, 'I don't believe it. I don't believe it.'

'No, Montagu, I swear to you, it is the truth,' the man with him said. 'The whole truth and nothing but the truth. I have it on the highest authority. Absolutely unimpeachable authority.'

'Well, I still don't believe it,' Montagu said. 'It's not *possible* to believe it. You'll be telling me next that Franklin is fit and well after twenty-five years and sharing his life with a little Eskimo bride.'

'He probably is, old man. And enjoying it more than he would London society with Lady Jane.'

Whirled through the throng, Adam was finally catapulted out of it into a part of the room where the crowds were thinner and it was possible to walk freely. In front of him was a languidly drooping young man, wearing a monocle, a moustache and a look of snooty disdain.

'Wemarkable! Weally quite wemarkable!'

The languid man was talking to an older and plumper companion.

Adam found it difficult to decide whether his speech impediment was natural or affected.

'Weginald Womilly was welating this extwaordinawy stowy about a woman he met in Wussia. Appawently, she…'

Adam was never to know exactly what the woman in Russia did because the speaker and his friend passed out of earshot. A faint fragrance of perfumed oil lingered after them. Adam's attention was now caught by the approach of Mr Moorhouse.

Mr Moorhouse's ancient dress coat was spectacularly creased; he looked as if several hefty men had recently forced him to the floor and sat upon him.

'Is he here, Mr Moorhouse?'

'Is who here, Carver?'

'The man who was asking for me.'

'Asking for you?'

Adam felt his patience with the forgetfulness of the elderly departing but summoned it back. 'The gentleman who visited the club last week and asked if I was there.'

'Ah!' Mr Moorhouse's face could have been used as an illustration of sudden enlightenment. 'Creech.'

'Creech?'

'His name is Samuel Creech.'

'I don't remember you telling me the name last week, Mr Moorhouse.' Try as he might to disguise it, Adam could feel a note of exasperation enter his voice. Mr Moorhouse did not appear to notice it.

'Didn't know it then, old boy. Baxendale's only just introduced me to the fellow. They're both over there. Somewhere.' The old man waved vaguely at the throng. 'Oh, I say, there's that bounder Burton over by the door,' he went on. 'Surprised he has the gall to turn up at a dinner for Speke, when you think what went on between them.' Mr Moorhouse's commentary was interrupted by a deep boom that echoed around the room. 'Ah, there goes the gong. Better move along, I suppose.'

The reverberation was heard twice more. The gong was one

that had been appropriated from a Buddhist temple in Kandy sixty years earlier by a founding member and brought back to London. Since then, it had been used to summon the members of the Marco Polo Club to dinner. As the echoes of its third rumble echoed in their ears, they began to troop into the large, wood-panelled hall in which their formal dinners were held.

* * * * *

The man serving at Adam's table was clearly unaccustomed to his duties. Instead of appearing discreetly and quietly at the diner's elbow to offer each dish, and then retiring, he arrived amidst a clatter of clashing plates and serving spoons. He then remained within touching distance of the table long after diners had helped themselves, as if intent on joining the conversation at an opportune moment. On two occasions during the opening courses, Adam's neighbour on his left irritably waved the man away, only for him to reappear seconds later, thrusting forward further plates of food with a threatening air.

Adam spent the first twenty minutes of the meal in conversation with Hoathly, a retired army officer, whose account of his travels in the Gold Coast had briefly excited the public a decade earlier. Hoathly was telling him, in greater detail than was necessary, about the funeral rites of the Ashanti. From time to time, Adam glanced at the man to his left who had finally persuaded the inexperienced waiter to keep his distance and was talking to his neighbour, a bearded giant who, Adam remembered reading in the press, had returned last year from a plant-hunting expedition up the Orinoco. What was the Orinoco man's name? Dawson? Davidson? As Hoathly prosed on in the background about death on the Gulf of Guinea, Adam struggled to recall. Dodson, that was it. William Dodson. He had just published a book entitled *Plant-Collecting Along the Lower Orinoco*, which Adam had seen in the window of Hatchards only the other day. It sometimes seemed as if every member of the Marco Polo apart from Mr Moorhouse had published at least one book about his travels. There was little wonder that Adam's own opus had long since ceased to attract attention. The competition was too much for it.

'Of course, when the king is buried, the sacred stool is ritually blackened and...'

Hoathly was still talking about the Ashanti. The man to Adam's left had now finished his conversation with Orinoco Dodson. He turned to his right.

'Your name is Carver,' he said, with an abruptness that suggested Adam had been disputing this. 'My name is Samuel Creech.'

Now that the man had turned towards him, Adam could see the distinctive scar above his eye that Mr Moorhouse had described.

'It is a coincidence that we should be seated next to one another, Mr Creech. I understand from my friend Mr Moorhouse that you have been asking for me.'

'It is no coincidence. I arranged it with Baxendale. I have matters of the highest importance to discuss with you.' Creech lowered his voice. 'I would have spoken to you before now but I could not persuade this gentleman to cease from his prattle of South American orchids.'

'I'm delighted to think that I might have some connection with matters of the highest importance,' Adam said. 'But I cannot, for the life of me, guess what they might be.'

'It is simple enough, Mr Carver. You went with Burton Fields to Macedonia, did you not?'

'I did indeed.'

'I believe you also did some travelling on your own account.'

'A little.'

'I think I recall from reading your book that you found shelter in several villages south of Salonika.'

'I did.'

'Koutles? Barbes? Do I recall the names correctly?'

'I'm flattered, Mr Creech. You have obviously read my book with great attention.' Adam smiled amiably at his neighbour. He was beginning to wonder where the conversation was leading. 'I can scarcely remember the villages in question myself.

They were little more than collections of filthy hovels.'

'But you were there for several days?'

'Yes, we saw the sun come up over the shanties on more than one occasion. Not quite Homer's *rhododaktylos eos*, as I recall.'

Creech, who clearly did not recognise the quotation, stared at the young man for a moment as if he thought he might have been taken suddenly ill.

'The dawn was not exactly rosy-fingered in Koutles,' Adam explained.

'Ah, of course. It is many years since I have read Homer.' Creech dismissed Adam's remarks with a shake of the head and continued with his interrogation. 'Professor Fields was not with you when you visited the two villages?'

'No – Fields stayed in our encampment further north.'

'No one was with you during your visit?'

'Only Quint. Only my servant.'

Adam was growing ever more puzzled by Creech's questions. Why, he wondered, was he interested in Koutles and Barbes, which Adam recollected only as dirty and impoverished villages he was glad to leave?

'A very great secret lies hidden in the hills where you travelled, Mr Carver.' Although he was still speaking in the ordinary, restrained tones of dinner-table conversation, Samuel Creech was clearly filled with barely repressed excitement.

He glanced over his shoulder, as if to see whether or not the over-eager waiter was still nearby, and then lowered his voice until it was little more than a fierce whisper. Adam had to strain to hear it above the din of the Marco Polo club dining room. 'It is a secret that has been lost in darkness for centuries. But I know of a manuscript that can bring it back into the light. Its revelation will be a sensation.'

Adam looked at his neighbour with surprise. There was an almost unhinged intensity to the way he spoke. He had seized Adam's arm in his agitation.

'What would this sensational secret be?' the young man asked after a pause. He looked down rather pointedly at Creech's hand on his arm. The older man let go his hold. 'What is it that lies hidden in the hills?'

'I can say no more here. Even in the Marco Polo, the walls may have ears. Perhaps especially in the Marco Polo.' Again Creech looked about him as if he suspected persons unknown were loitering with the intent of robbing him of his secret. 'But I need your assistance, Mr Carver. I need your knowledge of the region. No Briton has travelled there more extensively or more recently than you.'

'I will certainly offer any advice I can.'

'I have made several journeys into Turkey in Europe myself,' Creech said, 'but I have never been so far north as you and Fields.'

'Perhaps you should speak to the professor rather than me,' Adam said casually, still puzzled by the fervour with which his dining companion spoke. 'His knowledge of the hills of Macedon far outstrips mine.'

Creech waved his hand impatiently, as if the idea of speaking to Fields was one that he had considered and long ago dismissed. 'I have already consulted with those whose knowledge of the region is of the bookish variety; those who can tell me what it was in classical times. I need someone who knows the lie of the land as it is now.'

'As I say, sir, I will offer you what advice I can.'

'I want more than advice, Mr Carver. Not only do you know the area, you have archaeological training. I want you to join me in mounting an expedition to Koutles and Barbes. We must dig to reveal the sensation.'

There was a silence as Adam considered what it was that this strange man wanted from him.

'I am not sure that I can oblige you, Mr Creech,' he said eventually. 'I have work and interests in plenty to keep me here in London. I am not at all certain I wish to roam the wilds of Macedonia again.'

'You must join me.' Creech spoke as if these words settled the matter. 'Come and visit me at my house. Herne Hill Villa. It is on the left on the road that leads up the hill. Next Thursday at two in the afternoon. I will tell you more then. Believe me, Mr Carver, this is the most important opportunity that life has offered you so far. You must not spurn it.'

Having said, it seemed, what he wished to say, Creech turned back to the bearded giant and began to talk to him of carnivorous plants and their habits. Adam was now ignored. Only at the end of the meal did Creech turn to him again. He raised his glass of dessert wine. 'To the secrets of Macedonia, Mr Carver.'

Adam reached out his hand for his own glass. He hesitated briefly, as if doubtful of the proposed toast. Then he picked it up and touched it briefly against Creech's.

'The secrets of Macedonia, Mr Creech.'

CHAPTER FOUR

everal days passed and Adam found his mind turning frequently to Samuel Creech and to the secret the man claimed was hidden in the Macedonian hills. Adam remembered the country through which he and Quint had travelled two years earlier. He remembered it only too well. Could there really be something of value to be found in the ramshackle collections of hutches and hovels that made up Koutles and Barbes? What else had there been there? The surrounding countryside had been unusual, it was true. Covered with tumuli that had reminded him slightly of the long barrows to be found in the West Country. Had Fields spoken of them? He recalled that his friend and mentor had said that the French had dug in them recently but found very little. What could Creech know that those French archaeologists did not? The villages themselves had been habitations from a nightmare.

Adam remembered the scene when he had ridden into Koutles, Quint twenty yards behind him, grumbling relentlessly about the heat and the flies. He could close his eyes and immediately bring to mind the dirt and the degradation. The men and women, in filthy clothing, staring at them with undisguised suspicion. The sullen children, old beyond their years, who refused to return his smiles. It had taken an hour of negotiation with the *proestos*, the village headman, to win them even a place to stay for the night. They had been obliged to bed down in a poor cottage where eight people and two goats had huddled together in the same room to sleep.

The following morning, no one had been prepared to admit to

possession of any food. Requests for eggs, chickens, even bread and milk, had been met with denials that the villagers had any for themselves, never mind any to spare for idle travellers. The goats with which they had shared accommodation were, according to the *proestos*, dry and could give no milk. Used to the open-armed hospitality that most Greek villages had extended to them, Adam had been disturbed by the hostility at Koutles. He had hated the place, and he and Quint had lost no time in leaving it behind them the following day. Barbes, another wretched village built of mud and faggots, had been little more welcoming when they had passed through it. Why should Samuel Creech care a fig about Koutles and Barbes? Or wish to enlist the assistance of someone who had travelled there?

* * * * *

In the Chelsea studio of his friend, Cosmo Jardine, Adam was able to relax. He and Jardine had known one another both at Shrewsbury, where they had shared a study, and at Cambridge, where, although they had attended different colleges, they had met for dinner at least twice a week. Since Adam's return to London, the two men had fallen into an easy habit of association. Weeks might pass in which they saw nothing of one another but Adam knew that he was always welcome to call whenever he liked at the house in Old Church Street, which Jardine shared with two other impecunious artists.

'What is this masterpiece in the making?' Adam asked, indicating a small canvas propped on an easel in one corner of the room.

Jardine, wearing a loose-fitting white smock over his everyday clothes and carrying palette in one hand and brush in the other, was looking more like a *Punch* caricature of an artist than any real painter should.

'An oil sketch for my grand Arthurian work: *King Pellinore and the Questing Beast.*'

Jardine walked across his studio and joined Adam in front of the easel. The two men stood for a while side by side, staring at the helmeted head of a medieval knight.

'It is all wrong,' Jardine said at last. 'I need a model. I have even been thinking of asking you to sit for Pellinore, Carver.'

'My dear fellow, I would as soon be the Questing Beast. Although I wish you well in your chosen career and I would help if I could. Anyway, if you recall, I have already sat for my portrait. And it provided you with your only success at last year's Academy show.'

'Even though it was skied and one needed the neck of a giraffe to see it. Clearly you bring me luck.'

'However, I draw the line at impersonating an Arthurian warrior.'

'Ah, well. It was just a thought.'

The two men stood a little longer in front of the canvas, each wrapped up in his own thoughts. Jardine was the first to break the silence.

'I am to take tea with Mr Millais on Saturday.' The young painter was unable to disguise the hint of smug delight in his voice. Adam laughed.

'You are the most infernal name-dropper, Jardine. You speak as if this were some intimate tête-à-tête with Millais. Yet both you and I know that it is nothing but a regular "at home", and there will be a dozen aspiring artists at least dancing attendance on the great man.'

'None the less, I spoke no more than the truth. I shall take tea with the "great man", as you choose to call him.'

'You will be lucky to exchange more than a greeting and a farewell with him.' Adam looked across at his friend, noting the self-satisfied smile that had appeared on his face. 'Besides, I do believe that you go to see Mrs Millais rather than her husband.'

'And why not? She is a beautiful woman, Carver. Who would not want to feast his eyes upon her?'

'She is married and she is fifteen years your senior, Jardine. I think perhaps your chances of a romance are limited.'

'Ah, but she is a stunner none the less.'

'I am pleased to hear that Mrs Millais is as lovely as rumour paints her,' Adam said, taking a cigarette case from his pocket, then extracting a cigarette and lighting it. Smoke drifted upwards, obscuring the image of King Pellinore on the canvas. 'So many of these famous beauties are fabulous in the report but disappointing in person.'

'Not necessarily the case, old man. I saw Skittles once riding in the park,' Jardine said. 'Several years ago now. She was quite as handsome as even her most besotted admirer might claim.'

'Ah, the legendary Miss Walters. The most practised of the capital's courtesans. Or so I am told.'

'I have often wondered about the origin of her sobriquet. Why Skittles? I have asked myself.'

'She once worked in a bowling alley off Park Lane, I understand.'

'The explanation is as simple as that, is it? Well, like Effie Millais, she was a stunner.'

Jardine moved suddenly away from his failed likeness of King Pellinore and began to pace around the small studio, as if measuring its dimensions.

'By the by,' he said over his shoulder, 'while we are on the subject of feminine beauty, you must tell me more of the enigmatic charmer you mentioned the other day. The lady who came calling upon you. The lady who vanished.'

'There is no more to tell. She arrived unheralded and she departed as mysteriously as she arrived. I was away but a few moments to deal with Quint and his attempts to destroy my dark room. When I returned, she was gone.'

'You must have driven her away, Carver. A remark out of place. A breach of etiquette. You were ever a blunderer where the more ornamental sex is concerned.'

'Thus speaks the Lothario of Old Church Street, I suppose. You would no doubt have me believe that you would have won her heart in a matter of moments.' Adam was smiling at his friend's words as Jardine continued to walk restlessly around the room. 'I had no chance to exercise any charms I may possess. She was gone before I could attempt it. However, I can assure you that none of my remarks was out of place. And any breach of etiquette was entirely hers.'

The painter had returned once more to his canvas and was staring closely at it.

'It is no good,' he said, taking a step back from it. 'It looks more like the *carte de visite* of a provincial solicitor than it does the portrait of a medieval knight.' The young artist made a gesture as if he was about wipe his canvas clean immediately. 'Photography has caused much damage to the fine arts. Even I am not insusceptible to its malign influence.'

'You should be careful of remarks like that, Jardine. It is bad artists who belittle photography. They do so in the same way that stagecoach proprietors used to decry the dangers and inconveniences of travelling by the railway.'

Jardine, his head cocked to one side, was examining his painting from a different angle.

'Aha, we are embarking on that old argument again, are we?' he said. 'It threatens to become stale, Carver.'

'I tell you, Jardine, photography is the art of the future. The easel and the palette belong to the past'

'My dear fellow, we shall have to agree to disagree. As for me, I shall stick with my brushes and my oils.'

Adam turned his back on the painting of King Pellinore and made his way towards the small rosewood table in the corner of the studio where the painter kept a cut glass decanter of whisky.

'Actually, I have no wish to argue with you. I have enough to puzzle my poor head at present. The lady who disappeared is not the only mystery I have encountered. I seem to have stumbled into another of late.'

'Well, waste no time in setting it before me, Carver. I have a devilish liking for mysteries. Especially those which involve beautiful young damsels in possible distress.'

'Unfortunately, this one does not. Do you mind if I pour myself a drink?'

Jardine made a gesture to indicate that his friend should help himself to the contents of the decanter. Adam, splashing a generous measure of spirits into the glass, first raised it towards the artist in a mock toast and then drank from it.

'The circumstances surrounding it have been plaguing my mind for the last few days. It began with a gentleman, unknown to me, calling at my club more than a week ago.'

As Jardine nodded and made small noises of surprise or encouragement, Adam unfolded events at the Speke dinner and the story his odd neighbour at the table had told him. When he had finished, the painter remained silent, stroking his beard like an actor playing the part of a man in deep thought.

'I do believe I know this fellow Creech,' he said at last.

Adam looked across at his friend in surprise.

'Yes, I am almost certain it must be he who came calling upon me the other day in search of a painting to buy. He said he had been recommended to visit my humble studios by Burne-Jones. This surprised me since I don't suppose I have exchanged ten words with Burne-Jones in my entire life. It pains me to admit this but the name of Cosmo Jardine probably means as little to him as the name of, let us say, Adam Carver.'

'Your days of anonymity are doubtless numbered, Jardine. Your fame will soon spread beyond the boundaries of Chelsea.'

The artist bowed his head in ironic acknowledgement of the compliment.

'However, I am about to deepen your little mystery rather than solve it. The man who came to me was exactly as you describe him. The telling detail of the crescent moon scar on the brow surely proves it was he. And yet he was not calling himself Creech.'

'He was not?'

'No,' Jardine said, 'he introduced himself to me as a Dr Sinclair, recently returned to London after a long period spent healing the expatriate sick in Florence. I had no reason to doubt him. Of course, he knew nothing of art. Even though he had lived in Florence, it was clear that he could not tell a Whistler from a Watteau. But then, few of my few patrons could. In the event, he failed to join the select list of those who have acknowledged the genius of Cosmo Jardine with pounds, shillings and pence. He bought nothing.'

'But why was he calling upon you at all?'

'There is, I suppose, the smallest of possibilities that he was doing what he claimed to be doing. Looking to purchase a painting from one of London's most promising artists.'

'While calling himself Dr Sinclair, the physician returned from Italian exile?'

'Perhaps he really is Sinclair. Perhaps it is Creech that is the assumed name.'

'No,' Adam said, 'there is not the slightest of chances that he could become a member of the Marco Polo under a false name. It is difficult enough for a man to gain admittance under his real one.'

'Well, the problem has me floored.' Jardine was losing interest in the question of his caller's identity, his eyes returning to the picture propped on his easel. 'I would not have minded him calling himself the Earl of Derby or Giuseppe Garibaldi or even the Daring Young Man on his Flying Trapeze if only he had bought one of my paintings.'

'Things are bad?'

'Atrocious. I am suffering from a chronic atrophy of the purse. Ruin stares me in the face. If I don't find someone soon who is prepared to invest in my work and thus bring in the lucre, I will be forced to give up art altogether.'

'And what a loss that would be!'

'You may mock, Carver, but I am entirely serious. I shall be driven to such a desperate act by want of money.'

'What on earth would you take up in its place?'

Jardine shrugged. He picked up a brush, dipped it in one of the paints on his palette and dabbed at his canvas.

'Who knows? Journalism, perhaps? I could work as a penny-a-liner for the papers. I have an uncle who knows Sala on the *Telegraph*. Perhaps he can help me.'

'The job would destroy your soul in weeks, old man.'

'Then I shall be obliged to sail down under and skin sheep in New South Wales for a living.'

'The climate would not suit you. And the society there would not meet your exacting standards.'

'Very probably not. In which case, I must marry a woman with money.'

'Do you know any women with money?'

'Nary a one. But I am willing to devote time to winning the acquaintance of some.'

Adam continued to watch as Jardine moved back and forth in front of his work, occasionally putting paint to canvas.

'Was he making enquiries about me?' he asked after a moment's silence.

'What's that, old man?' The artist's attention had returned almost entirely to King Pellinore.

'Did Creech ask you anything about me?'

'Not that I can recall. Why should we have been talking about you, old chap? Your egotism grows intolerable. There are other subjects for conversation besides your good self, you know. We spoke of art. Or, rather, I did, and Sinclair-Creech had the manners and sense to listen.'

The two men fell silent. Jardine was mixing colours on his palette and Adam was raising his glass occasionally to his lips. After a few minutes, the painter heaved a great sigh of exasperation and threw his palette to the floor. He watched as it skittered towards the corner of his studio, depositing further splashes of colour on the already paint-stained boards.

'Damn this wretch Pellinore! He continues to look far more suburban than he does medieval.' Jardine wiped his hands on his smock. 'I have been imprisoned in this place long enough. I must break my bonds and seek out new entertainments. You will join me in a debauch this evening?'

'What kind of a debauch had you in mind?' Adam asked.

'Let us go and watch the mutton walk in the Alhambra.'

'It is a Tuesday. It will be a poor night to visit.'

'Gammon and spinach! Any night of the week, there are dozens of beauties in silks and satins trotting through its gallery.'

'The kind of beauties that can be bought.'

'Of course they can be bought. And sold. What else do you expect? Don't be such a damned prig, Adam.'

'I must confess to finding it a dispiriting spectacle these days,

Cosmo. The women half-dressed and the men half-drunk.'

'Ah, well, if you are not in the mood... You have to be in the mood for the mutton walk. That I will allow.' The young painter changed the subject. 'Do you ever meet any men from college these days?' he asked.

'Hardly a one. Since I returned from Salonika, I have lived a quiet and retiring life chez Gaffery. Mellor and Hickling must have learned of my presence in town. Lord knows how. But they left their cards at Doughty Street. I am ashamed to admit that I made no effort to see them. How about you?'

'I dine with Watkins and a few others at my club from time to time. And I ran across Chevenix the other day.'

'Chevenix? That was that wretched little tuft-hunter, wasn't it? Forever sucking up to any man with a title to his name?'

'That's the man.'

'What did he want?'

'Nothing. He was merely loitering about at the Strand end of the Lowther Arcade when I chanced to be walking that way. Waiting for an earl or a marquess to emerge possibly. We exchanged a few words.'

'What became of Markham, do you suppose?' Adam sounded eager to move on from the subject of Jardine's meeting with Chevenix.

'He joined the Colonial Office, I believe. Probably despatched to some distant outpost of the Empire to brutalise the natives as badly as he used to brutalise poor young devils like you and me at Shrewsbury. Or to drink himself to death.'

'He would be no great loss to society if he did so,' Adam said.

'His grandfather was a butcher,' Jardine added, as if this explained everything.

'Oh, for God's sake, Cosmo,' Adam said, '*my* grandfather was an ostler at a York coaching inn. Are we still to be judged by what our ancestors did when George IV was on the throne?'

For a moment, the artist looked disposed to argue his case but he decided against it.

'You are right, of course, my dear Adam,' he said, laughing. 'Democracy marches ever onwards and soon family will count for nothing. And yet there can be no doubt that Markham was a beast when he was a boy and he is almost certainly a beast still.'

'On that we can agree, if nothing else.'

'Chevenix is now at the Foreign Office.' Jardine appeared unwilling to forget about his encounter in the Lowther Arcade. 'You say you have not seen him of late?'

'I have not seen him since I came down from Cambridge.'

'That is curious. He has seen you.'

Adam said nothing.

'In those grand new buildings in Whitehall. He was clearly wondering what on earth you were doing there: the son of some jumped-up railway builder entering the hallowed portals of the Foreign Office. He didn't actually put it in those terms, of course, but the implication was there.'

Adam remained silent. He moved towards the easel and made a great show of peering at the canvas on it.

'I must confess I wonder myself what you might have been doing there,' Jardine went on. 'I told Chevenix that he must have been mistaken but he was most convinced it was you. He said he called out to you but that you ignored him. And disappeared into one of the offices at the park end of the building with someone he didn't recognise.'

Adam still made no reply.

'What is all this, Adam?' Jardine said, suddenly exasperated by his friend's silence. 'Was it you?'

'Yes, it was I.' Adam turned away from King Pellinore. 'I saw Chevenix but I had little desire to renew acquaintance with him. I did not hear him call out to me. I am sorry if I offended him.'

'Oh, Chevenix is not an easy man to offend. But what were you doing in Whitehall? Are you about to join the ranks of the Civil Service?'

'No, that is not very likely.' Adam laughed at the prospect. 'But I have a friend there who values my opinion on events in European

Turkey. On the strength of the Fields expedition, he believes me to be a greater expert on the subject than perhaps I am.'

'So you visit the FO to put them right on the subject of cruel Turks and liberty-loving Greeks, do you? It is not a role in which I had ever envisaged you, Adam.' The artist was clearly amused by the thought.

'It is nothing, Cosmo. Let us talk of something else.' Adam placed his empty whisky glass on the decanter tray. 'I have changed my mind. Let us go to the Alhambra after all.'

* * * * *

As he came down the stairs, Adam was forced to suppress a long sigh of irritation when he saw who was waiting for him at their foot. Standing at the door that led to her own rooms in the house was Mrs Gaffery. She was unmistakeably intent on serious conversation with him. Adam raised his hat politely and wished her good morning with more enthusiasm than he felt. His slender hope that he might be allowed to escape without talking further with his landlady was instantly dashed.

'I would like very much to speak to you, Mr Carver.'

'Nothing would give me greater pleasure, Mrs Gaffery,' Adam lied, 'but I am afraid that I am running late for an appointment.'

'None the less, I trust that you can spare a little time to join me briefly in my haven from the boisterous world.' Mrs Gaffery indicated the door to her rooms, which was standing ajar.

'I am exceedingly behind my time, Mrs Gaffery. Perhaps on another occasion?'

'I must insist on *this* occasion, Mr Carver.'

Adam suppressed another sigh and bowed to the inevitable. He followed his landlady through the door. He had never before been asked to enter her inner sanctum and he looked around the room with curiosity. It seemed to be no more than a reception room and there were doors in its far wall which led, he assumed, to Mrs Gaffery's bedroom and sitting room. A large jardinière stood in each corner of the room, flowers overflowing the metal container and trailing down the stand. On the table in the centre of the room, a glass dome covered a display of wax flowers. Beneath a window onto the street was another small table and on it another glass dome with a similar display. The bottom half of a second window had been transformed by the introduction of a Wardian case. In its airtight glass box, a dozen ferns of the greenest and freshest hue flourished. Jungles of vines and greenery bloomed on the wallpaper. The room was like a hothouse at Kew Gardens.

As Adam surveyed the floral abundance around him, Mrs Gaffery made her way to the central table. She stood by it as if poised to point out each of the wax flowers in the display case and identify it by name. Adam's landlady was a woman of generous proportions. When she entered a room, her substantial bosom sailed like a galleon before her, announcing to those it encountered that the rest of Mrs Gaffery would shortly be with them. Now that same bosom, Adam noted with alarm, seemed to be quivering with indignation.

'You are not, I hope, an advocate of the mad and wicked folly of women's rights, Mr Carver?' Mrs Gaffery's opening question was unexpected. 'With all their attendant horrors.'

She waved her hand towards one of the jardinières on the far side of the room, as if the attendant horrors might be gathering within it.

Adam struggled to frame a reply.

'I have often thought that, perhaps, we men have not always done justice to your sex, Mrs Gaffery,' he said eventually.

His landlady looked at him as if he had confessed to being Spring-Heeled Jack. 'Away with you, sir. You will be telling me next that you are a supporter of the dreadful Mr Mill.'

'I regret to say that I do not know enough of Mr Mill's ideas to express an opinion upon them, ma'am.'

'Let me assure you that his ideas are abhorrent to all right-thinking people, Mr Carver. That is all you need to know of them.'

'I am sure that you are correct in your view of Mr Mill, ma'am.

But I am struggling to understand their relevance to our present conversation.'

'The woman who called here on Tuesday morning… and on the previous Friday. I will not enquire further into her motives for visiting my house. Nor into yours for receiving her. I tremble at the very thought of what they might be. But I must insist that she does not do so again.'

A rosewood chiffonier stood against the opposite wall, its double doors slightly ajar. As if on castors, Mrs Gaffery moved smoothly across the carpet towards it and pushed them together. They closed with an unexpectedly loud crash. She ignored the sound and turned to glare at her lodger.

'I am not sure I follow you, ma'am,' Adam said, puzzled. 'You say that the young lady had been here on a previous occasion?'

'She had, sir. Alone and unchaperoned at both times. As you must know only too well.'

'But I saw the lady only once. On the Tuesday. I was away from the rooms all day on the Friday of the previous week. I was taking photographs of the new embankment.'

'Well, Quint must have opened the door to the woman.'

'That cannot be the case. Quint was also out. He went to Stepney to discuss the merits of a pot of half-and-half with an old acquaintance.'

'I know only what my eyes tell me, Mr Carver.' Mrs Gaffery was adamant. 'And they tell me that that young woman was coming down the stairs from your rooms at half past two o'clock on the afternoon of Friday last week.'

'But that is impossible. How can she have entered the house? Or entered the rooms?'

'Those are questions to which I have no answers,' Mrs Gaffery said, brushing invisible specks of dust off the top of the chiffonier and then turning to glare at her young lodger. 'I know only that the woman who visited you on Tuesday was also here on the previous Friday. I must ask that you promise me she shall be here no more. When my late and much lamented husband left me this house, he had no intention that it should become a haunt of single ladies and I must respect his wishes. She must come here no more.'

Her words brooked no contradiction. And so Adam nodded with as much deference as he felt able to summon and said nothing. Mrs Gaffery waved her hand in dismissal and moved towards an enormous aspidistra that was casting its shadow on the opposite corner of the room. Adam could see that his ordeal was at an end. Bowing politely, he took his leave, still pondering the puzzle of Miss Maitland's earlier appearance at his lodgings.

CHAPTER FIVE

On the Thursday that Creech had chosen as the day on which they should meet again, Adam made his way to Victoria Station and boarded the London, Chatham and Dover Railways train to Herne Hill. Quint, whose expressed wish to stay in Doughty Street had been ignored, was with him. The short journey out of town passed in silence. Adam replayed in his mind the strange conversation he'd had with Creech at the Speke dinner and pondered what questions he should ask the man. Quint, thwarted of further hours in the company of his foul-smelling tobacco, stared sulkily out of the train window. From the station, a short walk up the hill brought them to their destination, a large detached villa set back from the road. At the entrance to its grounds, Adam stopped. He stared up at the house, half-hidden by the elms and birches which protected Creech's privacy.

'We must get him to answer our questions, Quint.'

Quint, who did not know Creech and had no particular questions he wanted him to answer, said nothing. Adam began to stride purposefully up the villa's driveway. Quint followed, a step or two behind him.

'This here gent ain't going to want to see me.' Quint was still not entirely reconciled to losing an afternoon's lounging around the Doughty Street rooms. 'If he sees the two of us coming up his garden path, he'll most like set the dogs on us.'

'Nonsense. He is expecting me. If he's watching now and sees you as well, he'll just assume I'm too shy and retiring to visit on my own. Believe me, we'll both be as welcome as the flowers in May.'

Quint grunted, unconvinced, but he continued to follow Adam up the winding gravel walkway. The house at the end was a substantial, three-storey property. Its architect had attempted, unsuccessfully, to cross a Queen Anne country mansion with an ancient Greek temple. Pale pink brick on the façade contrasted with a white Doric-columned portico that looked as if it should be welcoming worshippers of Apollo to their rites.

The two men stepped inside the porch and Adam pulled vigorously at the bell. They stood for a minute, listening to it ring inside. No one came to the door. Nothing could be heard save the sound of a distant train making its way towards Kent and the cawing of rooks in the elms.

'Maybe he ain't in,' Quint suggested after another minute had passed.

'If he is not here, where is everybody else?'

'Maybe there ain't nobody else.'

'A man like Creech. Living in a house like this. He would have servants. Where have they gone?'

Adam tugged again at the bell-pull. They heard once more the muffled sound of ringing within the house. No further noise, no clicking of footsteps across parquet flooring, nor opening and closing of inner doors, could be heard after the bell ceased to ring. Herne Hill Villa, it seemed, was deserted.

'This is monstrous, Quint,' Adam said with mock outrage. 'A man invites us to his house. He specifies the day, the time. He speaks mysteriously of secrets that cannot be divulged. And yet when we come visiting at the appointed hour, he is nowhere to be found.'

'Could be he's round the back,' Quint said, jerking his thumb leftward to where the driveway curved around the side of the house.

'Unlikely, but we shall investigate. When the host flouts the laws of hospitality so egregiously by not being present, the guests are surely entitled to go in search of him.'

The rear of Creech's villa faced west and the afternoon sun was shining fiercely on the windows that opened onto the gardens. A neatly kept lawn extended some forty yards to a group of trees. In the centre of the lawn was a small fish pond. In the centre of that was a fountain in the shape of some indeterminate mythological beast. Was it supposed to be a griffin? Adam wondered, as he gazed at it. What watery connotations did a griffin possess? He gave up the conundrum and turned his attention to the back of the house. A series of five long glass casements let light into the rooms at the rear. Adam began to peer through each one in turn, using his hand to shade his eyes against the glare of the sun.

'Nothing and no one in sight,' he reported to Quint, who was trudging and muttering in his wake.

At the penultimate casement, he stopped and leaned further towards the glass, like a small boy pressing his nose against the window of a sweet shop.

'I'm damned if I can make anything out clearly with the sun as it is,' he said. 'There seems to be someone in this room, though.'

He stood there another thirty seconds, face fixed to the casement window. Then he stepped back swiftly. 'Break the glass, Quint.'

Out of habit and sheer cussedness, Quint was usually ready to dispute any orders given to him, but the urgency in Adam's voice was unmistakeable. Thinking quickly, Quint removed the boot from his left foot and used the heel to shatter the central panes in the window. Broken glass flew in all directions. Adam reached inside the frame, pulled at its handle and opened the casement. He stepped over the glass and into the room. Quint replaced his boot and followed him, scrunching fragments of glass beneath his feet as he went.

The room was long and, because the rays of the sun fell only on the first few feet of its length, it was dark. Creech seemed to have used the place as a library, and two massive tables with heavy, claw-foot legs sat in its centre. Bookshelves stretched from window to far wall along both sides. The sombre leather bindings of the volumes which sat on them added to the sense of gloom and claustrophobia. The smell of the books pervaded the room. A book was open, face up on the furthest end of the second table. A chair had been pulled up to the table and someone was sitting in it. But this person was not bowed over the book as if reading it. Instead, his head was thrown back at an awkward angle. As Adam and Quint approached him, he made no movement.

Samuel Creech was dead. Of that there could be no doubt. Two bullets, probably from a pocket pistol, Adam judged, had entered his forehead. One had exited through the back of his skull and looked to have lodged itself in a walnut secretaire and bookcase behind the chair in which he was sitting. The other was presumably still inside the skull. Creech was slumped leftwards in the chair, with blood and brain matter covering the back of it. The metallic smell of blood mingled with the sweet aroma of some pomade that he must have been using on what remained of his hair. It seemed unlikely that he would be answering any of Adam's questions now.

'There is little we can do for Creech, poor devil.' Adam looked down at the slouched and bloody figure of the man he had met at the Speke dinner. He reached out and briefly touched its upper arm. 'We need to contact the police. I shall walk down to the road and look for assistance.'

'You leaving me here with 'im?' Quint gestured at the corpse. He sounded unhappy at the idea.

'The man's dead, Quint. He can do you no harm. And whoever killed him is long gone.'

''Ow can you be so sure of that?'

'Feel the arm. Creech has clearly been dead for hours. Rigor mortis has already begun to set in. Who would stay for hours having killed him?' Confident in his conclusion, Adam turned the pages of the book on the table in front of the dead man. It was Henry Tozer's *Researches in the Highlands of Turkey*. Adam had read it himself earlier in the year. Tozer, he recalled, had described his own travels in the same Macedonian hills that had interested Creech so much. Creech had been pursuing his peculiar researches to the very end. On the table beside the book was a pair of binoculars, which Adam picked up. He turned them over in his hands, looking for the maker's name.

'Negretti and Zambra,' he said after a moment. 'They have an establishment in Cornhill. Creech wanted the best for himself. They have a great reputation, I believe. I have long been intending to make a journey to Cornhill myself to inspect their cameras.'

Quint, standing beside the bookshelves, continued to look unhappy at the prospect of being left alone with a dead man. Adam remained unmoved. His servant must stay in the house.

'There is no help for it, Quint. You must hold the fort while I look for reinforcements. Perhaps you should take the time to look around. Who knows what you might find? Creech is going nowhere and he is in no position to object to the invasion of his privacy.'

The manservant looked as if he was still disposed to dispute his instructions but eventually he moved towards the door which led out of the library. He cast a single reproachful look over his shoulder as he went, but Adam did not see it. He was striding back towards the window they had broken, and the distant sunshine.

* * * * *

'Every Englishman's home is his castle, eh? Isn't that what they say, sir?' The voice was as cheery as if its owner and Adam were conducting a friendly conversation over a glass of port. 'Well, this here dead gentleman's had his castle well and truly stormed, ain't he? By you, sir, if no one else.'

'Look here, Inspector. You're surely not suggesting *I* broke in and murdered Creech, are you? Why would I loiter around like a damn fool and answer your questions if I were a murderer? I'd be back in town and strolling down Piccadilly by now rather than standing here exchanging pleasantries with you.'

The man to whom Adam spoke was, like him, tall and well built. He had the kind of rosy red face that suggested long exposure to the elements and a greying moustache that bloomed and burgeoned luxuriantly around the lower part of his face. He was dressed in chequered trousers and a black jacket that seemed just one size too small for him. In other circumstances, he might have been mistaken for a country farmer on a visit to town, but there was sharpness in his eye that spoke of wide knowledge of the ways of the city. When he had arrived at Herne Hill Villa, accompanied by two constables, he had strolled around the downstairs rooms with the air of a man visiting an auction room before a sale, examining Creech's possessions with a critical eye as if trying to decide whether or not to place a bid on them. On reaching the body in the library chair, he had raised his hat as a token of respect and then peered closely at the wounds to the head. He had walked around the corpse, looking at it from all angles before bending to examine the bullet lodged in the secretaire. Only then had he bothered to introduce himself to the watching Adam. His name, he said, was Pulverbatch and he was an inspector in the Detective Branch of the Metropolitan Police. He wanted a little chat with the gentleman that had found the body. The little chat had gone on for some time, interrupted by occasional conferences between the inspector and his constables.

Now, as Adam was making his protestations, Pulverbatch was waving his plump hands in the air as if attempting to swat them like troublesome flies.

'Oh, no suggestion of murdering was meant to pass my lips, sir. None at all. But a body can't help a-wondering what you *was* doing here. Inside a house you probably ought to have been outside of.'

'I've told you once already, Inspector. I had an arrangement to see Mr Creech. I arrived at the appointed time but the place was deserted.'

'It seems the gentleman had sent his servants away for the day. One of 'em come back only a few minutes ago.'

'Does he know anything of what might have happened?'

'Constable Smithers has been a-talking to him. Says that the man looks about as comfy as a billy goat in stays but that ain't to say he's a-feeling guilty. That's the effect us gentlemen in blue and white has.'

Pulverbatch picked up *Researches in the Highlands of Turkey*, examined its spine, grunted and put the book back on the table.

'I'll be speaking to him myself in a little while. And he'll look even less happy when that happens. But, at present, I'm a-listening to you, sir. If you would be so good as to go on.'

'I looked through a window on the ground floor.' Adam ran his fingers through his hair as he continued. 'I could see that something was amiss. I could see someone sitting in a chair at the far end. He was not moving and his head was awry. I decided to break a window and climb in. It was Creech and he was dead.'

'As a doornail,' Pulverbatch said. 'Sitting in his library with his legs under his own mahogany when someone bursts in and strews his brains all around the room. So what did you do next, sir? When you realised he was dead.'

'I walked back to the road and stopped a gentleman in a fly who was passing. I asked him to send word immediately to the police that they were needed. Then I came back to the house and Quint and I waited here until you and your men arrived.'

'Ah, Quint. That would be *your* man, sir, would it? And where-abouts might he be while we're here chatting so amiably?'

'Quint is upstairs, I believe.'

'And what might he be a-doing upstairs?'

'I have no idea.'

Pulverbatch took a red cotton handkerchief from his pocket and wiped his forehead with it. He returned it to the innermost recesses of his jacket and sighed. 'Perhaps we should call him and ask him,' he said.

'By all means, Inspector.'

Pulverbatch ambled out of the room and made his way to the foot of the main staircase. He lifted his head and bellowed. 'You, sir, upstairs.'

The sudden roar echoed around the house. Quint would have had to be as dead to the world as Creech not to hear him, but there was no sound from the first floor.

The inspector bellowed again. 'Get yourself downstairs.'

* * * * *

Up on the first floor of Herne Hill Villa, Quint had heard Adam return. He had called down to him and had been given instructions to continue looking around the rooms upstairs. Twenty minutes

later, he had heard the arrival of Inspector Pulverbatch and his constables. Long familiarity with officers of the law meant that he had
had little difficulty interpreting the sound of the voices drifting up
the staircase; they had the characteristic tone of policemen wanting
to know what was going on. Quint had spent the hour since Adam
had left him to summon the police roaming the upstairs rooms.
He had found nothing that he would not have expected to find in
the house of a man like Creech. On several occasions he had come
across items of value – a gold watch, a silver cigarette case engraved
with the initials 'SC' – which he had seriously considered pocketing. Quint had no objections in principle to petty larceny but he
had finally decided that any monetary benefit from what he might
filch would be more than outweighed by the aggravation that would
follow if the filching was discovered. He had left the items where
they were.

Now, listening to the voices from below, Quint had already
decided that his only option was to join Adam and the policemen
on the ground floor. The roars from Pulverbatch merely confirmed
him in his decision. He took one last look around what was clearly
Creech's bedroom before leaving it. He caught his own reflection
in a large cheval glass which stood in the corner. Then, as his eyes
continued to scan the room, they fell on a small table to the left of
the bed. On it was an octavo-sized book bound in morocco. Seized
by a sudden impulse, Quint crossed swiftly to the table and picked
the book up. Opening it, he riffled briskly through its pages.

Quint had but the vaguest memories of his schooldays. This
was unsurprising since they dated only to his seventh year and had
lasted less than six months. He could just about recall a dark room
in Holborn where two dozen grubby boys sat unwillingly at the feet
of an elderly dame deputed by the foundling hospital to teach them
how to read and write. The elderly dame in question was usually
drunk, and drink made her either so tired that she fell asleep in front
of them or so furious that she belaboured any boy who ventured
within striking distance with her walking stick. Somehow, Quint
had emerged from his schooling not only with a grudging respect

for elderly dames in their cups, but with a basic knowledge of his letters. He could read. And what little he was able to read in this small leather-bound book suggested to him that further reading of it would be interesting. Here were Samuel Creech's own words. Here was his journal. Quint wasted no time in stuffing the volume into the depths of his coat pocket before making his way down the stairs and joining Adam to face the guardians of the law.

CHAPTER SIX

I do believe that that was not the first time you have encountered the inspector, Quint.' Back in Doughty Street, Adam was stretched out in a chair by the fireside. His feet rested comfortably on the fender and his hands were clasped behind his head. Quint was pouring whisky from a crystal decanter. The two men had been back in the rooms but a few minutes. The inspector had not kept them long once Quint had joined Adam downstairs. Policeman and manservant had eyed one another suspiciously as Quint had sidled into Creech's library but the interview between them had been brief. Quint had done little more than confirm what his master had said. When Pulverbatch had asked what the devil he meant by roaming around a house that was the scene of bloody murder, he had muttered about looking for signs of the murderer. The inspector had grunted as if he had heard likelier tales in his time but had said no more. Once names and address had been noted, he and Adam had been dismissed from the policeman's presence, and apparently from his mind, almost immediately. Their return from Herne Hill had been free of much conversation, both men sobered into silence by thoughts of Creech and mortality. Now, sitting once again by his own hearth, Adam had recovered his spirits.

'Oh, I knows Pulverbatch all right.' Quint handed his master the drink.

'I thought as much. You circled one another in that room like two prizefighters about to climb into the ring. And what do you know of him?'

Quint paused to consider the question.

'Well, he's what you might call a chickaleary cove is Jem Pulverbatch.' Seeing Adam's raised eyebrow, his manservant decided to expand his description. 'In other words, putting it pretty plainly, you'd have to get up *very* early in the morning to catch *him* on the hop.'

'But you have done so, Quint. I can deduce from the wicked glint in your eye that you have done so. You have the demeanour of a man who has bested a chickaleary cove.'

With something approaching a flourish, Quint brought the little leather-bound book from his pocket. 'I don't reckon Pulverbatch'll miss this. I found it up in Creech's bedroom.'

Adam took the journal from Quint's hand and began to flick through its pages.

'I should condemn your shameless thievery unequivocally, Quint.'

'You prob'ly should.'

'I should chastise you for stealing what might be evidence from under the eye of the law.'

'But you ain't going to.'

'No, you are right. I'm not. Despite the terrible death of the man Creech, I remain curious about the secrets he claimed to know. Perhaps it is *because* of his death that I remain so curious.' Adam had stopped at one page and was looking at it closely. 'This journal may hold the key to Creech's interest in those barbarous villages we visited in sixty-seven. So I propose to read it from cover to cover.'

An hour passed. Nothing was heard in the sitting room at Doughty Street save the sound of the small clock on the mantelpiece striking the quarter hours. Adam was engrossed in reading Creech's writings. Quint, who had an almost oriental capacity for withdrawing from the world when action in it was not required, simply stood by the door to the room and waited for Adam to finish. He appeared, when his master glanced up at one point, to have entered a state of near-trance. Eventually, the reading was over. Adam threw the book onto the side table beside his chair.

'Well, Quint, this is all very intriguing.'

'Thought it might be.' Quint emerged immediately from his state of abstraction. 'That's why I swiped the thing.'

'Creech, poor chap, wrote a damnably bad hand but I have managed to decipher nearly all the entries in his journal. In truth, it's not much of a journal. No revelations of his private life. Much of the latter part of it is a record of his dealings with a man named Jinkinson. Creech was paying Jinkinson. Paying him quite large sums of money. Two guineas a week at least for the best part of four months. Five guineas in one week. Creech records the transactions very carefully. Although it's not quite clear what they meant.'

'Maybe this Jinkinson had some hold on Creech. Maybe he was milking him.'

'No, I don't think so. He was paying him for something but I don't think it was that. Look at this entry. "24th July – Jinkinson reports as usual. All three subjects in the week. No change. Two guineas to Jinkinson." That doesn't sound like blackmail.'

'Paying him for something he was bringin' 'im?'

'Possibly, but there's no apparent record of anything. There are other names in the journal, however. Names I recognise. Lewis Garland. James Abercrombie. Sir Willoughby Oughtred.'

'Toffs,' said Quint shortly.

'I suppose you could call them that. What else? All Members of Parliament. All members of the Marco Polo, for that matter. But why are they in Creech's book? Look at this entry, for example. What do you make of that, Quint?'

Adam handed the journal to his servant, his finger indicating a particular point on the page. Quint took the book and painstakingly read the entry aloud: '"Lewis Garland to SJW, no purpose in visit save the usual, Abercrombie in Paris for the week, no contact, Oughtred followed to Westminster and to HH, no other excursions. Two guineas to Jinkinson." If you ask me, this Jinkinson's some kind of snooper.'

'Snooper?'

'Creech is giving 'im the rhino to watch what the toffs are doing.'

'That certainly does seem to be the most obvious explanation.'

'No knowing why he's got such a powerful interest in what they're doing, though.'

'No knowing why, as you say. And there is a further puzzle.' Adam took the notebook back from Quint and flicked through it until he reached the last page. He showed it to his servant. The page was empty except for a single row of scribbled symbols in the middle of it. Quint peered at them.

'Greek, ain't it?' he said. 'I'd reckernise them twisted letters anywhere.'

'Greek it is, although Creech writes as poor a hand in that language as he does in his own.'

'What's it say?'

'"Euphorion". As far as I can tell.'

'And what the bleeding 'ell does Euphorion mean?'

'A good question. It is a Greek name. Do I have a vague memory from my Cambridge days of a Greek poet named Euphorion? But why should Creech devote a page of his journal to the name of a Greek poet?'

'More bleeding questions. We could do with some answers.'

'We could, and I can think of one obvious way to go in search of them, Quint. Here is an address written in Creech's infernal scrawl. It makes its first appearance in these pages at the same time that Jinkinson does and I take it to be his. 12 Poulter's Court, Lincoln's Inn Fields. I have never before heard of Poulter's Court, Lincoln's Inn Fields, but I think I should pay it a visit as soon as possible.'

CHAPTER SEVEN

That night Adam slept poorly. He lay awake for hours in his room in Doughty Street, listening to the never-ending sounds of the city around him. Even in the small hours of the morning, London was never quiet. Traffic could still be heard on the Gray's Inn Road. The shouts of men and the braying of beasts still echoed down the darkened streets. Adam watched the shadows chasing one another across the ceiling and fell eventually into a fitful sleep. In his dreams, the figure of Creech rode a costermonger's ass whilst driving a herd of scrawny goats through the single muddy street of a Macedonian village. Fields, waving his mortarboard, was shouting the name 'Euphorion' over and over again. Slowly the face of Fields melted and was replaced by that of Adam's father, who was chastising his son for his failure to win the Chancellor's Medal for Poetry during his time at Cambridge.

In reality, as Adam was aware even within his dream, Charles Carver had shown little, if any, interest in poetry. He had shown little interest in any of the subjects that attracted his son. Bluff, occasionally brutal in manner, the railway entrepreneur had been proud of the education he could buy for his only child but indifferent, even antagonistic, towards the enthusiasms that education inspired in Adam. Money was the object of the elder Carver's fascination, and for years he had been enormously successful in accumulating it. Throughout the boom days of the 1840s and 1850s, when Adam was growing up, Charles Carver's fortunes had expanded as rapidly as the rail network which created them. Only in the following decade did he begin to skate on thin financial ice. By the time his son arrived at Cambridge in the autumn of 1865, his father, unbeknownst to Adam, was plunged into reckless investments in a series of ventures, all of which ended in disaster. While Carver Junior read Horace and punted on the River Cam, Carver Senior struggled to keep his head above the rising waters of impending bankruptcy.

Faced by the final destruction of his fortune and by exposure of the fraudulent means he had been using to prop it up, Charles Carver hanged himself in a room in the newly opened Langham Hotel. The scandal was largely hushed up, but the money to maintain his son at university was gone. In a matter of weeks, Adam had been forced to leave behind his comfortable life of wining, dining and classical scholarship at Cambridge to face the unexpected prospect of earning his own living. A few weeks later, he was with Professor Fields on a boat approaching the harbour at Salonika, their adventure in Macedonia about to begin.

* * * * *

Poulter's Court, when Adam found it the following day, turned out to be one of the less prepossessing addresses in the vicinity of Lincoln's Inn Fields. One entered it through a stone archway, which led into a small, paved yard. In that courtyard, the air was filled with the unmistakeable scent of neglected drains. Adam took another look at the paper on which he had written Jinkinson's address. The building for which he was searching was the third in a row on the left-hand side of the court. A tarnished brass plaque on its door announced that 'Jinkinson & Hargreaves, Private Enquiry Office' occupied the first floor. Adam pushed at the door and, slightly to his surprise, found that it was ajar. He entered and mounted the staircase. At the top of the first, uncarpeted flight of stairs was another door and another sign – this one wooden with painted lettering – which read 'Jinkinson & Hargreaves'. One of the nails holding the sign to the door had come out and it hung at an angle. Opening the door and going in, Adam nearly dislodged the wooden sign completely.

A boy of about fourteen was sitting at a desk, black with ink stains, in a small and otherwise unfurnished room. He was reading. As Adam approached him, the boy, apparently startled by the arrival of a possible client in Jinkinson's outer office, attempted to thrust what he was reading beneath the desk. He was too slow and the desk too flimsy to succeed in hiding the penny dreadful he was enjoying. Adam looked briefly at the cover. The title, *The Dead Monk's Curse*, was emblazoned across it in large black lettering, half obscuring a scene in which several figures in monastic dress were menacing a young woman whose upper garments had gone missing.

'I likes a good story,' the boy said defiantly, as if Adam was about to impugn his literary taste.

'It certainly looks exciting.'

'I likes it when the women gets the chop.' He leered at Carver, revealing an array of blackening and broken teeth. Adam decided to ignore this remark.

'May I speak to Mr Jinkinson?'

The boy said nothing.

'Or to Mr Hargreaves, perhaps?'

'Speak to Mr Hargreaves? Oh, that's a good 'un, that is.' The boy was clearly tickled by this idea. He laughed throatily and slapped his hand on the inky desktop. 'You can speak with 'im all right, but 'e might not do much speaking back.'

'And why would that be?'

'Cos 'e's dead.'

'Ah, that *would* make conversation difficult.'

'Bin dead more years 'n I've bin alive. Old Jinks only keeps the name on the plate cos he thinks two names is more respectable than one.'

'And what about "Old Jinks"? Is he in?'

'Oh, 'e's in all right.' The boy gestured towards another door, which presumably led to Jinkinson's inner sanctum. 'But you won't get much more sense out of 'im than out of 'Argreaves.'

'And why do you say that?'

'' E's been out on the spree, ain't 'e? 'E's so corned 'e can hardly stand.'

'None the less, I would like to speak to him.'

'' E's through there, then,' said the boy, thrusting his thumb once more towards the inner room and returning to *The Dead Monk's Curse*.

Adam pushed open the door the boy had indicated. He entered another, larger office. Across the room and behind a desk as ramshackle as the one under which the boy had thrust his penny dreadful, an elderly and paunchy man was asleep in a chair. He was snoring loudly. As a very young man, Adam decided, Jinkinson must have been mightily impressed by the swaggering worldliness of society swells. Perhaps he had admired their images in the windows of the print shops in St Paul's Churchyard. Now, ageing and decrepit as he was, he still dressed like an 1830s dandy down on his luck. Although they had certainly seen better days, his extravagantly coloured silk cravat and ornamented waistcoat would mark him out in the more sombrely dressed crowds of 1870. It was not, Adam reflected, the kind of outfit ideally suited to a private enquiry agent. Enquiry agents, he assumed, needed to blend into the background. Perhaps Jinkinson's flamboyant taste in clothing went some way towards explaining why, to judge by the shabby state of his office, he was not a very successful enquiry agent. And yet this was the man to whom Creech had paid all those guineas. Where, Adam wondered, had all that money gone? Not, it seemed, on the decoration of his professional premises.

As Jinkinson continued to snore, Adam looked about the office. It had, like its owner, seen better days. There was little in the way of furniture beyond a desk and a chair. To the left, a black mark on the ceiling indicated where a gas lamp had once been. The decoration consisted of two engravings on the walls. To Adam's left was a gloomy Dutch pub scene. Almost certainly, he decided, it was entitled *Boors Carousing*. The boors, three of them, all had pipes clamped in their mouths and were caught in the act of smacking their thighs as an indication of drink-fuelled abandon. On the opposite wall, a Spanish hidalgo stared haughtily at the viewer from the frame of his portrait. The overall effect of the two images was profoundly depressing. Looking back at the stout toper behind the desk, Adam noticed him open first one bleary eye and then the other, and struggle into something approaching consciousness. Jinkinson eventually looked at his visitor as if he had been half expecting him to come calling.

'You have the air of a varsity man, sir,' he said, loudly but irrelevantly.

'I was up at Cambridge for a few terms,' Adam acknowledged.

'Ah, Cambridge, Cambridge!' Jinkinson now had a dreamy look on his face, as if remembering happy days spent punting along the Cam to Grantchester. 'Always fancied myself as a Trinity man. But it was not to be. The streets of London have been my alma mater. Or should I say, my not so alma mater? Not such a nourishing mother at all, sir. London can be a cruel parent, indeed.'

Having said this, the ageing dandy seemed to have shot his conversational bolt. His eyes slowly closed and he began to nod off once more. Adam was about to cough to claim his attention but Jinkinson suddenly jerked back to life and stared sternly at him.

'What can I do for you, young man?' he asked. He appeared to be under the impression that he had never seen Adam before in his life.

'I am looking for a Mr Jinkinson, and I presume that you are he.'

'Presumption correct, sir.' The man attempted a polite bow to his visitor but his paunch and his position in his chair conspired to produce no more than a vague shifting of his bulk. 'You see before you the wreck of the human being that goes by the name of Herbert George Jinkinson. And you, sir? You are…?'

'My name is Carver. I have learned of your name and your address through a mutual acquaintance: Mr Samuel Creech.'

To say that Jinkinson was startled by the introduction of Creech's name, Adam decided, would have been a gross understatement. He seemed poleaxed by it. The blood drained from his face. A look of apparently intense pain twisted his features.

'Are you unwell, Mr Jinkinson?'

'It is no matter, sir.' Jinkinson struggled manfully to regain his composure. 'I am suffering from a derangement of my interior. No more than that, I can assure you. Would you believe that no food save a small milk pudding has passed my lips in the last twenty-four hours, and yet a storm still rages in the inner man?' He patted briefly at his sizeable stomach as if to calm the tempest. 'A Mr Creech, you say? I believe I have some small recollection of the name.'

Jinkinson's elaborate pantomime of a man struggling to retrieve a memory hidden in the furthest recesses of his mind was a performance worthy of the stage of the Lyceum.

'Ah, yes. I have it. A gentleman who lives out of town. Dulwich, perhaps? Or was it Herne Hill? I seem to remember I was able to do him some trifling service. Something to do with a missing watch. Not valuable, but a memento of a much-loved relative. I would have to consult my records to be certain.'

Jinkinson gestured towards what Adam had assumed was a large wastepaper basket overflowing with papers. The ageing dandy noticed his look of scepticism.

'The records need attention, Mr Carver. And that blackguard boy outside, Simpkins, is as idle as a painted ship upon a painted ocean. Some mornings you cannot stir him into action at all. No more than you can stir cold lead with a wooden spoon.'

'So you would have no notion why Mr Creech is dead? Murdered, in fact.'

Jinkinson had been stunned by Adam's earlier remark. He was rendered speechless by this one. His mouth opened and closed in a vain effort to find words. His face, naturally rubicund, was now so pale he looked almost dead himself.

'You are shocked, I see, Mr Jinkinson.'

The enquiry agent made a Herculean effort and recovered the power of speech. 'Who would not be, sir? The death of a fellow traveller through this vale of tears is always shocking. A murder is even more so.'

'And yet you knew the gentleman in question only slightly.'

'Hardly at all,' Jinkinson agreed quickly. 'But I am a sensitive man, Mr Carver. The years may have rolled over me but they have failed to harden my heart entirely. I have heard the swish of Death's scythe so many times and yet each new report of it still saddens me.' The sound of his own voice echoing sonorously around his office appeared to help Jinkinson recover his equilibrium. 'I learn of the sudden departure of some acquaintance – some *slight* acquaintance – and the tears start unbidden to my eyes. It is hard to be a sensitive soul in a world so indifferent to the feelings of the individual, but I have learned to live with that fate.'

With difficulty, Jinkinson heaved himself to his feet. He lurched to the left and seized hold of the edge of the table to steady himself.

'I cannot help but be curious, Mr Carver, as to why you are interested in Mr Creech and his death yourself. You are related to the gentleman, perhaps?'

'No, Mr Jinkinson, I am not.' Adam noticed the enquiry agent's relief at these words. He wondered how much, if anything, to tell him. He decided that the truth, if not the whole truth, should probably be divulged. 'I met him only the once. But the meeting was in curious circumstances. He spoke to me of secrets which I could help him to unearth. Secrets buried far away in European Turkey. We arranged to meet again at his house. When I arrived in Herne Hill to keep the appointment, I found him dead. With a bullet in his head and his brains scattered about the room.'

'Curious circumstances, indeed,' Jinkinson said, still clutching the table for support. He was clearly drunk, but he was equally clearly the sort of drinker who could function perfectly adequately with quantities of liquor inside him that would fell a lesser man. 'They almost remind me of the opening of one of those penny dreadful stories that wretched boy Simpkins will insist on reading.' Jinkinson pawed briefly at his silk cravat, as if he was unsatisfied with the way it was tied and was contemplating redoing it. 'Not, I hasten to assure you, that I have ever read any of them myself.'

'I thought perhaps that you might be able to throw some light on the mystery of Mr Creech's death.'

'Throw some light? I, sir?' Jinkinson appeared astounded by the suggestion. 'How could I do so? How have you travelled, physically and mentally as it were, from Mr Creech's bloody corpse in Herne Hill to my humble offices here in Poulter's Court? What connection – what mistaken connection – can you have made, I wonder?'

'There was a journal by Creech's bed. With notes in his handwriting. Your name and address appeared in it.'

'Easily explained,' Jinkinson said, waving his hands in the air as if they were about to do the explaining. He had entirely recovered his composure. 'As I have said, I undertook some investigative work for the unfortunate Mr Creech. He must have recorded our business in his journal. No doubt the book holds records of the gentleman's other dealings.'

'All the records in the notebook – and there are many of them – appear to refer to you.'

'Our business was trivial but it took some time to reach a conclusion.' Jinkinson smiled blandly. 'Mr Creech must have been a careful gentleman who recorded even the most trifling of transactions in detail.'

'Curious, however, that only your dealings with the gentleman were recorded in this notebook.'

Jinkinson made an elaborate performance of shrugging his shoulders. 'Curious indeed. Perhaps he kept a multitude of such journals. One for each of the individuals with whom he did business.' The enquiry agent gave another bland smile. He looked like a fat baby with the wind. 'But the death of Creech and all circumstances surrounding it are surely now matters for the police, are they not? Not for a private gentleman? Even one such as yourself, who had the shocking experience of finding the body weltering in its own gore.'

'There *were* a number of other names in Mr Creech's notebook,' Adam continued. 'Names of prominent men. Lewis Garland and Sir Willoughby Oughtred. James Abercrombie.'

'I thought that you said that only my own dealings with Creech were recorded.'

'All these men seemed to be linked to your business with Mr Creech in some way. Perhaps you know them?'

Jinkinson's repeat impersonation of a man racking his brains in search of elusive knowledge was once again worthy of an audience's generous applause.

'No, I believe not,' he said at last. 'I thought for a moment the name Garland was familiar to me, but I can only assume that I have chanced upon it in the newspapers. A gentleman of the turf, perhaps? Or a brother of the quill?'

'He is an MP. As are the other two gentlemen.'

Jinkinson smiled again as if all mysteries had been solved.

'I take little interest in politics, Mr Carver. There is little wonder that the names mean nothing to me.'

'But there they sit on the pages of Mr Creech's notebook, side by side with your own.'

'A puzzle, indeed.'

'What of the word "Euphorion", Mr Jinkinson? Does that recall anything to mind?'

For the third time in the conversation, Jinkinson was rocked on his heels and, for the third time, he recovered his poise swiftly.

'That would be a Latin word, would it, Mr Carver?'

'Greek, I believe.'

'Ah, well,' Jinkinson said, spreading his hands wide as if this explained much that was previously inexplicable. 'Unlike your good self, I have not had the inestimable benefit of a classical education. No sojourns by the Cam or Isis for poor Jinkinson, however much he may have yearned for them in his youth. The Thames alone has been his watery companion.'

'And the word means nothing to you? It was also prominent in the pages of Creech's notebook.'

'Not a thing, sir. Unless it be the name of some minor god? The men of ancient Greece had so many, I understand.'

'It is not the name of a god, Mr Jinkinson. Why would Creech record the name of a Greek god?'

'Why indeed?' The enquiry agent was swaying on his feet but was now, once more, entirely at ease. 'Why would he record any

Greek word? In my brief dealings with the gentleman, he did not strike me as much of a classical scholar.'

Adam was obliged to acknowledge to himself that the man was right. And there seemed to be no possibility that Jinkinson was about to admit to anything more.

'You are correct, of course, sir. I should leave all these matters to the authorities. And yet I was the man who found Creech. It was I who was told of secrets that needed revealing. I feel compelled to investigate further.'

'I can see the logic of your remarks, Mr Carver, but if I were you, I would allow the police to do their work unaided.' The fat enquiry agent hesitated briefly. 'I would stand aside and watch the professionals go about their work. No need to confuse their investigations with irrelevant details. Such as my insignificant business with the deceased.'

Jinkinson caught Adam's eye and held his gaze for a moment. The younger man smiled to himself, amused by the obviousness of the decaying dandy's concern that his name should not be mentioned to the police. Then he inclined his head briefly in acknowledgement that he had understood.

'You are correct again, Mr Jinkinson. The police will no doubt find the murderer without my assistance. And why should I muddy the waters of their enquiries with unnecessary information?'

The fat investigator breathed an audible sigh of relief. He swivelled his body sideways and, aiming his bulk in the direction of the door, set off towards it. When he reached it, after a brief and involuntary diversion towards the window overlooking Poulter's Court, he turned to Adam.

'Nothing would delight me more than to throw some light on this dark and terrible mystery, Mr Carver. But I fear I cannot.'

Jinkinson reached out and threw open his door. He called into the outer office. 'Simpkins, please show this gentleman out.'

The boy was still sitting behind his rickety desk. He had not yet finished reading his penny dreadful and seemed disinclined to pay much attention to his master.

'Simpkins, the size of your great flapping ears makes it impossible for me to believe that they have failed to catch my instruction. Mr Carver here requires to be shown to the street.'

'Gent showed hisself in. Would have thought the gent could have showed hisself out.'

'I want none of your impertinence, you young devil.'

'No, you wants none of it cos you've got enough of your own already, you old rogue.'

Simpkins, coolly defiant, did not even bother to raise his eyes from the page he was reading. Jinkinson made as if to move into the outer office and assert his authority more forcefully, but the sudden effort appeared to disorient him. He clutched at the door jamb and brought his hand melodramatically to his brow. He turned back into his own office to address Adam.

'This miserable boy will be the death of me, Mr Carver. I took him on only at the request of his poor mother, to whom I owed a trifling obligation. And hear the impudence with which he repays me.'

Simpkins snorted contemptuously.

'And he has as little wit about him as the pump at Aldgate.'

There was another grunt from the target of Jinkinson's wrath.

'There is no need to trouble the boy,' replied Adam. 'I can make my own way out, as he says. And it seems you can throw no further light on Mr Creech's death.'

'Alas, no!'

'Perhaps I can leave this.' Adam had squeezed past the elderly dandy and now, back in the shabby ante-room, he held out his card. 'If anything occurs to you, I can always be contacted in Doughty Street.'

'Of course, of course.' Jinkinson took the card Adam offered him and slipped it into a pocket in his waistcoat without looking at it. 'But I fear I will be unable to tell you any more. At any time in the future. I must say goodbye to you, Mr Carver. Business, with all its stern demands, requires my attention.' He pointed back into his office, as if to indicate the mountains of paperwork that awaited him.

Unable to tell me more or unwilling? Adam wondered. It seemed pointless to linger any longer in Poulter's Court. Or to ask any more about Garland and Abercrombie and Oughtred and Euphorion. The enquiry agent very obviously wished him gone and was intent on telling him nothing but half-truths and lies. Indeed, with a flourish of his fingers and a bow of his head as a farewell, Jinkinson had returned to his office and closed the door. Adam was suddenly left with only Simpkins and his penny dreadful for company. He moved towards the door to the stairs, pausing briefly at the boy's desk. Simpkins's eyes had come to rest on a page of advertisements. One had attracted his particular attention and his finger was tracing its words down the page. Adam could see that it was for a competition with a prize of half a guinea a week for life.

'Will you enter it?' Adam asked.

'Won't I just,' the boy replied, looking up for the first time since Jinkinson had interrupted his reading with the request that he show Adam out.

'And what would you do with such money, if you won?'

'I'd get myself as far away from that old wretch as I could.' Simpkins thumbed his nose scornfully in the direction of the door behind which Jinkinson had just retired. 'And then I'd eat pies every day, mister. Pies and sausage rolls. Wouldn't that be prime?' The boy's eyes misted over as he contemplated a future filled with such feasts. Adam left him to his dreams.

* * * * *

'Mr Jinkinson was a curious gentleman, Quint.' Back in his rooms, Adam was reclining in a chair. He had slipped so deeply into it that he seemed to be experimenting with the possibility of sitting comfortably on his shoulder blades. 'Terrible toper, obviously. His offices stank of liquor and he could barely stand upright. But a man of some education.'

'The best eddicated gents are often the worst lushingtons of all,' Quint said.

'True enough.' Adam spoke from the depths of the armchair.

'Cambridge was full of the most dreadful drunkards. You could scarcely walk down Trinity Street of a Saturday night without tripping over a dozen men in liquor, sprawled in the gutter. Most of them quoting Virgil at you.'

'What did this Jinkinson cove quote at you?'

'Nothing from the *Georgics* or the *Aeneid*, I regret to say. He told me that he'd had dealings with Creech in the past but they were finished. That he had no idea why his name featured so prominently in that notebook you swiped. He was lying, of course.'

'Ain't no surprise about that. Anybody'd lie if they thought they was being linked to a man with a pair of bullets in his napper. This Jinkinson cove'd be worrying about the gentlemen in blue and white coming calling.'

'I think he's safe enough from the attentions of the police,' Adam said. 'I doubt very much if there is anything to connect Jinkinson to Creech other than the notebook and we have that.'

'Ain't we telling Pulverbatch about it?'

'No, Quint, we are not.' Adam had hauled himself into a more conventionally upright position in his chair. 'I have thought long and hard about this and I have decided that we shall continue to pursue investigations of our own into Creech's death. In parallel with those of the police, but quite separate.'

Quint stared at his master with an unreadable expression. 'Well, don't ask me to be the one to give Jem Pulverbatch the news we've been 'olding back on 'im,' he said, after a short silence.

'The responsibility is all mine, Quint. You are merely a humble manservant obedient to his master's every wish.'

Quint grunted.

'Yes, I know,' Adam went on. 'The idea of obedience to *any* of my wishes is an alien concept to you. But how is Pulverbatch – or any other policeman – to know of the extent of your habitual recalcitrance?'

'I ain't got the first notion what you're talking of,' Quint said.

'But you are content that we should pursue our enquiries?'

The servant nodded.

'Good!' Adam clapped his hands together and leaped from the chair. 'So we are left to confront the puzzle of Jinkinson and what he knows and does not know. Why was he so unforthcoming?'

'He was probably trying to work out what you was after. And whether there was any tin to be had out of helping you.'

'Possibly.' Adam sounded unconvinced. 'In that case, he must have decided I had no tin to offer since he was exceedingly unhelpful. But I thought he was more scared than anything else. Maybe of the police. Maybe of somebody else.'

'Course he was scared. As I say, nobody wants his name spoke in the same breath as a dead man.'

'No, it was more than that, Quint. Jinkinson knows something that I should like to know.'

'He ain't about to tell you, though.'

'Most certainly not. Which is why I propose to follow him when he leaves his office tomorrow and see whether or not his actions reveal more of the truth than his words.'

CHAPTER EIGHT

Eight o'clock the next morning found Adam once more in the vicinity of Lincoln's Inn Fields. It was a surprisingly cold morning for June and he was shivering from the icy breeze that was blowing along the street. To his left, a small platoon of labourers from one of the gas companies had arrived to dig up the road. The men were shouting cheerfully at one another as they unloaded their tools from the back of a cart. From where Adam was standing, he could just see through the arched entrance that led into Poulter's Court. A minute earlier, Jinkinson had descended his staircase in company with his boy assistant and the two were now engaged in some kind of spat. Simpkins was pointing back up the staircase and gesticulating. Jinkinson aimed a cuff in the direction of his clerk's head but missed by a good foot. With a shouted instruction which Adam could not hear well enough to interpret, he set off down Serle Street in the direction of the Strand and Fleet Street. The boy returned to the office.

Jinkinson was clearly in good spirits. Once again he was dressed to stand out from the crowd in a mustard-yellow jacket and chequered trousers. For a man who had drunk so fully and so freely the previous day, he seemed remarkably cheerful. It was difficult to believe, Adam thought, that he was not suffering the pains of a hangover, but he showed no obvious signs of it. Nor were there indications of the fears that Jinkinson had showed when told of Creech's murder. A night's sleep seemed to have dispelled them. There was an unmistakeable spring in his step. He was not actively twirling the ivory-knobbed stick he was carrying as he walked, but he had the air of a man who would do so at any moment. Adam followed him at a discreet distance. Jinkinson showed no sign that he suspected or feared that anyone might be tailing him. Two urchins, amused by the colour of his jacket, pestered him as he walked, but he waved them amiably on their way.

From Serle Street he turned into Carey Street. Outside the door of a pub named the Seven Stars he stopped briefly, as if contemplating early morning refreshment. Instead, he crossed the road and walked into Bell Yard. There were few people about and Adam was no more than ten yards behind his quarry, but Jinkinson seemed still to be oblivious of his follower. Emerging onto Fleet Street opposite Middle Temple Lane, both pursued and pursuer were suddenly caught up in the bedlam of a London crowd as they turned towards Ludgate Hill. Traffic, funnelled through the bottleneck of Temple Bar, had come to a halt. Adam looked swiftly to his right where Wren's stone edifice squatted in the middle of the highway. Pedestrians, squeezed under its side arches, jostled past one another. A light, perhaps a gas lamp, could be seen in the room above the central archway, which was an office of Child's the bankers. He turned his attention once more to his quarry. Jinkinson had wasted no time in pushing his bulk through the crowds and Adam soon feared he would lose sight of him. He made his own way through the press of bodies, elbowing others out of the way before they elbowed him. As he walked on, the source of the chaos became clearer. There was another obstruction further up Fleet Street and the road had become a tangle of stalled vehicles. Omnibuses, cabs, horses and carts, waggons and drays had all come to a halt and their drivers, shouting and cursing, added their own contributions to the city's unceasing roar. There was no clear way across the street. Over the heads of the jostling men and horses, Adam saw Jinkinson dodging into one of the innumerable alleyways that branched off Fleet Street. For the moment, he was unable to follow him.

Eventually, Adam pulled himself free of the crowds and reached the spot where Jinkinson had disappeared. He was temporarily uncertain which way to go. Either side of a tobacconist's shop, two narrow lanes ran in parallel. Which one had the man taken? Adam had little time to decide. He chose the right. The roar of the traffic was left almost instantly behind. He had gone no more than twenty yards down the alley when another obstruction appeared. A boy, barefoot and filthy, stood in his path. He held out a hand so black with dirt that mustard and cress could have been grown in it, and begged for 'Just a ha'penny, sir.' The boy's clothing was astonishingly threadbare. He looked as if he had simply crawled naked through a pile of disintegrating rags and trusted to chance that some of them would attach themselves to his body. Only a handful had. Adam moved past him but the urchin followed, still calling for his halfpenny. Adam stopped and reached into his pocket for a coin. He held a penny in his hand so that the boy could see it.

'Did a gentleman in yellow pass this way?'

The boy grabbed for the penny. Adam moved his hand. The boy turned a grubby and sulky face up at him. Then he pointed to another, even narrower, alley, which branched off the first. Adam had not even noticed the entrance to this second alley.

'He went dahn there,' the boy said.

'Thank you. The penny is yours.'

The boy snatched it from Adam's hand before he had finished speaking and ran off. Adam turned into the second passage and found, to his surprise, that it doubled back on itself. Within moments, he was once more on Fleet Street. What was Jinkinson doing? Adam's first thought was that the enquiry agent had observed his follower and was attempting to shake him off but, as he looked up Fleet Street towards St Paul's, he saw the man still ahead of him. Jinkinson was loitering outside a barber's shop, standing beneath its red-and-white striped pole and peering intently into its window. Eventually he moved on and Adam was able to continue his pursuit. Passing the barber's, Adam looked briefly into the window himself but he could see nothing more interesting than a sign which advertised shaves at a penny and haircuts at twopence.

Jinkinson, twenty yards in front of him, suddenly dodged into the traffic that trundled towards Ludgate Hill. For a moment, Adam was seized by the mad thought that the man had decided to commit suicide by casting himself beneath the passing vehicles. However, it was almost immediately clear that Jinkinson was an experienced London pedestrian. The cries and shouts of enraged drivers drifted back to where Adam was standing, but Jinkinson, showing unexpected agility in one so fat, had glided through the traffic and had safely reached the other side of Fleet Street. Now, to the astonishment of his pursuer, he turned back towards the Strand and began to walk purposefully in that direction. Perplexed, Adam stood on the pavement opposite, jostled by the crowds and wondering what to do. He decided that he had little choice but to follow Jinkinson's example and cross through the traffic. Slipping between two cabs that had been forced to a halt, he evaded a cart piled high with baskets of fruit heading in the other direction and gained the far side. Jinkinson was still in sight but marching briskly into the distance. Within a couple of minutes, both the enquiry agent and his pursuer were past Middle Temple Lane and heading towards Westminster.

Jinkinson was now in a hurry. He increased his pace as he made his way down the Strand. He came to a halt briefly outside a London and Westminster Bank. Adam thought for a moment he was about to enter it, but the enquiry agent had no such intention. After looking down at his shoes and rubbing first one and then the other on the backs of his trouser legs, he hurried on. He crossed the entrance to Villiers Street and made his way past the French Renaissance frontage of the Charing Cross Hotel. Adam, still some twenty yards to his rear, was hard pressed to keep his quarry in sight as he walked into Whitehall. Jinkinson's stride had become unmistakeably purposeful. Within ten minutes he was in the middle of Westminster Bridge. There he halted and, leaning against the railings, looked down into the waters of the Thames below. Adam also stopped. Standing to one side of the flow of pedestrians across the bridge, he watched a man in a charcoal grey morning suit and top hat approach the enquiry agent. Jinkinson turned to greet him.

Even at a distance of fifty yards, Adam had no difficulty recognising the newcomer. Although he had never been introduced to him, he knew the man by sight from the Marco Polo. It was Sir Willoughby Oughtred. From where he was standing, he could see that Jinkinson and the baronet were already deep in conversation. They made an incongruous couple, one plump and yellow-waistcoated, the other tall and formally dressed. He could not, of course, hear anything of what they said but Jinkinson looked to grow increasingly excited. After a minute or two, he was waving an arm and seemed to be pointing across the bridge in the direction of the Clock Tower. Oughtred responded by leaning forwards and prodding the agent three times in the chest. He then turned on his heel and began to walk back towards the Palace of Westminster. As he passed Adam, the young man feigned extreme interest in the river and the curious patterns of the railings reflected on the water, but he need not have bothered. Oughtred, who looked furious, had no eyes for anybody around him. He marched on in the direction of Parliament Square and was soon lost to sight amidst the other pedestrians. Adam glanced back at Jinkinson, who had remained on the bridge. He decided he had seen enough for one morning. Hailing one of the many cabs that patrolled the area, he headed for home.

* * * * *

For the next five days, Jinkinson made few excursions from Poulter's Court without someone at his heels. The following morning it was Quint who stood near the archway and waited for the enquiry agent to emerge on his business. From that day onwards, he and his master divided the duties between them. On four of those days, Jinkinson did little but stroll through the streets that ran between High Holborn and the Strand, like a nobleman touring his estate. He nodded amiably to passing acquaintances and stopped to engage many of them in lengthy conversation. On several occasions, Jinkinson sang as he walked. He had a deep baritone voice and he always sang the same tune, treating his fellow pedestrians to an aria from an Italian opera Adam half recognised as the work of Donizetti. Was it, he wondered, *Lucia di Lammermoor*? The plump investigator peered from time to time into shop windows on his travels and rarely passed a public house without venturing inside to sample its ale. He chose to spend little time in the offices off Lincoln's Inn Fields. Only on the afternoon of the fifth day did he demonstrate any sense of purpose. It was Quint who was loitering near Poulter's Court when Jinkinson emerged at around three o'clock, and it was Quint who followed him down to the Strand. Back in Doughty Street, he reported his news to Adam while preparing a supper for himself of cold meats, bread and ale.

'It wears a man out, following old Jinks. Never was such a bugger for walking. And talking. Gawd, how 'e can talk. Gassing away at everybody he meets.'

'He's certainly a man of eloquence when given the opportunity.'

''E's like a sheep's head. All bleeding jaw.'

'True enough, Quint. But what did he do today apart from jawing?'

'Well, 'e sets off from Poulter's Court. Going at a good lick. Not like the other day when he was moochin' around like the bleeding Duke of Seven Dials. Off he goes down Chancery Lane with me a short 'op behind 'im. Into the Strand we goes and we ends up outside that pub on the corner of Fountain Court. You know the one?'

Adam indicated that he did.

''Ere we are, I thought. Ain't that just plummy?' Quint spoke with bitter sarcasm. ''E'll be in here the rest of the day and half the night and, by stop-tap, he'll be as drunk as a rolling fart. But, no, this is one pub he ain't going into. 'E stops outside. In fact, he moves round the side of the pub and stands leaning against the wall in the court.'

'Unusual, indeed, for our man to resist the lure of liquor. Was he waiting for someone, I wonder?'

''Ere, moisten your chaffer on this.' Quint handed Adam a glass of beer. 'There's more of the story to come. Jinkinson's standing there in the court and I'm a-loiterin' in the street, tryin' to keep half an eye on him, when this gent comes up the Strand from Trafalgar

Square end. All togged up to the nines like a right swell. And 'e joins our man in the court.'

'A swell, you say?'

'Thought at first he might be some Champagne Charley out on a spree. But 'e knows old Jinks.'

'So he was the man for whom Jinkinson was waiting? Any distinguishing marks to this swell?'

'Not so's you'd notice.' Quint shrugged. 'Enough moustache for ten men. Can't hardly see his mouth for lip-thatch. But nothing else.'

'And why was he meeting Jinkinson in some pub alley?'

'Old your 'orses. I'm comin' to that. Now Jinkinson don't know me, do 'e? There's no harm, I think, in getting a bit closer. So, I stagger into the court as if the drink has just took me and fall into a heap.'

'Quick thinking, Quint.'

'That's what I thought,' said Quint complacently. 'You get the picture, then. There's our man. And there's his friend, all dressed up like Christmas beef. Both of them standing in the court. And then there's me, playing the drunk and sliding down the wall. They give me a quick glance and then they forget me. They begin to talk. Whispering, mind you, but I can catch some of what they say.'

'And what do they say?'

'The gent's name is Garland. Mr Garland, I hear Jinkinson say, not once but several times. Same name as was in the book I filched.'

'Lewis Garland. He's an MP.'

'Well, this here Lewis Garland is fit to be tied. Angry as a dog chasing rats, by the sounds of 'im. Not that he raises his voice or anything. But I can tell 'e's raging.'

'He was threatening Jinkinson, was he?'

'I reckon so. But our man ain't too fussed. Sounds like 'e's doing a bit of 'is own threatening in return. Something about the papers and a scandal.' Quint sat down at the table with a plateful of food and fell upon the cold mutton and bread.

'And how did Garland respond to what our friend Jinkinson was saying?'

'He didn't say more 'n a few words. But he looked as if he was like to have forty fits, didn't 'e? Then Jinkinson was off again, yammering and chattering at 'im a bit more.'

'Could you catch any more of the conversation?' Adam asked.

'Not much.' His mouth full of meat and bread, Quint's voice was indistinct. Crumbs sprayed upon the table.

'You eat as if you'd had no sustenance in weeks, Quint. Lions rending the flesh from their prey have nothing on you attacking cold mutton.'

'All very well for you to say,' Quint responded, sounding aggrieved and still tearing chunks from the bread in front of him. 'You ain't the one who's been chasing old Jinkinson all afternoon and spent his time face down in the muck. You've prob'ly been greasing your gills down some chophouse.'

'Not guilty, your honour. However, your courage in casting yourself down amidst the inn yard's effluvia certainly deserves acknowledgement. Please accept my apologies. But do slow down, man, or you'll choke yourself and I will have no idea how to save you.' Adam took a long pull from his glass of beer. 'So, what more did you hear from Jinkinson and Garland as you were lying so selflessly in the gutter?'

'As I say, not much.' Quint drank his own ale. 'Our man, he says something about an 'arbour in the woods, whatever that might mean. Then there's some pretty choice insults exchanged atween the two of 'em. Not that I can hear 'em exactly on account of my ear's next door to a pile of horseshit, but I can get the general drift of 'em. Then Garland makes to leave. You come bothering me again, he says, and I'll darken your bleeding daylights for you. Or words to that effect. And he stomps off up the Strand in the direction he come from.'

'What about Jinkinson? What did he do?'

'What d'you think? He goes into the pub for a drop of the lush. And I picks meself up and heads back here.'

'Well done, Quint. Thanks to your initiative in hurling yourself into the filth of that pub yard, we now know that Jinkinson has approached two of the men who were named in that notebook. And at least one of them was extremely displeased when he did so. But why did he contact them?' Adam stared into his now empty glass of beer as if the answer to his question might be lurking among the dregs. 'To blackmail them, we must suppose.'

'What if this Jinkinson we've been trailing around town for days is the cove what killed Creech?' Quint asked. 'What if he was putting the squeeze on him as well, and things got a bit out of hand? You given that a thought?'

'I have, indeed.'

'Any result from giving it a thought?'

'I have come to the conclusion that Jinkinson is not the stuff of which murderers are made. He may well be a bit of a rogue, I grant you, but he is not the man who despatched poor Creech from the world. He was utterly astonished when I told him of Creech's death. He would have had to be a Kean returned from the grave to feign the surprise I saw on his face that day in his office.'

Quint stood and moved towards the fire where Adam was slumped low in the depths of his favourite armchair. He gathered up the empty glass that the young man had rested on one of its arms.

'You want another of these?' he asked, dangling the glass in front of his master's eyes. Adam shook his head. The servant retreated to the kitchen.

'You come up with any more ideas about Creech getting hisself killed, then?' he called. He returned to the sitting room clutching a green beer bottle and began to paw at its cork stopper. 'Like who might have done it?'

Adam shook his head again. 'No, I have not yet come to any conclusion about the identity of the murderer.' The young man gazed up at the ceiling. 'However, I have not been entirely idle while you have been trailing down the Strand after our friend.'

Quint grunted, as if to suggest that he wasn't sure he believed this. He had succeeded in removing the cork from his bottle and was now pouring its contents gently into his own glass. He stared at the beer with a look of intense concentration as he did so.

'I have travelled out once again to Herne Hill,' Adam continued. 'The place already looks nearly as deserted as a haunted house. Pulverbatch and his men appear to have no further interest in it. Its only inhabitant is a young man named John. He was one of Creech's servants. He is the only one who has not yet moved on to another situation, although he was eager to assure me that he has had offers from several most respectable families in the neighbourhood.'

'He's there on his own?' Quint looked up in surprise. He had almost finished his careful decanting of his beer into the glass. 'I raise my 'at to him. Wouldn't catch me lying down to sleep in a dead man's 'ouse.'

'Well, not everyone is as plagued by his imagination as you are, Quint. John is a phlegmatic character – a man unlikely to be troubled by the spirits of the dead.'

Quint grunted again and tipped half the contents of his glass down his throat.

'This 'ere John tell you anything?' he asked, after allowing his drink to settle.

'Not as much as I had hoped,' Adam admitted. 'Creech used an agency in Cheapside to hire his servants. None of them knew anything of him other than that he was a gentleman arrived recently in London from abroad. John thought he had been, and I quote his words exactly, "living with the heathen, sir". But John's ideas about geography were a bit hazy. He appeared to believe that Greece was in Africa.'

'Where were all the servants when Creech got topped?'

'He had given them the day off. John and the others thought that this was strange but none of them was going to turn his back on an extra day of freedom.'

'We was coming to see 'im. Maybe 'e didn't want his drudges to know about us.' Quint had picked up his glass and was staring reflectively at the liquid inside. 'This John say anything about visitors?'

'He had none.' Adam hauled himself to his feet and began to pace about the room. His manservant watched him, occasionally sipping at what remained of his beer. 'The consensus below stairs seemed to be that this was odd.'

'Sounds odd to me.'

'The desire for solitude is not always to be condemned as eccentric. There might have been perfectly innocent reasons why Mr Creech wanted to see no one.'

'Maybe,' Quint sniffed, 'but you don't believe that any more 'n I do.'

'No, you are correct. I don't.' Adam had stopped by the window. He twitched the curtain aside and looked down to the pavements below. Doughty Street, gated at both its ends, was quiet. Only a solitary man, dressed in a long black coat and carrying a malacca cane, was in view. Adam watched as the man made his way down the street and disappeared from sight. Then he turned back into the room. 'And our friend John did have one tale to tell of a visitor.'

Quint, who had finished his beer and had been engaged in pushing his empty glass aimlessly back and forth on the table, looked up.

'Anyone we know?'

'Difficult to tell. It was several weeks before the murder. Creech had given all the servants time off. Apparently, he did this fairly frequently. John would have been going to spend time with his sister and his young niece in Stepney. He had walked as far as the railway station when he remembered that he had a present for the girl which he had left in his room. He came back to the villa and let himself in at the servants' entrance.'

'And there was some'un else in the house.'

'You run ahead of me, Quint, but you are right. John heard voices coming from the library as he made his way past its door. And then the door opened and his master stormed out. He was furious already, and he was even more furious when he saw John. He ordered him to leave immediately. He was not to go up to the attics to retrieve what he had returned for. So the young lady in Stepney had to wait for her gift.'

'Did John see the cove Creech was with?'

'Sadly, he did not, but he heard his voice.'

Quint cocked his head inquisitively.

'He was a gentleman,' Adam said. 'The voice was that of a gentleman. That was all John could say.'

'That ain't a fat lot of 'elp.'

'Of no use to us at all, really. "Gentleman" is such an elastic term. But John did hear something of the discussion that was taking place just prior to his master emerging hotfoot from the library. I suspect that, although he would die rather than admit it, John had been loitering outside the door, listening to the conversation for some time.'

'Nosy little bleeder.'

'Absolutely. He was indulging in one of the worst crimes a servant can commit. But his sin provides us with a little more knowledge of Creech's mysterious visitor.'

'Did he 'ear his name?'

'Nothing quite so useful as that, I'm afraid. He heard voices raised in anger. He heard the word "gold" which, unsurprisingly, piqued his curiosity. He heard the unknown visitor shouting about travelling to Greece. Indeed, that was when I learned that John labours under the misapprehension that Greece is in Africa. He then heard Creech shouting back about going without him.'

'Without 'oo?'

'The enigmatic visitor, presumably.'

Quint sat back and twisted his face into an expression suggestive of deep thought and the careful consideration of different possibilities.

'I ain't sure we're any further on than we was before you spoke to this John cove,' he said after a moment. 'We still ain't got no name for the bloke Creech was raising his organ-pipe with.'

'No, we have not,' Adam agreed reluctantly. 'But we do have more knowledge than we had. We know that Creech spoke to someone else of travelling to Greece. Several weeks before he met me at the Speke dinner.'

The young man crossed the room and threw himself once more into the armchair by the fire.

'There is some connection between the argument that John witnessed and Creech's conversation with me at the Marco Polo. There must be. And the solution to the riddle lies with this name, Euphorion. I am sure of it.'

* * * * *

Adam stood outside the newly finished Italianate building which housed the Foreign Office and other government departments, and watched as his friend, the Hon. Richard Sunman, emerged from its interior. It was Sunman he had been visiting on the occasion when, if Cosmo was to be believed, his presence had been noted by that infernal bore Chevenix. It was Sunman who had first recruited him into the Foreign Office's ranks of unsalaried and unofficial travelling observers when he had been about to set out on his visit to northern Greece three years earlier. An older contemporary at Shrewsbury, the son of Baron Sunman of Petersfield had also been in his final year at Cambridge when Adam had arrived there. He had, to Adam's surprise, sought him out at his college and insisted that they should dine together. Adam, who had always been rather in awe of the languid young aristocrat, had agreed. He had assumed that Sunman had looked him up because they had both been favoured pupils of Fields.

In the confusion following his father's death, when Adam was obliged to go down from Cambridge, Sunman, newly ensconsed in the Foreign Office, invited him twice to meet him in his London club. On the second occasion, he had suggested that Adam might like to pass on any observations of Turkey in Europe he might make during his recently announced expedition with Professor Fields. After they had arrived in Salonika, Adam had dutifully despatched reports back to London. He had been uncertain what might or might not be of value to the Foreign Office so he had ended by sending enomously detailed accounts of very nearly everything he had seen and heard. On his return from Macedonia, he was at first doubtful that Sunman could have found these at all helpful but it soon became clear that his friend had been impressed by Adam's thoroughness. Several times in the last eighteen months he had, in the politest possible way, issued instructions that Adam should meet him in Whitehall. There he had, again with the utmost courtesy, questioned the one-time traveller closely on news from European Turkey. Now, for the first time, it was Adam who had sent word to Sunman and requested a meeting.

'Shall we take the air?' the tall and elegantly dressed young man asked as he approached, waving his arm vaguely in the direction of St James's Park.

'By all means,' Adam replied, falling in step with his companion. They crossed Horse Guards Parade and entered the park. As they strolled along the paths through the green trees and over the bridge across the lake, Sunman seemed disinclined to address the subject on which Adam had asked to see him. Instead he spoke lengthily and eloquently about Disraeli's novel *Lothair*, newly published and all the literary rage. Adam, who disliked the politician's fiction and had not read the book, grew impatient.

'Are you able to assist me with the business of this man, Creech?' he said eventually, breaking into his friend's monologue about Lothair and the women who competed for his attention. He was aware that he was being unconscionably rude but he could restrain himself no longer. Sunman glanced at him briefly but gave no other indication that he had noticed the abruptness with which Adam had spoken.

'A gentle word has been dropped into the ear of your acquaintance at Scotland Yard,' he said, as the two men turned into Birdcage Walk. 'Cumberbatch? Is that the fellow's name?'

'Pulverbatch.'

'Well, whatever he calls himself, he will not trouble you any further with impertinent questions. It has been strongly suggested to him that he would do better to share what information he has with you rather than to treat you as a suspect in the case.'

'I am grateful, Sunman.'

Adam was eager now to atone for his earlier impoliteness. He strove to locate a subject for discussion which his friend would find congenial. He found it in the Mordaunt divorce case, Sunman proving a surprising and well-informed connoisseur of society gossip. They walked on into Great George Street in animated conversation. As Westminster Bridge and Parliament came into view, they prepared to say their farewells.

'Oh, by the by,' Sunman said, a shade too casually, 'it seems that the fellow Creech used to be one of us.'

'One of us?'

'In the service. Years ago. He was at the embassy in Greece back in the forties.'

'But what the man was doing in Greece in the forties can scarcely have any bearing on his murder in Herne Hill in the year of our Lord 1870.'

'Don't know about that, old man. One or two rumours flying about.'

'Rumours?'

'Almost certainly nothing in them.' Sunman, so indiscreet a few moments earlier on the subject of the Prince of Wales's supposed *amours*, seemed unwilling to enlighten Adam as to the nature of the rumours. 'This fellow Creech left the service long ago. Before the war in the Crimea. Bit of a scandal, as far as I can gather. Something about being in possession of funds that he oughtn't to have been in possession of. You know the kind of thing I mean.'

The man from the Foreign Office looked at Adam, who indicated that he did, indeed, know the kind of thing that he meant.

'And yet I cannot believe that the events of a quarter of a century ago have any relevance today,' insisted Carver.

Sunman came to a halt and stood as though admiring the view of the bridge along the street.

'You may well be right. But the feeling is that there is no harm in his death being looked into.' The young aristocrat paused in his speech and looked around him, like a man in fear of being overheard. 'By someone other than Pulverbatch. In an unofficial kind of way.'

'So any further curiosity about Creech on my part would not be frowned upon by the powers that be?'

'Not at all, old chap. More likely to be smiled upon, I would say. The police are all very well, in their own way. But a fellow like yourself…'

'… might find something the police couldn't.'

'Exactly, old chap.'

CHAPTER NINE

'top here, cabbie.' Adam rapped on the roof of the hansom with his cane and the driver drew up at the kerbstones. They had just turned into High Holborn. Adam, who had hailed the cab outside the Marco Polo, now decided to leave it and walk the remainder of the journey to Poulter's Court. He was about to climb down when he became aware of sounds of disturbance further along the street. Shouts and cries and the noise of dispute could be heard amidst the usual, unending hubbub of the traffic. Up ahead, an omnibus had also come to a halt at the side of the road and the driver was engaged in a vigorous discussion with a passing pedestrian.

The debate involved much arm-waving by both men. Was the driver touting for business? Adam wondered. It was a common enough practice amongst the busmen who were rarely willing just to wait passively for passengers to present themselves. Yet this seemed a more personal argument. Customers already aboard the omnibus were beginning to get restless. Voices demanding that the bus get underway again could be heard. Up on the roof, half a dozen young men sitting back to back on the knifeboard bench were all shouting down to the driver.

The pedestrian, Adam realised as he peered from his cab, was Jinkinson. Still shouting and gesticulating at the omnibus, the enquiry agent now turned away from the altercation and began to walk back down the street. He saw the cab by the kerbstones and waved at it. His walk turned into something between a trot and a waddle as he approached. So eager was he to get into the cab that he stumbled as he hauled himself in. With a yelp of anguish, he fell into its interior, nearly landing in Adam's lap. He cried out in surprise.

'I beg your pardon most profoundly, sir. I had no notion that the cab was taken. I was so anxious to remove myself from a vulgar scene.'

'There is no need to apologise, Mr Jinkinson. I am happy to share a cab with an old acquaintance.'

'Do I know you, sir?' Jinkinson, settling himself on the well-cushioned cab seat, peered short-sightedly at the man he had joined.

'My name is Carver. I called upon you in Poulter's Court a few days since.'

There was a momentary silence and then Jinkinson spoke again, warily. 'Mr Carver, of course. I recognise you now. I must apologise again. I cannot think how I did not see you.' He took out a large polka-dotted handkerchief and mopped his brow with it. He was sweating profusely. 'My excuse must be my distress at the behaviour of those scoundrels in the omnibus.'

'The driver seemed angry with you, Mr Jinkinson.'

'His anger is as nothing compared to my own.' The enquiry agent's outrage overcame his wariness. 'The villain attempted to run his vehicle over me. Had I not moved quickly, I would have been beneath the wheels.' Jinkinson returned his handkerchief to his pocket. A trickle of sweat continued to run down his left cheek. 'When I attempted to remonstrate, I was met with nothing but vulgar abuse.'

'The average jarvey is certainly one of the most dangerous men in London. And one of the swiftest to indulge in invective.'

'They drive their chariots with all the fury of Jehu,' Jinkinson agreed, warming to his theme. 'The unhappy pedestrian is less than the dust beneath their wheels.' The enquiry agent caught Adam's eye and then swiftly looked away.

'However, I must not detain you with my complaints about these rogues of the highways. I shall leave you with apologies for disturbing you and seek out another cab. It has been a pleasure to renew our acquaintance, however briefly.' He began to shift his bulk across the seat and prepare to disembark.

'But our meeting is most fortuitous, Mr Jinkinson.' Adam placed a restraining hand on the investigator's arm. 'I was on my way to see you. I have one or two new questions to put to you. Ones which did not occur to me when I saw you in your offices last week.'

'I will answer them if I can, sir.' Jinkinson stopped his shuffling across the seat. He looked uncomfortable. Although a cool breeze was blowing through the hansom, he was still perspiring freely. 'However, I doubt if I can help. As I said when we met before, I know little of the unfortunate Mr Creech beyond what I told you.'

'My new questions do not necessarily concern Mr Creech. They involve a gentleman named Oughtred and a gentleman named Garland.'

Once again Jinkinson's inability to mask his initial response to Adam's words let him down. He struggled to replace immediate dismay with a semblance of bewilderment.

'I do not think I know the gentlemen in question.'

'Ah, but I think you do, Mr Jinkinson. I think that you have met with them both in the last week. I also think that it is time that cards were placed more openly on the table. Otherwise a police inspector at Scotland Yard by the name of Pulverbatch might well come to hear of you and your recent activities.'

There was a long pause during which Jinkinson twice appeared to be about to speak before thinking better of it. He drew several deep breaths and noisily exhaled them.

'Let us not be too hasty, Mr Carver,' he said at last. 'I must confess that I have not been entirely frank with you.'

'I had suspected as much.'

'I was not employed by Creech to locate his relative's watch.'

'It seemed to me unlikely that you had been.'

'My business with him was not as trifling as I may have given the impression it was.'

'I did not believe it could have been.'

Jinkinson began to pat his pockets, as if looking for something. Adam waited for him to speak again. After a few moments, the enquiry agent appeared to lose interest in his search. His hands dropped to his sides and he stared glumly out of the cab window at the passing traffic.

'You may not credit it, Mr Carver, but I have been a prodigious toper in the past.' Jinkinson now swerved in a new conversational direction. 'Rivers and lakes of liquor have flowed down my unregenerate gullet.'

'Many a man enjoys a drink, Mr Jinkinson.' Adam was surprised by the new turn the enquiry agent's confession had taken. He did not know quite what to say but this did not seem to matter greatly since Jinkinson ignored his remark anyway.

'I would be embarrassed to admit to you, sir, how many of the nights of my youth I have wasted at idle bacchanals. And the drink that was at those gatherings…' There was a look of the deepest nostalgia in Jinkinson's watery eye. 'You might have swum in it. If you'd a mind to do so.'

'We have all of us overindulged in our time, I am sure.'

'But those days are now gone.' The fading dandy appeared to have forgotten that the days of which he spoke included one from the previous week. 'I am now a man of sobriety and self-possession.'

'I congratulate you on your new status, sir.'

'Like prodigious topers, however, men of sobriety and self-possession need to live.'

'Undoubtedly.' Adam was still puzzled by the direction in which the conversation was moving. Jinkinson had now taken hold of the lapels of his lurid yellow jacket and had adopted the position of a courtroom lawyer about to embark on a particularly incisive address to the jury.

'To live, a man must earn money. In the sweat of his face shall he eat bread until he return unto the ground. There is no shirking honest labour simply because he has sobered up.'

'Certainly not.'

'There is more need of it. And so, when Mr Creech – God rest his soul – crossed my threshold in Poulter's Court and offered me money to follow certain gentlemen, how could I turn him away?'

'How indeed? And these gentlemen were—'

Jinkinson held up his palm to interrupt. He had not yet finished his little speech, the outstretched hand clearly said.

'How could I listen to the small voice of conscience that told me I should not? How could I turn my back on the pieces of silver the tempter offered?'

'You could not, Mr Jinkinson.'

'I could not,' the enquiry agent agreed. 'I have always been a man whom the gods of chance and fortune have shunned, Mr Carver. There's something about me like a stone round a drowning man's neck. It keeps me from rising. And yet here was a gentleman offering me money – good money – to do no more than follow certain other gentlemen.'

'And these gentlemen Creech wanted followed, they were both MPs? Sir Willoughby Oughtred and Lewis Garland?'

'And another member of our honourable legislature, Mr James Abercrombie. I tailed all three of them, yes.'

'Why did Creech want them followed?'

'That, sir, was not information that was ever vouchsafed to me.'

'Was he blackmailing these gentlemen?'

'I decided that it was in my best interests not to ask such questions, Mr Carver.'

'But you did follow them? The record in Creech's notebook seems to indicate that.'

'Oh, I followed them. On particular occasions. When Mr Creech – God rest his soul – asked me to do so.'

'And did you discover what Creech wanted to know? You could not have followed them anywhere but on the public streets. There must have been any number of places where you could not pursue them.'

Jinkinson shrugged. He returned to patting his pockets and this time he found the object for which he was looking. He extracted a silver snuffbox from the inner recesses of his jacket. He opened it and offered it to Adam, who shook his head. The enquiry agent took a pinch of snuff between thumb and forefinger and inhaled it forcefully up his right nostril. He was immediately seized by a furious coughing fit which threatened to send the rest of the contents of his snuffbox flying around the interior of the cab. Somehow he managed to wrestle the box shut, replace it in his pocket and take out the polka-dotted handkerchief again. This time he blew his nose on it several times.

'Excuse me, Mr Carver. Nothing like a pinch of snuff to clear the passages.' He seemed to have entirely recovered his self-possession.

'Did you discover what Creech wanted to know?' Adam asked again.

'I discovered a number of things. I discovered that Sir Willoughby Oughtred possesses more sidewhiskers than he does brains.' Jinkinson continued to dab at his nose with the handkerchief. 'I discovered that business at Westminster doesn't preclude a bit of further business in St John's Wood. For one MP, at least, if you catch my meaning, Mr Carver.'

'One of the men was visiting St John's Wood?'

'Lewis Garland. A particular house in St John's Wood. A particular person in St John's Wood. A very accomplished young nymph who kept him busier than he is ever kept by the affairs of the nation.'

'Aha, an arbour in the woods.' Adam recalled the words Quint had heard in the pub yard. 'I see. All very discreet, no doubt.'

'Oh, very discreet. There's a kind of covered walkway from the road to the front door.' Jinkinson gave a sudden snort of laughter. 'Convenient, wouldn't you say? A gentleman in a top hat gets out of the cab. One step and he's hidden from view. It could be anybody visiting. It could be the Archbishop of Canterbury or Mr Gladstone going to see the lady in question.'

'Was Creech interested in these visits?'

'You'd think he would be, wouldn't you? Supposing he was intending to extort money from him. A parliamentary gentleman who can't keep the member for Cockshire quiet, if you'll pardon the vulgarism.'

'But he wasn't?'

'He didn't seem to be. It was difficult to decide what Mr Creech was interested in. But he kept on handing me those pieces of silver. So I kept on following those gentlemen he wanted following.'

'As I have been following you.'

'I had no notion that you *were* following me.' Jinkinson looked surprised.

Adam was puzzled. 'But, that very first day I was in pursuit of you, you dodged down the alleyway by the tobacconists and doubled back on yourself in Fleet Street. I felt sure you must have seen me.'

'Merely my usual method of perambulating the city streets, Mr Carver. Turn and turn about. I find that a man in my line of business cannot be too careful.' Jinkinson paused and looked suddenly crestfallen. 'Although, in this instance, my precautions proved futile.'

Adam took pity on the downcast enquiry agent. 'Had it not been for a child begging in the alleyway on that first day, I should have lost you. The child had seen you and pointed me in the right direction.'

Jinkinson's face brightened. 'I am an old fox, am I not? I have my wiles and wits about me still.'

'You do, indeed. And I do believe that you have been employing them in an attempt to extract money from others.'

'That is possible, sir,' Jinkinson acknowledged. 'In this great city of ours, many of us have nothing but our wiles and wits to rely upon. To gain the wherewithal to live, I mean.'

'Not to beat about the bush, Mr Jinkinson, I believe that Creech may or may not have been attempting to blackmail the two gentlemen we have already mentioned. But that you certainly have been. Using the information you acquired when Mr Creech employed you.'

'I would not choose to use the word "blackmail", Mr Carver. Such an ugly, uncompromising word.'

'What word would you choose, Mr Jinkinson?'

'I would prefer to say that I have been striving to persuade the gentlemen that their interests would best be served if trifling sums of money passed from their possession into mine.'

Adam smiled and bowed his head in mock acknowledgement of Jinkinson's artful use of euphemism. 'And have you been successful in your efforts?'

'Alas, not yet. But I do have high hopes that the gentlemen in question will come to see reason.'

'You don't think that, perhaps, you are playing a rather dangerous game?'

'Dangerous?' Jinkinson looked genuinely puzzled.

'Gentlemen as powerful as Oughtred and Garland are not to be trifled with, you know. Not in any circumstances. And there is always the possibility that one of them might know more of Creech's death than he should.'

'No, no, no, Mr Carver.' Jinkinson waved a hand to dismiss the notion. He shifted about on the cab's leather seat, as if in preparation for leaving. 'You are barking up the wrong tree entirely with such a suggestion. Whoever killed the unfortunate Creech, it was not any of the gentlemen I have been meeting. A member of the House of Commons committing murder?' The enquiry agent was amused by the idea. 'In the past perhaps, but not in this enlightened era of ours. Probably some rogue entered his house with larcenous intent and did the poor man to death when he confronted him.'

'You have no certain way of knowing this. If Creech was a blackmailer, he may well have been killed by one of the people he was blackmailing. You take risks, Mr Jinkinson, if you take up where Creech left off.'

'The world is full of risks, Mr Carver. There is no possibility of avoiding them.' Jinkinson began to struggle to his feet in the confines of the cab. 'But I regret to say I can stay no longer to discuss them. I must say my farewell to you.'

Bent almost double to avoid striking his hat from his head as he exited, Jinkinson climbed out. He stood on the pavement, brushing snuff from his clothes, and then raised his battered black bowler to Adam.

'I do hope you won't feel obliged to let that police inspector you mentioned know about our conversation. If the gentlemen from

Westminster do not care to involve Scotland Yard's finest in their business, then why should we?'

'Why indeed?' Adam raised his own hat. 'Your dealings with Garland and the others are your own concern, sir. I shall tell no one of them.'

Jinkinson smiled and replaced the hat on his head at a jaunty angle. He reached across the wheel of the cab to offer Adam his hand.

'Goodbye, my dear Mr Carver. It has been a pleasure to renew our acquaintance. I have enjoyed our conversation. Confession, they say, is good for the soul and I have confessed so many of my little misdeeds to you. It is small wonder that I bid you adieu with such a light heart.'

With that, the enquiry agent was gone. Adam watched him disappear into the crowds that thronged the pavement of High Holborn and then rapped once more with his cane to attract the driver's attention.

'Doughty Street, if you please, cabbie.'

CHAPTER TEN

'ow went the Millais "At Home"?'

Adam was once again a visitor to Cosmo Jardine's studio in Chelsea. He was sitting in the room's only chair, smoking a cigarette. The painter was standing in front of his easel, applying the occasional brushstroke to *King Pellinore and the Questing Beast* and then standing back to judge the effect of each one.

'My dear Carver, I would ask you, as a friend, to question me no further about that particular event.'

'A social success of the first water, then?'

'A débâcle. The beautiful Mrs Millais – Effie, as I presumptuously think of her – was not present. For long periods of time, nor was Millais himself. I was left to exchange pleasantries with two watercolourists of almost preternatural stupidity and to drink tea that was even more insipid than the company. Do you know Hardisty and Hepworth?'

'I do not think I have had the pleasure of being introduced to them.'

'They are like the Siamese twins who held court at the Egyptian Hall last year,' Jardine said. 'Chang and Eng, the indivisible brothers. Hardisty and Hepworth are much the same. Where one goes, so too must the other.'

'I take it that they are not sparkling conversationalists.'

'They are not. But let us speak of something else. I cannot bear to be reminded of the occasion.'

'I shall torment you no longer with questions about it.'

'That would be a kindness much appreciated.'

'However, I have questions still about the gentleman who came to visit you, supposedly at Burne-Jones's recommendation.'

'Ah, Creech or Sinclair, or whatever he called himself.' Jardine took several steps back from his painting, staring at it as if it might move should he take his eyes off it. 'I have remembered one curious thing about his visit.'

'And what is that? What curious thing did he do?'

Jardine continued to address his remarks to his canvas. 'It was more what he said than what he did. If you recall, I told you that we spoke of art.'

'You said that you spoke of art. I assumed that that meant poor Creech had to endure a lengthy lecture on the evils of photography and the dangers it poses to the true artist.'

'Ah, you underestimate me, Carver. I do have other arrows in my quiver, you know. I believe on this occasion the subject of my disquisition was the purblind prejudice of the Academy. However, what I said is immaterial. It is what Creech-Sinclair said that signifies.'

'And that was?'

'At one point, when I had paused briefly to review my arguments in my mind, he suddenly asked me where I had been to school. I assumed that he was referring to my training in painting so I confessed that I was self-taught. But he was not. He was asking about Shrewsbury.'

'I am not certain that there is anything strange about that. There are many who believe that his school says more about a man than anything else.'

'When last we met, I think I said I did not recall him speaking of you. My memory played me false. He *did* mention your name. More than once, in fact. As if fishing for titbits of gossip and scandal.' Jardine glanced briefly over his shoulder. 'Of course, I refused to say anything that might incriminate you.'

'My thanks for your discretion.' Adam bowed ironically in the direction of his friend. 'I suppose that I should be flattered by his interest.'

'You were not the only person of my acquaintance in whom he was interested.' The painter returned to the examination of his canvas. 'He went on to ask me several questions about Fields.'

'About Fields?' Adam was surprised, but a moment's thought banished his surprise. At the Speke dinner, Creech had been asking him about the expedition to Macedonia. Of course he would want to know more of the leader of that expedition. The only puzzle was why he had chosen Cosmo Jardine to cross-examine.

'Yes, about Thomas Burton Fields. Once much-esteemed senior master at Shrewsbury School. Now Professor of Greek at Cambridge. And equally respected by all who encounter him there.'

'Why would Creech ask *you* about Fields?'

Jardine shrugged. 'I have not the slightest notion. I am not even sure how he knew that I am acquainted with the professor. Perhaps I mentioned it in the course of our conversation. But his questions were decidedly odd. Did Fields spend all his time in Cambridge? Did he have lodgings in London outside term? Did I see him in London? How he thought that I would be able to provide him with the answers to them, I do not know.'

The painter stepped back from his painting again and cocked his head to one side, as if he thought that seeing King Pellinore from an unusual angle might help him continue with the work.

'Well, of course I *was* able to answer the last question. I could tell him that I have seen the professor only once since leaving Cambridge. And that was at a dinner at the Garrick. We exchanged possibly two dozen words. Maybe three dozen, if you include the introductory How do you dos.'

'What on earth did Creech mean by asking whether or not Fields has lodgings in London?'

'I cannot imagine what he meant by any of the questions.' Jardine had taken a small brush from one of the glass jars in which all his brushes stood. He was concentrating on adding tiny details to the face of King Pellinore, his nose no more than a couple of inches from his canvas. 'In any case, I have more than enough difficulties over which to cudgel my brains without devoting time to thinking about the oddities of a gentleman who is no longer with us.'

'Difficulties, Cosmo? Amorous difficulties?' Adam was used to listening to his friend recount either long stories of the pursuit of largely unattainable young women, or equally extensive accounts of his capture of those who were only too attainable. He prepared to hear another.

'Would that they were. But they are financial. Some months ago I was obliged to attach my name to several bills and they fall due for payment at the end of the week. How the deuce I am to find the money to cover them, I do not know.'

'Will your father not stump up?'

'I fear I have tried Pater's patience once too often this year.' Jardine's father, the dean of a small West Country see, had never shown any noticeable enthusiasm for his son's choice of career. 'Several begging letters have winged their way towards the deanery already, and the summer is only just upon us.'

'You should endeavour to live within your means, Cosmo.'

'Don't, pray, be such a moralising old fraud, Adam. Have you no debts of your own?'

Adam thought a moment. It was true that he owed his tailor a trifle. He owed another trifle to the man who made his boots and shoes. And Berry Bros and Rudd had temporarily terminated his credit with them when his desire to put fine wines on his account had noticeably outstripped his ability to pay for them. Yet he did not consider himself much of a debtor.

'I have debts,' he acknowledged. 'But none which is pressing. What will happen to yours at the end of the week?'

'They will remain unpaid. And, as a result, I assume that I will be visited here in my sanctuary by nasty little fellows threatening all sorts of dire consequences if I do not immediately sell my furniture.'

'You have little enough furniture to sell,' Adam remarked, looking around Jardine's spartan studio.

'I suppose the matter would eventually come before a court.' The artist ignored his friend's comment. 'And I would be inevitably convicted and sent off to Botany Bay, or wherever it is they now send those who put their names to bills which they shouldn't.'

'I cannot promise to pay you a visit there.'

'I would not expect one. The climate, I am told, is atrocious and so, too, are the food and drink. The company is even worse. But enough of my troubles. You must tell me of yours. There is no better way of relieving one's own pains than by listening to the tale of someone else's.'

'I am not certain that I have any, Cosmo.'

'You stumble over a fresh corpse in some distant part of the metropolis and yet you claim to be free of troubles. I find that difficult to believe. Were you not called upon at the inquest? There was an inquest, I suppose?'

'There was. Two days after I found the body. Did I not speak to you of it?'

Jardine shook his head. He continued to peer at his canvas from a distance of a few inches, occasionally making the smallest of strokes with his brush.

'Well, I stood up and told my story. Quint told his. The police inspector, Pulverbatch, stood up and hummed and hahed about investigating this and ascertaining that. And the jury retired for about five minutes before returning a verdict of wilful murder by person or persons unknown.'

'So there was no suggestion that it might be *felo de se*? That Creech might deserve to have his body carried off to the crossroads? Is that what they still do to suicides? Off to the meeting of four roads and a stake through the heart to discourage the ghost from travelling?'

There was an awkward pause. Jardine suddenly realised that he had spoken lightly on a subject in which his friend might struggle to find any humour.

'I am truly sorry, Adam,' he said. 'I had forgotten for the moment… I have allowed my tongue to run away with me… Your father… '

'It is of no matter, Cosmo,' Adam said, turning away and looking out of the studio window. He was aware that he was not speaking the truth. Such casual mention of self-murder could still stir unpleasant memories. 'I cannot spend my entire life avoiding all talk of such things. It is years since my father's demise.'

'Nonetheless, I apologise.'

'Apologies accepted, old fellow.' Adam turned back to his friend. 'In truth, I am not certain what happens to suicides in these enlightened times. But there is no possibility that the man killed himself. I saw the body. The wounds were such that they could not have been self-inflicted.'

'What of this tippling private investigator you visited? Jenkins, was it?'

'Jinkinson.'

'Jinkinson, then. I stand corrected. Did he put in an appearance?'

'No, he did not. I am by no means certain that the police are aware of his existence.'

'Should you not alert them to his role in the drama?'

'I am not at all sure what his role is, Cosmo.' Adam lit another cigarette and inhaled deeply. He blew out a series of smoke rings and watched them drift towards the ceiling. 'I am inclined to believe that he knows nothing of the killing and that he could have made no useful contribution to proceedings at the inquest. However, the curious thing is that he seems to have disappeared.'

'Disappeared?'

'Quint and I followed him for several days after my first encounter with him. He was, in his own way, a man of regular habits. But we have not seen him in any of his usual haunts for nearly a week.'

'There you have the proof, then.' Jardine turned from King Pellinore and wiped his hand on his paint-smeared smock. 'Jinkinson was known to Creech. He was employed by him to engage in nefarious activity. Creech is murdered. Jinkinson disappears. Ergo, Creech was killed by Jinkinson. *Quod erat demonstrandum.*' The artist waved his brush in a triumphant conclusion to his reasoning and small flecks of paint flew into the air.

Adam shook his head. 'It is not as simple as that, Cosmo. Logic points in the direction of your argument, I allow. Perhaps I *should* just go to Scotland Yard and tell Pulverbatch what I have not so far told him. Yet there is something more to the story, I am sure of it.'

CHAPTER ELEVEN

'I ain't seen him, I tell yer.' The boy's voice quavered with indignation. 'How many more times I got to say it? I ain't seen the old fool in days.'

'But you have been coming to the office each day and opening up?'

'He give me the key last Michaelmas. I've been using it to let myself in. Old Jinks'd expect me to. Anyways, I got me own work to do, you know.' Simpkins spoke with a sense of his own virtue in insisting on coming in to the office.

Quint snorted contemptuously. Adam glanced sceptically at the copy of *Varney the Vampire or The Beast of Blood* which lay face upwards on the boy's desk.

'Can't work all the time, can I?' Simpkins said, noticing where Adam was looking. 'A man's got to have a bit of recreation, ain't he?'

A fly was buzzing around the room. The boy watched it move from desk to window frame and window frame back to desk. He rolled up his copy of *Varney the Vampire* and, as the fly settled on the desk for the second time, he swatted it. The rolled-up penny dreadful descended on the insect with a tremendous thwack. The buzzing was heard no more.

'Got the little bugger,' the boy said, with a leer of satisfaction. He inspected the remains of the fly, splattered across an illustration of a befanged Varney threatening a cowering female, before flicking them to the floor. 'Don't want you gents troubled by that bleeding buzzing.'

'Very thoughtful of you, Mr Simpkins. Where do you suppose Mr Jinkinson has been these few days past?'

After the chance encounter with the private investigator in the cab in High Holborn, Adam had thought it expedient to continue his efforts to learn more of Jinkinson and what he knew about the three MPs whose names had appeared in Creech's notebook. For this reason, either he or Quint had again been stationed at the entrance to Poulter's Court for several hours of every day. His own curiosity and his friend Sunman's suggestion that he should pursue his inquiries into Creech's murder combined to make it seem time well spent. They had watched Simpkins and the other clerks who spent most of their daylight hours in the offices surrounding the court as they came and went. Of Jinkinson there had been no sign. As Adam had told Cosmo Jardine the previous afternoon, the fat enquiry agent had disappeared. Eventually, the young man had decided that the time had come to confront the boy who guarded the entrance to Jinkinson's lair, and ask him what he knew of his master's whereabouts.

'How should I know?' Simpkins said, shrugging his shoulders. 'He don't tell me everything about his life any more'n I tell him everything about mine. Maybe he's gone off with that tart of his.'

'That tart? What tart?'

'The woman he's so spooney about. Ada, her name is.'

'And what can you tell me about Ada?'

'She's an obliging girl, Ada is.' Simpkins winked horribly. 'Ask her to sit down and she'll lie down. If you gets my meaning.'

'And where does Ada live?'

The boy shrugged again. 'She's a tart. She don't *live* anywhere.'

'But where would Mr Jinkinson go if he was visiting her?'

'I *told* you.' Simpkins had swapped his tone of indignation for one of exaggerated patience. Adam, he implied, was being extremely slow on the uptake. 'She's a working girl. He'd go where she'd go. And she'd go anywhere, if you takes my meaning.' Simpkins indulged himself in another ostentatious wink. In his own mind, he was now a man of the world exchanging pleasantries with another man of the world.

'How can you be so sure the lady in question is a working girl?'

'Well, old Jinks give her a sov at least twice to my knowledge.' Simpkins tapped the side of his nose. 'And I think I knows what he give her it for.'

'And what would that be, Mr Simpkins?'

The boy looked at Adam with withering pity. He shook his head wearily as if he could scarcely credit such naivety.

'What d'you *think*, guv?' he said. 'He's been paying her to get amongst her frills. And, if that don't make her a tart, I'd like to know what does.'

Adam realised he would get no further asking after Ada.

'I assume, Mr Simpkins, that you would have no objection if my associate and I were to have a look around your employer's office. It is important that we find him.'

'I ain't so sure about that.' The boy sounded doubtful. 'I don't know as you can just march in and start a-rummaging around in old Jinks's things.'

Quint, who had been quiet up to this point, was beginning to lose his patience. He made as if to raise his right fist. Simpkins noticed the movement.

'Although,' he added with alacrity, 'I suppose there ain't any harm in it.'

'None whatsoever,' said Adam soothingly. 'Indeed, there might be a half crown in it. For you, that is.'

The boy's face brightened. 'Well, in that case, it's a business transaction, ain't it? And old Jinks, he'd want me to look after his business transactions, wouldn't he?'

'Indubitably.' Adam slipped the coin into the boy's hand.

'Come this way, gents.' Simpkins opened the connecting door between his own office and his master's with a flourish. He ushered Adam and Quint inside with the dignified air of a butler inviting visitors into a stately home. 'I shall leave you to your rummaging. If you wants me, I shall be next door. Attending to matters appertaining to the private enquiry business.'

The boy left the room. Quint walked over to Jinkinson's desk and ran his finger across its surface. He examined the dust on his fingertip.

'He ain't lying. Been nobody here for days.' He wiped his finger on his jacket and looked around Jinkinson's shabby and sparsely furnished office. The carousing boors and the haughty hidalgo stared down from the prints on the wall. 'What exackly are we after, anyways? Can't hide nothing here. Or nothing *worth* hiding.'

'Some clue that might indicate Jinkinson's whereabouts.' Adam pulled at the handle of a drawer to the desk. To his slight surprise, it opened immediately. 'He keeps his desk unlocked, I see. Which suggests that he keeps his valuables elsewhere.'

'If he has any.'

Adam began to empty the desk drawer of its contents. A small saucer with the remains of several penn'orth of pickled whelks on it. A length of string and a lump of very ancient-looking sealing wax. A piece of writing paper on which Jinkinson appeared to have been practising his own signature. A chipped enamel vesta box. Quint picked the latter off the desktop.

'Like something I could buy in a cheap swag shop,' he said dismissively.

'You could find a similar one for sixpence at the Baker Street bazaar,' Adam agreed. 'And still have the change to take in the wax-works at Madame Tussauds while you were about it.'

The young man pulled the drawer entirely out of the desk. He shook it and the last of its contents fluttered to the floor.

'This is a curious thing for him to keep,' he said, slotting the drawer back into its place and picking up something that had fallen in the dust. He held it up for Quint to see. It was a fragment of cloth clearly torn from the corner of a larger piece, perhaps a sheet. Written on the fabric in black and seemingly indelible ink were the words: 'Stolen from Bellamy's Lodging House, Golden Lane'.

'Why would he have this?'

'Reminder of a client's address?' suggested Quint.

'It's an odd reminder to have. Why not just write the address down? And, in any case, someone living in a lodging house would be unlikely to have the money or the inclination to employ an enquiry agent. And why leave the lodging house with a sheet or a blanket or whatever this comes from?'

Quint was swift with an answer to the last question. 'Bedding gets thieved from these paddingkens all the time. Fetches a bob or two down any market. That's why the keepers of the kens mark it like that. Maybe Jinkinson has took to lifting the stuff. Maybe he's that desperate for rhino.'

'Why rip off just the corner?' Adam knew the answer as soon as he had asked the question. 'Ah, of course, it's the only means of identifying the lodging house to which it belonged. But why keep it? Why not simply throw it away?'

This time Quint had no ready answer.

'Maybe the boy would know,' Adam said.

The boy was no longer in the outer room. In the ten minutes that Adam and Quint had spent in the inner office, Simpkins had clearly decided that his work was done and had left.

'Where's that young varmint gone?'

'The half crown I gave him was doubtless crying out to be spent,' Adam said. 'Find the nearest alehouse and I wager you will find Master Simpkins.'

'There's the Seven Stars in Carey Street. That's just around the corner.'

'We shall try the Seven Stars first. I recall I passed it on the first day I was dogging Jinkinson's footsteps.'

* * * * *

A brewery dray had stopped in the middle of the street outside the pub. Its driver and his assistant had climbed out of their vehicle and were pulling down the ropes they would need to ease the barrels of beer into the cellar. The publican emerged carrying two tankards of ale for the men. It was clear that this would be no speedy delivery.

Adam and Quint walked past the dray and turned into the Seven Stars. Adam raised his hat to the landlord as they passed. The man nodded briefly. Inside the taproom, three young men with a fine sense of their own importance, articled clerks perhaps, stood by the bar with glasses of stout in their hands. They were shouting to one another about a river excursion they had made at the weekend.

'There ain't no fish dinner to match a Greenwich fish dinner,' the noisiest of the young men was proclaiming truculently as if the others might be prepared to disagree with him. 'And there ain't no Greenwich fish dinner to match the one they gives you at the Ship.'

Far from disagreeing, his companions hurried to concur with him. 'You ain't wrong there, Walter,' one said. The other raised his glass and saluted his friend's good taste

'That's the truth of it,' Walter went on, still seeming to detect a hint of dissent somewhere in the room. 'And anybody as argues differently ain't worth a cobbler's curse.'

Next to Walter and his friends, propped nonchalantly against the wooden bar and intent on giving the impression that he was as much a man of the world as they were, was Simpkins. He was drinking from a tumbler of gin and surveying the room with a lordly air. A cheap stovepipe hat was jammed on his head at what he clearly considered to be a jaunty angle. He didn't look delighted to see Adam and Quint again, but nor did he look worried by their appearance.

'You two are persistent gents. I'll say that for you.'

'We found this.' Adam showed the boy the scrap of cloth. 'We were wondering if there is some connection between your employer and this lodging house in Golden Lane.'

'Might be. Or might not be.' Simpkins gulped at his gin and made a smacking noise of appreciation, like a wine connoisseur savouring a particularly fine vintage. Walter and his two companions had moved away from the bar and taken seats by the window where they continued to talk cheerfully of whitebait and champagne.

'Does your employer have some secret that we should know?' Adam asked.

'Well, if it is a secret, I ain't being paid to keep it one.'

'So, enlighten us.'

'I might like to be paid to tell it, though.'

'I'm sure you would,' Adam acknowledged. 'But, if you recall, a half crown has already passed from my possession into yours. A half crown is a substantial sum of money. It should buy a deal of information.'

'That was for letting you into old Jinks's office. I reckon this is a whole new transaction.'

'Well, Mr Simpkins, I'm sorry to have to say that my friend and I' – Adam gestured towards Quint who was glaring at the young clerk with a peculiar ferocity – 'we reckon otherwise. We reckon it's all part of the same transaction.'

Simpkins glanced at Quint and decided against prolonging the discussion.

'All right, guv'nor. Worth asking but no offence intended. A man's got to make his way in the world, ain't he? Ain't nobody going to help him but himself, I reckon.'

'I see you are a disciple of Mr Smiles, Mr Simpkins.'

Simpkins looked puzzled.

'A gentleman who is an advocate of self-help.'

The clerk still looked puzzled. 'A man's got to help himself,' he repeated.

'Precisely. And the way you can help yourself in the present circumstances is to tell me all you know about Jinkinson and this Bellamy's Lodging House.'

'Don't know much.'

'Nonetheless, you can tell me what you do know. Has Jinkinson spent time there? Or does he own the place? Does it have any connection with the young lady, Ada, whom you mentioned earlier?'

Simpkins held up his hands as if to ward off the questions. 'I tell yer, I don't know much. All I know is Jinks has a few hole-ups. Places where he goes when people wants to find him and he don't want to be found.'

'And this Bellamy's is one of them?'

'I reckon so. Last year, round about July time, he went missing just like he done now. Some lawyer from the Temple was interested in a-talking to him. On account of Jinks'd took a guinea from him to track down a gent. And then gone and done bugger all but drink it.'

'And your master chose to lie low for a while?'

' "Simpkins," he says to me one morning, "it's time for me to go to ground." And that's the last I sees of him for a week. "But," he says before he goes, "a letter addressed to The Count at Bellamy's Lodging House, Golden Lane would likely find me." '

'The count? Who is the count?'

'Search me. Never seen any kind of count round the office, that's for sure.'

'And did you need to make contact with your master during the week he was gone?'

The clerk shook his head. 'Nah. The lawyer gent comes round a few times, swearing like a bargee and threatening 'e'd 'ave the peelers on us. But I reckoned old Jinks wouldn't want to know about that. Anyways, 'e come back before the week's out.'

'Did the lawyer ever have his money returned?' Adam asked, curious to know what had happened.

Simpkins gave a short laugh. 'You're joking, ain't you? A guinea? Jinks'd have sawed his own leg off rather than give a guinea back. The lawyer gent still comes round once ev'ry month or so. A-shouting and a-yelling. But it's more of a game now, if you see what I mean. 'E knows his guinea's gone.'

Simpkins downed his drink and held the glass up to the light coming in through the window, angling it this way and that as if searching for one small droplet of liquor that might still be lurking within it. Adam turned to the barman and ordered another tumbler of gin for the young clerk.

'What about this young woman Ada you mentioned?'

'Ada's all right. For a tart. It's her mother what needs the watching. She'd have the hair off a man's head if she could get a penny a pound for it.'

'Her mother?'

'Fat old witch,' said Simpkins unchivalrously. 'Round the office all the time, poking and prying.'

'So Ada's mother was looking to make money out of your master?'

Simpkins laughed. 'Do dogs bark at cats? Course she was.'

'You could see that she was intent on extorting as much cash from Mr Jinkinson as she was able?'

'Course I could.'

'And you said nothing to him?'

The clerk shrugged. 'Weren't much I *could* say. If the old fool wants to make ducks and drakes of his sovereigns and throw them all away, then he ain't goin' to stop just cos I've said something.'

'Was your master not aware himself of how venal Ada's mother was?'

Simpkins looked at Adam in bewilderment.

'Couldn't 'e see she was out to fleece him?' Quint interpreted.

'He ain't going to see it,' the clerk said. 'He's too busy casting sheep's eyes at Ada. Anyways, he has as much idea about women as a donkey has of Sunday.' The clerk spoke with the assurance of a practised and worldly observer of the opposite sex. 'I tell you, between them they had old Jinks's ballocks in a cloven stick. And the old hag at least was out to squeeze 'em. But 'e couldn't see it.'

* * * * *

'Maybe this girl Ada *has* been hawking her mutton on the streets. There's plenty what's forced to do it. On the other hand, she might not be a regular tart at all, whatever the boy says. She might be just some dollymop out for a good time. With an older gent what pays her way for her.' Quint had settled himself at one of the tables in a chophouse on Chancery Lane. He looked across at his master who had lowered himself onto the bench opposite him.

'Who can tell? She may be a veritable Thais, for all we know,' Adam remarked. 'Although old Jinkinson makes a poor Alexander, it has to be said. But it's most likely that she does sell herself somewhere on the streets.'

He gestured to the waiter, who approached and took their order.

'Perhaps we should look to find this woman,' he continued. 'The boy Simpkins may be correct. Jinkinson may have gone off with her.'

'We've lost old Jinks already. Now we're going to find a tart?'

Quint sounded disbelieving. "'Ow we going to do that? London's full of 'em.'

'Agreed. The Cyprian corps is everywhere. If a man walks from the top of the Haymarket to the top of Grosvenor Place, he will receive two dozen invitations to stray from the path of virtue in the course of five minutes.'

'Well, Ada ain't likely to be among those doin' the invitin' in the 'aymarket. More chance she's in some backstreet case-house somewhere.'

'You know best, Quint. I shall leave the job of finding her to you. I mean it as no insult when I say that you know the backstreets of the city better than I do. You should consider it as a compliment.'

Quint's expression suggested that he thought it a backhanded compliment at best. His eyes brightened when the waiter materialised silently at the table with their drinks. Quint raised his tankard immediately to his lips and took a long pull on it. Then he placed it with a flourish on the table.

'That hit the mark,' he said. 'And what'll you be doing while I'm off in search of a tart?'

Adam leant back on the bench and surveyed the chophouse. It was not yet midday and there were few people in the place. Three men were huddled over cups of coffee at the table next to them, conducting a conversation in conspiratorial whispers. Another man at a corner table – a junior clerk of some kind, judging by his dress – looked up briefly from his copy of *Reynolds's Weekly* and then returned to his reading.

'I shall endeavour to find out more about the mysterious Mr Creech. He is at the heart of everything that has been most puzzling in the events of the last few weeks. Who exactly was he? What mark did he make upon the world before his untimely death in that Herne Hill villa?'

'And 'ow you proposing to do that exackly? You didn' 'av' much luck the other day. Even his servants knew bugger all about 'im.'

'True enough.' Adam smiled. 'I am not entirely certain how I am to put flesh on Creech's poor dead bones. But I think I might begin by making enquiries of the men named in his notebook. He knew something of them. Perhaps they know something of him.'

'The nobs, you mean.'

'Sir Willoughby Oughtred. And Lewis Garland and James Abercrombie.'

'"Ow you going to get to speak to them?"

'They are all MPs.' Adam turned over in his mind the possibilities of approaching the three men in the Houses of Parliament. But would this be a suitable setting in which to ask them questions they might be uncomfortable answering? Perhaps less formal surroundings would be better. A thought struck him. 'We also know that Oughtred, Garland and Abercrombie are members of the Marco Polo. I wonder if Mr Moorhouse might be able to put me on the right track. He spends most of his waking hours in the club. And many of his sleeping ones, too. He knows everyone.'

The clerk at the corner table had finished reading his *Reynolds's* and was making his way towards the exit into Chancery Lane. He raised his hat as he passed them. Adam returned his polite salute.

'And how will you begin to look for Jinkinson's *femme fatale?*' he asked, turning back to his manservant.

'Maybe I should go back and have another word with that little ink-spiller in Poulter's Court. Put the fear of God up him. He might know something more about her.' Quint had clenched his fists and was examining them as if confirming their ability to put the fear of God up people.

The waiter returned with their plates of food. He banged them down on the table like a military drummer striking his instrument and walked off without a word.

'Simpkins?' Adam dismissed the idea. 'No. He's told us all he knows.'

'Just a thought. For half a farthing, I'd be happy to tan that young rip's arse.' Quint unrolled his fists and picked up his knife. He poked suspiciously at the meat on his plate. 'This is thin flank, by the looks of it.'

'Do stop complaining, Quint. We're not at Simpson's or Verrey's.

We're in a Chancery Lane chophouse. I had no idea you were so difficult a man to please at table.'

'I ain't.' As if to prove he wasn't, Quint began to shovel meat and mashed potato into his mouth at an alarming rate. He spoke between mouthfuls. 'I just likes to see some sign the meat come off a fat cow, not a scraggy dog.'

'I am sure the neighbourhood curs are safe enough from cook's attentions.' Adam picked up his own knife and fork and began to prod half-heartedly at the food. 'Although this is indeed an enigmatic dish the waiter has flung before us. Is it beef? Or is it pork?'

'Maybe neither. It tastes better 'n it looks.'

'It is a relief to hear you say that. Although, it would be difficult for it to do otherwise.' Adam took a mouthful of the food, grimacing slightly as he did so. He chewed and swallowed with the air of a man undertaking an unpleasant but unavoidable duty. 'But you have still not answered my question about looking for Ada.'

Quint ceased eating just long enough to lay down his fork and tap the side of his nose with his forefinger.

'Ain't no need for you to worry about that. It might take a few days, but I'll find her.'

'Very well, I bow to your superior knowledge. We shall meet back at Doughty Street at six. And let us both endeavour to avoid the eagle-eyed vigilance of Mrs Gaffery when we return there. I have no wish to endure another cross-examination of the kind she has been undertaking so regularly of late.'

CHAPTER TWELVE

I n the smoking room of the Marco Polo, the modern world with all its noise and bustle and distraction was kept firmly at bay. Deep in the embrace of one of its enormous leather chairs, Mr Moorhouse seemed to have entered a kind of tobacco-induced trance. On entering the room, Adam thought at first it was empty. Only when he noticed smoke signals arising from a distant corner and followed them to their source did he find his man.

'Ah, Carver. You'll join me, I trust?' Mr Moorhouse said, coming back to consciousness and waving to the seat opposite his own.

Adam sank into its enveloping depths and lit a cigarette. His companion seemed to have no desire for conversation. He was happy enough just to rest in silent harmony amidst the swirling clouds of smoke. Several minutes passed. Adam finished his cigarette and stubbed it out in one of the vast brass ashtrays the Marco Polo provided for its members. He began to suspect that Mr Moorhouse, although his eyes remained open, had fallen once more into a state of transfixion.

'The Glorious Twelfth,' the old clubman said suddenly.

'I beg your pardon, Mr Moorhouse?'

'Just thinking about the shooting. Glorious Twelfth. Start of the grouse season and all that. Exactly two months from today.' Mr Moorhouse took a long pull on his cigar and blew smoke in large plumes towards the ceiling. 'Never been much of a one for shooting,' he continued. 'Don't seem to have the eyes for it. Last time I went out with Oughtred on his moors, I shot one of the beaters.'

He paused and watched his smoke drifting through the air. 'Well, winged him. Fellow was awfully good about it. I gave him a guinea and he said no more.'

His sporting recollections seemingly at an end, Mr Moorhouse fell silent. Now that the old man had himself referred to Oughtred by name, Adam was quick to seize the opportunity to introduce the subject that was uppermost in his mind.

'You will remember a gentleman named Creech at the Speke dinner, Mr Moorhouse.'

Adam was far from sure that his elderly friend would, but he decided to give Mr Moorhouse's memory the benefit of the doubt.

'Creech? Tallish chap? With an odd scar?' Mr Moorhouse gestured vaguely towards his own eyebrows. 'Yes, I remember him. Seemed a decent sort of fellow.'

'Well, I'm sorry to have to tell you that he's dead.'

'Dead? Good God, that's a bit sudden, isn't it?' Mr Moorhouse appeared genuinely distressed to hear of the death. 'His heart, was it? Or an apoplexy, maybe? I always think those dinners are just disasters waiting to strike. All those steaming plates of rich food. And all those fine wines. I never take more than a few mouthfuls myself.'

'He was murdered, Mr Moorhouse.'

'Murdered?' If he had been upset by the news of Creech's death, Mr Moorhouse was utterly aghast at the mention of murder.

'I was unlucky enough to be the person who found him.'

'My dear fellow! How absolutely awful!' Mr Moorhouse was so cast down it seemed as if he might be about to shed tears of sympathy. 'Murder's a wretched business. I remember the Courvoisier case. The valet who murdered his master. You must recall it yourself.'

'It was before my time, Mr Moorhouse. I believe it was thirty years ago.'

'Was it? Was it really? As long ago as that. *Eheu fugaces*, eh, as old Horace said. Anyway, murder's a terrible thing.' Mr Moorhouse stared sadly into space. 'And the punishment of it. I saw

Courvoisier hang, you know. Outside Newgate. Thousands of people there, all howling for the man's death. Shocking state of affairs. Quite spoiled my opinion of my fellow man. Never been to another hanging since. Wouldn't go to one now if you offered me a hundred pounds.'

'There will be no more opportunity for you to go to one, Mr Moorhouse, even should you wish to do so. There are to be no more public hangings. The last to suffer that way was the Fenian bomber two years past.'

'Really?' Mr Moorhouse's ignorance of very nearly everything that had happened in the public world over the last ten years was remarkable. 'Jolly good show, if you ask me. Brings out the worst in people, a hanging.'

'I was obliged to give evidence at the inquest into Creech's death.'

'Very disagreeable.' Mr Moorhouse shook his head and made a grimace of sympathy. 'Never did like courtrooms and those sorts of places. Everyone's so deucedly rude in them. Asking all kinds of impertinent questions.'

'Of course, further details of Creech's life emerged in the course of the inquest.'

Mr Moorhouse seemed to have lost interest in the case. He was gazing into the middle distance. Perhaps, Adam thought, he was remembering some occasion in his past when he had appeared in a courtroom and faced impertinent questions. The old man had once confided in him that he had, many years earlier, made the mistake of affixing his name to a bill of exchange and lived to regret it deeply. Perhaps the regret involved appearing before an unsympathetic judge in a case of financial default.

'It seems Mr Creech knew several members of our club,' the young man remarked after a moment.

'Well, he'd have to know somebody here' – Mr Moorhouse, returning to awareness of his present surroundings, spoke mildly but with the air of a man pointing out the obvious – 'in order to be invited to the Speke dinner.'

'Well, he spoke of Baxendale to me. Said he'd arranged with him to be seated next to me. But I received the distinct impression that he had other friends in the Marco Polo.'

Mr Moorhouse blew a small cumulus cloud of cigar smoke into the air and waved his hand idly through it. 'Bound to be the case,' he agreed. 'Every chap you meet here always seems to know lots of other chaps you've already met.'

'Sir Willoughby Oughtred's name cropped up at the inquest in connection with Creech's.' Adam decided that a white lie was forgivable in the circumstances. 'And those of two other MPs: Lewis Garland's and James Abercrombie's.'

Mr Moorhouse made no reply. He had clearly recovered from his passing shock at the news of Creech's death. He smiled benignly at his companion but said nothing. Instead he took another puff on his cigar.

'You know Sir Willoughby, of course,' Adam prompted. 'You spoke of shooting on his moors just now.'

'Oh, yes. Met him many years ago. Not long after Pam came into office for the last time. My brother introduced me to him.' The old clubman settled even further into the depths of his armchair. 'Oughtred that is, not Palmerston. Never met *him*. Don't think I'd have wanted to.'

'I had no notion that you had a brother, Mr Moorhouse.'

'He's dead now.'

'I'm sorry to hear that.'

'Oh, no need to be.' Mr Moorhouse waved his hand through the cigar smoke again. 'He passed away in sixty-six. Poor Robin. Suffered frightfully with his nerves. He knew Sir Willoughby because they were both in the House. He introduced us at a dinner at some house in Curzon Street. I used to go to those sorts of things all the time then.' Mr Moorhouse spoke as if he could scarcely credit the reckless follies of his earlier self. 'Never go to them now. Never go anywhere now. I'd much rather just sit here and watch the world go by.'

It was beginning to look as if speaking to the old man would prove a fruitless exercise, but Adam decided to continue anyway.

'No hint of scandal attaches itself to Oughtred's name to the best of your knowledge?'

'Scandal?' Mr Moorhouse looked perplexed. 'What kind of scandal?'

'Financial, perhaps?' Adam was unsure exactly how frank he could or should be with the elderly clubman. What would he consider enjoyable gossip and what unforgivable indiscretion? Mr Moorhouse was shaking his head. 'Or marital?'

'Good Lord, no! Never heard anything of that kind. Oughtred would be the last person I would suspect of that sort of... aah, straying.' Mr Moorhouse continued to shake his head in vigorous repudiation of the suggestion that he might know anything that would sully the baronet's reputation. Suddenly, he leaned forward in his chair. 'Have you heard anything?' he asked.

'Nothing.'

'Pity! Always enjoy a bit of tittle-tattle.'

The old man fell back once more into the comforting depths of his leather armchair. He said nothing more. His eyes closed and, after a few moments, Adam wondered if he had drifted off into a light sleep. It seemed once more as if the idea of questioning Mr Moorhouse had not been an especially inspired one. Adam prepared to leave the smoking room. He had hauled himself to his feet, escaping the clinging embrace of his own chair, and was just about to head for the door when Mr Moorhouse opened one eye and spoke again.

'Plenty of tittle-tattle about that Garland fellow, of course.'

Adam promptly sat down once more.

'Never have taken to him,' Mr Moorhouse continued. 'Bit too fond of the sound of his own voice, if you ask me. Of course, not much point entering the House if you don't like listening to yourself pontificating. But people like that fellow go a bit far.'

'What have you heard of Lewis Garland, Mr Moorhouse?'

'Oughtred introduced us earlier this year. Fellow was prosing on and on about the state India was in. Pretty dull stuff, if truth be told, but when I ventured to express an opinion of my own, he was downright rude. Made it only too clear he thought I'd no notion at all what I was talking about.' The old man rescued a cigar which he had allowed to extinguish itself in one of the ashtrays and began fumbling in his pockets for his vesta. 'Not that I had, to be honest. Never considered myself an expert on the great subcontinent, but any real gentleman would have heard me out at the very least.'

'What is the gossip about Garland, Mr Moorhouse?' Adam pulled his own silver vesta box from his jacket and struck one of the matches.

'Oh, that!' The old man leaned forward towards the proffered light. He took a drag on his cigar and fell back in his chair. He blew out the smoke and then dipped his head forward once more.

'Women,' he whispered, so close that Adam could feel the old man's breath fluttering in his ear.

Mr Moorhouse collapsed back into his leather armchair with what could only be described as a smirk on his face.

'Garland has a reputation as a ladies' man, does he? I had heard something about a pied-à-terre in St John's Wood.'

'Ever come across Beattie here?'

'The name is familiar, but I have not been introduced to him.'

'Some sort of banker in the City. Terribly nice chap. Been a member of the club for years.'

'And he knows Garland?'

'Does business with him regularly. Something to do with a railway company. Garland's on the board. Maybe Beattie is as well.' Mr Moorhouse fluttered his fingers vaguely in the air. It was clear that he had only the flimsiest notions of what went on in the City. 'Anyway, he told me once about Garland's friend in St John's Wood. Not sure how he knew but he seemed very certain of his facts.'

'What did he tell you?'

Mr Moorhouse shuffled forwards in his chair. He looked to the left and to the right like a man preparing to cross a busy road and then leaned towards Adam.

'She's an actress.' He spoke as if this were the most surprising of all professions that Garland's lady friend might pursue. Adam, who had already heard of Garland's amatory arrangements from Jinkinson, was not surprised.

'Not just any actress,' Mr Moorhouse went on. 'Lottie Lawrence.'

Adam had heard the name. Had she not been one of the actresses in Fechter's company when he had charge at the Lyceum a few years earlier? Mr Moorhouse, who seemed by this point breathless with excitement at the thought of Garland's love life, immediately confirmed his memory.

'Beautiful woman. Saw her myself at the Lyceum. In *The Lady of Lyons*.' There was a pause as Mr Moorhouse drew energetically on his cigar. 'She played the Lady,' he added.

Adam took out his cigarette case, extracted a cigarette and lit it. He was half intrigued and half disappointed by his elderly friend's revelations about the identity of Garland's lover. It was interesting to learn that she was well known in her own right. Perhaps her fame as an actress granted first Creech and then Jinkinson an extra advantage in their financial negotiations with Garland. Perhaps, he thought suddenly, one or both of them had approached Lottie Lawrence herself in an effort to extort additional money from her. And yet he had discovered little more than he already knew about the amorous MP. He had learned a name. That was all.

'Is there anything more to tell, Mr Moorhouse?'

The old man appeared to have entered a pleasant reverie in which, perhaps, the images of the actresses he had seen on stage in a lifetime of theatre-going were drifting through his mind. He started when Adam spoke.

'What was that, old chap?'

'Did your friend Beattie let slip any further revelations about Garland?'

'None that I can recall.' Mr Moorhouse had decided that he had smoked his cigar to its end and was looking around for the ashtray in which to deposit the butt. Adam passed him the brass one from the small table by his side.

'But you said "women",' he remarked. 'You said that the gossip surrounding Garland concerned "women". In the plural rather than the singular.'

'Did I, old chap? Just my way of putting it, I suppose.' Mr Moorhouse was having difficulty dousing his smouldering cigar in the ashtray and his attention was concentrated on performing this task. 'Although, now I come to think of it, Beattie did say that Garland was a devil with his maidservants as well.'

The old clubman had finally succeeded in extinguishing the cigar and he turned to Adam with a look of triumph on his face and ash on his fingertips.

'A devil?'

'Always after them. Forcing his attentions on them.' Mr Moorhouse's delight in his victory over the cigar stub disappeared and he shook his head sadly. 'I do think behaviour of that kind is exceedingly caddish. Poor girls! They're not in a position to refuse his advances, are they? And the consequences can be so cruel. One fall from virtue and a woman's reputation is gone for ever.'

Mr Moorhouse had thoroughly depressed himself with thoughts of the moral dangers that threatened female servants. He sighed, as if at the wickedness of the world, and began to search his pockets for another cigar.

CHAPTER THIRTEEN

'*L e dimanche anglais*, eh, Quint! A phenomenon to make the heart sink and the soul quiver. What do you say to a Sunday excursion?'

Quint poured his breakfast tea into his saucer and raised it to his lips. He sucked in the liquid with a noisy slurp. His expression suggested that anything he might say to a Sunday excursion would be short and unprintable. The two men were sitting in the kitchen at Doughty Street. Adam had broken his own fast and was now watching Quint eat and drink. Undeterred by his manservant's lack of enthusiasm, he continued to speak.

'We know that our missing dandy has gone to ground somewhere. We know that part of an item abstracted from Bellamy's Lodging House, Golden Lane was in said dandy's office. Ergo, we reasoned, Mr Jinkinson had been in Bellamy's Lodging House in the past. The boy Simpkins confirmed our reasoning. So now the time has come to see if he has visited there again. The hour has arrived for us to travel to Golden Lane.'

'I ain't doing anything on a Sunday,' said Quint flatly. 'Sunday's a day for loafing and liquoring, not gallivanting around Golden Lane after some dozy old josser who's prob'ly fluttering after some judy in the streets.'

'Oh, Quint, Quint. You disappoint me. Have you lost the spirit of adventure which carried us both through the mountains of Macedon? What has become of all the daredevilry you showed in the land of Alexander and Aristotle?'

'I ain't lost a thing.'

'I think perhaps you have been corrupted by comfort, Quint. Two years in Mrs Gaffery's luxurious lodgings, and you have become a positive sybarite. The stout-hearted hero of yesteryear has departed for ever.'

'Ain't nothing departed, I tells you.'

'To Golden Lane, then.'

'Hold hard.' Quint's resolve to stay in Doughty Street was crumbling but he still had reservations. 'Ten minutes around Golden Lane looking like that and you'd not have the shirt left on your back.'

Adam glanced down at the immaculately tailored suit he was wearing. 'Ah, I need to be dressed in something more discreet?'

'You need to be dressed in something that don't scream, "I'm a swell. Come and wallop me."'

'Golden Lane is dangerous territory, then?'

'A sight more dangerous than the arse-end of Greece.'

'There were brigands in those hills we travelled, though.'

'Maybe. But you can whistle up worse brigands round Golden Lane any time you like. Wear those flash togs and you won't even need to whistle.'

'I yield to your greater knowledge of these matters, Quint. What do you suggest?'

'I got me some old fustian. Jacket and trousers. Had 'em for years. Thought they was about ready for Rag Fair but maybe they got one last wear in 'em here.'

Quint departed for his room and returned holding what looked more like a pair of dead animals than a suit of clothing. Very reluctantly, Adam took them and retired to change. When he entered the sitting room once more, he was wearing both the suit and a look of profound distaste.

'This is revolting, Quint. Little wonder that you were about to dispose of it.' He shook his shoulders in an attempt to settle the jacket more comfortably on them. Adam's manservant was several inches shorter than his master and there was little chance that any suit he had once owned would prove a perfect fit. 'It feels as if it contains a small menagerie of things that once crept and crawled on the face of the earth. And now they are creeping and crawling through the folds of the jacket.'

'It may not be what the quality wears,' said Quint, sarcastically, 'but it's the kind of thing the nobs round Golden Lane do. So, if you wants to look like you belong there, you'd better keep it on.'

Quint now made a great show of consulting the watch in his weskit pocket. He was mightily proud of this fob watch which, in one of his more expansively autobiographical moments, he had told Adam was a family heirloom inherited from his grandfather. In fact, he had chanced upon it many years earlier, stripping it from a corpse he had found washed up from the river at Rotherhithe.

'The time,' he announced, 'is now ten minutes afore ten. We can be in Golden Lane by eleven.'

* * * * *

As the two men walked down Golden Lane towards Old Street, Adam could see that a second-hand-shoe seller had taken possession of part of the pavement opposite. His stock of boots and shoes stood in a line along the kerb. It looked as if a small queue of the ill-shod had once stood there and that they had all been miraculously spirited away, leaving only their footwear behind. The seller had no customers. Indeed, the entire neighbourhood was surprisingly unpopulated. A costermonger's barrow laden with potatoes and turnips trundled past, the costermonger perched precariously upon it, encouraging his mangy donkey forwards, but there was little other traffic in the street.

The lodging house was a brick building halfway along Golden Lane. A wall ran along the side of it, topped with mortar and broken glass to deter any passing thief with a mind to climb it, although it was difficult to imagine that the building held anything much worth stealing. It looked exceptionally uninviting. A man would have to be desperate, Adam thought, to choose it for his accommodation. Several windows on the ground floor had broken panes. A dingy yellow blind was half pulled down one of them. On it the words 'Good Single Beds at Threepence Halfpenny' had been clumsily scrawled.

The door to the lodging house was open to the street. Adam and Quint entered warily and walked along a long narrow passage to what was, they quickly realised, the communal kitchen. At one end of the room was a large fireplace and around it were gathered a dozen men. Several held long skewers and were toasting bread over the flames. The men were all dressed in an assortment of filthy and mismatched old clothes. None of them looked as if he'd had recent acquaintance with soap and water. The smell in the kitchen was like a physical presence squatting in the corner of the room. Adam was about to take out a handkerchief and hold it to his nose but thought better of the notion.

The men took little or no notice of the arrival of Quint and Adam. Two glanced briefly over their shoulders. The concentration of the others was focused fiercely on their toasting bread. A staircase ran off the room to the left and, before Adam or Quint could hail any of those gathered round the fire, they heard the sounds of heavy footsteps coming down it. Judging by the reactions of those by the fireplace, the man who now entered the room was the power in the land. Unlike the arrival of Adam and Quint, this man's entry meant something to the lodgers. It meant that it was time to leave off what they were doing and fawn upon him.

'Morning, Mr Pradd.'

'You're looking well, Mr Pradd.'

'Pleasure to see you, Mr Pradd.'

'Would you be wanting a tot of something warming, Mr Pradd?'

A chorus of voices surrounded the man as he came into the kitchen.

Pradd ignored them all and concentrated his attention on the new arrivals. The lodging-house keeper wore a dirty shirt that might once have been white, and a pair of greasy black trousers held up by a leather belt. His face was slate grey, as if he had not ventured into the sunlight for several years and, during that time, all his colour had slowly seeped away. One of his eyes was quite clearly a product not of nature but of the glassmaker's art. This false eye moved as freely as the real one but, disconcertingly, the two eyes did not move in harmony. As the real, right eye focused on Adam and Quint, the false, left one was rolling upwards and examining the dusty rafters above their heads.

'Ain't no beds to be had here. We're full.'

'We require no accommodation, my good man,' Adam said. 'What we need is information. We are looking for someone who may have stayed with you in the last few weeks.'

'Oh, *hin*-for-mat-ion, eh? It's *hin*-for-mat-ion you wants, is it?' Pradd's mockery of the young man's all too obviously educated accent was met with howls of laughter from his sycophantic audience. It seemed as if they had seldom, if ever, heard a more crushingly comic response to a presumptuous remark.

'Well, I ain't so sure there's much hinformation to be had 'ere. And I ain't your good man neither. I ain't nobody's good man.'

'Of that I have no doubt. But if you want to keep your police licence, you would do well to be civil, at least to me.'

'I can be as civil as the next man, if I chooses.' Pradd's false eye rolled alarmingly in its socket. 'But maybe I don't choose. I ain't going to be vexed by every young pup what walks in off the street.'

Murmurs of approval came from his fireside supporters. The conversation was not going as Adam had planned. He glanced at Quint but his servant refused to catch his eye. There was to be no help from that direction. Adam was on his own. He was suddenly aware of how little experience he had of speaking to those outside his own class. He wondered what his next words should be.

'Perhaps you should reassess your decision,' he said after an awkward pause. 'Or *I* might choose to speak with my good friend Inspector Pulverbatch.'

Adam decided to introduce the police officer's name more out of desperation than hope. He was only too aware that, while struggling to sound authoritative, he was actually sounding priggish and petulant. However, the name of Pulverbatch seemed to have a magical effect. Pradd stared hard at Adam for a moment.

'You'd best come in 'ere,' he said and then turned abruptly on his heel. Adam and Quint followed. The lodging-house keeper led them to a small office to the right of the kitchen. The floor was covered in what had once been a plain green oilcloth. It was now black with dirt and torn in a dozen places. A cage containing two bedraggled linnets stood on a rickety table in one corner of the room. One of the birds made a half-hearted attempt at song as they entered. The only other furniture in the room was a small desk. Pradd went up to it and, opening a drawer, took out a black leather-bound book. He turned its pages and then thrust it ungraciously towards Adam.

'See for yourself 'oo's been staying 'ere.'

Adam took it and began to leaf through it. He laughed mirthlessly at what he saw there.

'You are obliged by the terms of the Lodging House Act to record the names of your guests, are you not?' he said.

'The book must have names,' the lodging-house keeper acknowledged with a surly edge to his voice.

'But these names' here' – Adam pointed to one of the pages – '"Admiral Tom", "Hindoo Bill", "Cock Robin", "Cock's Mate". You would surely not claim that these are the real names of your lodgers?'

Pradd shrugged. 'Ain't no business of mine what folks calls themselves. The book needs names. The book gets names. Right names. Wrong names. Who cares?'

Adam continued to look down the lists of names in the book. Many were, like the ones he had quoted, obvious pseudonyms. Others looked genuine, but there was no Jinkinson amongst them. Adam was about to give up and return the book to the lodging-house keeper, when one surprising name caught his eye.

'Ha!' he exclaimed. 'I think we have him, Quint.'

He pointed to the page where the name 'Count D'Orsay' was written in a flamboyant, copperplate hand.

'Ain't much of a billet for a count,' Quint said.

'No – and the real Count D'Orsay died in France twenty years ago. But I'm willing to wager a sizeable sum that the only person likely to appropriate his name for use in a place like this is the man we pursue. Remember what Simpkins said? A letter addressed to "The Count" would find him.'

Adam looked again at the entry in the lodging-house register. 'According to this, the count graced this establishment with his presence on two nights in the last week. He was here but two days since. What can you tell us of the gentleman in question, Mr Pradd?'

The lodging-house keeper, scenting the possibility of profit, had changed his demeanour. Sly ingratiation had taken the place of surly defensiveness.

'This 'ere count,' he said.

'What do you know of him?'

'Nothing much. But he might have left some things. Here in the house.'

'What sort of things?'

'Some val'able things,' Mr Pradd suggested hopefully.

'We can be the judges of that. Let us see what he left.'

The man seemed to be weighing up the potential advantage to be had either in showing what Jinkinson had left or keeping them to himself. In the end, he decided to let Adam and Quint see what he had. He moved across the office and pulled a small, brassbound mahogany box from beneath a rickety chest of drawers which was standing against the far wall. He put it on the table in the centre of the room. Then, suddenly dropping his left hand into the innermost recesses of his greasy trousers, he began a strange, writhing dance. His visitors watched him in astonishment.

'The bleedin' key's down 'ere somewhere,' he said.

Adam and Quint continued to watch as Pradd struggled to locate the missing key. Eventually, with a yelp of triumph, he pulled it from the innards of his trousers like a conjuror revealing a hidden rabbit. He thrust the key into the lock and the mahogany box opened. He took out a small cloth bag, unfastened the drawstrings that closed it and emptied the contents on the table.

'I've been keepin' these things what the count left. What he left under his bed,' he said. 'Keepin' 'em in trust, you might say.'

'Very praiseworthy, Mr Pradd.'

'Worth a bob or two, that is. Keepin' 'em in trust.'

Adam was turning over the handful of items the bag had

contained. There was nothing in it that warranted the lodging-house keeper's suggestion of value. There were two buttons which looked to have detached themselves from one of Jinkinson's flamboyantly coloured waistcoats, and a clay pipe. There were half a dozen small scraps of paper torn from a notepad, on which Jinkinson had scribbled some lines of verse. Looking closely at them, Adam realised they were taken from what could only be love poems. The enquiry agent had been lying on his bed in this seedy lodging house and writing love poetry. When he had been dissatisfied with the promptings of his muse, he had torn the paper into bits and thrown them under the bed.

'So you sure them things ain't val'able?' Pradd asked, reluctant to let go of his dreams of financial reward.

'They are merely buttons and bits of paper, Mr Pradd.'

'There's writing on them bits of paper, though.' Pradd, Adam decided, could not read. It would explain the ridiculous aliases in the register. Visitors to the lodging house could sign in under any name they wanted and the keeper would be none the wiser. However, illiterate though he was, he seemed to have an almost mystical belief in the power of words and writing. It explained why he had kept the tattered scraps of paper and why he continued to hope that they held some value.

'It's nothing of significance. Merely lines of poetry.'

'Ain't poetry of significance?'

'Very much so. I would not wish to denigrate the significance of the Muses. In the past, I have even been responsible for committing verses to paper myself.'

Pradd looked puzzled.

'In this particular case, however,' Adam went on, 'the poetry seems to be of importance only to the poet. And perhaps to the person the poet was addressing.'

The lodging-house keeper, realising at last that there was no profit to be made from the items he had preserved, began to put them back into the bag.

'Jest tryin' to be 'elpful.'

'You have been helpful, Mr Pradd. Most helpful. And now, before we leave you, we would like to see the bed where the count slept on the last night he was here.'

'Don't want much, do 'ee?' Pradd's brief dalliance with courtesy was over. Seeing his chance of reward disappearing, he reverted to his earlier bad temper. 'And I ain't got nothing to do, o' course, but run around after every nosey bugger as wants to know the far end of everythin'.'

'You are, I am sure, a busy man,' Adam replied, 'and I appreciate the time you have given us. But I must beg this one further favour of you.'

Adam held out a silver coin, which Pradd promptly pocketed. The gift seemed to do little to placate the man, since he turned on his heel without a word and marched out of his office. Adam and Quint followed as he left and headed up the stairs.

Once upon a time, the building had been a handsome dwelling place, but it had long since degenerated into a slum. Paint was peeling from all the walls. The landings were bare of carpets or any other covering. The glass on the windows that looked out onto the street was so grimy that only a little light could penetrate it. Several panes had been broken and inexpertly mended with balls of rags that had been screwed up and thrust into the openings. The stairs themselves looked half-broken and potentially dangerous. For one flight, the wooden handrail had disappeared and been replaced by a grubby length of rope. Adam could peer beneath it and down the stairwell to where one of the lodgers had left the kitchen fireplace and was looking up at the three of them mounting to the top floor. When he realised that Adam was gazing back at him, he returned immediately to the kitchen.

The dormitory where Jinkinson had slept was on the second floor. Pradd stood in its doorway and gestured towards its far corner. Adam and Quint looked in. A dozen dilapidated beds were crowded into a room that Adam, examining it with mounting disbelief, thought too small for one. Quint, more used to such scenes, was less astonished.

'He crams 'em in as close as barrelled herrings, don't he?' he remarked, noticing his master's surprise.

'But how can this be allowed? What of the regulations?'

Adam became aware of a noise like wheezing bellows at his elbow. It was Quint laughing.

'Bless you, guv'nor. The regulations are right enough. It's just that there's not that many regulators as is interested in 'em.'

'What about the book we saw downstairs?'

'The book must have names,' Pradd reiterated, as if Adam was questioning this requirement.

'The names go down in the book,' Quint said. 'If that's done, there's precious few regulators as'll look much further. What I can't fathom is why the gent would come here at all.'

'Maybe he brought Ada here. Unsavoury though the place is, it might have been the only place they could meet. It might have been possible for them to snatch some time together when the other lodgers were out.' Adam sounded doubtful that this was likely. Pradd was outraged by the suggestion.

'I keeps a very decent house here,' he said. 'If I finds *any* of 'em dancing the blanket hornpipe behind my back, they're out.'

'How can you prevent men and women from consorting one with another?'

Pradd stared at Adam in bewilderment.

''Ow can you stop 'em doing the double-buttock jig?' Quint asked.

'Can't always. But there's one floor for the men, one floor for the women. If any of 'em is ketched on the wrong floor, it's a ticket out the door for 'im. Or 'er, o' course.' The man thought a moment. 'It's mostly 'im, though.'

'Well, I can scarcely believe that Jinkinson would entertain his doxy here. We have reached a dead end, Quint.' Adam turned to leave. 'We have detained Mr Pradd long enough. We must go.'

* * * * *

Quint and Adam left Pradd and his lodging house and returned to

Golden Lane. As they turned the corner into Old Street, a man was waiting for them. It was the lodger who had left the fireside to watch them climb the stairs. Up close, Adam thought, he looked like an animated scarecrow. The man was exceptionally thin-faced, his cheeks so caved in he seemed to be permanently sucking at the air. In some long-vanished historical era, the object on his head had been a black felt billycock. Now it squatted on his greasy hair like a diseased cat about to spring on a mouse. The cuffs of his linen shirt, tattered and filthy, poked out from the sleeves of an ancient velveteen jacket. The brown corduroy trousers he wore had been made for a much taller man and had suffered some kind of abrupt amputation below the knee to enable them to fit. They were so patched with oddments of fabric cut from other garments that there seemed little original material left. The outfit was completed by a battered pair of black boots with holes in them from which small puffs of dust emerged as he shifted uneasily from foot to foot.

'You was asking Pradd about the count,' he said.

'You have good hearing, sir.'

The man made a vague gesture as if shyly acknowledging a compliment.

'Them walls at Bellamy's are so thin you can practically see through 'em, never mind 'ear,' he said. 'Anyways, I was stood by Pradd's office door on purpose. A-listening, like.'

'You were eavesdropping upon us, then.'

The tattered man made no attempt to deny Adam's accusation. He merely ignored it.

'He's a gent, the count,' he went on. 'A real gent. He can talk up a storm as well. He can flash the patter, the count can. Never heard a man like him.'

'He is a man of eloquence and education,' Adam acknowledged. 'And we need to find him. Do you know where he might be?'

'You ain't got nothing to do with the bluebottles? Or the debt collectors?'

'My dear sir, we are merely the count's friends. We have not seen him for some time and we are concerned about his well-being.'

'Cos the count's a gent,' the man repeated, still looking suspicious of their intentions. 'I ain't wanting to see him in trouble.'

'He is more likely to be in trouble if we don't find him.' Adam felt in the pockets of the fustian trousers he had borrowed from Quint and found a sixpenny piece. He held it out to the man. 'Maybe this will prove a token of our good intentions.'

The lodger seized the coin so swiftly that Adam scarcely registered that the man's hand had moved to take it.

'I don't want you thinking that I'd be telling you this just for the tanner.' Adam indicated that no thought could have been further from his mind. 'But, if you're looking out for the count, you might ask after him down the tabernacle.'

'The tabernacle?'

'The Tabernacle of the All-Conquering Saviour is what Dwight calls it.'

'And what is the Tabernacle of the All-Conquering Saviour?'

'Bunch of interfering busybodies,' the man said, in tones of disgust.

'But busybodies who interfere with the activities of the count?'

''E went to their meetings a few times. Quite a few times. But 'e liked his liquor. Them meddlers don't 'old with liquor.'

'Abstainers, eh? Not to be trusted, then.'

'They don't 'old with anything a man might do for a bit of fun. And every man needs a bit of fun.'

The lodger was evidently a champion of a man's right to do as he wished, unhampered by either busybodies or Tabernacles.

'Fun is very definitely something we all need,' Adam agreed. 'Where might one find this Tabernacle?'

'Just round the corner, ain't it? In Whitecross Street. Can't miss it. Sign's outside. And that oily bastard, Dwight, is always greasing his way around.'

'And Dwight is?'

''E calls hisself a reverend,' the lodger said in tones that suggested he was willing to dispute Dwight's right to do so. He continued to stand in the path as if half-expecting another coin to come his way. When he realised that none would be forthcoming, he took a step or two backwards and touched his forefinger to his ancient billycock. 'I'll be leaving you two gents. If you finds the count, tell him Ben Madden was asking after him.'

'We will and I thank you for your information, Mr Madden.'

The man made another vague gesture of farewell, then turned and began to trudge down Old Street towards Aldersgate. Adam and his manservant watched him depart.

'If ever a bloke looked as if 'e'd gone and 'opped 'is perch and was still walking around to save the funeral expenses, there he goes,' Quint remarked after a moment.

'He does look like a gentleman who has seen better days, does he not?'

'He soon had your sixpence, though.' Quint spoke in an accusatory tone of voice. 'He was on to it faster than a tom-tit on to a horse turd. And he ain't the first.'

Adam glanced sharply at his manservant. He was in no mood to indulge Quint's impertinence.

'It is true that, ever since we began our investigations, I have been doling out coin of the realm to the deserving and the not-so-deserving like Lord Bountiful. But they are my coins to dispense as I wish, Quint, so I will not listen to criticism from you. I am confident that one day my generosity will bring me my just rewards. Perhaps Ben Madden's information will prove worth a sixpence.' Adam paused before continuing, his tone now more conciliatory. 'What do you suppose the Reverend Dwight's Tabernacle is?'

'Just another mission. There's one down every street in this neck of the woods.'

'And they all attract a congregation?'

'Most of 'em do. Not that folk round here are that choosy. They'd as soon be Turks if you give 'em a bowl of soup and a hot potato.'

'Which the Reverend Dwight does.'

'Prob'ly.'

'You seem well informed about these missions, Quint. For a man not noted for his donations to charity and the poor.'

Quint shrugged. 'I'm not one to dole out pennies to every shivering Jemmy as sits bare-arsed in the street, if that's what you mean,' he said with marked emphasis.

'Mr Madden was neither bare-arsed nor sitting,' Adam reminded him.

'Ain't the point. I could prob'ly have told you about the missions and saved you a tanner.'

'True enough. You are a positive almanack of miscellaneous information, Quint. Sometimes I wonder that one small head can carry all you know.'

'It ain't so small,' Quint said, aggrieved.

'Perhaps we should visit the Tabernacle of the All-Conquering Saviour.' Adam thought for a moment. 'No, there is no need for you to accompany me. Make your way back to Doughty Street. I shall visit the establishment alone. Today is Sunday, of course. The reverend's busiest day. Who knows? Perhaps Jinkinson will be amongst the congregation.'

CHAPTER FOURTEEN

T he mission house was not an imposing building. A single storey of plain red brick, it was set back slightly from the others in Whitecross Street. On the opposite side of the street, a two-storey building had just recently been demolished. Nothing of it remained but one wall, the spectral outlines of staircases, floors and ceilings still visible on its crumbling bricks. Huge pieces of timber were propped against the remaining houses in the row in order to prevent them tumbling into the streets. As he approached, Adam could see that a service of some kind had recently come to an end. The Reverend Dwight's congregation was emerging into the Sunday afternoon sunshine. Adam was surprised by its numbers. At least fifty men and women had exited the Tabernacle, and in gloomy silence were going their separate ways. Adam recalled Quint's earlier remarks about soup and hot potatoes and decided that the reverend must have provided a generous supply of both. He hoped the congregation had had some bodily sustenance because they looked as if they were starved of the spiritual variety. Certainly, any they had received had given them little joy or uplift.

Adam watched as they trudged away from the mission house. Jinkinson was not among them. Their pastor was easy to identify. He stood just outside the door of his chapel, looking more pleased than pained to see his flock depart. The Reverend Elisha Dwight was an imposing young man. In contrast to the stooped and hunched figures leaving his Tabernacle, he was tall and solidly built. His pink cheeks and flourishing beard radiated the kind of health and well-being they would never possess. His black and perfectly fitting suit shone like the finest handiwork of a West End tailor.

Adam looked down at his own shabby and ill-fitting attire and wondered what the reverend would make of him. However, it was too late to worry that he was inappropriately dressed for a social call. He pushed his way though the departing congregation and approached the Tabernacle's minister.

'I believe you might be able to help me, sir,' he said.

'The Lord may help you, my good man, and I am but the poor instrument He uses for His soul-saving work.'

In their own way, Dwight's words were encouraging but his expression was one of irritation. He was not happy, his face said, to be accosted like this when his pastoral duties had temporarily come to an end. He looked like a man with his mind more on his dinner than on saving souls.

'I must apologise for the guise in which I present myself,' Adam said. 'This is not usually how I dress each Sunday.'

'The Lord in His infinite wisdom looks beneath the outward show and sees the quivering spirit lurking in the very depths of a man's being.'

'I'm sure He does, but it is not my quivering spirit that troubles me most at the moment.'

'How else, then, may I help you?' The reverend's patience was clearly fraying.

'My name is Carver. I am looking for someone. For a Mr Jinkinson of Lincoln's Inn Fields.'

The reverend started very slightly. He retained the forced smile which had decorated his face since Adam first saw him but it obviously took an effort to do so. He stared at Adam for a moment, pondering his options, and then gestured behind him.

'Let us enter the dwelling place of the All-Conquering Saviour, Mr Carver, and we will speak further.'

Two women, dressed all in greys and browns, were still loitering outside the door of the chapel. Despite the plain clothing they had chosen for church attendance, they were very obviously prostitutes.

The reverend waved them away. The Tabernacle, it seemed, was now closed for business. The women moved off with obvious reluctance.

'Poor, painted butterflies they are for the rest of the week.' The reverend had recovered his poise and his taste for fine language. He sighed unctuously as he ushered Adam into his chapel. 'Lost and polluted souls. Forced to tread the unforgiving stones that pave the streets of this modern Babylon. Condemned to a ceaseless round of dissipation that must end in everlasting damnation.' He spoke as if he personally would be willing to step in to save such straying sheep but a more unforgiving judge above might make his intervention useless. Eternal torment could well be their regrettable but unavoidable fate. 'Only on the Lord's day and in these humble surrounds do they cast off the gaudy trappings of sin.'

Adam took the opportunity to examine the humble surrounds of the reverend's domain. There was little to see. The walls of the Tabernacle were whitewashed and so too was the ceiling. Several rows of cheap wooden chairs stood in the centre. At the far end of the room was a long table. He felt the need to make some comment on the bare chapel but could think of nothing to say.

'Your altar, I presume,' he said at last, nodding in the direction of the table. It was the wrong remark to make.

'Indeed not, sir.' Dwight sounded deeply insulted. 'An altar is an example of Romish mumbo-jumbo. I will not have one here in my holy Tabernacle.' He cast his eyes heavenwards, perhaps, Adam thought, in search of any further popish practices hiding in the upper part of his chapel. 'That is our table of communion.'

Adam was unsure of the distinction between an altar and a table of communion but he chose to say no more on the matter. Instead, he launched himself immediately on the subject of his visit. 'I believe you know Mr Jinkinson, Reverend.'

Dwight allowed his eyes to roam around the confines of the building, as though the answer to Adam's question might be lurking in a corner of the room for him to discover. He seemed to be debating with himself whether or not to make any reply. The appearance of a stranger dressed in tattered fustian and yet speaking in the accents of the educated classes clearly puzzled him. He was curious to learn what Adam wanted but reluctant to commit himself too far by admitting too great an acquaintance with Jinkinson.

'I think I may have run across the gentleman in question from time to time,' he said cautiously, after a lengthy pause.

'He is one of your...' Adam wondered what the correct word might be. 'One of your flock.'

'Most certainly he is not, sir.' The reverend was swift to deny any pastoral connection with the missing man. 'Jinkinson is nothing but a blackguard and a rogue.'

'So you do know him.'

Dwight realised that he had now said too much to continue quibbling over the extent of his familiarity with the missing man. He bowed his head to indicate that, although it pained him to acknowledge it, he did indeed know Jinkinson.

'Do you have any notion, Reverend Dwight, where Mr Jinkinson might be? His friends have not seen him for several days.'

Dwight made no reply. Instead, he waved his arm towards a long, wooden instrument with a glass front, which was hanging on the right-hand wall of his chapel.

'Over there is what I call my spiritual barometer, Mr Carver. Come, let me show you how it works.'

Adam could see some kind of dial covered with writing on its front. He followed his host as the clergyman pushed past one of the rows of chairs and made his way towards the wall.

'When the pointer is directed to the right,' the reverend gentleman began to explain, 'it is moving towards glory of the spirit and contempt for carnal lusts. When it is in the middle, it indicates a soul in a state of spiritual indifference. When it travels towards the left...' Here Dwight heaved another of his unctuous sighs. 'It moves through all the stages of damnation.'

As the two men approached the spiritual barometer more closely, Adam could see some of the gradations on the left. Minus thirty – 'Visits to the theatre and the pleasure gardens'; minus forty – 'Parties of pleasure and drunkenness on the Lord's Day'. Minus seventy, which seemed to be the lowest point to which a lost soul could sink, was simply marked 'Perdition'.

Dwight paused for a moment. Adam wondered if perhaps he was about to tap the spiritual barometer as he might a more conventional instrument before taking its reading. But the minister merely peered briefly at the dial before carrying on.

'By my reckoning, Jinkinson has reached minus fifty-five, Mr Carver, and is heading ever downwards. Ever downwards. He is an ancient reprobate. When a soul is so lost, it matters not where its physical vessel might be.'

'So I would be right in thinking that you have no notion of his present whereabouts?'

'For all I know, he may have departed this transitory scene. If he left with his sins still fresh upon him, I tremble for his immortal soul.'

Dwight did not look as if he was trembling. If anything, Adam thought, he seemed rather stimulated by the thought of Jinkinson's possible damnation.

'But when did you last see him, Reverend?'

'In his unrepentant flesh? The day before yesterday. He came with a young woman.'

'With a young woman?'

'The old recreant must have added Lust to Gluttony and Sloth in his list of deadly sins. Like the women we saw at the door just now, she was a harlot.'

'Why did he come here, Reverend? Why should he wish to parade his sins before you?'

'He came first to the Tabernacle some months ago. In a state of inebriation.' Dwight twisted his face into an expression of distaste. 'He wanted to join our congregation. I told him to return when the light of reason had once more been lit within the darkness of his soul.'

'And did he come back when he was sober?'

'He did. And in a moment of weakness brought on by an over-abundance of God's celestial charity, I allowed him to attend our services.'

'And that was a mistake?'

Dwight made no reply. He returned instead to his spiritual barometer and stared fixedly at it, as if in hope of discovering an answer to the question. Adam began to wonder whether or not the reverend had quite forgotten him.

'The Lord demands that we should strive to ignore as much as possible the concerns of our all too perishable flesh,' Dwight said eventually. 'Jinkinson did no such striving. The man was an indurate and incorrigible sinner.'

Were we not, Adam asked himself, all sinners? And was the object of religion not to redeem us from our sins and their consequences? Did missions such as this one not exist to save sinners from themselves and accept them into fellowship? Yet the Reverend Dwight appeared to have other ideas about the purpose of his Tabernacle.

'Would I be correct in assuming,' Adam asked, 'that it was Mr Jinkinson's drinking to which you most objected, Reverend?'

From the evidence of his own words and the writing on his spiritual barometer, there seemed little doubt that the minister had a particular animus against alcohol.

'Strong liquor makes woeful wrecks of men, sir. Ay, and of women, too.' Fine words, it seemed, rarely deserted Dwight. Perhaps, Adam speculated, they were present even when careful thought was not immediately forthcoming. The minister was now well launched on the waves of his own oratory.

'Oh! Thou invisible spirit of drink,' he roared at Adam, gazing at the young man as though he might be the power he was addressing, 'if thou hast no other name to go by, let us call thee Devil.'

Adam prepared himself to endure more blasts of the reverend's rhetoric but Dwight turned abruptly on his heel and marched towards a door to the left of what he had called his communion table.

'I shall be with you again shortly,' he bellowed over his shoulder as he pulled open the door and disappeared through it.

Waiting for Dwight to return, Adam examined the prints that were hanging on the wall opposite the spiritual barometer. Most were illustrative of the dangers of strong drink. A woman sank to the floor holding her brow as a bearded gentleman with a glint in his eye drank furiously from a bottle. Small children clutched the legs of their father in fruitless efforts to keep him from entering a public house. The same father expired in a garret room stripped bare of furniture as wife and children wept in the corner. Death and degradation, it seemed, were the inevitable fates awaiting those who took too great an interest in the delights to be found in a bottle of gin.

The minister had now re-emerged from whatever back room he had visited. He hastened towards Adam, clutching a bundle of papers in his hands, and thrust them towards him.

'You will find these of interest, Mr Carver. Would that that scapegrace Jinkinson had taken the trouble to read them.'

Without thinking, Adam took what Dwight was offering him. It was a pile of perhaps half a dozen small pamphlets.

'Several small disquisitions I have written on the workings of grace,' the reverend gentleman said, a modest pride in authorship evident in his voice. 'Privately printed, of course. But I believe that reading them may help a man take his first uncertain footsteps on the path towards salvation.'

'You are very kind, reverend.' Adam could see no option but to take the booklets. He squinted at one of the titles. 'What We Must Do To Be Saved,' it read. 'I shall lose no time in perusing them.' He tucked the minister's literature awkwardly under one arm. 'But can you tell me no more about the man Jinkinson?'

'I have told you all I know, sir. The sinner came here. I showed him the light of the Lord. He turned his back upon that light and retreated once more into the darkness. There is no more to be said.'

Adam fumbled in his jacket pocket. 'Perhaps I can leave you something in return.' He held out his card to Dwight, one of several he had hidden in the darker recesses of Quint's fustian suit before leaving Doughty Street. Dwight took it and turned it over in his hand, as if he had never before seen a calling card and was unsure what it might be.

'One further question, reverend, and then I shall leave you in peace. Does the word "Euphorion" mean anything to you?'

'Euphorion?' Dwight was still twisting the card in his hand. 'That is Greek, surely?'

'A Greek name, I think. Perhaps a poet.'

'I fear my knowledge of Greek is limited, Mr Carver. So, too, is my knowledge of poetry. I have no time to think of dactyls and spondees when unhappy souls come daily to the door of my Tabernacle in search of spiritual nourishment.'

'Of course not. I quite understand that you are a busy man, Reverend. I must apologise for taking up so much of your Sunday afternoon.'

Adam, reaching up to doff his hat to Dwight in farewell, remembered at the last moment that he was bare-headed and transformed his movement into an awkward salute. The minister bowed his head slightly in response. Adam turned and made his way out of the Tabernacle of the All-Conquering Saviour and into Whitecross Street. It had not, he thought, been a particularly successful visit. He was little more knowledgeable about Jinkinson's whereabouts than he had been earlier in the day. It was time to make his way back to Doughty Street.

* * * * *

'What's the 'oly roller got to say for himself, then?' Quint asked, as he ushered his master into the sitting room.

'Nothing very illuminating. He knows Jinkinson and disapproves of him heartily. But he doesn't know where he is. He believes him to be an awful example of the destructive powers of the demon drink. The Reverend Dwight has a strong objection to the demon drink.'

Quint grunted and raised his eyes to the ceiling. 'Another of them interfering bastards as wants to snatch the working man's beer out of his hands, then.' He spoke as if the interfering bastards might be hiding behind the furniture in the rooms, waiting to leap out and seize his tankard. 'I hate 'em.'

'Probably. But he is firmly of the belief that he is doing work the Lord has called him to do.'

'I particularly 'ate the buggers as reckons they've got Gawd Almighty on their side.'

'Certainly Dwight seems to assume a high degree of intimacy with the Lord of Hosts. Like the Prince of Preachers, Mr Spurgeon, he has the habit of addressing Him as if He were sitting at the back of the meeting room and cheering his every word.'

Quint decided there was no more to be said of the Reverend Dwight. Instead, he handed Adam a letter and a telegram. 'This 'ere missive come with the one o'clock post,' he said as the two men walked into the sitting room.

'What about the telegram?'

'The boy brought it about 'alf an hour since. 'E was wanting to wait for a reply but I told 'im you wasn't around.'

Adam picked up a brass letter opener in the shape of a miniature sabre from his desk and slit open the letter. He began to read it.

'This is from the stunner who visited us the other week, Quint. And left us so abruptly.' Adam read on in silence for but a moment. 'This is extraordinary! She wants to meet me again: "... affairs to discuss of consequence for both of us." And – even more extraordinary – she is suggesting that we meet in Cremorne Gardens.' Adam waved the letter in front of Quint's nose.

'It's signed "Emily Maitland". Which I thought at the time was a curious name for a lady who was so obviously from the Continent.'

Quint only grunted in reply, as if both her suggestion of a meeting place and the name she was choosing to adopt merely confirmed suspicions he had held of the woman from the moment he had opened the door to her.

'Cremorne Gardens, though!' Adam looked at the letter again, half expecting to see that he had misread the name of the place where Miss Maitland was proposing to meet him. 'Does she not know the place? A single lady arranging to meet a single gentleman by the dancing platform at Cremorne Gardens. Does she have no care for her reputation?'

'Maybe she ain't got none.'

Adam ignored Quint's comment.

'Perhaps, as a visitor from abroad, she has no notion of the impropriety of meeting a gentleman alone in such a place.'

'Who can tell wiv a foreigner?' Quint said. It was very clear that the unfathomable ways of those unfortunate enough not to be English held little interest for the manservant.

'I shall accept her invitation, unconventional though it is. The letter has come from Brown's Hotel, which is presumably where she is staying. I shall write back to her there and agree to meet her as she requests.'

'What about the telegram?'

'Ah, I had almost forgot it.'

Adam unfolded the telegram the boy had delivered. Its wording was as laconic as such messages tended to be. He showed it to Quint: 'New developments Creech killing. Request immediate attendance Room 311 Scotland Yard. Pulverbatch.'

'The detectives at the Yard keepeth not the Sabbath day, I see,' Adam said.

'You going to join 'em?' Quint asked.

'Curiosity dictates that I must. But, equally, I must first rid myself of these pestilential clothes of yours and take a bath.'

CHAPTER FIFTEEN

A sergeant ushered Adam into Room 311. Inspector Pulverbatch was sitting at a large, baize-covered desk in the middle of what proved to be a comfortably furnished office. On the wall behind him was a portrait of the queen, looking much younger than the middle-aged widow of Windsor she had become. Little more than a girl, she nonetheless stared down at the inspector with an air of faint disapproval. Carver approached the desk.

'How are you today, Inspector?'

'A touch liverish, Mr Carver, if truth be told, but I have news as makes a dicky liver seem a trifle. You got my telegram, I'm reckoning.'

'I did, indeed. And hastened to follow your instructions and present myself here at the Yard.'

'Not every day as I send out a telegram to all and sundry in a case. But, with a gent like yourself, I thought I'd make an exception.' Pulverbatch, beaming with self-satisfaction, now looked anything but liverish. He seemed in the peak of health.

'A gent like myself?'

'A gent who has been making his own enquiries. On the sly, you might say, if you was so inclined.' The inspector continued to smile broadly. 'Not that I am so inclined. But I'd hate to think of you toiling away at your investigations for no reason, Mr Carver.'

'I am not sure that I take your meaning, inspector.'

Adam was wary in his reply. How much, he wondered, had the police officer learned of his recent activities? According to Sunman, a gentle word had been dropped into Pulverbatch's ear that he should share information with him, but there was no reason to believe that the inspector would relish doing so. However, Pulverbatch seemed to have decided to adopt an attitude of benevolent bonhomie. He wagged his forefinger at Adam in mock admonition.

'I ain't such an ass as anyone can ride me, Mr Carver. I know you've got friends in higher places than what I get to visit. But I also know what you've been a-doing of late. I know you've been speaking with that fat fool Jinkinson. Much good it'll do you.' The inspector settled his hands comfortably on his embonpoint. 'Because I know one more thing. I know the man as killed your friend Creech. So you can stop ferreting around like Paddington Pollaky on the case.'

'I'm not certain that I could say Creech was ever a friend,' Adam said. 'And I know of Mr Pollaky and his private enquiry office only through the newspapers. But I am delighted to hear that you have learnt the identity of the murderer.'

'We've not just learnt about the villain,' Pulverbatch declared. 'We've got him. Got him sitting in a room not five yards from where the two of us is having this little chat. Clanking his cuffs and brooding on his misdeeds.'

'I congratulate you, Inspector.'

Pulverbatch inclined his head, as if to demonstrate a modest conviction that congratulations were entirely in order.

'I don't mind admitting it to a gent like yourself, Mr Carver, who won't hold it against a man, but there've been times in the last few days when I've been well and truly fogged.'

'We have all been fogged, Inspector.'

'That's as may be, Mr Carver, but I'm the man as is paid *not* to be fogged.' The inspector leaned across the desk and pushed a pile of papers to one side. He took a small pistol from his pocket and placed it on the green baize. 'And I'm happy to report that I *ain't* fogged now.'

'That is the murder weapon, is it?' Adam looked at the small gun with distaste.

'That is, indeed, the pistol as blew out a portion of the poor gentleman's brains. We found it in a hedge further down Herne Hill.' Pulverbatch picked up the pistol. He pointed it briefly in the direction of the ceiling and then replaced it on the desk. 'Don't look much more than a toy, do it?'

'And what about the man who used it? You say you have him in your custody?'

By way of reply, the inspector stood up and beckoned Adam to follow him. He made his exit from Room 311 and walked along the corridor outside. Adam was just behind him as he opened a door into another, smaller room where a uniformed constable stood guard over a shabbily dressed man, sitting at a desk. At a gesture from the inspector, the constable left the room. The man behind the desk stared vacantly into the middle distance. There were two other wooden chairs in the room and Pulverbatch, waving Adam into one, settled himself into the other. He pushed it back on to its rear legs and pointed across the desk.

'This is the cove as killed Mr Creech. This is Thomas Benjamin Stirk, of Monmouth Street, Seven Dials. Take a bow for the gentleman, Stirk.'

Adam looked doubtfully at the man who sat in cuffs opposite him. Stirk was round and red of face. He was wearing a dirty fustian jacket and a pair of dilapidated flannel trousers which might once have been blue. At the inspector's words, he ceased gazing into the air and concentrated on his two visitors. He nodded cheerfully at Adam, who turned to look at Pulverbatch.

'He's a lot like a winter's day, ain't he?' the inspector remarked. 'Short and dirty.'

'He seems... ' Adam was unsure what exactly to say. He was still trying to work out how much Pulverbatch knew about Jinkinson. Did he know about the blackmail? Was he aware of the notebook with the names of Garland and Oughtred and Abercrombie in it? Of Euphorion? He realised that the inspector was waiting politely for him to finish his sentence. 'He seems rather a mild sort of fellow for a murderer, Inspector.'

'Looks can be terrible deceiving, Mr Carver. He's a villain, sir, a light-fingered rogue. Ain't nothing and nobody safe when Stirk's around. If his mother was a cripple, he'd steal her crutches.'

'Thieving is a long way from murder, though, Inspector.'

'But he's a pugnacious varmint is Stirk, sir. A very pugnacious varmint. You'd be surprised to hear what Stirk is a-capable of. He'd kick a man's lungs out, soon as look at him.'

Stirk was now grinning broadly. He looked as if he thought Inspector Pulverbatch was providing him with a particularly impressive character reference.

'So, Mr Stirk is a gentleman you've arrested before?'

'Oh, yes, sir. We've put our 'ands on Stirk more times than you've had kidneys for breakfast.'

'But what would a man from Seven Dials be doing in Herne Hill?'

'He's a traveller, is Stirk, sir. He travels many a mile round London to perpetrate his villainies. Lambeth, Peckham, Hammersmith, Islington. Don't matter to Stirk. Last time we had him in here, he'd been putting his murderous thumbs round a man's windpipe down Bethnal Green way. Flung his victim down on the cobblestones and kicked his eye out, sir. The eye was a-hanging on the poor fellow's cheek.'

Apparently enjoying this brief résumé of his recent career, Stirk looked across at Adam and nodded again, as if confirming Pulverbatch's description of events. He seemed almost to be expecting some kind of applause.

'Gin is Stirk's downfall.' Inspector Pulverbatch now sounded almost sorry for his prisoner and his shortcomings. 'He thirsts after gin like a tiger after blood. Look at him now, sir. Like a lamb, ain't he? But give him liquor and it's a different matter.' Pulverbatch shook his head and made a whistling noise. 'Ferocious, he is, once the liquor seizes hold of him. He'd sell his own mother for the money she'd fetch in old bones when the gin fever is on him.'

'After he'd pawned those crutches of hers, I suppose,' Adam remarked. 'I have no doubt that this gentleman is the terror you describe. But how did you succeed in tracking him down?'

Pulverbatch clasped his hands behind his head and leant back so far in his chair that Adam began to fear he was going to fall off it. He had the air of a grandfather about to launch on the telling of a fairy tale to an admiring circle of grandchildren. As he leant backward, Stirk leant forward as if to catch every word the inspector might say. He continued to grin, as if enjoying the performance of some music hall comedian. Adam was beginning to suspect that the man the police had arrested was little more than a simpleton.

'Imagine London as a thick forest, sir,' Pulverbatch said. 'A villain may hide himself there, among the trees, like a wild beast in the jungles of Africa. And many of them are just that. Wild beasts like Stirk here. But I've got the means to track 'em down, Mr Carver. I'm the hunter in the forest, sir. The hunter in search of his prey.'

'But how do you know this particular prey is the man who killed Mr Creech? As I have said, he does not look the part to my eye.'

'Ah, but if you'll forgive my impertinence, sir, yours is the eye of the average man. Here at the Yard, we don't see things like your average man. That's what the likes of you and Paddington Pollaky don't seem to understand. We're what you might call specialists, sir. We have to be in possession of special facts what the average man don't have. We have to be able to distinguish between a vast array of villainies.'

Pulverbatch, warming to his theme, was clearly enjoying himself.

'The man's a thief, your average cove says. Not good enough, says I. Not good enough at all. What kind of a thief? That's the question. There's your cracksmen and your rampsmen, your bludgers and your bug-hunters, your drag-sneaks and dead-lurkers, your till-friskers, toshers, star-glazers, snow-gatherers, snoozers, stick-slingers and skinners. Which variety of villain is your man?'

Exhausted by his own eloquence and still rocking back on his chair, the inspector fell silent.

'I can see that your profession is one that requires subtle discrimination,' Adam said after a brief pause.

'That it does, Mr Carver, that it does.'

'And yet I cannot see the relevance here. We're not talking about a bludger or – what did you say? – a tosher. We're talking about someone who shot Mr Creech.'

'The same principles apply, sir.'

'Has Mr Stirk admitted his crime?'

Pulverbatch allowed a brief grimace to pass across his features. He rocked forward again on his chair and his feet dropped to the floor. He crashed his fists on the table with a sudden force that made both Adam and the man Stirk start in surprise.

'That he has not. He's as stubborn as an ox in denying it. But I'll have the truth out of him.'

'Perhaps you have already had the truth out of him, Inspector. Perhaps he had nothing to do with the murder.'

Pulverbatch glanced at Adam, as if to confirm that this was an average man speaking whose opinion was not to be compared to that of a specialist, and then turned to his prisoner.

'Look at me, Stirk.' At the sound of his name, Stirk, who had followed the conversation between Adam and the inspector with every sign of enjoyment, now shifted uncomfortably in his chair. His eyes swivelled around the room, looking anywhere but at Pulverbatch. 'I say, look at me.'

Very unwillingly, Stirk forced himself to return the inspector's gaze.

'Do you see any green in my eye, Stirk?'

The man made no reply.

'Well, do you?'

'No, Mr Pulverbatch.'

'Don't be giving me any more of this gammon you've been giving me so far, then. I know you broke into that house. I know you shot that poor gent when he come across you. You know I knows. So let's be hearing you say it.'

'I can't have kilt a gent in 'Erne 'Ill, Mr Pulverbatch.' Stirk still looked surprisingly cheerful, considering the circumstances in which he found himself, but he sounded puzzled. 'I ain't never been in 'Erne 'Ill. I ain't even sure where 'Erne 'Ill is. Anyways, I told you. I was in The 'Are and 'Ounds down Borough Market that day. There's dozens can tell you that.'

'You see, Pulverbatch, he has an alibi.'

The inspector snorted.

'I've looked into this alibi of Stirk's, Mr Carver, and it just won't wash. It ain't worth a jigger. The regulars in the Hare and Hounds all lie as fast as a horse can trot. They'd swear the devil had been drinking with 'em and couldn't have been in hell, if the fancy took 'em to aggravate us. I can tell you plainly, Mr Carver, Stirk could have been in Herne Hill as easy as you or I.'

Pulverbatch sighed deeply as if distressed by the dishonesty of the Hare and Hounds' clientele.

'Now, I'm not claiming that he's the chief villain of this piece.' The inspector sounded indignant at the very idea that Adam might believe he was. 'Of course I ain't. Somebody put him up to visiting Herne Hill, but Stirk ain't saying who that somebody was.'

'So, what do you propose to do now, Inspector?'

Pulverbatch made no reply. He left his chair and walked behind his prisoner who smirked uneasily and twisted his head to follow the policeman as he moved around the room.

'Screever!' Pulverbatch yelled suddenly. The door to the room opened and the constable appeared once more. 'Take this rogue back down to the cells.'

Screever hauled the prisoner to his feet and the two of them left the room. As they passed down the corridor, Adam could hear Stirk, in a bemused tone of voice, repeating to the constable his earlier assertion that he 'ain't never been in 'erne 'ill'. Pulverbatch sat himself down in the chair his suspect had just vacated and drummed his fingers on the table. For a minute or two, he gazed into the middle distance as if he had just realised that Scotland Yard and the city were the very last places he wanted to be and he was dreaming instead of green fields and shady woodlands. Adam was just beginning to feel slightly uncomfortable and was considering making his farewells when the inspector roused himself from his reverie.

'Remember the old saying, Mr Carver,' he said, with renewed energy. 'The bird that can sing and won't sing, must be made to sing. Never fear, sir. We'll have Stirk singing like a linnet before the day is out.'

'But what if he's singing the wrong tune, Inspector? Or just the tune he thinks you want to hear?'

'He's our bird, sir. Have no doubt about it. Never was such a one for villainy and violence, I do believe. No need for you to be a-chasing old Jinkinson halfway round town. That fat fraud ain't got anything to do with this case.'

'And yet you will admit that it may be difficult to prove your case against the man you've got?'

'Not in the slightest, sir. We'll put an end to Stirk, don't you worry about that. We'll have the drop creaking under his feet before the month is out. And before he goes, he'll tell us who sent him out to put the threateners on poor Mr Creech.'

CHAPTER SIXTEEN

T he following day, Adam took lunch in a chophouse he knew off the Strand. He sat alone at one of the tables in the rear of the restaurant. Few other customers were there. A mournful-looking man dressed in black was at the next table, eating his meal as if doing so was more of a penance than a pleasure. Adam's mind was no more on his food than his neighbour's. The steak with oyster sauce, which in normal times he would have relished, he scarcely tasted. The piece of Stilton he left largely untouched on the plate. The waiter, clearing the table, scowled as if personally affronted by Adam's poor appetite. Adam hardly noticed. He was thinking about all that had happened in the last two weeks. At the beginning of the month, he'd had no more pressing concerns than his growing debt to his tailors. Now there were a dozen unanswered questions and more to plague him.

Some were related to the death of Creech and the mysteries that still surrounded it. Others forced him to think uncomfortably about the whole course of his young life. Adam mostly considered himself a contented man. It was true that his career at Cambridge had unexpectedly left the rails when Charles Carver had put an end to his life. Adam had been obliged to face up not only to the loss of his father but to the sudden ruination of all his plans for the future. Gone were any dreams of academic glory. Gone was even the chance of finishing his degree. No money had been left to support him. Yet he had, he thought, coped admirably. Professor Fields had, of course, come to the rescue with his invitation to accompany him to European Turkey, but it was Adam himself who had made the most of the opportunities the adventure offered. It was Adam who had responded so wholeheartedly to their travels and had even recorded them in a book, which had earned him a certain, albeit fleeting, celebrity. Since his return to London, he had cultivated his new interest in photography and had found much fulfilment in his self-imposed task of recording the buildings that were so swiftly vanishing from the city.

And yet at times – and this was one such occasion – the young man found himself curiously dissatisfied with his lot. For all his inability to make significant progress with his portrait of King Pellinore, and for all his mounting debts too, his friend Cosmo Jardine at least knew what he was: a painter, for better or worse. But what was he himself, Adam Carver? What was he to do with the rest of his life? He may have lacked the entrepreneurial and commercial skills of his father, but he had his own talents, he knew. Where, though, did any of them lead? How could he make the best of them? Should he determine to travel again? To visit more unfamiliar and unexplored locations than European Turkey? Could he make a more concerted effort to earn money from his abilities as a photographer or writer? Perhaps, he thought, half smiling at the idea despite his present glumness, he should follow the example of Jinkinson. Could he be, he wondered, some sort of enquiry agent *manqué*? He had certainly enjoyed the drama and the excitement of the last fortnight. He felt flattered that Sunman had asked him to look into the circumstances of Creech's demise, just as he was fascinated by the murder itself. And there was the enticing prospect, too, of discovering the real identity of Emily Maitland, who was clearly not all she seemed.

As always, Adam concluded this examination of his own charac-ter by drawing no conclusions beyond the decision that he would continue on his current road and attempt to resolve the present mystery. What an intriguing mystery it was! There was the matter of Creech and the secrets of which he had spoken. Why had the man been so eager to meet him? Why had he approached Jar-dine under an alias? Could Creech have been nothing more than a deluded obsessive? Or had he been a genuine scholar who had truly stumbled across something remarkable? No, Creech had been no scholar. Adam remembered the man's puzzlement when he had quoted one of the most familiar of all Homer's phrases to him. And did scholars pay private enquiry agents to follow Members of Parliament in pursuit of information with which to blackmail them? It seemed unlikely.

The waiter, while clearing the evidence of the earlier course, had left the plate with the cheese on the table. Adam picked up the knife and cut a sliver of Stilton. He ate it absentmindedly, still mulling over the questions which troubled him. Would Creech have been killed if there had not been something in his story? Or did his talk of secrets in the Macedonian hills have nothing to do with his death? His apparent activities as a blackmailer offered a more likely motive for murder than enigmatic talk of a mystery hidden in an ancient manuscript. And yet surely it was too much to believe, as the police seemed to, that his death was the result of a botched burglary? Unless Stirk had been hired by one of Creech's victims to break into the house and steal some incriminating evidence the blackmailer possessed, and had killed the man when he confronted him. Pulverbatch seemed to believe in some such sequence of events, but Adam found it difficult to agree with the inspector's version of what had happened. Who in their right minds would employ a simpleton like Stirk to undertake such a task?

Then there was the distracting puzzle of Emily Maitland. She was a beautiful woman. Adam was disinclined to admit, even to himself, how much time he had spent in picturing her in the days since she had so unexpectedly visited his rooms. Her trim figure flitted regularly through his imagination. Her Titian hair and dancing green eyes were rarely far from his thoughts. He was therefore delighted that she had asked to see him once more. But behind the pleasure he gained from recalling her visit, there were nagging questions about the young woman. What had been the true reason for her visit to Doughty Street? And was Mrs Gaffery correct in saying that Emily had been there not once but twice? Perhaps he would have answers when he met her again, in Cremorne Gardens.

Adam pushed aside the cheese plate. He rested his head in his hands. So many riddles already and now there was another one. What had happened to Jinkinson? Was the enquiry agent's disappearance significant? Men and women vanished into the vast, anonymous sprawl of London every day of the year. Many did so of their own volition. Jinkinson himself had done so in the past. Perhaps the plump and dilapidated dandy was merely in flight from some pressing creditor or overly importunate client. The boy Simpkins had said that his employer had a history of temporarily vanishing when trouble came knocking on the door of 12 Poulter's Court. Even now, as Adam stared at the crumbling Stilton in front of him, Jinkinson might be drinking cheerfully in some out-of-the-way haunt and regaling his fellow topers with tall tales.

The mournful man on the neighbouring table had reached the end of his penitential meal. His plate was empty. He paid the waiter and left. On his table Adam saw a copy of the morning newspaper which had been forgotten. He thought briefly of calling after the man but decided against it. He stretched his arm across to the table and picked up the newspaper. He began to turn the pages, his eyes flickering idly from column to column. The news today, he thought, was little different from the news of a week ago, the last time he had bothered to look at a newspaper. Prussian and French politicians were still squabbling over who should sit on the Spanish throne. As if it was of any real concern to either of them. It would presumably not be long before one side or the other found the pretext for war. The pages were also full of tributes to Dickens, who had recently died, worn out by his creative exertions, at the age of fifty-eight. Adam, who had never forgotten the sheer joy of reading Pickwick and *David Copperfield* when he was no more than a boy, had been saddened when Jardine had told him of the author's death a few days earlier. But now he could not concentrate on all the columns of praise for the great humorist's genius. Instead, his eye was drawn to a few short paragraphs at the bottom of a page that were headed: 'Outrage in Herne Hill'.

'We are given to understand,' the article began, 'that a man well known to Scotland Yard as a most audacious villain has lately been apprehended in reference to the brutal murder which was committed in Herne Hill earlier this month.' Adam read the rest of the piece and threw the newspaper to one side in exasperation. What did these scribblers know of what they wrote? How wonderfully they combined ignorance with arrogance in their presumption that they knew more than they truly did. In his indignation, he forgot altogether that, on his return from European Turkey, he had himself earned sums of money as a newspaper scribbler and that he continued to place articles in the press from time to time. One not so long ago in the very newspaper he had just cast aside. He picked it up again and looked at the article for a second time: 'That renowned and perspicacious agent of the law Inspector James Pulverbatch...' He could not continue. Perhaps Pulverbatch did merit the adjective 'perspicacious' but what did he know of this case? How could he believe that the half-witted Stirk could be the perpetrator of the crime at Herne Hill?

* * * * *

''Ere, mister.'

Adam looked down at the ragamuffin standing by the entrance to the Marco Polo. The boy was dressed in jacket and trousers of threadbare black cloth and wore a look of scowling concentration on his face. Adam was surprised that Gilzean, the Crimean veteran who was the club's doorman, hadn't moved the child on, but there was no sign of the old soldier.

'The other gent told me to give you this.'

'What other gent?'

'And you'd give me another sixpence.'

'Who said this?'

'On top of the sixpence he give me.'

'Who was the gentleman who told you this?'

'He says to say Quint and you'd know him.' The boy was holding a grubby scrap of paper. Adam took it from him and looked at it. Quint was not the best penman in London but he was able to scrawl enough words to convey his meaning. 'Charing X Otel. 8 oclock. See yew ther. Owtside.'

'You was to give me a sixpence, he says.'

'Did the gentleman named Quint say no more?'

'Just to give me a sixpence.' The boy was single-minded in his pursuit of his earnings, Adam thought, as he reached in his pocket.

'Here,' he said, holding out a shilling. 'Take this. I haven't a sixpence about me.'

'Thanks, mister.' The boy looked at the more valuable coin. He seized it and then turned and ran off as quickly as he could, probably terrified that Adam might change his mind and demand the money back.

CHAPTER SEVENTEEN

'Was you in search of *poses plastiques*, gentlemen? Very voluptuous ladies, sirs, but entirely artistic. Only poses from the Greek and Roman. This way, if you please, gentlemen.' The speaker was short and fat, flesh pouring into the inadequate container of a corduroy suit and spilling over its confines. He had red eyes, a bulbous nose and a mouth from which vile exhalations of poorly digested meat, gin and tobacco issued forth to assail passers-by as relentlessly as his patter. He gestured leeringly towards a darkened doorway behind him. 'Beauties fresh from the bagnios of Paris, sir. All as nature intended them to be.'

Quint took Adam's arm. The young man looked too much like what he was, an innocently basking dolphin amid a sea of sharks. His manservant manoeuvred him past the foul-breathed tout.

Evening was falling and the two men were making their way through a warren of narrow streets and ill-lit alleyways off the Strand. Unaccustomed to this secret London behind the façade of the better-regulated streets and squares he usually frequented, Adam was lost. They had entered the maze soon after he had descended from a cab outside the new Charing Cross Hotel and found Quint waiting for him there. Quint had said little in greeting but beckoned him to follow. Almost immediately, Adam had lost track of where he was, rapidly resigning himself simply to continuing on the twisting and turning route on which his manservant led him. Other than the belief, founded more on faith than evidence, that the Strand was somewhere to his right and Covent Garden somewhere to his left, he had no idea where he was. Slightly to his surprise, he found the sensation of being so lost in London exciting rather than disconcerting.

They may have been striking out beyond Adam's beaten path but, for others, this was clearly home territory. The streets were crowded. Men, women and children, nearly all poorly dressed, hastened along them. Shops were still open. Suits of clothes, like emaciated corpses on a gallows, hung from a rail above one of them. Further along the narrow street, a butcher had removed the burners from his gas lamps in search of brighter illumination for his premises and great tongues of flame shot into the air. Glistening pigs' heads revolved in the light he had created, which also shone on the sides of beef and mutton lying on his stall, revealing every vein and lump of fat in them. Next door to the butcher's was a bookmaker's whose shopfront was lit with almost equal brilliance. A blind beggar stood outside it, as if bathing his body in the light he could not see. Somewhere an unseen street organ was playing and its jingling music could just be heard above the constant roar of the crowds.

People were intent on their own business and swarmed purposefully through the streets. On several occasions, Adam was obliged to move swiftly to avoid collisions. The barker for the *poses plastiques* was not alone. Others of his ilk begged and cajoled the crowds to enter the halls of entertainment that employed them. On one particularly squalid lane, a series of luridly coloured posters invited passers-by to enter a cheap theatre and enjoy performances of 'Red-Handed Ralph, the Fiend of Shoreditch'. On its corner, where it crossed another alley, a family of street acrobats was performing its routine. Paterfamilias, dressed in an outfit reminiscent of a pantomime harlequin, held a long wooden pole upright, its base lodged firmly in his waistband. Perched precariously near its top, his two small children, a girl and a boy, adopted a series of poses and attitudes. All three wore expressions of extreme ennui on their faces. Few passers-by had stopped to watch and those that had seemed as bored as the performers. Amidst the swirling crowds, Adam, so obviously well dressed and well fed, was feeling uncomfortably conspicuous.

'Where are we going, Quint?' he asked.

'A tarts' academy off Holywell Street.'

'Holywell Street? That's the one where the shops sell…' Adam seemed unsure of how to describe what the shops sold. 'What would you call it? Literary curiosa?'

'Dirty books is what I'd call it,' Quint said. 'And them as wants to do more than just *read* about rogering can pop round the corner and visit this 'ere case-house I'm telling you about.'

'And where is this case-house?'

'We're just about there.' Quint threw his answer over his shoulder before making an abrupt dog-leg turn into an alleyway which, to Adam's eyes, was even less prepossessing than the ones along which they had already walked. A runnel of water, or more probably water and other liquids, raced down its left side. On Adam's right, a solitary gaslight threw its dim illumination on house fronts and the occasional shop, still open for whatever enigmatic business was conducted on its premises. Away from the hustle of the marginally broader lane they had left so suddenly, there were few people about and those that were ignored them. Quint stopped at the door of one of the houses, apparently indistinguishable from the others, and pushed it open. It seemed that they had reached their destination.

As the two of them stepped inside, Adam was surprised by what they found. A narrow passage led from the door towards an inner darkness. A smell, a potent combination of mouldering plaster and the sweat of a thousand human bodies, hung in the air. Yet the walls of the passage were covered in billowing drapes of brocade, all in the newly invented and modish colour of mauve. Quint moved determinedly along the mauve tunnel and Adam followed. Light soon began to appear in what had been darkness and the passage opened out into a square, high-ceilinged room. The mauve drapes had disappeared and the walls here were painted an eye-catching shade of egg-yolk yellow.

The room was entirely empty save for a man who stood, arms

folded, by a staircase, which Adam assumed led down into rooms beneath street level. He was enormous, towering several inches above Adam, who topped six feet himself. His shaven head sat atop a body that more resembled a bear's than a man's; a bear dressed, for some unfathomable reason, in a black moleskin jacket and trousers. Like Mr Dickens's celebrated character, Wackford Squeers, the giant had but one eye, and the popular prejudice runs in favour of two. That one eye was bloodshot and staring, and a watery mucus appeared to be streaming from its corner. Where its partner had once been, there was no patch, no glass replacement, not even a gaping socket. Instead, a film of skin seemed to have stretched itself somehow across the space where the missing eye should have been. Adam could see what looked like small veins of blood pulsing on the skin. A prizefighter, he thought, or an ex-prizefighter. What other profession could produce such a particular combination of muscular development and physical disfigurement? Some sign, almost imperceptible, passed between Quint and the Cyclops. What was it? A slight nod of the head? A brief movement of that single, staring eye? Adam wasn't sure, but whatever it was, it meant entry to the otherwise forbidden rooms below. He and Quint were allowed to shuffle past the Cyclops and to descend the staircase.

'People here know you then, Quint?'

His servant shrugged. 'Plenty of people know me. Here and there and elsewhere.'

As the two men walked down the stairs, the chattering of female voices rose from beneath their feet. Another door confronted them. Quint threw it open. Adam's first thought was that the room was on fire. A fug of smoke hung in the upper air. The hubbub that had reached their ears on the stairs was now deafening. Shouts and screams of raucous laughter mingled with random cries and yells and, if Adam was not mistaken, the sound of at least one woman sobbing.

'What is this filthy den, Quint? And why are we here?'

As Adam looked around, he was repelled and intrigued in equal measure. The room was full of whores. It was early in the evening and few of their clients could be seen. Adam noticed only three men, soldiers of some infantry regiment, who were sharing drinks with their chosen tarts before retiring to less crowded quarters. One of them, more drunk than his fellows, was swaying on his chair, his uniform unbuttoned almost to his waist. The other women in the room were sitting in small groups around an assortment of tables and boxes. Some were obviously ageing veterans of the streets or 'virgins' whose maidenheads had been miraculously renewed a hundred times. Others looked like country girls, so recently arrived in town that the scent of hops and apples might still have clung to them. Yet others were raddled scarecrows whose faces bore the scars of a thousand brief and largely brutal encounters. Nearly all had glasses in front of them and pipes or cigarettes clamped in their mouth, adding their own small contributions to the rolling smoke clouds above them.

'It's that one over there, guv'nor.' Quint pointed to the far corner of the room where a woman sat alone at one of the tables. 'I found her. Her name's Ada. She's the one Jinkinson's been seeing.'

Ada was petite and dark-haired and dressed far more demurely than most of the other women in the room. A pair of pearl-grey shoes peeped out from beneath a similarly subfusc dress. Were it not for the surroundings in which they had found her, Adam would have taken her for a maidservant or shop girl. As they approached her, she glanced in their direction and then looked swiftly away.

'This is Mr Carver, Ada,' Quint said, attempting to sound as benevolent as he could. 'He wants to ask you some questions.'

The woman now turned again to look at them. Her face was ghostly pale and her mournful brown eyes made Adam think of some dog awaiting its master's instruction. She said nothing and showed no curiosity about Adam's identity. She cast down her eyes and continued to sit patiently, hands clasped on her lap, seemingly uncaring as to what might come next.

Adam was distracted by the unfamiliar surroundings in which he found himself. His entry had not gone unnoticed and several of the women had made lewdly suggestive invitations to him as he passed.

He was unused, even in his ventures out on the town with friends like Cosmo Jardine, to hear women speak so crudely. To his surprise, Adam had sensed himself blushing slightly as he heard them. Now he made an effort to compose himself.

'Good evening to you, Ada,' he said.

The girl made no reply. The young man pulled up a chair from the next table and sat down opposite her. 'I am making enquiries about a gentleman named Jinkinson and I think you might be able to help me. Are you willing to help me, Ada? Are you happy to answer my questions?'

She nodded, her eyes still lowered.

'Do you know Mr Jinkinson? He has offices in Poulter's Court. Near Lincoln's Inn.'

The woman nodded again.

'We are looking for Mr Jinkinson, Ada. He has not been seen in Poulter's Court for several days. Do you know where he is?'

Ada looked up at Adam as if she was about to speak but then thought better of it. She lowered her eyes again and shook her head.

'We do not mean Mr Jinkinson any harm, Ada. Indeed, we wish him well.'

'Don't know where 'e is, sir.'

'But you are fond of Mr Jinkinson?'

"E's a gent, sir.'

'You would not want harm to come to him.'

'I could tell 'e was a gent, sir. First time I met 'im,' Ada went on. 'On account of 'is hands were so white.'

She paused as if the meaning of Adam's previous remark had only just struck her.

''Arm, sir? What 'arm?'

'There may be people looking for him who have less concern for his welfare than we do. It would be better for Mr Jinkinson if we found him than if they did.'

Adam felt that this was a pardonable exaggeration of the facts. After all, it might well be that there were others looking for the enquiry agent and, if there were, the likelihood was that it would be with unfriendly intent. But his words had no effect on Ada. After her brief flurry of animation at the thought of harm coming to Jinkinson, she had returned to her original state of passivity.

'Don't know where 'e is, sir,' she repeated. 'I ain't seen 'im for weeks.'

Adam ran his hand through his hair and tried another tack. Perhaps the girl might know of the old dandy's favourite places in town.

'Did you ever spend time with Mr Jinkinson? Did he take you on any excursions? On the river?'

The girl shook her head.

'Or to one of the dance halls? To Highbury Barn, perhaps?'

'I ain't never been to Highbury Barn, sir.'

'To a public house, perhaps?'

But Ada had decided that she would say no more. She stared down at her hands in her lap and refused to look at either of the men. The noise in the rest of the room was even louder than when they had entered. Raucous singing now rose from the table where the three soldiers were carousing. Adam wondered whether there was anything he might say that would prompt the woman into speaking.

'Did Mr Jinkinson ever speak to you of another gentleman, a gentleman named Garland?'

Ada continued to gaze at her red and chapped hands. She said nothing but an unmistakeable look of fear passed across her face. She shook her head again, more violently than before. Adam had a sudden moment of inspiration. He remembered his conversation about Garland with Mr Moorhouse. He recalled the rumour about the MP that he was a 'devil with his maidservants'.

'Did you work once for a gentleman named Garland, Ada?'

Adam could see that tears were now falling silently down the girl's cheeks, but she still said nothing. She continued to shake her head. It was obvious enough what the answer to his question was. He could not bring himself to press the girl further. He stood up and motioned to Quint that they should leave. One last question now occurred to him and he turned again to the girl.

'Did Mr Jinkinson ever speak Greek to you, Ada?'

The young prostitute did now look up. She was bewildered. Her eyes flickered back and forth between Adam and his servant.

'For gawdsake, guv,' Quint said. 'The girl ain't going to know Greek from the bleating of sheep on the way to Smithfield.'

'Did Mr Jinkinson ever use odd words in your hearing?' Adam persisted. 'Words that you couldn't understand?'

''E was always using funny words.'

'Words that were not English?'

Ada shrugged helplessly.

'Were they French, perhaps?'

''E was parleyvooing with some Frog waiter down Dean Street once,' Quint remarked conversationally. 'When I was after him.'

'Never mind that now, Quint. I wish to know what Ada heard him say, not you.'

But the girl was growing even more anxious under the inquisition. She looked desperately at the manservant.

'She don't know what you're talking about, guv.'

'I think she does, Quint.'

The girl was now moving her hands restlessly in her lap. Quint, glancing over his shoulder from time to time, had seen a new development that demanded their attention.

'Harry Fadge has come downstairs, guv. I reckon maybe we ain't welcome no more.'

The one-eyed giant who guarded entry to the brothel had indeed descended to the cellar room and was moving purposefully towards them. He looked displeased and his displeasure, as Quint knew and Adam guessed, was not something to be ignored.

'You have nothing more to tell us, Ada?'

'Let's go, guv. Let's go while we've still got the legs to do the going with.'

Unceremoniously thrusting aside those unlucky enough to find themselves in his path, Fadge was now only a few tables away from them. One of the soldiers, pushed in the chest, attempted to remonstrate with him. Fadge stopped briefly and, without saying a word, threw a punch which immediately felled the infantryman. The soldier tumbled to the floor amidst screams from the women at his table. Fadge continued on his way. He appeared to be snarling and shaking his head, his resemblance to a bear in killing range of its prey even more marked than before.

'Ada?' Adam prompted.

'Yew Ferrion,' the girl said. ''E was always talkin' about some bloke called Yew Ferrion. How he was to be all right once he found out about Yew Ferrion. That's foreign, ain't it?'

'Thank you, Ada. You have been most helpful.'

With as much dignity as he could muster in the circumstances, Adam retreated by a roundabout route towards the door, holding out his hands towards Fadge in what he hoped was a placatory manner. Quint, with the unerring instinct for self-preservation that had been the cornerstone of his career thus far, had already disappeared. Fadge continued to bare his teeth and growl unmistakeable threats. Deciding that dignity was a luxury he could no longer afford, Adam turned and ran for the door, stopping only to overturn one of the tables in Fadge's path. Followed by the protests of half a dozen whores outraged by the loss of their drinks, he reached the stairs and raced up them. He charged through the egg-yolk yellow room and the mauve tunnel and into the street. He had no idea of the direction in which he should run. For several minutes, he dodged first left and then right through the backstreets until he ended in a cobbled courtyard. He appeared to have left the pursuing Fadge far behind him. From here, a dozen or more narrow crooked alleys ran off in every possible direction. Adam stopped to consider which one of them to choose. He was still standing, panting with exertion and debating whether one of the filthy little lanes was likely to lead back to familiar territory, when Quint appeared suddenly at his shoulder.

'Thought you was never going to get out of there,' his manservant remarked. 'Bow Street's this way.'

* * * * *

'I am ashamed of our cowardly withdrawal.' Returned once more to streets he knew, Adam had regained lost courage. He was now regretting their hasty retreat. 'Should we have allowed some decayed bruiser to frighten us, Quint? Some brothel bully with one eye? We were just beginning to get the girl to talk.'

Quint, who had seen plenty of bare-knuckle men fight, from Bendigo and Ben Caunt to Sayers and Heenan, wasn't so sure that Fadge was the duffer Adam was implying.

'Maybe you fancy swapping haymakers with an old pug, guv, but I don't. Didn't you see what he did to that soldier boy?'

'What had stirred the man to action? Why did he come roaring at us like the bull of Bashan when he had welcomed us to that den only a few minutes before?'

Quint shrugged. 'Dunno, guv. I reckoned I'd squared it with 'im. But he must 'ave twigged me.'

'Twigged you?' Adam was puzzled. 'What was there for Fadge to twig?'

Quint, looking as close to sheepish as he was ever likely to get, scratched his chin and refused to meet Adam's eyes.

''E may have found out I didn't exackly tell him the truth.'

'And what is the truth?'

'It took me bleeding ages to track that girl down, you know.' Quint thrust his hands deep into the pockets of his blue fustian trousers and stared at his master with sudden defiance. 'In and out of pubs and case-houses, asking questions here and there. Do you know 'ow many women there are on the grind called Ada? Bleeding 'undreds.'

'I appreciate your devotion to the task I set you, Quint, but you leave my question still unanswered. What did you say to that doorman?'

'Well, I found the right Ada. Found out she was spending time in that knocking-ken. So I told Fadge you had a liking for a shy tart. That Ada'd tickle your fancy.'

Adam laughed. 'Well, I am not certain that I approve of your decision to impute particular tastes in women to me, but I cannot see the difficulty.'

'I said as how you'd pay a bit extra for extra time with her.'

'But he allowed us hardly any time at all. And none of it in private.'

'In fact, I give 'im some extra rhino. A sov.'

'You gave that man a sovereign?' Adam was aghast.

'Don't worry, guv.' Quint held out his hands in a placatory gesture. 'It was a crooked sov.'

'Aha, a light begins to dawn. Do you think that perhaps, in the interval between allowing us to pass into the cellar and descending the stairs himself, Mr Fadge had discovered that he had been cheated?'

'Could be,' Quint acknowledged reluctantly.

'Do you think passing a crooked sovereign to a former prize-fighter was a good idea?'

'I thought it was safe enough.' Quint was indignant. He sounded as if he was outraged that Adam was questioning his judgement. 'There ain't too much milk in Harry Fadge's coconut. He was on the wrong side of the door when brains was being handed out, wasn't he? Then what few he 'ad were knocked from 'ere to 'Ounslow and back in the ring. I didn't think he'd notice it was bent.'

The two men turned into Long Acre. The streets were busy with people and they were obliged to dodge their way through the crowds. Many were dressed for the theatre. A sandwich man, with boards back and front advertising the latest comedy at the Gaiety, trudged mournfully past. Two small boys, eager to take advantage of the sandwich man's inability to retaliate, followed him, jeering and aiming kicks at the board on his back. He ignored them. He looked as if he was so lost in melancholy contemplation that he had not even noticed their presence.

'My throat is parched, Quint. There is a coffee stall over there. Let us stop for refreshment.'

The two men crossed Long Acre to the point where it was met by Bow Street. There stood a wooden hut, open on one side and tented over with tarpaulin, from which a large-faced woman dressed in a man's greatcoat was selling coffee. A line of people waited to be served. Adam and Quint queued for a few minutes and then were able to hand over a penny each for a tin mug of oily black liquid. Adam sniffed suspiciously at the drink.

'So, having found her, what was your opinion of Miss Ada, Quint?' he asked.

'She's a nice bit of goods. Ain't no surprise if Jinks was sweet on her.'

'I think perhaps he was. Although, I suspect his original motives in approaching her were more mercenary than amorous.'

Quint's face arranged itself into an expression that said, as clearly as if he'd spoken, 'I ain't got a bleedin' clue what you're talking about.'

'He thought she might have information he could use to make money,' Adam said. 'By the by, the boy Simpkins spoke of a mother. Ada's mother. Did you locate her during your investigations?'

'Ain't seen no sign of her. But Ada spoke of her when I first found her. Far as I can tell, she's too fond of the lush. Any penny she earns goes on gin. And any penny Ada earns.'

Quint took a drink and almost immediately spat most of it onto the ground.

'Jesus Christ, that's like cat's piss.'

'Probably more acorn than coffee bean in it,' Adam commented. He sniffed his own mug again and then, turning from the stall, poured its contents into the gutter. 'We have now spent two pennies and a counterfeit sovereign this evening, and we have received very little benefit from our financial outlay.'

Quint was still making elaborate moues of distaste. He spat twice more on the ground. Adam placed the two mugs back on the counter of the coffee stall and bowed to the proprietress, who was scowling at them.

'In all likelihood, it's the mother who insists that her daughter continues to sell her body, then?'

'Maybe, maybe not.' Quint had finally recovered from his mouthful of coffee. From personal experience, the manservant was much better acquainted with life on London's streets than his master. He doubted that Ada and her mother had much choice when it came to earning their money. 'We ain't no closer to finding out where old Jinks has gone, though.'

'I think that the girl probably does know where he is but, out of loyalty, she has no intention of telling us.'

'She didn't tell us much about anything.'

'Ah, but what she didn't say may tell us something. I am certain that she once worked for Lewis Garland. Her face betrayed her when his name was mentioned.'

'Maybe she did. Maybe that's why Jinks was after her in the first place.'

'My conjecture exactly. We are two minds with but a single thought. I believe Garland had his way with her and then cast her onto the streets. Jinkinson discovered this while he was following the man at Creech's behest, and sought out Ada in order to gather more incriminatory material on the fellow. Either on behalf of Creech, or for his own benefit after Creech was killed.'

The two men left the coffee stall behind them and walked towards Drury Lane. Crowds of theatregoers swirled around them. In the noise and bustle of the London evening they had to shout to make themselves heard.

'You reckon Jinks was blackmailing this Garland bloke?' Quint roared.

'Why else would they have met in that pub yard? And yet there is something more. I am sure of it.'

'What sort of something?'

'Something that is linked with the Greek name in Creech's notebook. Even Ada mentioned Euphorion. Who else could the mysterious foreigner "Yew Ferrion" be? Why does his name keep recurring in our search?'

'You've got that Greek bloke on the brain,' Quint said, deftly dodging a drunk who came careering along the pavement towards him. 'But 'e ain't at the bottom of this, if you asks me.'

'Well, I do ask you, Quint. Who or what is at the bottom of this?'

'Rhino. Sovs,' Quint shouted, patting his pocket. 'Money. Creech was after it from them toffs and now Jinks is after it.'

'You may be right, I suppose.'

'Of course I'm right.'

'In which case, I think perhaps my next task should be to speak to those "toffs" you mention.'

''Ow you going to do that?'

'Send in my card to them. When they are at the House, perhaps. Or in their homes. I can think of no reason why they should not see me.'

Adam recalled his earlier doubts about the advisability of seeking out the three men in the Houses of Parliament. They now seemed overly finical. Speaking about Garland and Oughtred to Mr Moorhouse at the Marco Polo had proved interesting enough, but the time had come to seize the bull firmly by the horns. He should face them on their own ground and learn, once and for all, what they knew about Samuel Creech and his activities.

CHAPTER EIGHTEEN

'Any new developments in the case of that poor man Creech?'

In the smoking room of the Marco Polo, Mr Moorhouse was once again sunk in the depths of his favourite leather armchair. He gave the impression that he had not stirred from there even once in the days since Adam had quizzed him about Lewis Garland. He had merely accumulated ashtrays which were positioned around him like fire irons around a hearth. Adam, who had joined the old man after lunch, watched him aim his ash at one of them and miss.

'The police have taken a man named Stirk into custody,' he said.

'They've got the murderer, then?'

'They think they have.'

'But you're begging to differ?'

'I have met Stirk. He is little more than a drunken dolt. Like critics claim of Mr Darwin, he may well have had a gorilla for a grandfather. There was a picture of one in the *Illustrated London News* the other week and it was Stirk to a T.'

'Some of these African beasts are murderous brutes, though.'

'Well, the gorilla may or may not be. Du Chaillu and the other experts seem to differ on the subject. But Stirk certainly isn't. Whatever the police believe, Mr Moorhouse, he cannot possibly be the killer.'

'So the real perpetrator is still on the loose? Hands steeped in gore and all that.'

'I believe so.'

'Goodness gracious.' Mr Moorhouse looked shocked. He groped for the small glass of port that was resting on the table beside his chair. 'Anybody got any plans to do anything about it?'

'Well, I have been endeavouring to discover more about the man Creech in the hopes of learning reasons why he might have been killed. I have only had limited success as yet. But I believe that I cannot simply leave everything to the police. Not if they insist on believing in the guilt of this man Stirk.'

'Absolutely not,' Mr Moorhouse agreed, sipping at his port. 'Can't have murderers stalking the streets as bold as brass.'

The old man replaced his glass on the table. Ash dropped from the cigar in his other hand. Some of it fell onto his lap and he brushed what he could away.

'Doubtless you will be spending the rest of the day in hot pursuit of the guilty party,' he suggested after a moment's silence. He seemed to be envisaging Adam chasing a blood-soaked killer through the London streets. He looked as if the image was a rather thrilling one for him.

'I hate to disappoint you, Mr Moorhouse, but I have no notion of the identity of the guilty party. Only that it's not the man the police have in custody. In any case, I have another appointment to keep. I am going to Cremorne Gardens.'

'Cremorne, eh?' Mr Moorhouse looked down at the ash still on his trousers. 'Saw a chap go up in a balloon there once. Years ago. Must have been fifty-four.' He screwed up his eyes with the effort of recollection. 'Or was it fifty-five? One or the other, anyway.'

'A fine sight to see, no doubt,' Adam said politely.

'Not really. Bit of a tragedy, actually. Chap fell out of the basket when it was just clearing the trees. Broke his neck. He was French, I think. Brassy. Or Brissy. Some name like that. It was in all the newspapers. You probably read about it at the time.'

'I cannot remember doing so.' Adam decided that it was too much trouble to remind the old man that he would have been no more than a small boy at the time.

'Or was it Brossy?'

'Bressy, perhaps?'

'No, no, no.' Mr Moorhouse sounded uncharacteristically assured. 'Definitely not Bressy.' He seemed to have lost interest in Creech's murder. 'As you say, fine sights to see at Cremorne, I've no doubt. Don't let my experience put you off going.'

* * * * *

As he emerged from the Marco Polo, Adam hailed a cab. The driver, an elderly gnome with a bulbous nose, looked as if he might have been lucklessly patrolling the streets in search of fares since daybreak. Adam climbed in and they set off down Piccadilly in the direction of the park. The hansom seemed even older than its driver. Inside there were rips in the leather of the seats and it smelt as if the previous fare had spent his entire journey sweating and breaking wind. Adam considered asking the ancient driver perched above him to pull over so that he could leave and take another less-reeking vehicle to Chelsea, but decided to stay where he was. He settled gingerly on the torn leather and pulled Emily Maitland's letter from his inside pocket. He read through it once again. It was perhaps the fifth time he had done so and it revealed no more than it had done on first perusal. She apologised for leaving Doughty Street so abruptly. She begged for another meeting with him at which she would explain the reasons for her departure. And, most extraordinarily of all, she suggested that they should rendezvous at the dancing area in Cremorne Gardens.

Strolling among the trees and past the geranium beds after the decrepit cabbie had dropped him at the gates of the gardens, Adam wondered again if Emily was aware of the place's ambivalent reputation. Perhaps she had only been there in the early afternoon. He knew from personal experience that Cremorne Gardens after sunset was a very different place from Cremorne Gardens during the day. He had strolled through them on more than one evening with Cosmo Jardine, in search of fun and temporary company. The atmosphere changed markedly as the evening wore on. The families in search of innocent pleasures disappeared, as did the children eager to see the beasts in the menagerie. The American Bowling Saloon lost its patrons. Instead, with lawns and flower beds and gravel walks undergoing a transformation in the flickering light of the gas lamps, Cremorne became the haunt of hundreds of ladies of easy virtue and their would-be clients. It was not a place for a respectable young woman, even one who had been prepared to flaunt convention and turn up, unchaperoned, at a young man's rooms. Adam stopped and pulled his silver watch from his top pocket. It was not yet six and there were hours of summer daylight left in which to enjoy the more innocent pleasures of Cremorne. If Miss Maitland had no concerns about visiting, then why should he entertain any on her behalf?

He took a seat at one of the tables overlooking the dancing area. Behind the railings which fenced off the floor and the tiered and fretted pagoda where the orchestra played, only a couple of dozen couples were dancing. It was early yet. Adam ordered a bottle of ale from the waiter and looked about him. Two elegantly dressed swells, arms linked, sauntered past, talking loudly about the play they had seen the previous night. Above him, he could also hear raised voices, possibly those of squabbling lovers, coming from one of the upper-floor supper rooms. At the next table was another man, alone like Adam. He was holding a battered nosegay of flowers which he was picking apart and scattering on the ground. He looked to be half-drunk. The air was suddenly full of shrieks of laughter from the dancing platform as the orchestra struck up a swifter tune and the dancers picked up their pace.

'Such indecorous antics, eh?' Adam's neighbour remarked, with a slur and a bitter smile. Adam glanced at him but the man clearly expected no reply. He threw the remains of the nosegay to the floor and, rising unsteadily to his feet, stumbled off. Adam watched him go and then returned to his scrutiny of the people walking round the circular palisade that fenced off the dancing area. He had chosen his seat with care. It provided a clear view of all the paths that converged here. Even at a distance he was able to recognise the young woman who had visited him in Doughty Street as she approached.

He felt his heart beat faster and his spirits lift as he saw her. She was truly a beautiful woman.

She was dressed from head to toe in fine white muslin and was holding a white parasol above her head, as if the noonday sun was still blazing down on Cremorne and she needed all the protection it offered. She was stepping out with an almost manly confidence and pace. Heads in the crowd turned as she passed. Adam rose from his seat. As he did so, Miss Maitland noticed him and gave a slight wave of her parasol. She quickened her already swift pace and arrived by the table breathless and laughing.

'I was stricken with a sudden fear that you might not be here, Mr Carver. Or that I might not be able to find you. There are such crowds in the gardens.'

'There are always crowds almost everywhere in London, Miss Maitland.' In truth, Adam had been thinking only a moment or two earlier that Cremorne was quiet for a June evening. 'It takes time for a stranger to accustom himself – or herself – to the hustle and bustle of the city.'

He motioned towards one of the cushioned wooden chairs by the table and the young woman, closing her parasol, took it.

'I do not think I shall ever be anything other than a stranger in London. I am rarely allowed out to see any of it. My mother is convinced that I must be chaperoned everywhere I go. If I am not, she believes I will end by running off with a shoe-black off the streets.'

'Yet here you are in Cremorne Gardens. Unchaperoned.' And you visited a gentleman's lodgings in Doughty Street, equally unaccompanied, Adam thought, although he said nothing of it.

'I have given my mother the slip. She has gone to see her banker in Lombard Street, leaving me, as she thinks, reading a novel in our rooms at Brown's. I took a cab ten minutes after she left.'

Adam could not help but laugh at the conspiratorial air with which the young woman made her confession.

'Was it awfully improper to suggest meeting you here?' Emily asked after a moment's pause.

'A little unconventional, perhaps.'

'I am quite certain that I have done any number of things that were awfully improper in the weeks since I arrived in town. There are so many more rules in London than there are in Salonika. But I grow very weary of them.'

She heaved a great sigh as if to indicate the extent of her weariness.

'Am I not to enjoy the freedom that men take for granted, Mr Carver? Can a respectable young lady not walk where she wishes without attracting sullen stares or unwanted conversation?'

Adam was unsure what to say. The truth was that an unaccompanied lady in the streets of London was only too likely to attract exactly the kind of attention Emily described. Or worse.

'And yet I trust that I have not been *too* forward. Too...' She paused to search for the word. 'Too unmaidenly.'

'I am certain you are incapable of appearing unmaidenly, Miss Maitland.'

'I shall have to do as you have done, Mr Carver,' Emily said, laughing. 'Write a book about my travels! The adventures of a naive young girl from Salonika in the wilds of London!'

'And of what have your London adventures consisted?' Apart from visiting gentlemen unannounced, Adam thought to himself.

'Very little, if truth be told.' Emily looked cast down at the thought of all the adventures she had been missing.

'There must be something to fill the pages of this book you will write.'

'Well, we have been to the theatre on several occasions. We went to the Queen's last night. *Lady Audley's Secret.*' She used the tip of her parasol to trace some pattern in the gravel around her chair. 'Such a dismal drama. Nothing but murder, bigamy and madness. We were greatly disappointed by it. Although the ladies' hats were much to be admired.'

'I am sorry that your visit to the theatre was not a success.'

'Oh, you should not be.' Emily laughed. 'No play can be considered a complete failure if one comes away from it with a new idea for a bonnet.'

'I have to confess that I have never gone to a play and studied the hats of my neighbours with any great attention.'

'You certainly should do, Mr Carver.' Emily sounded as if she was recommending a moral duty that was not to be lightly shirked. 'Hats are fearfully revealing. I think that you can judge much about a person's character from the shape of his or her hat. Take the hat belonging to the gentleman in the blue jacket who is standing by the little gateway onto the dancing platform. The black coachman's hat.'

Adam turned his head very slightly so that he could see the person Emily meant.

'And what does that hat tell you about its wearer?'

'That the gentleman in question is not a gentleman at all. That he is not to be trusted.' Emily was firm in her conviction.

'And does my own headgear reveal anything about *my* character?' Adam asked. The young woman put her head on one side and pretended to consider the question.

'That you *are* a gentleman and that you *are* to be trusted, I would say.'

Adam smiled. He tipped the headgear in question, a low-crowned grey top hat, in Emily's direction.

'Thank you kindly, miss,' he said, ironically. 'And is there anything which you would care to entrust to such a trustworthy gentleman?'

'There is certainly a secret which I should entrust to somebody,' the young woman said, looking at him with disconcerting directness. 'But I am not yet certain that the gentleman in question is that somebody.'

'Is there anything the gentleman in question could or should do to assist you in reaching the certainty you seek?'

'Not at present. There is nothing to be done.' She looked away towards the dancing platform. Adam was left to contemplate her profile and struggle to think of more to say. Emily showed no signs that she would be the one to renew the conversation.

'How long will you and your mother remain in town?' he asked after half a minute's silence, which had seemed to him like half an hour.

'Who can tell? Perhaps a week. Perhaps a month. I suppose we shall be gone before the end of August. Surely everybody has left by then?'

Adam thought the streets of London would probably be no less crowded at the end of August than they were in the middle of June. Besides, he wondered whether Emily and her mother were quite so conversant with the higher echelons of society as her remark seemed intended to suggest.

'You will return to Salonika, perhaps? I am sure that Salonika offers society to entertain your mother and yourself,' Adam said. On the basis of his own experience of the city, he was unsure of any such thing but thought it politest to claim otherwise.

'Society!' Emily said, with great scorn. 'Nothing but a set of old frumps and foozles, I can assure you. Nobody talks about a thing but the price of this and the price of that and when the next ship from Constantinople is due. I have been like to scream with boredom the entire time we have lived there.'

'I am sorry to hear that, Miss Maitland. So there is little to draw you back to Salonika.'

'Not a thing. My mother is considering the possibility of travelling to Switzerland. She thinks a month amongst the glaciers would be of inestimable advantage to the health of us both.'

'And do you agree with her?'

'A daughter should probably always agree with her mother. But I am inclined to believe that we will thrive well enough without the benefit of mountain air and Alpine walks.'

Since they had first begun to talk, Adam had noticed that Emily's feet had been restlessly tapping beneath the table. Now she began to wave her arm in time to the music drifting over from the bandstand.

'We must dance before we leave, Mr Carver.'

Adam was startled. He had not thought that they were leaving. He still had no notion about 'the affairs of consequence to us both' of which Emily had written in her letter. He had assumed that he had been summoned to Cremorne Gardens to hear more of them. Now, after little more than idle chatter about hats, the theatre and the Alps, together with an enigmatic remark about a secret that should be told, the young woman was talking of dancing. And of leaving. In his surprise, he scarcely noticed that she had been so forward as to suggest taking to the dance floor herself.

'I am no dancer,' he said. 'My left foot rarely seems to know what my right foot is doing.'

'This is a galop,' Emily replied. 'And the galop is no dance. At least, not one worthy of the name. Little more than a dash down the room, a swift turn, and then a dash back. Even so poor a dancer as you claim to be can take the floor for a galop.'

'There is no "down the room and back" at Cremorne, Miss Maitland. As you can see, the dancing area forms a circle round the orchestra.'

'Then we shall go round and round,' she said firmly, standing and holding out her hand.

With the young woman already on her feet, Adam could not be so churlish as to refuse. He pushed back his chair and stood himself. The two of them moved through the gathering crowds to the circle of the dance floor. It was not a galop that was now playing as they made their way through one of the gaps in the low fence that surrounded it. The orchestra, doubtless sweating from their exertions in the raised box above the dancers, had turned to a slower measure. Adam took the young woman into his arms and the pair of them began to swirl decorously across the circle. He was acutely aware of the pressure of her body in his arms. Should his hand be *there*, he asked himself, as they swept past two flagging couples, perhaps themselves exhausted by the galop? Should he move it higher? Lower? No, definitely not lower. He wondered how closely he could hold her without causing offence. It was not a dilemma that he had faced before. With the girls that he and Cosmo picked up in the dance halls in town, and indeed occasionally at Cremorne, it was not a question that arose. Provided he paid for their drinks and their supper, he could hold them just as tightly as he wished. With the young ladies he had partnered on the rarer occasions he had attended what might be called a society ball, the etiquette was also clear. The young woman was to be held with lightest of touches, like a porcelain figurine in the delicate hands of a connoisseur. But where did Emily fit into the social equation? She was undoubtedly a lady. Everything about her appearance proclaimed that fact. And yet what lady would have come unannounced and unaccompanied to Doughty Street? What lady would have chosen to meet him in the early evening at Cremorne Gardens? More questions raced through Adam's mind but Emily herself answered many of them by moving closer into his tentative embrace.

'You have deceived me, Mr Carver,' she said with a smile. 'You dance very well. Your left foot knows *exactly* what your right foot is doing.'

'No, it is partnering you that has worked a miracle, Miss Maitland. I assure you that I am usually as clumsy as a carthorse when I dance.'

The two of them moved beneath the large sign that read 'All the Nations of the World are Welcome to Cremorne' and continued to circle the orchestra. At this time of the day, only a handful of couples were dancing. Other groups of men and women, and some solitary men, strolled around the perimeter fence, watching those who had taken to the floor. Adam felt proud to be seen with such a beautiful woman as Emily but his curiosity about her remained. He decided that directness was, perhaps, his best policy.

'I am puzzled by the affairs of consequence to us both to which you referred in your letter, Miss Maitland. I am uncertain what affairs we can have in common.'

'Oh, the dance floor is no place to talk of them!' Emily moved even closer into his arms. Adam was only too aware of the warmth of her body pressed against his as they completed a first circuit of the orchestra and embarked upon another. However, he was determined to find out more about his mysterious partner.

'I was delighted by your visit to my rooms in Doughty Street,' he persisted, 'on the day that Quint's clumsiness with the plates seemed to frighten you away. But I was perplexed as to the reason for it.'

He paused and strove to catch the young woman's eye. She looked away from him, as if scanning the rows of spectators for a familiar face.

'And for the call you made upon me the previous Friday,' he added.

Emily now turned her head and stared at him, almost sullenly. As if by mutual agreement, the two of them began to move even more slowly than the music demanded. After a moment they came to a complete halt. Another couple, surprised by their stopping, nearly collided with them, before laughing and reeling off at an angle.

'My landlady, Mrs Gaffery, saw you come down the stairs,' Adam said. 'I do believe she has as many eyes as Argus Panoptes.'

Emily continued to gaze at him. For a few seconds, he thought that she was about to speak. Instead, she leaned in towards him, her head uptilted and her lips slightly parted. Adam's own head moved downwards. They began to kiss. To his surprise, the young man felt Emily's tongue enter his mouth, gently probing. He responded. For what seemed to him like many minutes, they stood entwined on the dance floor. Then Emily broke free from his embrace and began to make her way swiftly towards one of the breaks in the perimeter fence. Rooted to the spot, the taste of her still within his mouth, he watched her go. She did not look back. He debated whether or not to follow her. By the time he decided that he should and must, she had disappeared from sight.

CHAPTER NINETEEN

At Sir Willoughby Oughtred's house in Eaton Square, a pigeon-breasted and melancholic servant, whose face suggested profound disillusionment with the world and all it contained, took Adam's card and disappeared. Left in an entrance hall tiled in squares of black and white marble, Adam felt like a chess piece awaiting the next move in a complicated game. The servant returned in a surprisingly short time and led him up to a first-floor drawing room. Sir Willoughby was already there, warming himself in front of the fireplace. Above his head, on either side of the hearth, were portraits of disgruntled-looking men in eighteenth-century costume. Adam assumed they were earlier baronets. The Oughtreds were an ancient family, so ancient that even the present-day members of it had lost track of its exact origins. They had not come over with the Conqueror. That, at least, was certain. In fact, when William the Bastard had crossed the Channel, he had found that the Oughtreds were already there. They had been waiting for him and, in alliance with King Harold, had attempted to bloody his nose. When this failed, one Oughtred had disappeared into the East Anglian fens with Hereward the Wake. Over the centuries, having made their peace with the Norman invaders, the Oughtreds had quietly prospered. They were granted land in Lincolnshire by Henry I. They fought on the side of this Henry and several of those that followed him in wars against ambitious noblemen. They were granted more land in Lincolnshire.

By the time of Henry VIII, the Oughtreds already had more acres in the county than they really needed, but as stalwart supporters of the king they accepted thousands more which had once belonged to the monasteries. During the Civil War and the rule of Cromwell, their fervid royalism proved costly to them for the first time in several hundred years. Several Oughtreds were obliged to join Charles II in impecunious exile in the Netherlands but luckily this proved to be only a temporary downturn in their fortunes. In the two centuries since the Merry Monarch's triumphant return to his throne, they had continued to sit comfortably in the upper ranks of English society. They had faced only minor setbacks. In the reign of George III, one Oughtred had sunk so low as to marry a brewer's daughter. The social stigma had been unavoidable but the young woman in question had brought compensating gifts to the marriage and to the Oughtred fortunes. A quarter of a million pounds of them, in fact.

Today, the family was as ubiquitous in the life of the nation as it had ever been. Half a dozen Oughtreds or more were currently serving in the army and were kept busy dealing with potentially restless natives in the furthest-flung corners of the empire. At least three were in the Church and one held a bishopric. And Sir Willoughby Oughtred sat in the House of Commons, as he had done since the day after his twenty-first birthday many years before, helping in his own particular way to shape the laws that governed his fellow Englishmen.

Some of this was known to Adam and passed through his mind as the sad servant ushered him into Sir Willoughby's presence and withdrew. He looked at the Oughtred portraits and at the head of a stag which held pride of place above the hearth, its glass eyes visibly protruding as if it had met its death by strangulation rather than shooting. He tried not to feel intimidated by the weight of Oughtred history hanging in the air of the vast drawing room.

The present baronet looked little less pop-eyed than the stag and just as dissatisfied with the world as his ancestors in the portraits. He had a glass in one hand and was puffing on a large cigar. Neither appeared to be giving him much pleasure. He took the cigar from his mouth to greet his visitor.

'Come in, Carver. Bargate here will get you a drink. Whiskey and soda do?'

Sir Willoughby spoke as if it would have to do because no other drink was on offer. Bargate, a man who looked no less doleful than his fellow servant but several decades older, emerged from the shadows in which he had been lurking. He set off towards the decanters. Bald and astonishingly wrinkled, his head jutting forward as he shambled across the room, he was like a 200-year-old tortoise, stripped of its shell and sent out into the world to serve drinks to its betters. The baronet returned the cigar to his mouth. A blast of smoke erupted from it and hung in clouds in the air. These clouds seemed, suddenly and miraculously, to gain motive power from somewhere and began to make their way towards Adam. In seconds his head was swathed in them and he was hard pressed not to break down in a coughing fit.

'I knew your father, Carver,' the baronet said. 'Saw a lot of him when he was putting together that Lincolnshire Railway Company. But I do not believe I have had the pleasure of meeting you. Came across your name in the papers, of course, when you returned from European Turkey. Even had Bargate buy that book of yours. Never got round to reading it, mind. But we haven't been introduced. Have we?'

The MP sounded suddenly uncertain, as if aware that he met dozens of people in the course of an average day and that he couldn't trust himself to remember every single one of them.

'No, sir, we have not met.' Adam fought his way out of the poisonous miasma of Sir Willoughby's cigar smoke in order to reply. 'Although we have acquaintances in common. And we are both, I believe, members of the Marco Polo.'

'Ah, the Marco Polo. Were you at the Speke dinner?' The MP did not bother to wait for an answer. 'The food was foul, was it not? Lord knows who the chef is. Some filthy Frenchman, I suppose.'

Sir Willoughby waved his hand towards the centre of the room where a round mahogany table stood, surrounded by half a dozen chairs.

'Shall we take a seat?'

Again without waiting for an answer, and looking far from confident that it would support him, Sir Willoughby walked across and lowered himself gingerly into one of the chairs. Adam pulled another out from the table. Bargate reappeared to hand him his drink.

'How can I help you, my boy?' The MP was clearly prepared to cast himself in the role of a benevolent father figure, ready at all times to dispense his wisdom to the younger generation.

Adam hesitated. How much should he tell Sir Willoughby? He was aware that he might blunder unwittingly onto treacherous ground. Yet questions had to be asked. If the baronet found some of them offensive, there was little Adam could do about it.

'Little to do with the Marco Polo, sir. Although it was at the Speke dinner that the story began.'

Sir Willoughby looked politely puzzled. What story beginning at the Speke dinner could possibly have anything to do with me? his half-raised eyebrow seemed to say.

'It was there that I met a gentleman named Samuel Creech.'

In an instant, the baronet's expression changed from puzzlement to curiosity. He looked long and hard at Adam and then turned to his servant.

'Leave us, Bargate,' he said. As the doddering retainer made his slow way to the door, Adam and Sir Willoughby stared at one another in silence. The younger man felt uncomfortable. It was a relief to him when he heard the door to the drawing room close.

'Creech is dead,' the baronet said. 'Slain in some outrage in the suburbs.'

'Yes, that is so. He was murdered on the Wednesday of last week. It is evident that you knew the gentleman in question.'

'Most certainly I knew Creech. I knew him for forty years and more. We were at school together.'

'May I risk an impertinent question and ask how you learned of Creech's murder?'

'Impertinent or not, I cannot see its significance.' The baronet thought for a moment. 'Either I read about it in the *Morning Post* or a mutual acquaintance told me.'

'Could that mutual acquaintance have been Lewis Garland or James Abercrombie?'

'It might have been Garland, yes. Abercrombie is out of the country.' The baronet was beginning to sound annoyed. He was not a man used to being questioned in so direct a manner. 'It might have been someone else entirely.'

'But Garland and Abercrombie both knew him?'

'Certainly they knew him.' Sir Willoughby spoke now as if Adam was insisting on displaying almost inconceivable imbecility. 'We were all four at Eton at the same time. Garland arrived the year before me and Abercrombie the year after, but we were all there together.'

'I have arranged to see Mr Garland at the House later in the week.'

Sir Willoughby grunted as if to suggest that Adam's social calendar was of little interest to him.

'Sound enough fellow, Garland,' he said grudgingly. 'Although bit too much of a reading man. When we were at school. When we were up at Trinity. Probably reads too much now, to judge by his speeches in the House. All very well being on nodding terms with the classics but a gentleman shouldn't make a fetish out of them. Nobody wants Homer dropped into a debate about married women's property. Not sure anybody wants a debate about married women's property at all, but that's a different matter.'

'So I am right in thinking, sir, that you and Creech and Garland and Abercrombie have known one another for many years?'

'Have I not already said as much?' The baronet was becoming very irritated. 'Look, what is all this about, Carver? I agreed to see you out of respect for your late father. I assumed you had something to say that related to the railway company. To the dealings I had with him before his unfortunate demise. And yet all you do is ask me questions about someone from my schooldays. Some poor devil who has met a dreadful end.'

'It was perhaps not reported in the press but Creech's body was found by a visitor to his house. I was that visitor.'

'Good God!' The baronet seemed genuinely shocked by Adam's revelation. 'But what has all this to do with me? I assume you cannot be scouring London for every one of Creech's old school friends in order to tell them the unhappy news. Why have you come to me?'

'I found something else at the house. A notebook with transactions in Creech's handwriting. Transactions with a private enquiry agent named Jinkinson.'

Silence descended again on the room. Adam could hear nothing but a clock ticking quietly in the background.

'I ask you again.' Oughtred took another pull on his cigar. 'What has this to do with me?'

'Your name appeared frequently in the notebook.'

'I cannot imagine why. I have scarcely seen Creech more than half a dozen times in twenty years. He spent much of that time abroad, I believe.' Sir Willoughby's voice was now icy. 'And I have never had any dealings with any enquiry agent of any name.'

'I am sorry to have to say this, sir, but I find that statement rather difficult to reconcile with the evidence of my own eyes.'

For a moment, Sir Willoughby looked as if Adam had slapped him across the face. He had been leaning forward in his chair to reach for his drink. He stopped and pulled back. Red dots of colour appeared on his cheeks.

'What do you mean by that, you impudent young cub? Are you accusing me of being a liar?'

'I hope not, sir. I hope there is some simple explanation for events. But I was in contact with the enquiry agent, Jinkinson. I followed him one day as he went about his business. He met you on Westminster Bridge. I saw the two of you in conversation together.'

'The devil you did! And you *are* accusing me of being a liar. I tell you I have never met this man. Have you sunk to such a level that the word of a gentleman is not good enough for you?'

Sir Willoughby stood up and walked to the bell-rope by the fireplace, which he pulled sharply.

'I have rung for Bargate to return. I must ask you to leave my house.'

'But this man Jinkinson has gone missing, Sir Willoughby. He has not been seen for more than a week. Perhaps the conversation you had with him might throw some light on his disappearance.'

'I doubt that very much. I suggest you leave at once, sir. I have no time for Jinkinsons and those who skulk about the city in pursuit of them.' The door opened and the antiquated servant reappeared. 'Bargate, Mr Carver is leaving. Be so good as to show him out.'

Adam had no choice but to pick up his hat and depart. He strove to look the baronet in the eye before he left, but Sir Willoughby had already performed the aristocratic trick of dismissing from his attention anything or anyone he no longer wished to acknowledge. Adam had ceased to exist for him. The young man could only turn and follow Bargate, leaving Sir Willoughby alone with his ancestors. Enveloped in cigar smoke from head to foot, the baronet remained standing impassively beneath the portraits of long-dead Oughtreds.

CHAPTER TWENTY

'And so this man Creech or Sinclair or whatever he chose to call himself was a blackmailer?'

'It looks very much like it.'

Cosmo Jardine laughed. He and Adam were sitting in the painter's studio. The rays of the setting sun were drifting through the room's large windows and falling unforgivingly on *King Pellinore and the Questing Beast*. The young artist was staring intently at his painting. As Adam spoke, he stood and moved towards his easel. He picked up a sheet from the floor and threw it over the canvas, hiding the image of the Arthurian knight.

'It is just my confounded luck,' he said. 'The only man to show any interest in my paintings in months and he turns out to be a wrong 'un. And then he is discovered dead only days after visiting me.'

'You do seem to make a poor choice of potential patrons.'

'Creech-Sinclair chose me, if you recall.' Jardine returned to his chair. 'Who was the not-so-gentlemanly gentleman blackmailing?'

'He was paying the man Jinkinson to follow three MPs. So the assumption must be that he had knowledge of all three of them that they would not want made public. Or was assuming he'd get that knowledge.'

'Who were these men with secrets to hide?'

'Willoughby Oughtred. James Abercrombie. Lewis Garland.' Adam counted them off on his fingers.

'There are Oughtreds everywhere, aren't there? Not sure I've heard of a Willoughby Oughtred, though.' Jardine stretched out his legs and stared at his shoes. 'Abercrombie is some man of business, isn't he? Richer than Croesus. Garland I know. His constituency includes some of the same verdant Cotswold acres as my father's see. What has Mr Garland been doing to attract the attention of a blackmailer?'

'If Jinkinson and my other informant are to be believed, he is keeping a mistress. In St John's Wood.'

Jardine laughed again, louder than before.

'How drearily predictable,' he said. 'But what if Lewis Garland does have a bit of muslin on the sly? That is not exactly news that would rock the nation to its foundations.'

'No, but embarrassing enough for him that he might wish to pay to keep it quiet. I don't suppose your father and his fellow clergy would be delighted to know that their representative in Parliament has a fondness for bedding actresses.'

'I cannot see how this matters very much.' Jardine, smothering a yawn, was unconvinced. 'Men of the cloth can be surprisingly tolerant when it comes to such affairs. At least when gentlemen like Garland are involved. They find it easier to turn a blind eye than to cast the first stone.'

'In the great scheme of things, Cosmo, it may not matter much. No doubt all will be one a hundred years hence, but for the moment, I would say that it matters a great deal to Lewis Garland. I bow to your superior knowledge of ecclesiastical opinion but I still think that he would not wish his constituents to learn of his misdeeds. And if ensuring that meant paying a blackmailer, he might just do so.'

'I suppose that you are correct,' Jardine acknowledged. 'But our parliamentary Lothario would scarcely go so far as to kill said blackmailer.'

'No, that is true. I suppose he might hire someone to do his killing for him.'

Jardine waved his hand in dismissal of the idea. 'You have spent too long in the lands ruled by the Turk, Adam. That sort of thing might happen in Constantinople or Salonika but you are in London now. Prominent men don't hire assassins to dispose of their enemies.'

'No, you are, of course, correct. It does seem unlikely.'

'Impossible. I suppose one could just about imagine Mr Disraeli hiring bully-boys to kidnap Mr Gladstone and cast him into the Thames in a sack, but there is no other politician capable of such ruthlessness.'

Jardine lit a cigar and blew smoke towards the windows.

'I must give up that theory, then,' Adam said. 'Creech's death must have some other explanation.'

'And you are the man to smoke out the truth, are you? To sneak surreptitiously through the city streets in pursuit of the villains and unmask them for the murderous swine they are?'

'I am not sure I am able to do much in the sneaking line. I am under surveillance myself. The widow Gaffery twitches her parlour curtains every time I leave the house. She is convinced that I am smuggling women in and out of my rooms with the sole aim of ruining her reputation with the neighbours.'

'And are you?'

'I have no opportunity to do so.'

'And yet it would be so easy. A cab pulls up at the door. The door is opened. There is a rustle of skirts and another young maiden is hurried into the love nest of the gallant Adam Carver.'

Adam laughed. 'It is a pretty picture you paint but it would not be possible. Not in Doughty Street.'

'Ah, I had clean forgot. Doughty Street is none of your common thoroughfares to be rattled through by cabs. It has a gate at either end to prevent any rude incursions by *mobile vulgus*.'

'Precisely. And besides, as I say, La Gaffery stands guard at all hours like Cerberus at the gates of Hades.'

'Not three-headed, surely?'

'No, but quite as fierce and just as relentless.'

'But you escape her vigilance occasionally, do you not? You have opportunities to pursue your curious investigations into the death of Creech-Sinclair?' Jardine held up his hands, fingers splayed, and examined them in the light. Traces of paint, relics of his morning's work, remained on them. 'I must confess that I find it difficult to understand your continuing interest in the whole sordid business.'

There was a slight pause. The artist looked enquiringly at his friend.

'I find it difficult to understand myself, Cosmo,' Adam said eventually. He remained half-puzzled about his own motivations in making his enquiries. Was he driven to these investigations by boredom? He had not been aware of late of any particular feelings of ennui. He had found a genuine sense of purpose in his photography and in his plans to record the disappearing architecture of the city. However, there was no doubt that even the capture of the most artistic image of a half-timbered building in the city was not as exciting as the pursuit of a murderer. As he spoke, he felt his determination to find the truth about Creech grow. 'Somehow I feel half-responsible for the man's death. That if he had not spoken to me at the Marco Polo, he would be alive still.'

'I cannot see how the two events can be connected.'

'No more can I – but the feeling remains.' Adam was hauling himself onto firmer ground, reaching more confidently for justifications for his actions over the last weeks. 'And I dislike mysteries. There is mystery surrounding this man's death. And now a new mystery with the seeming disappearance of this enquiry agent Jinkinson.'

'The truth is, my dear chap, that you have too little to occupy your time.' Jardine had found a rag and was wiping his paint-stained fingers. 'All those months with nothing to do but tote your camera round town and take sun-pictures of ancient buildings. And then along comes this villain, Creech-Sinclair, and gets himself killed. Little wonder that you seized upon the opportunity for a little excitement.'

'Perhaps you are right, Cosmo.' Adam smiled at his friend.

'I *am* right. Depend upon it.' Jardine threw the rag into a corner of his studio. 'But I gain no satisfaction from being so. With the blackmailer dead, my search for a rich art-lover must continue.'

* * * * *

The following evening, Adam was ushered into a wood-panelled room deep in the hidden recesses of the Houses of Parliament where Lewis Garland was waiting for him. The walls of the room were covered with paintings of politicians from the last century and the MP was gazing intently at a full-length portrait of Pitt the Elder. He looked as if he was memorising the face in case he met the long-dead prime minister in the streets and needed to recognise him. He turned as Adam approached him and pointed up at Pitt.

'There was a man with whom to reckon, eh, Mr Carver? I should have relished facing him across the floor of the House. A worthy opponent. Worthier than some of those in government today.'

Garland was a tall and vigorous man in his late fifties. He was languid in his speech and movements and yet carried with him an air of barely suppressed energy. His moustache was as abundant as Quint had said it was. Despite Garland's years, his hair was also so black that Adam was certain he must be dyeing it. It was blacker than nature ever intended the hair of men in their fifties to be.

'You wrote in the note you sent me that you wished to talk about a gentleman named Samuel Creech. I understand that Mr Creech has been found dead. Murdered.'

'He was indeed. But you knew him.'

'As you say, I knew him. But I am not entirely clear how you and Creech are connected.'

As concisely as he could, Adam described the meeting with Creech at the Marco Polo, the curious conversation between them, the journey out to Herne Hill and the discovery of the body. He said nothing of the notebook or of the names within it. Garland listened impassively. When the story was finished, he gave a chilly smile before making any comment.

'A strange encounter indeed, Mr Carver. I do not know how it is that you have discovered that Creech and I were acquainted, although it is no particular secret. I knew Sam Creech for many years. Since we were both boys. And God knows that is a long time ago.'

'Have you seen him in recent months?'

Garland looked up at Pitt the Elder once again.

'An interesting face, is it not? Strong features but a look of melancholy, would you not say? Around the eyes?'

Adam agreed that there was a suggestion of melancholy in the portrait.

'What is it exactly that you want to know, Mr Carver?' the MP asked.

'I want to know why Creech was killed. There is also a gentleman named Jinkinson who had something to do with Creech and who has now disappeared. I want to know what connection this man had with Creech and where he has gone.'

Garland walked away from Pitt the Elder and waved his hand dismissively.

'Sam Creech's death is no doubt a great tragedy. But you should leave the investigation of it to the police. They are the experts in murder, are they not? As for this other man – Jinkinson, did you say his name is? – he might be anywhere. London, as I'm sure you have noticed, is a large city. It is a place in which it is only too easy to disappear. People do so every day.'

Adam had already decided he would not allow himself to be browbeaten by the older man. He was determined to stand his ground in this encounter.

'Nonetheless, I cannot help feeling – perhaps foolishly – that Creech died because he was in contact with me. An d that Jinkinson's disappearance is linked to my visit to his offices. I want to know the answers to my questions. I want to know more about Creech. Perhaps I will then be able to discover why he was killed.'

'We should be careful in deciding what it is we want, Mr Carver. Perhaps you know the story of Colonel Pierpont?'

'I have never heard of the gentleman,' Adam said stiffly. He was aware that Garland was, in some subtle way, laughing at him.

'The colonel was a fellow member of my club in Pall Mall. The Marco Polo – I seem to recall that you are also a member. Anyway, several years ago, he developed a fear of crossing over to St James's Square. Too much traffic for the poor man. He paid for a small island to be constructed in the middle of the street. Somewhere he could stand and look in all directions before venturing on the second half of the journey across the road. When it was built, Pierpont was delighted. He rushed out of the club to admire it. Alas, he was so excited, he failed to notice the cab travelling along the street. Pierpont never reached his island. The cab knocked him down and he expired the same day from his injuries.'

'A sad story, but I fail to see its relevance to our conversation.'

'Pierpont should have been more careful in choosing what he wanted. Had he not wanted his island so much, he would have been with us still.'

Garland looked at Adam and then gave a barely perceptible shrug of the shoulders.

'Ask your questions, Mr Carver, if you must. I can see that you will not be satisfied until you have done so. But I do not think I will be able to help you.'

'Creech was a man who had no obvious source of income. And yet he lived in some style in Herne Hill. How did he do so, do you suppose?'

'London is full of men with no obvious source of income. They are called gentlemen.'

'But where did he get his income?' Adam persisted.

'I do not know. I do happen to know that Creech stayed at the Langham when he first came to town last year. What does that suggest to you?'

'That money was little object to him.'

'Precisely.'

'But why was money suddenly no object to him? He was a man who had spent most of his career drudging in foreign climes for a meagre salary. Did he receive an inheritance? Was there money in the family that finally came to him?'

'Money can come from a thousand different sources.' Garland paused and seemed to be considering whether or not to say anything more. After a moment, he continued. 'If you wish to know the truth, Mr Carver, then most of Sam Creech's money probably came from blackmail. He was a blackmailer.'

Adam had been prepared for any number of possible replies to his questions, including this one, but he was still surprised to hear it directly from Garland's lips. He was surprised that the MP should state the facts so openly.

'And was he blackmailing you, sir?' he asked, after a moment.

In the silence that followed, Adam could hear the gentle hissing from the gaslights in the room. He wondered what the answer to this question would be, but when Garland spoke, the MP continued as if it had not been asked.

'Blackmail is a nasty word, of course, but then Creech was a nasty man. He was a nasty little boy, if it comes to that. When we were at school, it was always Creech who would tell tales on his fellows if he thought he could get away with it; Creech who would bully the smaller boys most cruelly; Creech who would suck up to the powerful and spit upon the meek. I was not in the slightest degree surprised when I learned that he had turned to extortion in his more mature years.'

'But whom was he blackmailing? And what did he know that enabled him to turn to extortion?'

'Everyone has his secrets, Mr Carver. A determined blackmailer does not usually need to look far for material with which to work.'

'So Creech knew of matters of which others would have preferred him to be ignorant.'

'I have no doubt that he did. He would have been a poor extortionist without access to the secrets of others.'

'Would the secrets Creech had gathered have died with him? Or could someone else be in possession of them?'

'That I cannot tell you.'

'Perhaps Jinkinson has come into possession of them and has decided that he too will embark on a career as a blackmailer.'

'Jinkinson?' Garland looked puzzled at first, but understanding soon dawned. 'Ah, yes, the man in yellow.'

'So you acknowledge that you met him outside a public house in the Strand?'

'You have been following me, Mr Carver?' The MP sounded more amused than affronted.

'I was interested in Jinkinson. It was he that my man was following.' Garland nodded to himself, as if all was explained.

'Yes, I met the fellow,' he said. 'In the Strand, as you say. You would not expect me to entertain the canary-coloured jackanapes here, now, would you? Or in my house in Bruton Street? I had my doubts about meeting him at all.' Garland flicked invisible specks of dust from the sleeve of his morning coat.

'The man is a complete fool. His business demands subtlety and subterfuge and he dresses in such a way that he would stand out in the crowd on Derby Day. God knows how Creech came across him. His taste for the low life must have grown since last I saw him.'

'But you met Jinkinson and spoke to him. I wonder why you felt the necessity to do so.'

Garland looked sharply at Adam. He made as if to move closer to him and then stopped.

'I can only say to you, Mr Carver, what I said to the canary man. You would do well to look after your own business and refrain from concerning yourself with mine.'

Adam decided to change tack. 'I have spoken recently with Sir Willoughby Oughtred,' he said. 'I have been asking him very much the same kind of questions I have been asking you, Mr Garland. I am not trying to poke my nose where it is not wanted. I am merely seeking to find out more about the circumstances surrounding Creech's murder.'

'You have seen Oughtred, have you?' Garland laughed. 'You know him from the Marco Polo, I assume.'

'I had never met the baronet before. Although he knew my father.'

'Of course, I had forgotten. You are the son of Carver of the Lincolnshire Railway.'

Garland moved towards the large mahogany table in the centre of the room. He began to run his hand across its surface as if he was polishing it. 'And what did you think of Oughtred, I wonder?'

'Sir Willoughby is a fine example of an old-fashioned English-man,' Adam replied cautiously.

The MP laughed again. He continued to rub his hand across the wooden grain of the table, as if admiring its smoothness.

'Spoken like a diplomat, Mr Carver. He is exactly that. Perhaps a little too old-fashioned.'

'I am not sure I catch your meaning, sir.'

'Let me put it this way, then.' Garland turned to look at Adam. 'All right-thinking men know that the country's present and future fortunes are tied up with cotton and coal and railways rather than with corn. Your late father was one of those in the vanguard of the nation. Oughtred belongs with those bringing up the rear. He firmly believes that the rot set in as long ago as thirty-two, with Grey's Reform Act, if not earlier, and that the country has been going downhill ever since.'

'And yet, like yourself, he has his seat in this House. He is one of the nation's legislators.'

'In my humble opinion, the trouble with Parliament is that there are still more MPs whose wealth and position depend, as Oughtred's does, on agriculture and not industry.'

Garland, Adam thought, did not look like a man who had ever held a humble opinion in his life. He assumed he was not going to begin to do so now. The tall MP continued to speak.

'He is a dear man but no one could say that he is the brightest baronet to be found in the pages of Burke's. Indeed, there are some who might claim that he is among the dimmest. Let me be perfectly honest with you. I have known Willoughby, as I have known Creech, for four decades. He is a man who cannot add two to three and be sure of getting five. He is not only suspicious of abstract thought, he is incapable of it. In his heart of hearts, he believes that intellectual endeavour of all kinds will lead inevitably to the levelling of classes and the destruction of society. However, his pedigree predates the Plantagenets and he owns half the acres of Lincolnshire. And so...' – Garland shrugged his shoulders – 'he takes his seat in the House and his place in a dozen boardrooms is guaranteed. Well, I suppose there is one thing that can be said for poor old Willoughby. He may be mediocre, but at least he's reliably mediocre.'

The MP moved closer to Adam and rested his hand on his arm.

'We have strayed from our original topic of conversation, Mr Carver. And I have been woefully indiscreet about my old friend. I must trust you to repeat nothing of what I have said when you leave this room.'

'It will go no further, sir, but can you not tell me whether or not you have seen this fellow Jinkinson again? Do you know where he is?'

Garland turned away in exasperation.

'You are persistent, Mr Carver, if nothing else. I will grant you that virtue, if virtue it is. But it is not the most gentlemanly of activities, detective work, is it? Scurrying about London asking all these impertinent questions.'

Adam made no reply.

'Do you really think I have nothing better to do with my time than to keep track of some buffoon like Jinkinson?' Garland asked after a brief pause.

'But he was seen in your company little more than a week ago.'

'I am in the company of many in the course of a week. The man's probably off on some backstreet bacchanal in St Giles. I neither know nor care where he is. You should not bother with him yourself, Mr Carver. Forget about him. Forget about that old villain Sam Creech. Clap the extinguisher to your curiosity. It's a terrible thing to say but Creech may well have deserved the fate he met. Leave the policing to the police and the detecting to the detectives.'

CHAPTER TWENTY-ONE

he following morning, Adam was sitting in his study reading Richard Burton's *Wanderings in West Africa*, when Quint's large and shining head appeared round the edge of the door.

'There's some Bible-grinder asking to see you,' he said, his face twisted into a gargoyle expression of distaste. 'Leastways, I reckon that's what he is. He's got a white choker round his neck and looks about as cheery as an undertaker's mute.'

'You have no time for evangelists, Quint?'

Quint snorted dismissively. 'I ain't one for all that gospel-gab,' he agreed. 'Most of these tub-thumpers have less sense than a coster's jackass. This one seems harmless enough. Although he's got eyes like cod in a Billingsgate basket.'

'Show him into the sanctum sanctorum, then.'

The visitor was, as Adam had already guessed, Elisha Dwight. The reverend entered the room warily, as if he half expected it to be filled with unrepentant sinners intent on tempting him from the path of righteousness. When Adam gestured towards the only chair he could offer visitors, Dwight wasted no time in plumping himself down in it. His smooth, round face was flushed and he looked acutely uncomfortable. He had a white cravat wrapped round his throat, which Adam thought must be intended to denote his clerical status. It was so tight that any attempt Dwight might make to move his head to the left or to the right was fraught with the danger of strangulation. He could only stare fixedly ahead of him.

'I am delighted to see you again so soon, Reverend,' Adam said amiably. 'How can I help you?'

'I have been wrestling with the minions of Satan, Mr Carver.' Dwight spoke as if this was one of his regular pastimes.

'Which minions would those be, Reverend Dwight?'

'The imps of temptation.' The clergyman, rubbing his hands and gazing at the books on Adam's shelves, sounded very unhappy. 'The demons that demand lies. Lies in the service of the Father of Lies.'

'I am sorry, Reverend, I do not quite follow you.'

'I did not tell you the truth, the whole truth and nothing but the truth when you came to see me the other day. The minions of Satan wish me to persist in my deceit but I have fought them and won.'

'I am glad to hear it.' Adam was beginning to tire of his visitor's orotund sanctimony. He wished the clergyman would say what he had to say without further ado. Dwight had travelled halfway across London to tell him something. Why did he not just go ahead and do so?

'I know more of Jinkinson than I admitted.' Dwight pulled at his cravat like a man awaiting a hanging with a noose round his neck. 'I have decided that I should tell you the more that I know.'

'I am all ears.'

'Jinkinson is a sinful man.' Dwight returned to rubbing his hands together, as if washing them with soap and water from a bowl set down in his ample lap. 'He has long been a drinker and a degenerate. His home has more often been the low tavern and the penny gaff than the Tabernacle of righteousness.' The clergyman spat out his words like oaths. 'He is a slug in the Lord's vineyard, Mr Carver.'

'You are surely too harsh on him, Reverend Dwight.' Adam began to wonder whether this pompous young minister really did have much to reveal about Jinkinson's whereabouts. Perhaps he had walked from his Tabernacle all the way to Doughty Street merely to insult the plump enquiry agent a little more than he had done the previous Sunday. 'There is no harm in the occasional indulgence in alcohol. And the penny gaffs do no more than bring colour and excitement into lives that have little of either.'

This, Adam realised immediately, was the wrong thing to say.

'Filthy songs. Filthy dances.' Dwight was suddenly overwrought. His Adam's apple wobbled furiously behind the tightly tied cravat. 'And filthy men and women watching them. That's your penny gaffs for you, sir. They disgust me. They should disgust every Christian soul in the realm.'

Taken aback by the minister's sudden wrath, Adam hurried to placate him.

'I know little of them, Reverend Dwight. I am sure you are correct and that the virtuous should avoid them. In any case, it is unlikely that Jinkinson has taken refuge in a penny gaff.'

'No, but I believe I know where he will have gone.' Dwight had regained control of himself as rapidly as he had lost it. His hand reached up to his throat to adjust his cravat.

'Mr Jinkinson has spent many years pursuing that will of the wisp, Pleasure, through the giddying labyrinth of Dissipation,' Dwight said, sternly. The minister's voice, Adam thought to himself, possessed the ability to add invisible capital letters to so many of the nouns he used. 'He has struggled with the Demon Drink throughout the time he has attended the Tabernacle. When he falls from grace and returns to his wine-bibbing, there is one sink of iniquity he frequents. He may well be there now. It is a public house in Wapping called the Cat and Salutation. He pays the landlord for a room and there he drinks his immortal soul towards the pit.'

* * * * *

The street in Wapping was almost deserted. Adam watched the yellow light from the side lanterns on the cab which had dropped him there flicker briefly in the evening gloom and then disappear. Two men, standing a dozen yards away beneath the street's solitary gas lamp, were conducting some mysterious business of their own. They glanced briefly at Adam and then turned their backs to him. Closer to hand, a woman was making her unsteady way along the pavement ahead of him. She was wearing a shapeless black bonnet that even her grandmother might have considered somewhat dowdy, and was reeling with drink. As Adam watched, she pitched forwards and sideways, only recovering her balance at the last minute. Her black bonnet fell into the gutter but she did not seem to notice it had gone. Following behind her, he stooped briefly to pick it up. It was the work of a moment to overtake the woman and hand it back to her. She took the hat and gazed bleary-eyed at him. She attempted to say something but drink defeated her. Frustrated, she turned and staggered into the wall of one of the soot-blackened houses that lined the street. Adam moved forward as if to help her but she waved him away and sat down in the doorway. Within seconds, she appeared to be asleep. Adam left her to her stupor and walked on. There was almost a spring in his step. He felt, he realised, oddly enlivened by venturing so far off the paths he usually trod in London.

The Cat and Salutation was at the end of an alleyway running off the street that opened out into a small, cobbled court. Another solitary gas lamp stood at one end of the cobbles and cast its light on the pub sign. The tavern looked an uninviting refuge for even the most desperate of drinkers. Adam approached the entrance, his heels clicking on the cobblestones.

An old woman was sitting on a wooden bench outside the pub. She was fat and dirty. A faded green rag was tied beneath her jaw and over her head, and a short pipe was clamped in the corner of her mouth. She glared at the young man.

'Sing you a song for a glass of the blue, sonny,' she offered, truculently.

'That's very kind of you, ma'am, but I cannot linger to hear you at present.'

'You could jest get me the gin.'

'Alas, I have no time to do that either.'

'Pox on you, then.'

The old woman removed the pipe from her mouth and spat a great gob of phlegm on the cobbles at Adam's feet. He picked his way around it and made his way into the Cat and Salutation. The alehouse was small and gloomy, little more than a square box with dingy, red-curtained windows. It seemed to lack most of the amenities usually associated with a good pub. A few tables and benches were scattered around it. A bar ran along most of the left side of the room. At each of its ends stood an earthenware spittoon filled with sawdust. Behind it were a row of bottles on a shelf, a couple of barrels of beer resting on wooden supports and a torn poster advertising the merits of Reid's Matchless Stout. The Cat and Salutation also seemed to lack any of the jolly atmosphere traditionally associated with alehouses. In fact, it was very nearly empty. A long-faced man with a squint was sitting at one of the tables, drinking from a pint tankard and eating bread and cheese. With one arm he created an encircling barrier around his food, as if expecting a thief to snatch it away from him at any moment. With the other he tore at the bread and cheese and stuffed lumps of both into his mouth. Adam was astonished by the ravenous relish with which he ate. The man looked up briefly as Adam entered and then returned to his food. Next to him was a younger man, little more than a boy, with untidy, straw-coloured hair and a look of distraction. This youth had wrapped a small comb in tissue paper and was blowing through it. Adam could just about make out the tune of 'Lilliburlero'. As he looked in his direction, the boy stopped blowing and dropped the comb and paper into his lap. He grinned at Adam, revealing stained and blackened teeth.

The only other person in this first room was the man behind the bar but, through a door at the back, Adam could see another room. In it was a billiards table and two men were moving around it, cues in hand. One settled to play his shot. He was tall and so fat that he had great difficulty bending over the table. His opponent had noticed Adam enter the bar and he muttered something in his companion's ear. The fat man heaved his bulk off the baize and looked back into the bar room. Wagging his finger at the man who had whispered in his ear, he left the table. A small white, strikingly ugly terrier trotted after him as he exited the billiard room and approached the bar.

Several of his chins wobbling with the effort of moving, he was smiling a ghastly smile of greeting. 'Six penn'orth of hot brandy and water here, Toby. And whatever this gentleman is having.' He looked questioningly at Adam.

'That is kind of you, sir, but—'

'No buts, guv'nor. I insist on standing you a drink. The least I can do for a young gent what comes down Wapping way.'

'Thank you. I'll take a half pint of your...' Adam looked again at the poster behind the bar. 'Your matchless stout.'

'That's more like it,' the fat man said, flicking his fingers at Toby the barman, who began to pour the drinks. 'Not often we get visitors down the Cat. Not visitors like yourself at any rate.'

'Like myself?' The ugly terrier was nipping at the bottoms of Adam's trousers and he was struggling to concentrate on what was being said.

'Down, Billy. Leave it, sir, leave it.' The dog barked once and then retreated. The fat man moved closer, bringing a strong smell of corduroy, sweat and cheap pomade with him. 'Of a gentlemanly nature. Of a not-usually-seen-in-this-neck-of-the-woods nature.'

'I'm looking for someone, Mr...?'

'Brindle, guv. Jabez Brindle. At your service.'

Jabez Brindle looked, Adam thought, as if he was never at anyone's service but his own. He was not an attractive man. Even had he shed several stones and thus returned himself to the average weight of a London publican, he would have attracted no admiring glances from the ladies. His head was shaven and his nose was flatter than noses are meant to be. He had the look of a man for whom violence was a first resort, not a last.

'And who would you be looking for, I wonder?' Brindle's voice was quiet but carried the hint of a threat. 'Ain't very likely to be any others of a gentlemanly nature in the Cat. No gents here, Toby, eh?'

The barman guffawed at the very notion.

'I'm looking for—'

But Adam had no chance or need to reveal who he was looking for. At just that moment, a door from the street opened into the billiard room and a familiar figure lumbered into the pub. It was Jinkinson, looking very much the worse for wear. His shoulders slumped, his yellow silk cravat twisted into a knot beneath one ear and his plaid waistcoat spotted with the stains of drink and dirt, he was a picture of unrelieved misery. He took off his hat and was about to place it on the billiard table when he glanced through the connecting door towards the bar and saw Adam. His reaction was immediate. A look of mingled surprise and fear appeared on his face and he turned to flee.

Adam moved swiftly to follow him but, surprisingly, Brindle was even swifter. He stuck out his leg and sent the young man tumbling. As Adam fell, his head struck a glancing blow on the rim of one of the tables. Briefly stunned, he was unable to rise. He could only rest on all fours and endeavour to gather his briefly scattered wits. The great full moon of Brindle's face suddenly appeared, sideways, in his field of vision. The fat man was leaning over him.

'Very clumsy for a handsome gent, ain't you? You really should mind where you're going. Or you'll be doing yourself a severe mischief, you will.'

Adam pushed Brindle away and struggled to his feet. Having allowed Jinkinson his escape, the fat man seemed uninterested in stopping Adam from following him. Instead he began to laugh, great heaving waves of laughter rising from the pits of his stomach. Adam staggered from the bar room into the billiard room. He reached a hand to his head. He could feel blood on his fingers. He must have grazed his brow on the table as he fell. It was nothing serious, he decided, but he did feel decidedly dizzy. Shaking his head to clear it, he exited through the door Jinkinson had used and nearly found himself in the river. At the back, the pub was propped on thick wooden pillars which rose directly out of the Thames mud. Only the narrowest of footpaths ran between the back wall of the Cat and Salutation and the ooze of the river.

There was no sign of Jinkinson. Rackety wooden railings stretched along the water for twenty yards. There was a gap in the middle of them where the rotting wood had given way. Holding a handkerchief to his nose, Adam glanced into the filth below. Had Jinkinson, he wondered, fallen into the Thames as he came dashing out of the pub's rear door? There was no evidence that he had. Masses of green weed floated on the surface of what was, to judge by the smell, a potent mix of water and human effluvia. What looked unpleasantly like a dead dog, swollen with putrefaction, had washed up against the post which marked one end of the railings. Adam could hear squeals and the splashing of water as rats, alerted to his presence, made off into the darkness.

He began to walk warily along the pathway, his feet squelching in mud and possibly worse as he did so. Suddenly, there was a sound which could only be a pistol shot. It reverberated from building to building and along the riverbank. It was followed almost immediately by several more and by a long cry of pain. Adam stopped and listened. Did the noise come from close to hand or much further away? He could not be certain. He set off in the direction from which the shots seemed to have sounded. He had gone about fifty yards when, in the half-light, he stumbled over something. It was something large and soft. Something that was lying half in and half out of the water. It was a body.

Gingerly, Adam reached down and took hold of the shoulder. He rolled the body onto its back. Grunting with the effort, he pulled it out of the mud into which it was sinking and hauled it towards the top of the bank. In the faint light from the distant gas lamp, he could just make out the features. It was Jinkinson. The enquiry agent was alive but only just. Blood oozed through his waistcoat and onto Adam's hands. He was struggling to say something. His mouth opened and closed but no sounds emerged. His eyes were fixed on a point behind Adam's left shoulder. He looked as if he was concentrating intently on some object that was slipping out of focus and out of view. His legs were twitching and splashing in the murky Thames water. As Adam battled to haul him further out of the riverside filth, the light left the enquiry agent's eyes and he died. Adam was left to clutch the substantial shell of Jinkinson's body, but whatever had once animated it had gone. The old dandy, it seemed, had tied his last cravat.

Half-crouched in the mud, Jinkinson's corpse at his feet, Adam heard the sound of movement behind him. He swung round and was in time to see a dark figure, twenty yards away, silhouetted against the wall of one of the riverside houses.

'You there,' he shouted. 'Stop, I say, stop!'

The figure turned briefly in his direction. There was something disconcertingly familiar about it, but before Adam could think what it might be, the man moved into the darkness between two buildings and disappeared. Adam briefly contemplated the idea of pursuit but he decided against it. He turned back to the dead body in the Thames mud. He wondered how long it would be before others joined him on the riverbank. At present it was as if he was stranded on the shore of Crusoe's desert island but appearances, he knew, were deceptive. There were doubtless a dozen dives and pubs within a few hundred yards of here. And out on the river, even amidst the darkness, there would be boatmen and scavengers. Plenty of people would have heard the shots fired. The sound of shots, however, might not be so uncommon in the neighbourhood that they would attract immediate attention. And curiosity, in the circumstances, might prove dangerous. Minding one's own business in the worst areas of Wapping was probably thought conducive to a longer life. On reflection, Adam decided that he had time to search the body before anyone joined him.

It was not a pleasant job. Jinkinson's body was warm and fleshy. Stifling his nausea, Adam felt hurriedly through the pockets of the enquiry agent's mud-stained and bloody clothes. It took him but a short time. Whatever possessions Jinkinson had owned, he had not been keeping many of them about his person. Trouser pockets surrendered only a cambric handkerchief and the stub of a pencil. The lower pockets of the plaid waistcoat held nothing. Inserting his fingers into the waistcoat's top pocket, Adam could feel something in it. Whatever it was, it proved difficult to grasp and his thumb and forefinger pursued it vainly around the recesses of the pocket for a while before they closed on it. Finally, he pulled it out. It was a visiting card. Adam took a box of matches from his pocket and struck one. The card was battered but largely dry and, in the wavering light of the match, he could make out the name 'Lewis Garland' printed on it in a bold and simple font. Adam turned the card over. At first, he thought the reverse was plain, but holding it nearer the light, he could see that one word had been written on it in pencil. The word, in English capitals, was 'EUPHORION'.

It was the same word or name that had appeared in Creech's journal. Now, more than ever, it seemed to Adam to lie at the heart of the mystery that had led him to this dismal stretch of the Thames. The mystery that had cost both Creech and now Jinkinson their lives. The enquiry agent had denied all knowledge of Euphorion. So for that matter had the Reverend Dwight. But Ada, poor girl, had recognised the name, even if she had transliterated it as 'Yew Ferrion'. She had spoken of Jinkinson's belief that it held the key to riches. Now here were those same nine letters on a card belonging to Lewis Garland, whom Quint had observed meeting the enquiry agent in the pub yard near Fountain Court. And Garland, along with Sir Willoughby Oughtred and James Abercrombie, had been mentioned in Creech's journal.

Adam struggled to make sense of it all, his thoughts twisting and turning in search of a theory that might explain the few facts he had. His speculations were interrupted, however, first by the match burning out and then by a sound from behind him. He spun round quickly. For all he knew, Jinkinson's killer might have returned. A man was standing a few feet away in the mud of the footpath. He was holding a bull's eye lantern in his hand and appeared to be swinging it aimlessly from side to side. As it swung, its light flashed back and forth, first blinding Adam as he stood over the body and then illuminating the man who held it. It was Toby, the barman from the Cat and Salutation.

'Mr Brindle. He ain't going to like this,' he said.

'No, well, I doubt Mr Jinkinson is entirely delighted by the turn events have taken.' Adam swiftly pocketed the card with its enigmatic message. 'Come over here. We need to get the body out of this filth. We'll have to carry it to the pub.'

CHAPTER TWENTY-TWO

‘Seems to be some kind of attraction between you and those what have passed over to the other side, don't there, Mr Carver?'

Despite the gloom of both the surroundings and circumstances, Inspector Pulverbatch was in a jovial mood.

'Some kind of fatal attraction, you might almost say.'

'Our paths do seem destined to cross, Inspector, do they not?'

Adam was bone weary and still covered in the mud of the river. He had rather liked Jinkinson and had been distressed to stumble across him, dying in the river's filth. Now Pulverbatch's cheerfulness was the latest in the series of misfortunes the evening had inflicted on him.

'Does Scotland Yard,' Adam asked, 'have no one other than your self to investigate murders?'

The two men were sitting in the bar of the Cat and Salutation. Apart from a constable standing guard at the door and the corpse of Jinkinson lying beneath a sheet on the billiards table, they were alone. Complaining bitterly, Brindle and his cronies had been ushered out into the courtyard where another constable was watching them.

'Oh, dearie me, yes,' Pulverbatch replied. 'Plenty of detectives at the Yard capable of looking into a murder or two.'

Before despatching Toby to join his employer and his customers outside, Pulverbatch had instructed the barman to pour him a half-pint of stout. He now picked it up and examined it against the light, as if looking for flaws in the glass.

'But only me what's got an interest in the Cat and Salutation already,' the policeman continued. 'So when word reaches me that someone's gone and found a dead body outside that very same public house, I'm all ears. And then I further hears that that someone is none other than your good self. A man as has come across another body in Herne Hill nary a fortnight ago. A man as has friends in high places. *Very* high places, judging by what Dolly Williamson himself tells me. Well, you can imagine how interested I was.'

Pulverbatch raised his stout to his lips.

'If you'll excuse me, sir, I'll just put this where the flies won't get at it.'

For twenty seconds, nothing was heard but the sound of beer being emptied down Pulverbatch's throat. Then, with a sigh of appreciation, the inspector finished his drink and slammed the glass on the pub table with sufficient force to make Adam start.

'Well, that slipped down like soapsuds down a gully hole.'

'I'm delighted you enjoyed it, Inspector.'

Puverbatch ignored Adam's sarcasm.

'So, you've been a-drinking and a-gassing with Jabez Brindle and his pals, have you?' he remarked. 'Well, they're a bad lot, as the devil said of the Ten Commandments.'

'You make our meeting sound like a social occasion, Inspector. I wouldn't describe it like that.'

'How *would* you describe it, sir?'

'I received information that a gentleman whom I was anxious to meet might be staying here at the tavern. When I entered the place, Mr Brindle introduced himself to me.'

Pulverbatch nodded slowly. He seemed to be turning over in his mind the veracity or otherwise of Adam's tale.

'This man Brindle is known to you, is he?' the young man asked.

'Oh, yes, we know Jabez Brindle down the Yard.' The inspector paused and picked up his glass from the table once again. He tilted it slightly and examined it as if there might be more beer in it that he had somehow missed. Satisfied at last that there was no more drink to be had, he replaced it on the bar table. 'Want to know what we know of him, Mr Carver? I'm supposed to tell you all I know, now ain't I?'

Adam indicated that he was.

'Well, for one thing, he's a bit of a student of the four kings is Mr Brindle.' Pulverbatch mimed the dealing of cards. 'Bit of a dishonest student, in fact.'

'A card sharper?' Adam was surprised. 'Surely someone with your position at the Yard has more important tasks to perform than preventing some tuppenny ha'penny rogue from cheating at whist?'

'True, Mr Carver, true.' The inspector sounded satisfied that Adam had recognised his status in the force. 'But there's a bit more happening at the Cat and Salutation than a few dodgy hands of cards. There's goods going in and out of the place as shouldn't be going in and out.'

'But that must be the case with any number of the public houses in this part of London, I would have thought.'

'There's some rummy places along the river, that's for sure, sir.' A tiny puddle of beer had spilled onto the table. Pulverbatch dipped his finger into it and began to trace out patterns on the wood with the beer. 'The sort of places a gent like yourself shouldn't go.'

'Perhaps you are right, Inspector,' Adam acknowledged. 'And yet it was the Cat that was attracting your attention. Even before a *corpus delicti* was established.'

The policeman rubbed his hand across the table, obliterating the liquid shapes he had been creating. He looked up at Adam, beaming with delight.

'Never met a man with such a mouthful of half-crown words at his disposal as you has, Mr Carver,' he said. 'It's a treat just a-sitting and a-listening to you. Even when I ain't got the first notion what you're talking about. Which, right now, I ain't.'

'I was simply curious, Inspector,' Adam said, holding to his line. 'You seem to have had your eye on Brindle's pub long before any crime other than cheating at cards was committed. Before the body was found.'

'Oh, that's easily explained, sir. As I said, there's business going on in the Cat that shouldn't be going on. Brindle works for a bit faker, passing dud coins into circulation. Not that we can ever catch him at it. He's up to every dodge you can think of – and plenty you can't – is Jabez Brindle. Not to mention, we're pretty certain the faker's got a man inside the Yard.'

'He's corrupted one of your officers?'

'As the song says, sir, "There's sure to be a bobby as is ready for a bob." Not all of us are able to resist the lure of filthy lucre.'

Pulverbatch now rested his hands on the table like a pianist about to begin playing. He was looking closely at his fingers splayed across the wood. For a moment, it looked to Adam just as if the inspector was counting them to make sure he had the correct number.

'I'm sure you'll excuse me for asking, Mr Carver,' the policeman said, after a pause. 'All part of my job and no offence intended. Not to you nor to those friends of yours.'

'None will be taken, Mr Pulverbatch.'

'I have to know what you've a-been doing since we last had the pleasure of exchanging our thoughts about the world.'

Adam sighed. He had been expecting this but, weary as he was, he felt barely able to satisfy the inspector's curiosity. He wondered where to begin his story and what to omit from it. He looked across at Pulverbatch, who was still examining his fingers. He decided to tell something of what he knew about Jinkinson without revealing how the enquiry agent's name had first come to his attention. The inspector listened to the story without interruption, nodding to himself from time to time as if Adam's narrative merely confirmed what he had already suspected. When it came to an end, he leaned back in his chair. He blew the air from his mouth like a small boy attempting to whistle for the first time.

'I thought that Jinkinson might have something to do with Creech's death,' Adam said. 'That is why I followed him. And why I endeavoured to find him once he had disappeared.'

'Very interesting, Mr Carver, very interesting. All these fine gents that friend Jinkinson was seeing.' The inspector ran his hands through his hair as he spoke. 'But I don't reckon as how he could have anything to do with the murder out at Herne Hill. I showed you the man we collared for that one, sir.'

'I regret to say this, Mr Pulverbatch, but I have no confidence that you have the right man behind bars.'

'Oh, it was Ben Stirk as shot Creech, all right.' The inspector's confidence remained undented. 'Although, I suppose this Jinkinson fellow might have put him up to it. Who shot Jinkinson, though? That's the question.'

Pulverbatch gazed into the middle distance like a philosopher contemplating a particularly knotty problem in metaphysics.

'So, remind me again,' he said eventually. 'Where did you say you was last night?'

'With Mr Garland.'

'Ah, yes. In the Palace of Westminster, no less. And the night before?'

'Visiting Sir Willoughby Oughtred.'

Pulverbatch nodded again. 'And what about the night before *that*? I don't remember as how you mentioned that night.'

'Quint and I went to Holywell Street.'

'Holywell Street?' Pulverbatch sounded surprised. 'Full of Jew clothesmen and nasty bookstalls, ain't it? What would a fine gent like you be doing in Holywell Street?'

'We were looking for a young woman named Ada.'

'Ah, a whore,' the inspector said, as if all was now clear to him.

'Ada is a young lady who has fallen into misfortune,' Adam said. 'We were interested in her because she was acquainted with Jinkinson.'

'And did you find her?'

'We did, but she did not know where Jinkinson was.'

'But this reverend, this Dwight gent, he *did* know.'

'He gave me the name of this tavern. Soon after I arrived here, Jinkinson turned up. When he saw me, he ran.'

'And got himself shot in the mud for his troubles. Now, who might have been a-chasing poor Mr Jinkinson, I wonder?'

'Can the landlord of this place not throw some light on the mystery?'

'We won't get anything out of Brindle. No point even attempting it, Mr Carver. Might just as well try and roast snow in a furnace.'

'What about the barman? The one who turned up with the lantern. He must have followed me out onto the bank. Did he see nothing?'

'Toby, you mean?' Pulverbatch looked doubtful.

'Is that his name? Yes, I seem to remember Brindle calling him that.'

'Well, we've asked him, of course. But old Toby's attic ain't exackly well-furnished, if you take my meaning, Mr Carver.' The inspector tapped the side of his head as he spoke. 'He's a bit of an innocent abroad, sir, an innocent abroad. And he thinks the sun shines out of Brindle's fat arse, if you'll pardon the indelicacy. Brindle could send him out to buy a pennyworth of pigeon's milk and all he'd ask for would be the glass to put it in.'

'So there is nothing to be gained from interrogating the barman?'

'No, there's no point in talking to a soft Sammy like him. You might just as well try and teach a pig to play on the flute.'

'So, the landlord is a villain and the barman is a dunce. Where does that leave us, Inspector?'

'Difficult, ain't it? Brindle won't tell us much about what happened here in the Cat. He lies just for the fun of it. And, other than your good self, the only witness we've got to anything as happened by the river is about as sharp as the corners on that there round table.'

'We appear to be stumped, then, Inspector.' Adam stared at the mud caked on his trousers. He was so exhausted that he could think of little but his own fireside at Doughty Street and a large glass of brandy and water.

'Oh, I wouldn't say that, sir. There's a little life in us yet. A few paths we can stroll down to see what's at the end of 'em.' Pulverbatch, Adam thought, continued to sound appallingly cheerful. 'Now, one of the few things Brindle is saying is that this man Jinkinson was renting a room here in the Cat. He says as how Jinkinson come here to drink. Used to drink a lot, the late gentleman did, according to Brindle. "I've seen him so grogged he was down in the street and lapping the gutter." Those was his exact words, I seem to recall.'

Pulverbatch paused, as if he expected Adam might say something.

'The room's up those stairs over there.' The inspector gestured through to the billiard room where a rickety flight of stairs disappeared upwards. 'Now, as I say, Brindle's got as many faces as a churchyard clock. I'd trust him about as far as I could fling a bull by its tail but I'm not sure he'd lie about that. Why should he? Ain't no crime in renting out a room. So what say you and I go and take a peek in Mr Jinkinson's hidey-hole?'

Adam was about to reply when, behind the inspector's back, the door to the bar opened and a boy of about twelve entered. He began to make his way furtively towards the body on the billiards table. Adam merely gazed at the scene and could hardly bring himself to draw Pulverbatch's attention to the intruder. There was no need.

'Hook it, you young prig,' Pulverbatch roared over his shoulder. 'Ain't nothing here for the likes of you. If I sees you still there when I turn round, you'll be in quod before you can remember what your name is.'

The boy made a gesture of contempt in the policeman's direction, but deciding that discretion, in this instance, was definitely the better part of valour, he beat a swift retreat. Pulverbatch remained in his seat, his hands still resting on the table. Adam was left to wonder how he had known the boy had come into the bar.

'Always the same with a dead body and young cubs like that,' the inspector said. 'Like a honeypot for bees. They always wants to take a look.'

With a sudden sigh, Pulverbatch lifted his hands from the table-top and hauled himself to his feet. Adam, his limbs now aching from his exertions by the river, did the same. The two of them made their way into the adjoining room, skirted the billiards table with its white-sheeted burden and climbed the stairs to the next floor.

Two doorways opened off the first-floor landing, one to the right and one to the left. Without hesitation, Pulverbatch opened the one on the right. The room they now entered was surprisingly spacious. It had no floor covering other than a small square of drugget in the middle.

The bed stood behind a dirty chintz curtain in one corner. The only other item of furniture was a battered chest of drawers in the opposite corner, above which hung a small looking glass in a chipped gilt frame. The inspector went over to it. He began to pull out the drawers one by one, peering into them.

'What does Brindle say of Jinkinson?' Adam asked, now determined not to surrender to his tiredness. 'Why did he offer him refuge?'

'According to him, he was acting like the Good Samaritan did.' Pulverbatch continued to examine the contents of the chest of drawers. 'Him in the Bible as picked up the man by the roadside and dusted him down and took him home to heal his wounds.'

Adam pushed the chintz curtain to one side and sat down on the bed.

'So Jinkinson came to him in trouble and Brindle, out of the goodness of his heart, said to him, "I have a room above my tavern, my good man. For the payment of a small sum per week, you may have the use of it."'

'That's about the size of it, according to Brindle.'

'I don't think that can be what happened, do you, Inspector? Mr Brindle does not seem the type of man to do things out of the goodness of his heart.'

Pulverbatch paused before he slid the final drawer back into place, a smile playing briefly across his face. He was clearly amused by the possibility, however remote, of Brindle acting with good intentions. But his expression hardened once again.

'Lord love us, Mr Carver,' he said. 'We both know gammon when we hear it, and that's pure, unadulterated, one hundred per cent gammon. Brindle had some other reason why he was a-helping Jinkinson. And it weren't one the Good Samaritan would have recognised.'

'I 'ope you ain't goin' to believe everything that shark Pulverbatch tells you.' The remark emerged from the darkness outside the Cat and Salutation as Adam left the pub to make his way back to Doughty Street. It was followed by the substantial figure of Jabez Brindle, who trundled into the light still shining from one of the ground-floor windows. ''E'd lie as soon as look at you.'

The fat man looked as weary as Adam felt but he was still grinning gamely. His ugly little white terrier was still at his heels even if it seemed to have lost much of its earlier aggression. It made no attempt to bite at Adam's ankles but stood cocking its head towards its owner as if listening for what he might have to say.

'That is more or less what the inspector said of you, Mr Brindle.'

'Thought 'e might. Pot calling the kettle black arse, if you ask me.'

The publican was wearing a battered chimney-pot hat which wobbled unsteadily on his head. He reached up to right it and then seized Adam by the arm. The young man tried to shake him off but Brindle's grip was like a vice. He began to guide Adam away from the Cat and Salutation.

'Which is why,' Brindle added, 'I thought as 'ow it might be useful for you and me to have another chat before you went back west.'

The steps of both men echoed across the cobbles. It was well after midnight and the only other person in sight was a street scavenger who was standing under a gas lamp and ladling manure into his cart.

'I am more than willing to hear you out, Mr Brindle, but I must insist that you leave hold of me.'

The publican grinned again and dropped Adam's arm.

'No offence intended, Mr Carver. It is Carver, ain't it? Old Jinks mentioned your name.'

Adam brushed the sleeve of his coat where Brindle's sweaty fingers had impressed themselves on the material.

'You knew Jinkinson well?' he enquired.

'Poor old Jinks.' Despite his words, the fat man looked serenely untroubled by the private investigator's departure from the world. 'Known him for years. 'E's been coming down the Cat since you was just a young nipper caterwauling in your ma's arms.'

'So he knew you well enough to confide in you?'

'Don't know as 'ow you'd call it that. But 'e often come to the Cat when he wanted to lie low for a bit.' Brindle shrugged. ''E paid me well enough for the room so I ain't going to be too partickler about what he wants to lay low from.'

'And that's why he was with you tonight?'

The publican nodded.

'Turned up a couple of nights ago. Said 'e needed a room to stay in to keep out of trouble. Someone was after 'im, 'e thought.'

'After him?'

'That's what 'e says. Somebody like yourself. Of a gentlemanly nature.'

'I cannot believe that it was I he feared.'

'No, you ain't much for anybody to fear,' Brindle agreed. 'Not even for Jinks.'

'Did anybody visit him while he was with you?' Adam asked, ignoring the implied insult. He began to wonder whether he and Pulverbatch had misjudged the publican. Perhaps there was no further mystery about Brindle's motives for sheltering Jinkinson. He did it because he had known the enquiry agent for many years and Jinkinson paid him money for the room. The Cat and Salutation was like Bellamy's Lodging House. A refuge when Poulter's Court became a place to avoid. 'Did he see anyone other than your regular drinkers?'

The fat man shook his head. 'Didn't even see them. 'E spent all 'is time up in that room above the billiards. Didn't come out until an 'our before you arrives. Then 'e goes out for a walk. Needs some air, 'e says.'

'And returns at the very moment that I was speaking to you and Toby.'

'That's about the size of it. 'E must 'ave panicked when 'e saw you. Runs out but 'ooever was after 'im was waiting further along the river. You know the rest.'

The two men had left behind the quiet alleys in which the Cat and Salutation lay hidden and now emerged in a busy and well-lit thoroughfare. Even at this hour, wagons, carts and cabs, both pouring into the city and out of it, streamed past them. Adam peered to his left, looking for landmarks he might recognise. Was this, he wondered, the Ratcliffe Highway? His knowledge of this part of the city was so regrettably poor, but he assumed that it was.

'Now I got that pig Pulverbatch and his little band of piglets swarming all over my crib,' Brindle went on, raising his voice to compete with the noise of the passing traffic. 'And that ain't something I appreciates.'

'The inspector is investigating a murder, Mr Brindle. I doubt he's interested in your assorted crimes and peccadillos.'

'You're as green as duckweed, ain't you,' the publican said, almost admiringly. 'It's the killing as don't interest Pulverbatch that much. One body more or less pulled out of the river ain't goin' to worry him. Especially some private sniffer on 'is uppers like old Jinks. But 'e's been itching to find a reason to come grubbin' around the Cat and now 'e's got one.'

Adam decided directness was his best policy.

'What if the murder of Jinkinson was connected to the murder of another person? A person of greater social standing?'

'You mean that cove in 'Erne 'Ill?' Brindle asked, enjoying Adam's look of surprise. 'Oh, I know about 'im. I know Pulverbatch 'as got Ben Stirk lined up for a bit of dancing on nothing down Newgate way as well.'

'You know Stirk?'

'Let's go over there,' the publican said, gesturing towards a shop doorway further along the highway where a shabby vendor had set up his steaming potato can earlier in the evening and was still standing, close to half past midnight, in the hope of trade. 'I could do with a bite of supper. And I'll let you know what else I knows.'

After a minute, Brindle had been served his food, hauled from the can and then sprinkled liberally with salt. Holding the potato in his right hand, he blew on it three times and then bit vigorously into the brown skin and white innards. Between mouthfuls, he continued to speak.

'First thing you 'ave to remember, sonny, is that Pulverbatch ain't about to admit 'e knows next door to bugger all about this 'ere killing in 'Erne 'Ill.' Brindle sprayed small fragments of hot potato in Adam's direction. 'That's a place full of coves with plenty of ready. When someone gets topped in a neck of the woods like that, 'e knows 'e'd better find a daisy-brain to take the drop as soon as 'e can. Otherwise all 'ell will be bustin' out. That's where poor Ben Stirk comes in.'

'So Stirk is no more than a scapegoat?'

'Ben's just the nearest dumb gawk that Pulverbatch can lay 'is 'ands on. 'E'll end up sold like a bullock in Smithfield.'

Brindle took a last bite of his potato and threw the remaining bits of skin over his shoulder.

'If that is the case,' Adam said, 'we must do something to help him.'

The publican waved a fleshy arm in dismissal of the idea. 'Ain't a thing as *can* be done,' he said, picking at his teeth.

Adam was about to dispute this but Brindle held up his hand to silence him.

'Second thing you need to know,' he went on, 'is that old Jinks didn't have no visitors at the Cat. But 'e did send out a message. Paid Toby to trot 'alfway across town to deliver it.'

'A message to whom?'

'I ain't at all sure why I should tell you this. Maybe it's on account of I'm too kind-hearted.' Brindle smiled like a crocodile scenting its lunch. 'Maybe it's because I could do with Pulverbatch out of my 'air. And this might be a way of arranging it.'

The publican pulled an old silver turnip watch from his waistcoat pocket and took a swift look at it.

'It's a-getting late, Mr Carver. Time for all of us saints and sinners to be in bed. So I'll jest tell you one last thing and then I'll be off. Old Jinks, 'e sent a message to a very important gent. An even more important gent than your good self. 'E sent word to an MP, did Jinks. An MP called Garland.'

With that, the publican raised his chimney-pot hat and then waddled off in the direction of the river.

* * * * *

It was eight o'clock on the following morning and Adam had recovered some of the spirit which his adventures in Wapping had knocked out of him. Sitting at the breakfast table as Quint busied himself in the kitchen, he was looking through what the day's first post had brought him.

'A bill from some importunate tradesman. In all likelihood my tailor, who will have to be paid soon before he decides that he has no alternative but to involve the law in our business transactions. A communication from my cousin Richard. Probably news of distant relations about whom I neither know nor care. Or possibly a begging letter. In either case, it can be safely ignored for the present. Something from my publisher. Unlikely to be good news.'

Adam sifted quickly through his correspondence, throwing the letters one by one to the far end of the table. He held the last one up to the light from the window, looking more closely at the inscription on it.

'Aha, I do believe I recognise this handwriting.'

'Ain't another from that young tart what come calling here the other week, is it?' Quint called. 'The one you went dancing with at some twopenny hop?'

'Cremorne Gardens, Quint. We took to the dance floor at Cremorne Gardens, not some twopenny hop. No, it is not. The postmark looks to be Cambridge. And speak more respectfully of Miss Maitland. She is a lady, not some trollop you might find parading down the Haymarket. No, the day before yesterday I wrote to Professor Fields.' Adam brandished the letter and shouted over his shoulder. 'Today I have his reply. I am invited to my alma mater to meet with him. You will, of course, accompany me.'

Quint, entering the room and handing Adam a plate of devilled kidneys with mushrooms, looked less than thrilled by the prospect.

'I ain't so sure old Fields'll want to see me again. If you recall, last time he saw me, he told me I was a damned rogue.'

'Well, so you are, Quint, but your friends have never allowed that fact to stand in the way of their affection for you. If *you* remember, Fields called you a rogue—'

'A damned rogue,' Quint insisted.

'He called you a damned rogue because, on the night before you and I were to leave the expedition and sail from Salonika, you stole a pouchful of his favourite tobacco.'

Quint watched solemnly as Adam picked up his knife and fork and began to attack his breakfast.

'I 'ad no choice,' he said, mustering what dignity he could. 'There were nothing else but that Turkish filth to be 'ad. I deserved a good smoke before we sailed.'

'That was not how the professor saw matters, but I am sure that he has now had time to forget – or at least to forgive – your misdeeds. More than two years have passed since we departed from Salonika.'

Quint looked less certain that his theft of the tobacco was now consigned to the realms of history.

'So, we're off to Cambridge, are we?' he said. 'And what are we a-going to do when we gets there?'

'There are questions to ask the erudite professor. Including, of course, the question of the mysterious Euphorion of whom we have heard so much.'

' 'Ow the devil we going to get there?'

'You speak as if I were proposing an expedition in search of Dr Livingstone. We have only to look in *Bradshaw* to discover the times of the Cambridge trains. And now, if you please, Quint, I would be grateful if you would cease your questioning and allow me to enjoy these excellent devilled kidneys you have provided.'

'If that's what you wants,' the manservant said, although clearly he continued to harbour nothing but doubts about the wisdom of an excursion out of town.

'It is,' his master replied, and turned his attention exclusively to his breakfast.

CHAPTER TWENTY-THREE

'**F**ast, ain't it,' Quint said, peering out of the carriage window as the Hertfordshire countryside raced past. 'On some railway journeys the delays are such that you rid yourself entirely of the restless spirit of the age. But on the London to Cambridge run…' Adam left his sentence unfinished, thinking that the speed of the train spoke for itself.

'What we doing exackly, charging out of town like this?' Like most Londoners, Quint was deeply suspicious of the world beyond its streets and thought that all that life offered could best be enjoyed within hearing distance of Bow Bells.

'We are heading, I hope, in the direction of enlightenment.'

The grimace on Quint's face suggested that he thought they were unlikely to reach their destination very easily.

'I ain't so sure why we need enlightening. Why don't we just turn our backs on everything and go back to taking sun-pictures of old buildings like we was doing before?'

'The train is slowing. We are coming into a station,' Adam said, leaning forward in his seat and peering ahead. 'Royston, I think.'

The train was indeed arriving in a station. The first-class carriage in which Adam and Quint were travelling juddered and came to a halt at the platform. A man and a woman, well-dressed and prosperous-looking, approached the carriage door but stopped when they saw it was already occupied. Adam raised his hat politely. The man did the same and reached for the door handle. The woman, who was gazing at Quint with the kind of appalled fascination that visitors to the Zoological Gardens bestowed on the monkeys there, tugged swiftly at his arm.

'We shall look for another carriage, Henry,' she said, and the two moved further up the platform.

'I'm disappointed in you, Quint.' Adam was accustomed to the effect his manservant often had on his social betters and felt no need to make any remark on the couple's behaviour. 'Two men are dead. We cannot just carry on as if nothing had happened.'

'We ain't got no real business with dead men, though. We just had the bad luck to find 'em. Why'n't we leave it to Pulverbatch to lay hands on whoever killed 'em? He's already got that Stirk cove.'

'Mr Stirk could not have killed Jinkinson. Even the inspector recognises that, since he was holding him in custody at the time I was stumbling across poor Jinks. And, despite what Pulverbatch says, Stirk is about as likely to be the murderer of Creech as I am. As the Archbishop of Canterbury is.'

'What we planning on doing then?'

'We are doing more than planning, Quint. We are already turning our minds to the curious events that have overtaken us.'

With another judder, the train began to leave the station. 'Let us consider what we know and what we can deduce. And a few leaps of deductive reasoning are surely acceptable.' Adam settled himself deeper in his seat. 'When I sat beside him at the dinner at the Marco Polo, Creech spoke to me of a manuscript. Of a manuscript which, he claimed, holds a great secret. A secret which rests in the hills of Macedonia. He wanted my assistance to discover the secret. A week later, you and I made our way to Herne Hill to visit Creech.'

'But he was already croaked.'

'Croaked, indeed. And when we found Creech, we also found a notebook.'

'It was me what found it,' Quint pointed out.

'As you say, you were the man who laid hands upon it and let no one try to take the credit from you. However, the importance of the notebook lies not so much in the identity of its finder as in what it contained.'

'Jinkinson's name. And word of all them comings and goings by the toffs.'

'In addition, there was the word "Euphorion" written in the middle of one of the pages in Greek script.' Adam had slipped further and further down the seat until he was almost staring upwards at the roof of the carriage. 'So, Jinkinson was employed by Creech. For purposes not yet entirely clear.'

'‘E was gathering all the juicy titbits so's Creech could rook the toffs.'

'That seems most likely, I grant you. In the light of what we now know about Lewis Garland's relations with the actress in St John's Wood, Lottie Lawrence. But it is not certain. The purposes may have been connected, for all we know, to the great secret. Anyway, I go to see this Jinkinson. I beard him in his Lincoln's Inn den.'

'And 'e says, "I ain't never 'eard of this Creech gent. You've got the wrong cove altogether when you come calling on me."'

'He says almost exactly that. But, of course, we do not believe him. We give no credence whatsoever to his evasions and mendacities. We follow him through the streets of the city and find the proof that he has been misleading us. We see him talking to Sir Willoughby Oughtred and Mr Lewis Garland. Not gentlemen usually to be found in Jinkinson's social circle.'

'Toffs,' said Quint, who had evidently taken a great liking to the word.

'Exactly. But, after a few days, our quarry eludes us. He disappears.' Adam had made a steeple of his fingers, resting his hands on his chest, as he continued to gaze upwards. 'Despite this setback, we are men of resource. We refuse to believe that, even in the dark morass that is London, a man can simply disappear. We ask questions of those who knew him. We follow his trail through the streets of the city. We make enquiries of those who know him.'

'I find his tart,' Quint said.

'You find Ada,' Adam acknowledged. 'She will tell us nothing of the whereabouts of her ageing paramour but she does mention the fact that he has been talking of how his future fortunes may depend on a foreign fellow named, she believes, Yew Ferrion. Eventually, thanks to my encounters with the oleaginous Elisha Dwight, we track Jinkinson himself down.'

'And then 'e gets croaked as well.'

'Very true, Quint. The poor man is murdered by the river, even as I am slipping and sliding in the mud no more than a few dozen yards from where he meets his wretched end.' Adam remained silent for a moment, still resting back in his seat, before hauling himself into a more upright position. 'When I found Jinkinson on the river-bank, he had about his person a card. The word "Euphorion" was inscribed on it just as it was in Creech's notebook. Euphorion, I am certain, is the name of a Greek writer. In the absence of any other thread to guide us through the labyrinth, it is reasonable to assume that the manuscript of which Creech spoke was a manuscript of a work by Euphorion.'

'Sounds right enough to me. Who's this Euphorion cove, though?'

'As I say, I cannot be certain that my memory is not playing me false but I seem to recall, from the dim distant days when I read such things for fun, he wrote poetry.'

'What's there going to be in a load of old Greek poems?' Quint asked with some contempt. 'What's a poet going to know as nobody else did?'

'*Rem acu tetigisti*, Quint.'

'Ain't no point you speaking that Greek bollocks at me.'

'Latin.'

'Latin. Greek. Don't make no odds. It's still double Dutch.'

'*Rem acu tetigisti*. "You hit the nail on the head." In colloquial translation.'

'Why you don't just speak the bleeding Queen's English like the rest of us, I don't know.'

'The benefits of an expensive education, Quint. I cannot let it go to waste. Besides, I know how much it irritates you.'

Quint merely grunted.

'That old beggar Fields'll know more about Euphorion, will he?'

'Correct, Quint. If by "that old beggar Fields", you mean Thomas

Burton Fields, the much esteemed and admired Professor of Greek in the University of Cambridge; my mentor in the study of the classical civilisations; the leader of the expedition into European Turkey which did so much for both our fortunes. Hence our journey out of town on this bright and beautiful morning. We must hope that Professor Fields can answer some, at least, of our many questions.'

Quint grunted again and, settling deeper in his seat, closed his eyes as if to sleep. Adam took a copy of Swinburne's *Poems and Ballads* from his pocket and opened it. He began to read but it was soon clear that not even the verse in that daring volume could hold his attention. His eyes kept straying from the page to the passing landscape and then to the recumbent figure of Quint, sprawled in the seat opposite.

'Tell me more of what you know of Pulverbatch, Quint,' he said eventually, casting Swinburne's lyrics aside.

'He's a downy one,' Quint said, reluctantly opening one eye.

'So you remarked when first we encountered the inspector. But I need more information than that. Where does he stand in the Scotland Yard hierarchy, for example? What is the extent of his powers? I noticed that man Pradd at the lodging house knew his name. And feared it.'

Quint opened his other eye and sat up.

'Pradd knows what side his bread is buttered. I reckon Pulverbatch answers only to "Dolly" Williamson. And "Dolly" answers to no one but the top nob himself.'

'Dolly Williamson? I do believe Pulverbatch spoke of him when we met one another at the Cat and Salutation.'

'Chief Inspector Frederick Adolphus Williamson to the likes of you and me. Head of the detective force at the Yard.'

'He's the real power in the land, is he?'

Quint nodded.

'And Pulverbatch is his man?'

'That's what I hear. That's why he goes strutting about like a crow in a gutter.'

Adam stared up at the luggage rack above his head as if in search of enlightenment there. Presumably it was Williamson to whom Sunman or someone else at the Foreign Office had spoken on his behalf. That explained Pulverbatch's willingness to share so much information with him on the night Jinkinson had died. But it did not explain everything about the inspector's behaviour.

'I cannot yet understand why the inspector is so convinced that Stirk is the killer,' he said eventually.

'It's the easiest answer, ain't it?' Quint replied.

Adam raised a querying eyebrow.

'Pulverbatch is like a bleeding gravedigger, right,' his manservant went on. 'He's up to his arse in business and 'e don't know which way to turn. 'E can't get any kind of 'andle on 'oo done for Creech. And old Dolly Williamson is screaming at 'im to get someone behind bars for it. So 'e picks up an old lag like Stirk and pins it on 'im.'

'Would Pulverbatch do something so reprehensible, do you suppose?'

'Of *course* he would,' Quint said, sounding as if he could scarcely credit his master's naivety. ''E just wants things sorted so Dolly ain't giving him an 'ard time.'

'Perhaps you are right, Quint.'

'Course I am.'

'But, if it is the case, then Jinkinson's murder makes the inspector's life more difficult. The two killings must be linked and Stirk was in custody at the time of the second.'

'Pulverbatch'll put his 'ands on somebody else for doing away with Jinks. Mark my words. Probably that noddy of a barman.'

Adam didn't like to admit it but it did look as if Quint might be correct. He picked up the volume of Swinburne poetry again and leafed through its pages, but his mind was elsewhere.

'I still cannot see exactly how far Garland and Oughtred and Abercrombie have been implicated in all this,' he said, after a moment.

'They were in that book of Creech's, weren't they? Like three jolly butcher boys, all in a row. 'E was fleecing 'em. All three of 'em.' Quint sounded like a man willing to brook no argument. 'And when one of 'em ain't too keen on being fleeced no more and blows 'is brains all over 'is furniture, then up steps old Jinks to take 'is place. And then, bugger me, if 'e ain't sent off to make worm food as well.'

'Well, Jinkinson did more or less admit that he was extorting money from them.'

'And that toff Garland I saw with 'im, 'e more or less owned it. When you met 'im. A penny gets you a pound old Jinks was croaked by one o' them three.'

'Hold hard, Quint. Your horses are racing away with you. For a start, at no time did Garland state unequivocally that *he* was being blackmailed. He merely said that Creech was a blackmailer.'

'There you go.' Quint shrugged as if the point was too obvious to pursue further.

'*Quod erat demonstrandum*, you reckon. Creech was a blackmailer. He knew all three men. Ergo, he was blackmailing them and one of them killed him. Jinkinson took over the blackmailing business. Ergo, he was killed for the same reason. A reckless leap or three in the deductive process, Quint old chap.' Adam tucked Swinburne back into his pocket. 'We must not make a Procrustean bed of our theories and force the facts to fit them.'

'I ain't making any kind of a bed. I'm jest telling you what's likely to 'ave fallen out.'

'If Creech *was* squeezing his old schoolfellows till the pips popped out,' Adam said, 'what secrets did he know about them?'

The manservant shrugged again. 'Tarts,' he said. 'Tarts is at the bottom of these affairs. Nine times out of ten, anyways.'

'Well, a nymph of the bedroom was almost certainly involved in Garland's case. Jinkinson told me that he was a regular visitor to a pied-à-terre in St John's Wood. Mr Moorhouse said that the lucky lady was the actress Lottie Lawrence. I doubt if Garland would have wanted word of his fair friend to circulate widely.'

'Or reach them as voted for 'im.'

'True. Accusations of adultery seldom assist a promising political career. So Garland may well have been vulnerable to a blackmailer who knew of his visits to St John's Wood. But I doubt if Sir Willoughby is a man for the ladies, Quint.'

'He may not seem one for chasing after Haymarket ware. But there ain't no telling just by looks,' Quint said. 'What about this Abercrombie cove?'

'James Abercrombie. Another MP. I've seen him occasionally at the Marco Polo. Moorhouse even introduced us earlier this year.'

'' 'E the sort to be gallivanting with the tarts?'

'As you say, Quint, it's difficult to know from the mere look of a man. He's out of town at present. Out of the country, as far as I can gather. Unlike Oughtred and Garland, who are members of the Marco Polo on the strength of one journey made decades ago, Abercrombie is a man who has genuinely travelled to the ends of the earth. Twenty years ago, he went to the gold diggings in Ballarat.'

'That's in convict land, ain't it?'

'It's north-west of Melbourne, yes. Abercrombie spent six months there. From what I have found out, it was the making of him. When he went to Victoria, he was nearly forty and had failed in every venture he'd ever undertaken. When he came back, he was a rich man. He bought an estate in Norfolk, married an earl's younger daughter and entered Parliament as a Palmerston supporter after the war in the Crimea. He's been there ever since. However, he's a restless man. He spends part of each year travelling Europe and the Levant. Interestingly, he has journeyed at least once into the areas of Turkey in Europe we know from our own adventures. He is thought to be somewhere in that part of the world now.'

Quint sat scratching his head, like the caricature of a man deep in thought.

'Maybe 'e's got some secret from the diggings 'e don't want known,' he said at last. 'Maybe Creech got to 'ear of it and was rooking 'im on the strength of it. Maybe 'e killed a man for his gold.'

'A moment ago you said a tart would be at the bottom of it.'

Quint thought again. 'Could be a tart from down under that come looking for him. On the grounds that 'e was the gent that first 'ad 'er. And set 'er on the downward path. Maybe it's Ada.'

'What a sensational imagination you are developing, Quint. A respectable and wealthy MP with murder in a distant land on his conscience. Young women of lost virtue travelling across the world to confront their seducers. You should be supplying plot lines to Mr Collins or Miss Braddon.'

'Well, it's possible, ain't it?'

'Anything is possible, Quint. But we have met Ada, have we not? I don't think she much resembles a vengeful maenad from the Antipodes, do you?'

'Whatever one of them is.' Quint was reluctant to relinquish his theory but he could see that the young girl in Holywell Street made a poor candidate for a leading role in it. 'She ain't too likely to be from convict-land, though.'

'No, she isn't.' Adam drew a silk handkerchief from his pocket and began to polish a button on his waistcoat. 'Anyway, did we not decide we knew the man who ruined her?'

Quint, who had assumed that the conversation was at an end and was about to close his eyes once more, looked unimpressed.

'Who? Jinkinson?'

'No, not Jinkinson. Garland. Remember our conversation at the coffee stall. Ada used to work as a parlour maid, did she not?'

'That's what she says when I first found her.'

'Did she tell you anything more?'

'Not as I can recall just now.'

'Well, try to recall what else she might have said, Quint. It could be significant.'

Quint screwed up his face as he struggled to remember.

'Must have been near Piccadilly,' he said. 'On account of she says something about walking in Green Park.'

'And Mr Moorhouse, in addition to being indiscreet about Lewis Garland and Lottie Lawrence, told me that Garland has a reputation for seducing the more attractive of his servants.'

'Plenty of toffs do,' Quint said.

'And Garland has a house in Bruton Street.'

'Which ain't far from Piccadilly. But all the houses round there belong to nobs. Ada may not have been working at Garland's.'

'She knew Garland's name, I am sure. She reacted to the mention of him. It would explain a great deal if she had once worked for him. It would explain the connection between Jinkinson and the girl. He knew about her. He went in search of her. We've been thinking that Jinkinson was amorously involved with Ada.'

'That young rip Simpkins said he was soft on her.'

'Perhaps he was wrong. Perhaps Jinkinson was only interested in Ada because she added to his weaponry in a confrontation with Garland.'

CHAPTER TWENTY-FOUR

n elderly porter was sleeping peacefully in the little gatehouse attached to the college. As Adam and Quint passed by, the porter shifted slightly in his seat and let out a deep sigh of contented slumber. They walked on past a carefully manicured lawn surrounded by medieval buildings, through a short, wood-panelled corridor and into a second quadrangle. Half a dozen begowned undergraduates were strolling through it, and Adam approached one of them.

'I am sorry to trouble you but I am looking for Professsor Fields. Does he have rooms still in the Fellows' Building?'

The undergraduate, who had been lost in his thoughts, started at the sound of a voice. He looked first at Adam and then, with greater curiosity, towards Quint, who had stopped in the middle of the courtyard and was scratching his buttocks.

'That is my servant Quint,' Adam said. 'He is mostly harmless. Perhaps you know Professor Fields?'

The undergraduate turned back to Adam. 'Yes, of course. My apologies. I was thinking of something else. I have just seen the professor. He and Mr Dandridge went through into the Fellows' Garden no more than two minutes ago.' He pointed towards a tall wrought-iron gate at the far side of the quadrangle. 'You may wish to wait for them.'

'I think we shall follow them into the garden.'

The undergraduate looked as shocked as if Adam had proposed assaulting a member of the royal family.

'You can't do that, sir. Only Fellows are allowed in the Fellows' Garden.'

'Oh, I think a special dispensation can be made in this instance,' Adam said, raising his hat to the young man. 'Many thanks for your information.' He beckoned to Quint and the two of them made their way towards the gate into the garden. The undergraduate watched them go, a puzzled look on his face, but made no attempt to stop them.

Once they had passed through the gate, they halted and looked around them. Some fifty yards away were two men, both dressed in the billowing black gowns that denoted their status as academics. One was prodding the ground with a walking stick and gazing down at the grass as if he was making an inventory of the wildlife sheltering in it. The other was waving his arms and talking relentlessly.

'Stay here a while, Quint,' Adam said. 'I shall go and interrupt the professor in his conversation.'

At Cambridge, Adam remembered, there had been plenty of students who never attended a single lecture. Several of the dons had matched this undergraduate idleness by never bothering to deliver one. Fields, however, had not been so remiss. He had always been a great deliverer of lectures, not all of them confined to the lecture hall. It looked very much as if he was in the midst of addressing one to his companion.

As Adam approached across the lawn, this companion looked up and caught sight of him. He spoke briefly to Fields but his remark did nothing to stem the tide of the professor's eloquence. Fields continued to flap his hands in the air and hold forth. Adam caught the occasional word in both English and Greek. He was standing next to Fields before the old scholar noticed him.

'Ah, Adam, you have arrived at an opportune moment. I have been telling Dandridge here of your letter. And of the extraordinary tale it told.'

The other don made a slight motion of his head in greeting. It was clear that Fields was too distracted to make a more formal introduction. Adam returned the acknowledgement.

'We have been talking of the poet Euphorion.' The professor spoke as if the ancient Greek was a slightly disreputable don at another college. 'We have gathered together the knowledge we have of him.'

'It is little enough,' his companion said, smiling benevolently at Adam. 'Only fragments of his works have survived. But a few scattered leaves can possess as much beauty as a mighty tree, do you not think, sir?'

'Dandridge has written verse himself,' Fields went on, in a tone of voice that suggested this was a scarcely credible activity for any sane man to undertake.

'I have rested in the groves of Helicon in my youth,' the other man acknowledged, with noticeable self-satisfaction. He nodded his head repeatedly as if to confirm to himself that he had indeed done what the professor claimed he had. 'I think I can say that I tasted briefly of the fountain of Hippocrene.'

'And no doubt it was like sweet wine to your lips, Dandridge,' Fields said dismissively, scarcely bothering to hide his contempt for his colleague. 'But we can spend no time on reminiscences of our gilded youth. Adam here has a mystery to solve. Men have died and he needs to know why.'

'Must he know why?' Dandridge asked mildly, his round red face still wreathed in smiles. 'Perhaps the dead should be left undisturbed by such enquiries. Remember what Palladas says. "Weep not then for him who departs from life, for after death there is no other accident."'

Fields snorted derisively. 'It's difficult to believe that either victim would have been so philosophical as he saw his own death approaching. But I cannot stay to argue the point, Dandridge. Adam and I will leave you to the contemplation of mortality.'

Fields turned and strode off. Adam stayed briefly to raise his hat politely to the other don. Then he followed him.

'The man's a fool,' the professor hissed as they made their way towards where Quint stood. 'As an undergraduate, he published a volume of execrable verse. Hexameters to make Virgil turn in his grave. And more than a hint of that unspeakable vice that so sullied life in Plato's Athens.'

'But you chose to speak to him of Euphorion.'

'He is well-read in the lesser Greek poets,' the professor conceded. 'Ass though he is. I thought it might be of benefit to ask him about the versifier you mentioned. I will tell you later the little I learned from him.'

Adam wondered how the professor could have learned anything, however little, from Dandridge since he had appeared to allow his fellow don no opportunity to speak, but he said nothing.

As they approached the gate leading out of the Fellows' Garden, Adam's manservant, who had been slouching against it, stood up straighter and watched them warily. He looked to be wondering whether or not the professor might still be harbouring a grudge against him for the loss of his tobacco two years earlier.

'Ah, the valiant and faithful Quintus is with you still, I see. *Fidus Achates*, indeed,' Fields said. 'How are you, my good man?'

The valiant and faithful Quintus, looking far from pleased to be so described, acknowledged Fields's condescending nod with a grunt. The incident with the tobacco was, it seemed, forgotten. Fields returned his attention to Adam.

'I have learned something more of Euphorion.'

'What have you learned of him?'

'You must be patient, Adam. I shall tell you all I know this evening, after we have dined.'

CHAPTER TWENTY-FIVE

I n the evening, Quint was banished to take his food with the college servants. The meal was a cheerless affair. The servants ate on benches lining a long table in a dank and ill-lit room off the kitchens. The bill of fare consisted of a watery soup made from pea or possibly green cabbage, a plate of grey, stringy meat of uncertain origin, and a cold, collapsed fruit pie. Pints of weak beer provided the only liquid accompaniment to the repast. Few of his fellow diners bothered to address Quint and those that did spoke in a thick Cambridgeshire accent he could barely understand. After several failed attempts at communication, Quint fell into sullen silence. The college servants soon chose to ignore him. He watched them morosely, while struggling to separate the small amounts of meat from the large amounts of gristle on his plate. They were a pretty poor crew, these porters and kitchen staff, he decided. Anyone with a bit of bounce in him, he thought, would long since have left this dead-and-alive hole in the Fens and headed for London. Yet here were these benighted sods cheerily gobbling up tough meat and downing horse piss they called beer as if there was nothing better anywhere in the world. Not for the first time, Quint despaired of his fellow man.

Meanwhile, Adam and Fields had joined the academic throng in the hall. Unsurprisingly, they fared rather better than Quint – not least in terms of drink, since the college possessed one of the university's finest wine cellars – and it was only after several strenuous hours of eating and imbibing and exchanging Cambridge gossip that they were able to escape to the professor's rooms. Fields's servant had ensured that a fire was waiting for them and they sank gratefully into the comforting depths of two decrepit leather armchairs which stood one on each side of the hearth. Clutching tumblers of brandy and water, they were now ready to discuss what had brought Adam back to Cambridge.

Fields began with characteristic briskness.

'So, young Carver, to return at last to your letter. I understand that, since our meeting at the British Museum, you have been involving yourself in the most thrilling of adventures in the great metropolis. Mysterious men importuning you to help them. Corpses littering the pathways where you tread. We can only dream of such excitement here by the waters of the Cam. Here we lead lives of almost monastic quiet. Dullness, some might say.'

'Nonetheless, sir, you may be able to throw some light on at least one of the mysteries which now surround me.'

Fields's angular face, illuminated by the glow of the fire, wore an expression which was hard to interpret. Was he genuinely eager to hear more? Or was he being no more than ironically indulgent towards a young man who had recently been a favourite student? Adam was unsure, but continued with what he had to say.

'I think I described in my letter how I followed the enquiry agent Jinkinson out to a pub in Wapping. How I stumbled across him only moments after he had been shot.'

The professor nodded.

'As I wrote in my letter, I found this on the man's body.' Adam held out the visiting card. 'As you can see, the word "Euphorion" is inscribed on it.'

'But, if I understand you correctly, this was not the first time you had come across it.'

'No, indeed. I found the same word, in Greek characters, in a journal belonging to Creech, the man who was so interested in our travels in Macedonia. I thought I recalled a Greek poet of that name.'

Fields took the card and examined it briefly before returning it. 'As I said to you this afternoon, I have been looking into the question of Euphorion, with some small assistance from Dandridge.' The professor put considerable emphasis on the word 'small'. 'There are several writers of the name. Euphorion, son of Aeschylus, son of the great Aeschylus, is recorded as having taken first prize in the Athenian Dionysia in 431 BC. But none of his work survives. Better known – and probably the man that you have been struggling to pluck from the waters of Lethe – is Euphorion of Chalcis, third century BC. Meineke published fragments of his verse in Germany some thirty years ago.'

'I was correct in my recollection, then. There was a poet of that name.'

'Your memory served you well. Much better than time has served Euphorion of Chalcis. He raised no *monumentum aere perennius*, no monument longer lasting than bronze. His poetry is either lost or all but forgotten.' Fields sipped at his brandy. 'I cannot see why this man Creech would have noted down the name of an obscure Greek poet.'

'No, he did not seem a very poetic soul.' Adam stared into his own glass, as if looking for the answers to his questions in its contents. He found only a further question. 'But there are others by the name of Euphorion, you say?'

'One at least. Euphorion of Thrace,' Fields said. 'Author of a text entitled *Ellados Periegesis*. He is an exceedingly obscure writer. Never studied at either of the universities. I find it difficult to guess what his name could mean to Creech. Or to an enquiry agent, whatever one of those might be or do.'

'*Ellados Periegesis*. "The Description of Greece". That is surely the same name given to the work of Pausanias?'

Adam knew the writings of the Greek geographer and traveller of old. He could recall translating several pages of Pausanias's lengthy account of his visit to Delphi as punishment for some schoolboy transgression involving a cricket ball and a broken window.

'Yes, Euphorion was a slightly younger contemporary of Pausanias,' Fields said. 'Second century AD. Most of his work is a direct plagiarism of the older man's but written in even less elegant Greek.

Which probably explains why Euphorion's work is largely ignored by scholars.'

'But there is no mystery about this man's writings? Creech kept talking of a secret within the manuscript. What secret could there be hidden in an ancient travel book?'

'No particular secret of which I know, but there is one fact about this Euphorion which may be relevant.'

'And that is?'

'There are only half a dozen passages of his book which are not very obviously borrowed from Pausanias. All of these refer to areas in which the older writer did not, as far as we know, travel.' Fields paused for a moment. 'All are in Macedonia.'

Adam sat in silence for a minute, thinking of the implications of the professor's remarks. Perhaps Creech had read something of the Macedonian villages he had mentioned at the Speke dinner in the pages of Euphorion. Yet the man with the crescent scar had seemed no student of the classics. Adam remembered again his failure to recognise a commonplace phrase from Homer.

'Has Euphorion's book always been available to scholars?' he asked eventually. 'Modern editions have been published, surely?'

'Indeed, they have. Not many – but Aldus Manutius the Younger published a critical edition in Venice in the late sixteenth century. The work of a scholar named Palavaccini. That is the *editio prin- ceps*. And a gentleman at the University of Edinburgh named Robert Munro produced another, some time in the 1760s or 1770s.'

'So any secret in the book has been hiding in plain sight for nearly three hundred years. What about manuscripts?'

'Only three survive. All from the Byzantine centuries, of course. Your late acquaintance may possibly have discovered another. One hitherto unknown to scholars. That is a possibility.'

'I have no idea whether or not he possessed a manuscript. He spoke merely of knowing about one. He spent much time in the East. He might have come across one in Constantinople, I suppose.' A sudden recollection struck Adam. 'Or Athens. Sunman at the FO told me that Creech worked there before the war in the Crimea.'

There was a pause. Adam speculated again about the depth of Fields's interest in the subject under discussion. Maybe he was only indulging a favoured former student, but the professor seemed to have devoted some time to unearthing the information about Euphorion of Thrace.

'I am forgetting,' the young man said after a moment. 'Creech must know you. He was asking after you in London. He spoke of you to Cosmo Jardine.'

'Jardine? Is that young rogue still wasting oil paint and canvas somewhere in Chelsea? Why would this man Creech ask Jardine about me?'

'I have no notion.'

'Nor I. I have never come across the man.' Fields, Adam noticed, was almost too firm in his denial. He wondered briefly if the older man was telling him the full truth.

'When he visited Jardine's studio, he was calling himself Sinclair.'

'The only Sinclair I know is a fellow of Magdalene who wrote a very bad book on the Nicomachean Ethics.'

'Well, Creech certainly gave Jardine the impression that he knew you.'

'He did not, but my name must have been familiar to him. He must have wished to speak to me of our travels in European Turkey.' The professor shifted in his seat, as if struggling to find the most comfortable position in it he could. 'If he wished to consult with a junior member of the expedition such as yourself, he must have been even more eager to pick the brains of its leader.'

'Perhaps he thought you might be able to provide him with information about Euphorion.'

'That is certainly a possibility.' Fields was yawning. His interest in Adam's tale seemed to be fading. 'Well, it seems that Euphorion may have cost him his life. And the life of at least one other man. Or am I indulging too freely in melodramatic speculation?'

Adam thought a while before replying.

'No. I believe a manuscript could have been the reason why Creech and Jinkinson were both killed. This morning I was of the firm opinion that their deaths resulted from their attempts to black-mail someone. But now I am not at all sure that there is not some strange connection between their deaths and this ancient writer.'

'I can help you to research Euphorion of Thrace further,' Fields said. 'If you think it would be valuable to do so, of course.'

'It can do no harm to learn more of the man. Who knows? A little more information may throw light on the puzzle.'

'I cannot be certain without checking, but I believe the library will have a copy not only of Munro's Edinburgh edition but of the earlier volume as well. The college has rather a fine collection of Aldine books.' The professor yawned again and placed his empty glass carefully on the table by his chair. 'But looking for them is a task for the morning. At present the chimes of midnight are upon us and it is time to retire. You have a room awaiting you in First Court, I believe.'

* * * * *

'There is a passage here in Latin. It is not part of Euphorion's Greek text.' Sitting at a reading desk in the college library, Adam looked up from the book he was examining. The professor, hunched over his pocket volume of Thucydides, did not raise his head from its pages. Adam watched his old mentor turn a page in the book. Not for the first time, he wondered how old Fields really was. Fresh-faced on his arrival at Shrewsbury School and first encountering him, he had thought him ancient, a man long teetering on the brink of the grave. Fields had left Shrewsbury for the professorship at Cambridge when Adam was in his final months at the school. A year into his own soon-to-be-interrupted Cambridge career, Adam had had chance to think again about the professor's age and had taken ten years off his original schoolboy's guess. Then the two of them had been companions on the expedition into Turkey in Europe. After two months of trekking the arduous terrain of Alexander's one-time kingdom and watching Fields take each day's travel in his stride, Adam had been obliged to revise his opinion again. Now, poring over the volume of *The Peloponnesian War*, the professor looked every inch a decrepit and decaying scholar, but Adam remembered well enough the vigour he had shown during their months away from civilisation.

'It will be a note of exegesis by the editor,' Fields said, head still bowed over Thucydides. 'It was a common practice in the Aldine volumes.'

'No, I do not think that is what it is. Not exactly, anyway. "*In hoc libro dignissimus et famosus Euphorion...*"' Adam began to translate. '"In this book, the most worthy and renowned Euphorion listed the villages and towns and cities of the fair land of Greece which he had visited and recorded their places of worship and their ancient traditions."'

'I doubt very much Euphorion himself had visited many of them.' Fields's tone was dismissive. 'He was mostly copying what Pausanias had already written.'

'Perhaps not. There is more to this Latin note, though. The Aldine editor, assuming it was he, writes of the manuscripts he has seen.'

'The three of which I told you.'

'Possibly, possibly not. "In one manuscript only does the most worthy Euphorion write of the golden treasure that lies hidden where the ancient kings buried it. Of this treasure I have learned no more and I have chosen therefore not to transmit to posterity words which are most probably but lies and idle fantasies." What do you make of that?'

The professor finally looked up from his volume of *The Peloponnesian War*. He took the Aldine book from Adam and read the passage himself.

'Hmm, interesting. What could have been the treasure to which the manuscript referred?' He gave the book back to Adam. 'But, as Palavaccini says, probably no more than an idle fantasy of hidden riches.'

'But what if it was more than fantasy? What if one of the manuscripts of *Ellados Periegesis* did contain details of some ancient treasure? And what if Creech had come into possession of it? That would be reason enough to speak of a "very great secret".'

Fields waved his hand in dismissal. 'There can be nothing in the three manuscripts,' he said, with apparent certainty.

'Perhaps there is a fourth manuscript,' Adam went on, his excitement growing as his thoughts raced ahead of him. 'Last night, you said yourself that Creech might have found another.'

'I said it was a possibility, Adam. I do not believe it is particularly likely.'

'I am not sure that it is not the only explanation. Other scholars have no doubt seen the three manuscripts that are known to exist and found nothing in any of them which can possibly justify the remark about the golden treasure. Ergo, there must be another manuscript. One which Palavaccini saw in the sixteenth century but which had disappeared by the time Munro put together his edition two hundred years later. Creech must have seen that missing manuscript. He must have known where it is. Or was.'

'As I say, it is not beyond all bounds of possibility that another manuscript exists.' Fields still sounded dubious. 'This man Creech might have read it and realised what he was reading. But it still seems improbable to me.'

Adam thought for a moment.

'I don't think Creech was sufficiently a scholar to have read the manuscript himself. I remember at the Marco Polo dinner he did not seem to recognise a very familiar phrase from the *Iliad*. He must have had someone whose Greek was very much better than his own to translate it for him.'

'Creech's Greek may have disappeared with the passage of time. I know of men who were fair enough scholars in their youth who could not now construe a Greek verse if their lives depended upon it. Some of them continue to teach in the university. However, as I have said, we do not know that such a manuscript exists.'

'You must admit, Professor, that there is – at the very least – a possibility that one does.'

'I have acknowledged as much already, Adam. But I will go no further than to reiterate that it is only a possibility. Nothing more.

If another early manuscript of Euphorion does survive, it cannot be anywhere in Western Europe. Scholars would know of it.'

'Creech might have seen it in Greece or Turkey.' Adam felt a rising certainty that he was correct. 'He spent much of his life in the lands of the Ottoman Empire.'

'That is true.' Fields seemed to have caught some of the excitement which was stirring his one-time pupil. His voice now possessed an animation it had not so far done. 'There are undoubtedly manuscripts that have never been properly catalogued or recorded. In obscure libraries and isolated monasteries.'

The professor stood. He thrust his small volume of Thucydides into his jacket pocket.

'We must both read more of Euphorion, Adam. There is a riddle here to be answered.'

'I shall continue to read here this afternoon.'

'No, no, you must return to London. There is a train at three.'

Fields retreated into the darker recesses of the library. Adam could hear him moving books on one of the shelves.

'I could stay longer in Cambridge,' he called.

'There is no need for you to do so, my boy.' A book fell noisily to the floor. There was a muffled curse and then the professor appeared again by the reading desks, holding an old volume bound in calfskin. He blew gently on it and coughed as clouds of dust rose from it. 'Here is a copy of the Munro edition. No one has looked at it for decades, it would seem. Possibly since it was first published. Take it back to town. I cannot countenance the borrowing of one of the college's Aldine volumes, but the Munro is another matter. Perhaps there is some further clue to be found within its pages.'

'And you shall read the Aldine edition here?'

'I shall.' The professor ran his hand through his hair where much of the dust from the book had settled. 'I shall also make more enquiries of my confrères at high table. I shall even speak to Dandridge again. Together you and I will get to the bottom of this mystery.'

CHAPTER TWENTY-SIX

'Word from Cambridge, Quint,' Adam said, waving a letter in his manservant's direction. 'It can only be from the professor. Who else would write to me from the college? And in such a wretched scrawl.'

Quint, standing by the window and staring down into Doughty Street, said nothing. His interest in Cambridge and the professor, his attitude very clearly said, was limited.

Adam opened his letter and began to read it.

'You must depart on a quest for provisions, Quint,' he said after a moment. 'Fields intends to visit this afternoon. We must offer him some refreshment after his journey. He has news to deliver to us and a proposal to make, he says. The least we can do in return is set afternoon tea before him.

Adam placed the letter by his plate and turned to look at his manservant.

'Cucumber sandwiches are still de rigueur on such occasions, are they not?' he said. 'And muffins, perhaps. Or scones? I leave the choice to you. The baker's on the Gray's Inn Road sells both, I am sure.'

'We paying with ready gilt?' Quint asked, turning from the window. 'Or we still looking for tick?'

'I think we shall make Mr Gregory's day and pay him for once with coin of the realm.'

Adam took a florin from his jacket pocket and spun it through the air. His manservant caught it and pocketed it in one swift motion.

'What a ferocious woman your landlady is, Adam! Medusa shaking her serpentine locks at Perseus could scarcely be more terrifying. Unlike the hero of old, I possess no mirrored shield but I have escaped her petrifying gaze. Somehow I have mounted the stairs to your rooms unscathed.'

As he entered the sitting room at Doughty Street, it was clear that Fields was in an exuberant mood. There could be no doubt that he had awakened that morning in the best of spirits and the journey from Cambridge had done nothing to dampen them. Not even a close encounter with Mrs Gaffery had been able to dent his ebullience. He shook hands with Adam as warmly as if they had last seen one another a year ago rather than a week, and nodded amiably at Quint, who was still employed in ferrying the materials for afternoon tea from the kitchen. The professor skipped around the manservant like a small boy and moved towards the side table where Quint had placed muffins for toasting and a plentiful supply of butter, jams and preserves. Fields gazed down at it as if he had never seen such riches spread before him.

'A feast fit for Lucullus,' he exclaimed. 'The recipe book of Apicius himself does not contain anything more appetising.'

'It ain't finished yet,' Quint said, attempting to elbow the professor out of his path, but Fields was not to be moved.

'What have we here?' he asked, seizing a jar from the table and peering at its label. 'No less than the honied wealth Hymettus yields, I do believe.'

'It is honey certainly, sir,' Adam replied. 'But I think it is more likely to have come from the beehives of Kent than from the slopes of Hymettus.'

'No matter. It will be equally agreeable, I am sure.'

Waving Quint on with his work, Fields retired from the side table and sank into one of the armchairs by the hearth. A small fire was burning there and the professor held out his hands to warm them as if it were December rather than July. Forgetting for the moment that he was guest rather than host, he gestured to Adam to join him. Smiling to himself, the young man obeyed. He settled himself in the other chair.

'However, we are not here solely to indulge in the Epicurean pleasures of the table,' Fields said. 'I have no doubt that, like me, you have now spent much time with Euphorion. I had thought that there could be no more tiresome guide to the ancient lands of Greece than Pausanias but I was mistaken.'

'His Greek is certainly more workmanlike than elegant,' Adam acknowledged. He patted a leather-bound book that was resting on a round walnut wine table by his chair. 'I have read the Munro edition you lent to me.'

'And you found nothing further to pique your curiosity?'

'No, I could find no references to treasure or to anything else that might have excited Creech's interest. But you said yourself that you had found nothing in Munro's volume. What of the older edition, the Aldine? Did you read that again?'

'I did, but there is nothing beyond that enigmatic reference to the golden treasure that lies hidden where the ancient kings buried it. The one you saw when you came to Cambridge.'

'So, we are at a dead end.' Adam was disappointed. He had hoped so much that Fields might have something new to tell him. 'There is nothing more to be learned from Euphorion.'

'I would not go so far as to say that.' Fields was almost hugging himself with delight.

'You have discovered more of our mysterious author?'

'I have done more than that. I have located another manuscript.' The professor looked about the room with the air of a man expecting a hidden audience to reveal itself and burst into sudden applause. 'I sent a telegraph to an old friend in Athens. Professor Masson at the French School there.'

'He knew of another manuscript?'

'He did not. He is an archaeologist. His interest lies in the Eleusinian Mysteries. He believes that he has found a shrine to Demeter on the road from Athens to Eleusis.' Fields waved a hand in dismissal of his friend's archaeological concerns. Shrines to Demeter, he seemed to suggest, were pretty small beer in comparison with what he and Adam were chasing. 'But he made enquiries on my behalf. And he is of the opinion that there is another manuscript of Euphorion's work in the Greek National Library.'

'And it is one that is unknown outside Greece?'

'There can be no doubt about it. Scholars in the West know of three manuscripts only. One is in the Harleian collection in the British Museum. Another is in Paris. The third belongs to Sir Granville Tukes of Tukes Hall in Buckinghamshire. It has been in the family for at least a century and a half. If Masson has really found another, it is a new one.'

'Although Palavaccini may have known of it in the sixteenth century?'

'That is certainly a possibility.'

Adam took a muffin from a plate that Quint thrust unceremoniously in front of him. He placed it on a toasting fork and pointed it towards the flames of the fire.

'And yet this manuscript that your friend has located must have been in Athens for some time?'

'Not necessarily. You forget that the modern Greek state has been in existence for a few decades only. The National Library is also a young institution. The Euphorion manuscript must have only come into its possession recently.'

'So where was it before that?'

The professor shrugged. 'Who can tell?' he said. 'A monastery library, perhaps? They will have some record in the National Library of its provenance, I assume. I am not sure that it is of any great import. It is enough that it is there now.' He paused. 'I do believe that muffin is toasted more than adequately for consumption.'

Adam, who had forgotten his toasting duties while thinking of the manuscript, pulled the fork from the fire. He scrutinised the muffin impaled on it.

'I have allowed it to burn.'

'It will serve its purpose.' The professor seemed untroubled by the muffin's blackened state. Lifting it off the fork, he helped himself to the butter and honey that Quint had set out on the small table beside his chair and began to eat it with apparent relish.

'There is but one way to learn more of this mysterious manuscript that Louis Masson has unearthed,' he said between mouthfuls, spraying crumbs carpetwards. 'And that is to travel to Athens and inspect it.'

'I do not see how that is easily possible.' Adam was surprised by the professor's sudden enthusiasm for another journey to Greece. He was not even sure he wanted to leave London in the near future. He had returned to his photography and his dark room was filling up with plates awaiting his attention. Nor had he lost all hopes of meeting once more with Emily Maitland. 'We cannot drop everything and make our way across Europe in pursuit of one manuscript.'

'Why not? The long vacation is nearly upon us. What better way for me to spend my time than in journeying to Greece in search of mysterious manuscripts? The college would be only too delighted if I could unearth some others that were equally unknown.'

'It is a long journey to make on what might turn out to be a wild goose chase.' Adam continued to sound doubtful.

'Nonsense, my boy. We can be in Athens within ten days if we so desire,' Fields said. 'If we make our way to the south of France, we can take the steamer from Marseilles to Malta. And then on to Athens. Or we could go by rail to Trieste and then join an Austrian ship to Greece.'

'That would probably be cheaper.'

'But the Malta route would be more convenient and comfortable. And I am inclined to think that convenience and comfort should trump expense.' The professor leaned forward, dripping butter from the muffin he was eating onto the lapels of his jacket. His eyes were shining with excitement. 'Shall we go? The two of us? And the bold Quintus, of course. It will not be so challenging an expedition as the one we made in sixty-seven but – who knows? – the results may prove more rewarding.'

Fields's enthusiasm for the journey he proposed was oddly

infectious. Adam, who had been about to recite a list of objections to the plan, began instead to consider its benefits. Within the hour, it had been decided. The two of them, with Quint in tow, would depart for Athens as soon as the long vacation began.

CHAPTER TWENTY-SEVEN

s Adam and Cosmo Jardine entered the Café Royal, the artist was telling his friend of some social excursion he had made the previous evening.

'The champagne tasted like varnish and as for the girls...' He grimaced.

'As bad as that?' Adam asked.

'Worse.'

They made their way to one of the tables.

'There's that fellow Gilbert,' Jardine said, nodding towards a florid and heavily moustached man in his early thirties who was sitting nearby with a group of other men.

'Should I know him?' Adam asked.

'He writes lyrics and one-acters for German Reed – the musical entertainments in the Gallery of Illustration, that theatre just around the corner. If you recall we saw one together last year. Some nonsense about haunted castles in Scotland and pictures coming to life and stepping out of their frames. Was it entitled *Ages Ago*? Something like that.'

The moustachioed gentleman inclined his head ever so slightly in response to Jardine's greeting.

'He knows you, it would seem,' Adam remarked.

'I was introduced to him at Gatti's the other night.'

'I remember the piece we went to see now. Nonsense, as you say, but enjoyable nonsense.'

'Gilbert is a talented man. No doubt the world will hear more of him before long.'

A waiter materialised at their table. He took their orders for coffee and disappeared as swiftly and silently as he had arrived.

'So this is to be our last meeting for a while,' Jardine said. 'Before you shake the dust of England from your feet for several months?'

'Yes, Fields has arranged it all. As soon as the long vac is upon him, we travel once again to Greece.'

'And which of the beauties of ancient Hellas draws you there this time?'

'We go to Athens. Whether we travel further depends on what we find there.'

Jardine raised his eyebrows questioningly.

'We shall be on the trail of lost manuscripts,' Adam said. 'Of this writer Euphorion I have mentioned. Fields has an acquaintance in the French School at Athens who claims to have seen a manuscript of which Cambridge scholarship knows nothing.'

'I thought that anything of which Cambridge scholarship knew nothing was scarcely deemed knowledge.' The young painter crossed his arms behind his head and leant back against his seat. 'Well, it is not a journey I envy. Although I shall be sorry to see you go. London is a dreary enough place as it is in the summer.'

'You will have no distractions. There will be no excuses for not finishing *King Pellinore and the Questing Beast.*'

'True. Although I seldom find it difficult to fashion an excuse for not working. But I shall miss the mysteries which seem to have followed you around town in the last month: the maiden in possible distress; the men murdered just as you were eager to converse with them.'

'I fear that they must all remain mysterious, Jardine.' Adam sounded sombre and downcast. 'The maiden in possible distress, together with her mother, has disappeared from Brown's.'

'She deserted you on the dance floor at Cremorne, did she not?' the painter remarked, with the slightest hint of malice in his voice.

'Not quite on the dance floor,' Adam said defensively. 'We spent some time together. We talked of several inconsequential subjects. We danced. And then she said that she must return to Brown's before her mother returned from Lombard Street. We walked together to the gate where the cabs gather. As you can imagine, I offered to accompany her back to her hotel.'

'Of course. The very least a gentleman could do. But she spurned your offer?'

'She did. "I'm not in the least bit afraid of a London cab by myself," she said, and before I could make any reply, she had climbed into one. In truth, she all but jumped into it and shouted for the cabbie to take her to Albemarle Street. She disappeared in the general direction of town within seconds.'

Adam was only slightly ashamed of himself for providing this largely fictional account of Emily Maitland's departure. Cosmo's curiosity about the young woman was obvious but his friend felt little urge to satisfy it. He was so far from understanding Emily's motivations himself that he had no desire to tell Jardine any more and then be obliged to listen to the discourse on the fickleness and unpredictability of women that the painter would inevitably give.

'So Cinderella had to flee the ball.' Cosmo continued to probe for further information.

'And long before midnight's witching hour. It was barely seven in the evening. The gardens were only beginning to grow busier.'

'This capricious belle of Cremorne left you none the wiser as to her reasons for seeking you out in the first place?'

Adam shook his head. The ghostly waiter shimmered into view again, served them with their coffee and departed.

'You have visited Brown's in the days since?'

'Twice. I was there only yesterday.' In truth, Adam had been to Albemarle Street more than twice since the meeting at Cremorne but he was embarrassed to admit to his friend how frequently he had haunted the hotel in hopes of catching a glimpse of Emily. Indeed, he was shy of admitting even to himself how eager he was to see her again. 'But they are no longer there. I can only assume that they must have done as Miss Maitland suggested that they might and travelled to Switzerland.'

Jardine took a silver cigarette case from his pocket. He selected a cigarette, tapped it gently on the case and put it in his mouth. The waiter, miraculously reappearing from whatever spectral limbo he inhabited when his services were not required, held out a match. Jardine sucked in smoke from the first pull on the lit cigarette and blew it out. He nodded his thanks to the waiter, who left them once again.

'Meanwhile the dead men are doing no talking,' the artist said.

'Indeed not. The police inspector in charge of investigating their deaths, who is either one of the greatest fools in Christendom or a man of subtle and devious wisdom – I cannot decide which – appears to have convinced himself that Creech was killed in the course of a bungled robbery. Quint believes that he is interested only in pinning the murder on somebody. Anybody would do and this man Stirk has simply been singled out as the unfortunate sacrificial lamb.'

Jardine shrugged his shoulders, as if to say that, in this wicked world, Quint's theory might well be true.

'And the other man?' he asked.

'The inspector seems to care little for the fate of poor Jinkinson. He was associating with villains and received much what he deserved for doing so. That appears to be the police opinion on the matter.'

'But you have not been content with the police view of the killing.' Jardine blew out smoke again and sipped at his black coffee. 'You tell me that you have played the intrepid explorer and ventured into the city's most abandoned and desolate regions. With Quint as your improbable Virgil, you proved a latterday Dante and descended into the pits of hell in search of news of the lost soul of this fellow Jinkinson.'

'If you consider Holywell Street and the Palace of Westminster to be the pits of hell,' Adam said.

'Oh, I do. Particularly Westminster.'

'Certainly one of its inhabitants seems to have played the very devil with at least one poor woman.'

'I would be astonished if only one of the members of the House had proved a devil with the women.'

'Well, there is but the one of whom I know. As you say, doubtless there are plenty of others. But I am sure it was Garland who ruined Ada.'

'The woman your late friend Jinkinson was seeing?'

'The very one. I am convinced that she was Garland's maid and that he seduced her. Then he turned her out of his house.'

'And Jinkinson was employed by Creech to find her.'

'Jinkinson discovered a great deal about Garland's women. He located the pied-à-terre where Garland kept the actress he visited. He told me about that love nest himself. But he omitted to mention Ada.'

Adam now reached over to extract a cigarette from his friend's case which was still lying on the table. Before he had completed the manoeuvre, the waiter was there again, holding a flaming match. The man was certainly earning his tip.

'Was this enquiry agent tupping the girl himself, do you suppose?' Jardine asked.

'Simpkins – the boy Jinkinson employed – assumed that he was. But I think it unlikely that he was right. Jinkinson merely suggested Ada join him in a plot to take her revenge on her seducer.'

'And she was eager to do so.'

'Perhaps, perhaps not. I believe Ada was past caring about revenge. But she has a mother. Quint tells me the mother is an avaricious old soak. She probably saw an opportunity to extract money from her daughter's disgrace.'

'What a quagmire you have stumbled into, Adam. Death and deception on all sides. It will be a relief for you to swap such dark scenes for the bright light of Greece. When do you go?'

'At the end of the month.'

'You will be able to renew your activities on behalf of the Foreign Office. Did you not tell me that the great panjandrums there valued your opinions on matters Greek and Turkish?'

Still curious about their conversation some weeks ago, Jardine was very obviously fishing for more information about the exact nature of the relationship between his friend and the people he had been seen visiting in Whitehall. Adam was unwilling to satisfy his curiosity. The truth was that he had visited Sunman soon after the professor had first mooted the journey to Athens. The languid young aristocrat had encouraged the idea that despatching his thoughts and impressions of the Greek capital back to London might be a valuable one while simultaneously suggesting that it was entirely Adam's decision whether or not he should do so. 'Always glad of an extra pair of eyes in a place like Athens, old man, but no need to put yourself out too much.' Those had been his exact words, Adam recalled, but he felt no urge to report the conversation to Cosmo.

'I doubt the great panjandrums will be hanging on my every word,' he said mildly.

'I shall have no opportunity to see you again before you go,' his friend continued, seeming to realise that he would learn no more. 'I would raise a glass to the success of your expedition with Fields but there is no glass on the table at present. This will have to do as a substitute.'

Cosmo Jardine lifted his coffee cup into the air. Adam smiled and followed suit. The two young men touched the delicate porcelain cups carefully together.

PART TWO

ATHENS

CHAPTER TWENTY-EIGHT

A dam awoke with the sound of one of the tunes he had last heard at the Cremorne Gardens in his ears. At first he imagined that some Athenian hurdy-gurdy player had added the Pretty Kitty Quadrille to his repertoire, but even within a delicious state of half-sleep, he was aware that the song was only in his head. He continued to lie beneath the sheets, enjoying the memory of Cremorne and his encounter with Emily Maitland. He remembered the warmth of her body pressed against his as they danced and the unexpected but delightful touch of her lips to his.

Two weeks had now passed since he had left England in the company of Quint and Fields. The journey to Greece had unfolded much as the professor had predicted on the afternoon he had eaten burnt muffins in Adam's rooms in Doughty Street. They had travelled through France at breakneck speed in order to catch a steamer from Marseilles to Malta. A short stay there had been enlivened only by an altercation on the Valletta waterfront between Quint and a sailor which had escalated from mutual insults in English and Maltese to a sudden and inconclusive bout of fisticuffs. The three men had then travelled onwards to Athens. They had docked at Piraeus three days earlier and had been driven from there to the Hotel d'Angleterre in Constitution Square. Fields had insisted, at some length, that this was the finest hotel in Athens and that its manager, Polyzoïs Pikopoulos, was a particular friend of his. They could not think of staying anywhere else. In the three days they had been there, 'Polly', as every English guest appeared to call him, had been a model of respectful politeness, but there had been not the slightest indication on his part that he knew Fields of old or that he could distinguish him from any of the many other Englishmen who passed through his hotel.

On the second day after their arrival in Athens, Adam and the professor had visited the latter's friend at the French School. To Adam's amusement, Professor Masson had fitted almost exactly the caricatured image of the average Frenchman presented in the comic papers. He was small and moustachioed and exceedingly voluble. He waved his arms vigorously and very nearly unceasingly, like a man trying to pluck a swarm of flies from the air. He spoke torrentially of his own impending excavations near Eleusis and it was only with the greatest difficulty that he could be brought round to the question of the Euphorion manuscript. At this point his face had fallen and he had slapped his forehead as if he were close to distraction. He was wretched, he was *desolé,* so *desolé.* His friends, his *chers amis,* how could they forgive him? He had brought them to Athens on what they would call a chase of the wild duck. There was no manuscript of Euphorion? *Au contraire,* there were *two* manuscripts of Euphorion. *Mais, hélas,* they were both the *wrong* Euphorion. They were the work of Euphorion the poet not Euphorion the traveller. How could his *chers amis anglais* forgive him? Even more importantly, how could he forgive himself? His life had become an insupportable misery to him. It had been a full thirty minutes before Adam and the professor had been able to extricate themselves from the conversation and leave. By that time the diminutive Frenchman had succeeded in forgiving himself and was discoursing happily on the worship of Demeter in sixth-century Athens. The two Englishmen had returned to their hotel in a dejected mood to contemplate the chase of the wild duck on which they had come all this way across Europe.

A bell somewhere in the city was chiming eleven when Adam finally emerged from the bedclothes and stumbled towards the luridly floral washbowl and jug the hotel provided for his ablutions. It was close to noon when he finished dressing and made his way down to the hotel restaurant. The place was almost empty. Only a handful of tables were occupied. The professor was sitting at one of them, drinking coffee. He waved cheerfully at Adam. His recovery from the disappointments of the previous day seemed complete.

'There you are, my boy. While you have been such a slug-a-bed, wasting precious morning hours in the arms of Morpheus, I have been busy. I have seen Masson again. I have spent time at the National Library. For an institution that has been established for no more than a few decades, it is an admirable one.' Fields, whose usual opinion of everything in Athens less than two thousand years old seemed to be one of contempt, was in a surprisingly gracious mood.

'As I have had occasion to remark before, sir,' Adam said, joining the professor at the table, 'there is more now to the city than just the ancient sites.'

'And, as I have had occasion to reply, nothing of any significance, my boy.' Fields was amiably dismissive. 'The delights of the National Library notwithstanding, the modern town is but a mushroom growth of the last forty years. Since the moment it became the capital of a newly liberated Greece. There is nothing of any consequence intermediate between us and the age of Plato.'

'But we have seen so much ourselves of a new Athens taking shape. And we have been here but a few days.'

'It is true that the city is expanding. By the hour, it sometimes seems. But Greece has no modern history of such a character as to obscure its classical past.'

It was becoming a familiar argument to Adam and one that he knew he could not win. He turned briefly to survey the restaurant. There was a solitary waiter in evidence, a tall and gangling youth, and he indicated to him that he, too, would welcome coffee.

'Your visit to the library has proved useful, has it, sir?'

'Enlightening, if not of any immediate use. Our French friend Masson did indeed mislead us. The manuscripts of which he wrote to me so excitedly are fine specimens of Byzantine calligraphy from the time of the emperor John Komnenos. But, as he told us yesterday, somewhat belatedly, they consist of the work of Euphorion of Chalcis.' Fields picked up a spoon and began to stir his coffee vigorously. 'Fragments from an epic poem which is shockingly poor. And lines of amatory verse which are merely shocking. I am surprised that the scribe, who was almost certainly a cleric of some kind, could bring himself to write them down. But that is by the by. The point is that they are not by our Euphorion.'

The long-legged waiter sidled awkwardly to the table and served Adam his drink. It was a small cup of what looked like boiling mud. The young man stared at it, black and bubbling, and braced himself to raise it to his lips.

'I have also paid a visit to the embassy and arranged to see someone there,' the professor went on. 'Samways. Felix Samways. He was up at the college not so many years ago. Perhaps you recall him?'

'I have no memory of anyone of that name.'

'He must have been before your time. The man's a fool but even fools can have their uses. He is attached to the embassy.' Fields took a napkin and dabbed at his lips. 'With luck, he will be able to expedite any journey out of Athens we might wish to make.'

'What journey out of Athens might we wish to make?'

'Who can tell where we might wish to travel?' The professor replaced the napkin on the table. He had adopted an air of mystery like a stage magician about to pull a rabbit from a hat. 'But this Dilessi business earlier in the year has made it exceedingly difficult for us to come and go as we please. After the kidnapping and murder of several Englishmen so close to Athens, no one is eager to allow others to leave the safety of the city. A voice raised in our favour at the embassy might well prove invaluable.'

'But where might we wish to go?' Adam persisted. 'I would think that our only journey should be back to England. After our disappointment with Masson, what is there to keep us here?'

'Why should we not stay a while longer? The land where Pericles ruled and Plato thought must always have a strong claim on our hearts,' Fields said, picking his teeth as he spoke.

'I do believe that you have learned something more at the National

Library, Professor.' Adam swallowed a mouthful of the hot mud and found it surprisingly flavourful.

'I have spoken with the librarian there. He is a charming man. He had a suggestion to make.'

'And that was?'

'That there are manuscripts still awaiting discovery and proper cataloguing in many of the Greek monasteries. That we might wish to mount an expedition in search of some to take back to Cambridge.'

There was a silence as Adam thought about this.

'What of these monasteries?' he asked after a few moments. 'Is the librarian right, do you think? Is it possible that they could contain unknown manuscripts? Lost manuscripts?'

'Possible, yes, but I do not know that it is likely.' The professor seemed suddenly deflated. His earlier enthusiasm had evaporated. 'I did look into the matter before I left Cambridge.'

'And what did you learn?'

'A Swedish traveller named Bjornestahl examined some of the monastic libraries in Thessaly about fifty years ago. He found little of any interest. Musty volumes of the Greek Fathers. Some manuscripts and codices, but none of any considerable value. Everywhere he found signs of damp and neglect.'

'Perhaps the monks were unwilling to show an outsider what they really owned.'

'Perhaps. But scholars have long ago lost hope that a forgotten library might hold some genuine treasure.'

'Who knows? Maybe we will stumble upon the lost books of Livy.'

'No, they are gone for ever.' Fields sounded like a man regretfully acknowledging an inescapable truth. 'As are the missing plays of Aeschylus and Aristotle's book on comedy. We shall find nothing so remarkable.'

'But there might be the work of some lesser author still to be discovered.' It was Adam whose enthusiasm was now growing as the professor's shrank. 'An author like Euphorion.'

'I cannot bring myself to believe even that.' The professor stared into the bottom of his cup and stirred the dregs of his coffee. He appeared to discover new hope there. 'Although, it is true that Bjornestahl did not include all the monasteries of Thessaly in his survey.'

'So, there is a chance that there is something still out there.'

'A chance, yes. A systematic search of the monastic libraries might reveal hitherto unknown manuscripts. Who knows? Even lost works by ancient authors.'

'Then we must go,' Adam said, decisively. 'We have come too far to do no more than return to London with our tails between our legs.'

The professor shrugged, whether in agreement or disagreement Adam was not entirely certain, then got to his feet.

'There is something,' he announced rather too loudly, 'that I must fetch from my room.'

Adam followed Fields's progress through the hotel's restaurant, which was fuller than it had been when he had first come down. Several tables were now taken by those intent upon lunch. Adam looked across at a young English couple whose behaviour suggested they were newlyweds on their honeymoon. Further away, two middle-aged men, Americans to judge by their accents, were talking noisily about stocks and shares. Another man entered the restaurant and, at first, Adam assumed he was planning to join the two Americans. He moved in their direction. As he did so, Adam saw to his astonishment that the man was Lewis Garland. The MP strode confidently past the American businessmen and took a seat at a more distant table. He waved to the tall waiter who set off towards him like a contestant embarking on a foot race. Adam took the opportunity to head for the nearest door. He had no desire to engage Garland in conversation but he could not help but wonder what on earth could have brought the man to Athens.

CHAPTER TWENTY-NINE

The man hailed Adam and the professor as soon as they entered the house in the Square of the Mint that served as the British embassy. He was wearing a blue blazer with brass buttons and a pair of white duck trousers and was about to leave the building. He looked more like a sailor recently come ashore after years at sea than a member of the British diplomatic service.

'Apologies for the outfit, gentlemen,' he said, looking anything but apologetic. He seemed to have forgotten, possibly deliberately, that he had an appointment to see them. 'Not really on duty at present. Taking a boat to Aegina this afternoon, but I thought I'd exchange pleasantries before I went.'

He shook hands with Fields and then held out his hand to Adam.

'You must be Carver. Don't think we met in Cambridge.' He paused. 'Or did we? I'm constantly coming across chaps who claim to have known me at college and I haven't the faintest recollection of them.'

'No, we were up at different times, I think. I went down in the summer of sixty-five.'

'Oh, different epochs altogether, then. I was a year into the dreariest of postings in Copenhagen in the summer of sixty-five. Ever been to Copenhagen?'

Adam indicated that he hadn't had that pleasure.

'Wretched weather. So damned cold most of the time,' said Samways, taking a handkerchief from his pocket and dabbing at one of the buttons on the cuffs of his jacket. 'Can't recommend it.'

'I have no plans to visit Copenhagen at present, but if I do ever go, I shall remember your warning about the temperature.'

The young man from the embassy ignored Adam's remark. He continued to polish the brass on his sleeves.

'Not that Athens is much better,' he said. 'Choking in dust in summer, drowning in mud in winter.'

'But surely proximity to the glory that was Greece is worth a bit of discomfort, Samways, is it not?' Fields said, drily.

'Not too sure about that, Professor.' Samways tucked his handkerchief back into the top pocket of his blazer. 'You may keep the glory that was Greece, in my humble opinion. Smacks too much of the classroom. Your natural habitat, of course. Myself, I can't wait to get a posting to somewhere with a climate that agrees with me more.'

He smiled at Adam and the professor with a look of immense self-satisfaction on his face, as if he was expecting them to rush to agree with him that the glories of Greece were much overrated.

'And where would you prefer to be posted, Mr Samways?' Adam asked.

'Ah, there you have me, old boy.' Samways was still inspecting the gleaming brass buttons on his sleeves, moving his arms to admire the light flashing off them. 'Paris is obviously out. Still surrounded by Bismarck's bully-boys. No doubt the French will be at each other's throats before long. Murdering one another in their beds and that kind of thing. As is their wont. I'm none too fond of any variety of jabbering foreigner, if truth be told, but Johnny Crapaud quite takes the biscuit, don't he?'

Satisfied that his buttons were shining with sufficient brightness, the diplomat hauled another white cambric handkerchief from his trouser pocket and began to wipe beads of sweat from his brow. His thoughts were still running on his next posting. 'Vienna? Berlin? Germany seems to be quite the coming place, don't it? Wouldn't mind going anywhere I shan't have to deal with all these tourist pilgrims mooching about with a volume of Homer in one pocket and Byron's verse in the other.'

'I would have thought that tourists would be in short supply after the Dilessi affair,' the professor said, doing little to disguise his low opinion of Samways. 'Few things do so much to deter the average traveller as kidnap, murder and brigandage.'

'Oh, I don't know. Being captured by brigands isn't all bad, you know,' the diplomat said cheerfully, as if he was planning on being abducted himself in the near future if only he could find the time in his busy calendar. 'Bags of fresh air to breathe and fresh game to eat. Set of picturesque rogues for company. Then, when family and friends get the money together for a ransom and aforementioned picturesque rogues release you, you've got a story to dine out on for years to come.'

'The poor devils who were murdered at Dilessi would probably disagree with you,' Fields said pointedly.

'Oh, no doubt, no doubt.' Samways waved a languid hand in the air. 'Always exceptions to any rule. Poor Herbert and Vyner just had the most terrible bad luck. Problems with the ransom money and all that.'

'And yet the countryside will still be dangerous for travellers.'

'Safe enough for Englishmen, if you want my humble opinion. Despite all this Dilessi business. It's not often a Greek's going to take a potshot at you. For one thing, he's aware of the fact that nine times out of ten either he's going to miss or his gun won't go off. Whereas, if you take a potshot back at him, the likelihood is the gun *will* go off and you *won't* miss.' Much to the irritation of both Adam and the professor, Samways continued to be fascinated by the buttons on his blue jacket and was still moving his arm back and forth as if to find the point at which they glinted most attractively in the sun. Fields glared at him like a schoolmaster about to rap a naughty pupil's knuckles smartly with a wooden ruler. 'Not to mention all the infernal fuss caused if an Englishman does get himself killed. Herbert and Vyner are shot and look what happens. People galloping like mad hither and yon. Arrests and beatings by the dozen. The game's not worth the candle. As I say, those chaps were just damned unlucky.'

Fields, whose face had been turning a peculiar shade of red as he listened to Samways, looked likely to roar at the embassy man in reply. Adam, noticing the professor's poorly suppressed rage, hastened to intervene.

'Dilessi has undoubtedly been the scene of a tragedy,' he said smoothly, 'and yet it is not the subject we came here to discuss. If I understand the professor correctly, you are the one man in Athens who may be able to help us. In our quest for manuscripts. We need the help of someone like yourself who knows the town inside out.'

Adam's flattery worked. Samways's delight in being considered the one man in Athens capable of offering assistance was obvious. His self-regard, already enormous, visibly increased. He drew himself up to his full height and looked around the lobby of the embassy as if inviting the admiring glances of anyone who might be passing through it.

'If I say so myself, I *have* become something of an authority on the place. I may not like the town but I'm here now. Representing queen and country and all that. So I reckon it's my duty to learn all I can about it.'

Fields made a strange snorting noise. Adam was once more swift to speak.

'Your knowledge of Athens and its inhabitants will doubtless prove invaluable to us. We are looking for someone to advise us on the sale of ancient manuscripts. A Greek, if possible. Perhaps someone from your large acquaintance in the city springs to mind?'

'Been thinking about that since the prof first spoke to me the other day.' Samways beamed at his two visitors. 'It seems to me that the man you need is Alexander Rallis.'

Fields made a heroic attempt to control his temper. 'And who is this Rallis?' he demanded.

'He's a decent sort,' Samways said. 'About as close to a gentleman as you're likely to get in Athens.'

'We have certainly met very few gentlemen since we arrived in the city,' Fields said, pointedly. 'Either Greek or English.'

'What more can you tell us about him?' Adam asked, hurriedly.

'Not a lot, old boy.' Samways had entirely missed any hint of irritation or innuendo in the professor's comment. 'His father was a government minister back in the days of Good King Otto. Left politics after Otto was forced to abdicate and head back to Bavaria. Rallis senior retired to his estates outside Athens.'

'And what of Rallis junior?'

'He's a lawyer. Greek lawyers usually cause nothing but trouble, but he don't. Quite the reverse. He's even helped us with some tricky business.'

'Why should we have need of a Greek lawyer?' Fields asked, the little patience he had been able to muster for their conversation with Samways ebbing away. 'We have no intention of falling foul of the law while we are in Greece. We are here to investigate the country's antiquities. As I told you, Samways, we are looking for manuscripts.'

'Absolutely. That's why Rallis is your man.'

'We don't want legal manuscripts.' Fields raised his voice in his annoyance.

'No need to get in a bait, Professor.' Samways seemed to notice the older man's simmering temper for the first time. 'Alexander's not just a lawyer. That's the point. Did I not say? He's a bit of a scholar as well. Has some connection with the university, although I'm never quite certain what it is exactly. If anyone knows where to find musty old parchments with Greek poetry and whatnot on them – and I understand that's what you're looking for – then Rallis does.'

Adam glanced at Fields. The professor's intense irritation with the embassy man seemed to have rendered him unexpectedly speechless. His eyes spoke volumes but his lips were clamped shut. It was, Adam thought, best that they should remain so.

'How shall we make ourselves known to the gentleman?' he asked Samways. 'Perhaps you might be able to arrange a letter of introduction?'

'No need for that, old man. There's a reception in the embassy the day after tomorrow. For some rich merchant we want to butter up. Rallis will be there. Why don't you both come along and I'll introduce you to him there.'

'That would be most kind of you, Samways.'

'Don't mention it, old chap. Always glad to give people like yourselves the benefit of my knowledge. Anyway, must dash now. Don't want to miss that boat to Aegina.'

Waving his arm in farewell, the diplomat almost ran from the building. Adam and the professor followed him into the sunshine.

'We will meet this fellow Rallis,' Fields said, as they watched Samways climb into a carriage standing outside. 'If even that insufferable little pup recommends him, he must be a man of some consequence.'

Fields paused and stared gloomily about the square.

'Unless, of course, he turns out to be as big a damned fool as the man who's recommending him,' he said.

'That would be difficult, would it not?'

'It would be very nearly an impossibility that one city the size of Athens should include two men of such idiocy,' the professor acknowledged. 'But I doubt that Samways has come to an opinion about Rallis alone. Others at the embassy must think highly of him.'

'And, as a rule, they think little of most Greeks,' Adam remarked. 'If there is one subject on which all the foreign residents of Athens agree, it is the rascality of the natives. French, Italians, English, Germans, Americans – they seem to argue about everything else, but there they speak with one voice.'

'That is true. It is rare to find a Greek they admire. So we shall come to this reception on Friday and we shall talk to Mr Rallis.'

* * * * *

'The parliament building was begun more than ten years ago.'

Adam and Fields were sitting outside a café at the junction of two roads. One led back towards the Angleterre. The other, which they faced, provided them with a view of the Acropolis and the Parthenon silhouetted against the horizon. The professor had embarked upon one of his favourite topics of conversation – the decadence of the modern Greek when compared with his ancient ancestors.

'They talk of its opening next year but will it do so?' he continued, picking up his cup and looking at its contents dubiously. 'This is Athens. The home of idleness and procrastination. Who knows?'

Fields sipped at his coffee. Adam, who knew better than to engage his companion in debate on this particular subject, stretched back in his seat and clasped his hands behind his head. He gazed at the distant temple to Athena on its hill and thought idly of the history it had witnessed over the centuries. The sound of the professor lecturing became no more than a background buzz requiring only the occasional, random interjection in reply. The dust rose and the Athenian traffic, its carts and carriages and pedestrians and animals, continued to thunder past them but Adam felt himself tempted towards sleep. He closed his eyes.

'Be off with you!'

Adam opened his eyes again in surprise. An ugly dark-haired woman and a child were standing by the table, hands outstretched. The professor was waving them away with a theatrical gesture, like a father in a Drury Lane melodrama dismissing his erring daughter from his sight. Carver offered a ten-lepta coin to the girl who was barefoot, filthy and dressed in torn clothing. She snatched it and the two grubby figures moved on.

'You should not encourage them, my boy. They will batten upon your weakness and you will never see the back of them.'

'I can see the back of them now, sir,' Adam remarked mildly, watching as the beggar-woman and her daughter walked away.

'Ah, you may be flippant but, mark my words, they will return. Or others will do so. Give but once to these Athenian mendicants and you will be pestered throughout the rest of our time here.'

The young man doubted Fields was correct. He had given freely to the city's destitute since they had arrived and he had never seen the same beggar twice. He gazed down the narrow street ahead of them. A sad procession of emaciated horses, a dozen or more of them, was being led down it. Their destination, he thought, was almost certainly the knacker's yard. The horses, with the man leading them, turned to the left. The traffic, which earlier had been so busy, had almost disappeared. The road ahead was clear for the best part of a hundred yards. The only vehicle that could be seen was a wooden cart, drawn by a sturdy-looking chestnut horse, which was trundling steadily towards them. Adam turned in his seat and peered through the window behind them into the gloom of the café.

'I suppose we should pay mine host and return to the hotel.'

'I shall not accompany you back to the Angleterre, my boy. I shall visit my friends at the National Library again.'

'I do not believe the waiter plans to venture outside again for the rest of the day.' Adam stood. 'I shall beard him in his den.'

He brushed aside the curtain that hung across the café door and entered. Almost blinded by the change from light to darkness, he squinted into the interior. There were several rickety tables inside but only one was occupied. Two middle-aged men in shabby suits, wreathed in the smoke from their cigarettes, stared expressionlessly at Adam. As his eyes adjusted to the shadows, an older man emerged from the innermost depths of the building, smiling and nodding. Adam paid him for the drinks and turned to leave. He glanced through the window. The professor was standing with his back to the street. He was patting the pockets of his jacket as if he suspected that the beggar-woman who had importuned them might also have been a pickpocket and he was in danger of having lost his wallet.

'*Antio sas.*' Adam tipped his hat in farewell at the two shabbily dressed men at their table. They made no reply but continued to draw impassively on their cigarettes. He pushed aside the flimsy drape that separated the darkness of the café interior from the morning sunshine. As he did so, he heard a rumbling like distant thunder. It was so like thunder, he later remembered, that he was about to look up to the heavens in search of the clouds that must have materialised so suddenly. Instead, he could only stare in horror at what was racing towards them. Fields was still lost in his own world, his back to the street. Behind him, and approaching at tremendous speed, were the chestnut horse and its wooden cart.

In the short time Adam had spent paying the café owner, something must have disturbed the beast and sent it careering across the junction of the two roads. Realising that it was charging towards a collision, the horse suddenly veered leftwards but, as it did so, the barrow it was pulling spun round in the direction of the café front. There were yells of warning from passers-by but the professor, still oblivious to the uproar behind him, made no movement.

Adam acted without thought or hesitation. Instinct replaced reasoning and he hurled himself towards Fields, like a swimmer diving full-length into a river. His outstretched arms struck the professor in his midriff. Both of them were propelled sideways just as the cart crashed into the table where they had been sitting. Momentum drove it on and clean through the window of the café with a terrific noise of shattering glass and splintering wood until finally the vehicle came to a halt. Adam, now sprawled across the professor's body, felt a waterfall of tiny shards of glass shower down upon them both. He continued to lie there, aware now of the frantic whinnying of the chestnut horse and a hubbub of voices in the background. To his relief, he could sense Fields breathing heavily beneath his weight. He moved his arms and legs gingerly. Miraculously, there seemed to be no great damage. The café owner had emerged from the wreckage of his business together with his two customers, apparently unhurt and shocked, not into silence, but into voluble complaint and indignation. All three men roared and yelled. Picking himself up, Adam could hear loud demands that the owner of the horse and cart should make himself known to them. They were also threatening such retribution that he doubted anyone would step forward from the crowd that had gathered. Indeed, the driver of the cart had vanished. His vehicle was scarcely worth claiming. It had all but disintegrated in the impact. The chestnut horse had bolted up the street.

Amidst the continuing clamour, Fields pulled himself groggily to his feet.

'Are you hurt, Professor?'

'I think not.' The old scholar raised his hand to his brow. He looked curiously at a red smear on it. 'There is blood here but no serious injury. What happened? One moment I was thinking of the library manuscripts and the next, like Icarus, I was plummeting earthwards.'

'A runaway horse.' Adam kicked aside fragments of wood and glass and picked up his hat from where it had fallen. 'An accident.'

'Possibly.'

'What else could it be?'

For once, Professor Fields was silent.

* * * * *

The large room on the embassy's ground floor was already crowded when Adam and the professor arrived in the Square of the Mint. Most of the men in attendance were dressed in black tie and jacket. A few of the Greeks, wishing perhaps to advertise their patriotism, wore what had come to be seen since the War of Independence as national dress: richly embroidered velvet jackets, two or three inside one another, accompanied white *fustanelles*, bound round the waist by leather belts. One fierce-eyed individual even had a silver dagger and scabbard hanging by his side, as if to suggest that he was a warrior chieftain only recently descended from his mountain hideout. Samways, appearing briefly to point out the more interesting guests to them before pushing his way back into the throng, identified him as a journalist on one of the city's more radical newspapers.

'They're like the damn Scotch,' Fields said with disgust as he watched Samways's back disappear into the crowd. 'Marching around in their ridiculous kilts, pretending to be great heroes.'

The embassy man was not gone for long. Within a couple of minutes he had returned, forcing his way through the crush of people in the company of the man Adam and the professor had come to meet. Rallis was one of the majority that had chosen western dress. Indeed, his immaculately tailored suit would not have looked out of place in Piccadilly or Bond Street. He was of medium height and olive complexion. Samways had told them that the lawyer was not yet out of his twenties, but his jet black hair was already receding and his high forehead gave him the look of an older man. He bowed deeply on introduction but made no attempt at first to shake hands with them. Adam had the feeling that, just as they had attended the reception to judge him, Rallis was there to assess them. He might meet with their approval but there was no guarantee that they would meet with his.

'I am delighted to meet you, gentlemen. Mr Samways has told me much about you.' Rallis now reached out his hand to Adam. 'I trust that you are enjoying your visit to Athens.'

'It is a city that every lover of truth and beauty must enjoy,' Adam said. 'But we are finding the heat near intolerable. We are not used to such temperatures as yet.'

'Ah, the heat, yes. It is fierce, is it not? Enough to drive a man as mad as the March hare.'

'You have a fine grasp of a good old English simile, Mr Rallis,' the professor said, shaking the Greek's hand in his turn, and was rewarded with the briefest of smiles.

'Oh, Alexander speaks English better than I do,' Samways said. 'He lived in London in the early sixties.'

'I was there as a very young man.' The Greek spoke as if he was now full of years and looking back on his distant past. 'I was a student but I was also busy with the task of persuading your fellow countrymen to support the rightful claims of my people.'

Adam raised an eyebrow enquiringly.

'Our claims to land that should be Greece but which is ruled by the Turk,' Rallis continued. 'It is what we Greeks call the *Megale Idea*, the Great Idea. We long for a time when the nation will encompass all Greeks.'

'Dreaming that Greece might still be free and all that?' Samways said, clearly bored, his eyes idly roaming around the room.

'A part of Greece is already free, Mr Samways. But the kingdom of Greece is not the whole of Greece. The Greek is not only he who inhabits the kingdom. The Greeks of Ioannina, of Salonika, even the Greeks of Constantinople, do they not deserve their freedom? What kind of a Greece is it that does not include Mount Olympus?

Where the ancient gods look down on a land ruled by Turks?'

Rallis was growing warm in his enthusiasm. His voice was raised above the ordinary level of social conversation, so much so that several people in his vicinity turned their heads to look at him.

'All sounds a bit too political for me, old boy,' Samways commented. 'We embassy chaps should always steer well clear of politics.'

'I see it is the same with the English as with the French or with the Germans. I discovered that it was so when I was in London,' Rallis said. He had noticed that he was attracting attention and had lowered his voice. He was now smiling to take any sting from his words. 'You are always kind enough to allow us a glorious past, but it is seldom you concern yourselves with our future.'

'The future's no business of ours, Alexander old chap. Difficult enough keeping up with what's going on in the present.' Samways had seen someone he wished to flatter on the other side of the room and was eager to extricate himself from the conversation. 'I shall leave you with these two gentlemen. Although I suspect that they will prove to be like the rest of us. More interested in the past than the future.'

Rallis watched the English diplomat push his way through the crowd and then turned to Adam and the professor.

'I think that Mr Samways, perhaps, does not always concern himself even with my country's present. But he is a good man.'

Fields snorted. 'Felix Samways is what he always was. A man with more money than he has brains. But he recommends you, Mr Rallis.'

The Greek bowed his head as if to suggest that this recommendation merely proved the diplomat's essential goodness.

'He is very kind. However, for what is he recommending me? Not for legal work, he tells me. He speaks instead of ancient manuscripts. I must confess myself puzzled. But I am also intrigued. What manuscripts do these English gentlemen seek? I wonder to myself.'

'The story is a long one, sir. But it is one that you should hear. It begins in London at a dinner in my club. A gentleman named

Samuel Creech introduced himself to me.' Adam took Rallis gently by the arm and, with the professor on his other side, guided the Greek lawyer towards a less crowded corner of the room.

CHAPTER THIRTY

itting towards the back of the little Anglican church of St Paul's, listening as best he could to the preacher's quiet drone, Adam was able to survey the English community in Athens at worship. It was not, he decided, an altogether prepossessing sight. He could see Samways, stifling a yawn, in one of the pews further forward. Looking beyond the young diplomat, he could see more men he assumed were attached to the embassy. Some he recognised from the night of the reception. Others in the congregation, well-fed and well-dressed men and women with a look of indestructible self-satisfaction in their eyes, he took to be businessmen and their wives. One white-bearded old man, sitting stiffly to attention near the front, might have been one of the generation of English Philhellenes who had fought on the Greek side in the War of Independence. Bored by the service, Adam indulged himself in idle speculations about the life the elderly gentleman might have led. He might have witnessed the kind of adventures in the 1820s of which the young man had dreamed as a boy. He might have been one of Byron's comrades at Missolonghi or a man who had sailed with the British fleet at the Battle of Navarino. These thoughts were enough to distract Adam slightly from the tedium of the service. He had not wished to attend St Paul's this Sunday morning but the professor had insisted. Fields, it seemed, was too busy to go to church himself, but it was imperative that Adam should go.

'There are few more revealing sights than our fellow country-men at prayer,' he had said. 'You will lean more about the English

Athenians in one hour at St Paul's than in a week spent observing them elsewhere.'

Adam was unsure that he wished to know much more about the English in Athens than he knew already. He was very certain that the professor was wrong in his assumption that they would best display their true characters while worshipping their god. However, he had chosen not to argue with Fields and had dutifully made his way to the Anglican church for the morning service. Now, here he was, crammed uncomfortably into a wooden pew, wondering anew why he had come. His eyes moved on from the ageing Philhellene and further towards the front of the congregation. He almost exclaimed aloud in surprise at what he saw. Sitting in a pew immediately beneath the pulpit was Emily Maitland. She was leaning forward, her lips slightly parted, listening to the sermon with more apparent attention than it deserved. Seated next to her, his face set in a faintly mocking smile, as if he could scarcely credit what the preacher was saying, was Lewis Garland.

Adam was astonished to see them together. The MP's presence in Athens was, of course, no great surprise. Adam had seen him in the restaurant of the Angleterre earlier in the week. At the time, the young man had made every effort to avoid Garland's notice, slipping out of the room before the MP had spotted him. An encounter just at that time, Adam had thought, would have proved too complicated to negotiate. He had told Quint of his sighting, but not Fields. Yet what was Emily doing in the city? This was Athens, not Switzerland or Salonika. And why was Garland in the company of the enigmatic young woman who had visited Adam in London? How did an English businessman and member of the House of Commons know her? Was she another of his conquests? It was not a pleasant notion. As the clergyman continued to mumble relentlessly about the wages of sin, Adam found he could not begin to bring his thoughts into order or to find adequate answers to all the questions that filled his mind.

When the service finally stumbled its way to its conclusion, he was the first on his feet and the first to make his way into the bright sunshine of the Sunday morning. His initial thought was to avoid coming face to face with Garland and Emily. If they had not seen him, what purpose was there in renewing acquaintance with them? If Emily was indeed one of the ageing Don Juan's paramours, why torment himself with meeting them together? He began to walk away from St Paul's, but he had gone no more than a hundred yards when curiosity and the overwhelming desire to speak to the young woman got the better of him. He turned and retraced his steps. The English expatriates were still trooping out of their church. The street was filled with their carriages. Ahead of him, Adam could see Lewis Garland escorting Emily towards a black landau. He hastened to intercept them.

'Good morning, sir. I trust that you are enjoying your visit to Athens.'

The MP smiled wrily as he shook the hand Adam proffered.

'Miss Maitland said that she was sure she had noticed you among the congregation, Mr Carver. But we could not, at first, see you as we left. And – forgive me for saying this – I had not put you down as a regular churchgoer.'

'You are right, sir, I am not. But I was told that I could not miss the Sunday service at St Paul's. That everybody would be here. Well, everybody English, that is.'

'And, as you can see, your informant was correct. Everybody *is* here.'

Adam turned and raised his hat to the young woman.

'I expected you to be taking the fresh mountain air by now, Miss Maitland. When we met last, I understood that you and your mother were soon to travel to Switzerland.'

'Our plans were never set in stone, Mr Carver.' Emily flushed very slightly as she replied. 'After some consideration we decided that we should return to Salonika. But we have chosen to visit friends here in Athens for a week before we travel further north.'

She looked at him almost defiantly, as if he might be tempted to dispute her statement.

'I had not realised until a few minutes ago that you and Miss

Maitland knew one another, Carver. She tells me that you met in London.' Garland made his remark seem a casual one, but there was no disguising his curiosity about the circumstances in which Adam had encountered the young lady.

'We were introduced by friends of my mother's, were we not, Mr Carver?' Emily was swift to intervene. 'In Kensington.'

'Yes, of course, Kensington.'

'As I was saying to my godfather' – Emily inclined her head towards the MP – 'it was at an afternoon tea party. In aid of charity.'

'And what charitable organisation is it upon which you bestow your patronage, Carver?' Garland asked. 'I do not think that you mentioned its name, Emily.'

Adam struggled to think of some philanthropic body that he, together with Emily and her mother, might plausibly patronise.

'The Society for the Employment of Necessitous Gentlewomen,' he said, after a lengthy pause.

Emily stifled a giggle, transforming it into a genteel clearing of her throat. Garland raised his eyebrow and looked from the girl to the young man and back, but could scarcely express the disbelief he clearly felt.

'What did you make of the preacher here at St Paul's, Carver?' he asked, changing the subject. 'Is he a bawler, would you say? Or more of a squeaker?'

'I'm not sure I catch your meaning, Mr Garland.'

'Every reverend gentleman I have ever heard is one or the other. Either they bawl so loud you need earmuffs or they squeak so you can't hear more than one word in ten.'

Adam laughed. 'The gentleman who has delighted us this morning is more of a squeaker, I would say,' he suggested.

'I agree with you. Squeak, squeak, squeak. I was unable to follow his argument. Or even to hear it. His text appeared to be from Ecclesiastes and to refer, as one might expect from that depressing book, to the vanity of human wishes, but whatever benefit there might have been in his thoughts on it was entirely lost on me. What about you, my dear? Did you gain wisdom and insight from the preacher's sermon?'

'There is always wisdom and insight to be gained from a sermon, Mr Garland, is there not?' Emily said, looking as if this were the last thing she truly thought.

The older man smiled. 'So we are always led to believe, my dear,' he said, 'but you will excuse me for a moment. We must be on our way.'

He turned to beckon his driver towards them. Adam and the young woman looked at one another but said nothing. The black landau began to approach.

'And how is your man Quint, Mr Carver?' Emily said hurriedly, eager to fill the sudden silence. 'Is he here in Athens with you?'

'He is, Miss Maitland. And, arrived in the birthplace of democracy, he has proved even more of a free spirit than he was in London. It is sometimes difficult to look at the pair of us and decide which is the master and which the man.'

'You have encountered Carver's servant, Emily?' Garland said, turning back to them and seizing on the girl's remark. 'Was he also devoting his time to the assistance of necessitous gentlewomen?'

Emily said nothing. She looked at Adam.

'He was waiting with a cab when I left the tea party,' the young man said. 'Miss Maitland was good enough to condescend to speak briefly to him then. He has not forgotten it. He will be gratified that you remember him,' Adam added, certain that Quint would be nothing of the kind.

The carriage, with its two greys, now stood close to them. One of Garland's servants was sitting with reins in hand. Another had climbed down from the landau and opened one of its doors.

'I am sorry that we cannot stay longer, Carver,' the MP said. 'No doubt you and Emily would find further Kensington memories to share. But we have a luncheon appointment that cannot wait. Perhaps we will see you again. You are at the Angleterre, I assume?'

Adam nodded.

'You must tell Polly to serve you one of his best bottles of burgundy at dinner tonight and charge it to my account.' Garland took Emily's hand to help her into the carriage. 'He has a habit of forcing his guests to drink the most filthy wines if he is not watched carefully.'

'Goodbye, Mr Carver,' the young woman said, as she settled into her seat. 'It has been a pleasure to meet you again in so unexpected a fashion.'

Adam raised his hat as Garland climbed into the landau and tapped the driver on the shoulder with his stick. The horses were eager to be on their way. The carriage moved abruptly into the road and departed in a flurry of dust. Adam caught a last view of Emily, her head turned to look at him and her hand waving farewell.

* * * * *

'Garland? That's the MP chappie, ain't it? My pater knows him, I think.' Samways, seated behind a large desk in an airless office in the embassy, was red in the face and sweating fiercely. On the wall behind him was a portrait of the queen. The artist had caught Victoria at one of her sterner moments and she looked to be scowling down on her perspiring representative in Athens.

'He is in the House, yes.' Adam turned his eyes away from the glowering queen and glanced briefly from the one window in the room. He could see the leaves of a tree fluttering in a light breeze outside and hear the faint noise of traffic in the square below. 'But he is in Athens at present. I saw him at St Paul's on Sunday.'

'Oh, I know he's in Athens, old boy. Saw him at the service myself.'

'And you know where he is staying in the city, do you?' Adam had assumed that Garland was staying at the Angleterre but enquiries had shown this assumption was wrong. He was now hoping that the man at the embassy could help to locate him.

'Might do, old boy.' Samways moved a bronze inkstand from one side of his desk to the other. He stared at it, as if judging the aesthetic effect of shifting its position, and, clearly dissatisfied, moved it back again. 'Might do. But I'm not sure I ought to let you in on the secret.'

'It *is* a secret, is it?'

The embassy man smiled slyly. 'Not sure I'd go so far as to call it that,' he said, tempting Adam to remark that that was exactly what he *had* just called it.

'Did I, old boy? Just a turn of phrase. It's not a secret. Or at least not a secret that the embassy wants kept. But Garland himself might not want you knowing it.'

'This is not a matter of any great consequence, Samways.' Adam tried to make his voice as casual in its tone as he could. He sensed that, if the man from the embassy thought there was much significance in his enquiry, he would not tell him what he wanted to know. It seemed there must be some hidden motive behind Garland's arrival in the city, some reason for his visit of which the embassy was aware. Why else would Samways be so circumspect? 'I met Garland at my club in London last month. The Marco Polo. I thought I would leave my card. But it is of no great moment. If you do not know where he is staying…' Adam rose from his seat as if to leave the room.

'I did not say that I didn't.' Samways's desire to appear a man in the know was at war with his belief that discretion on the subject of Garland was required. He reached an arm across the table as if to seize Adam by the hand and prevent his departure. Discretion, it seemed, had lost.

'Look, I'm sure you're a man who can keep his mouth shut, Carver, when it's required.'

Adam agreed that he was.

'Garland's here on a delicate mission. Not many people know he's here. Can't tell you more than that. Probably shouldn't have told you anything at all. But you're a college man, ain't you? If I can't trust an old college man, who can I trust?'

Adam assumed that the question was a rhetorical one and left it unanswered.

'And if you know Garland of old, no harm in telling you he's staying here at the embassy.'

'At the embassy?' Adam was surprised.

'Thought he'd be more inconspicuous here than at the Angleterre. He's only here for a few days. If you want to leave your card, I'll make sure he receives it.'

Adam reached into his pocket and took out his silver card case. He opened it and handed one of the cards to Samways. The diplomat turned it over suspiciously, as if he thought it might have some hidden message scribbled on its rear face, and then placed it in a small tray on his desk.

'When you saw Garland at St Paul's,' Samways said, 'you must have seen the girl who was with him.'

'There was a girl with him, yes.'

'Quite a stunner, ain't she? She's staying here as well. Calls herself his god-daughter.' Samways leered unpleasantly. 'Ain't heard that one before.'

Adam felt a strong temptation to lean across the desk and punch the embassy man on the nose, but he resisted it.

'She's very beautiful, certainly. Do you know anything more of her?'

Samways shook his head.

'Garland has a reputation, though, don't he? Randy old devil. He's old enough to be her grandfather, never mind her godfather.'

CHAPTER THIRTY-ONE

The young Englishman drew a long breath as he reached the top of the Acropolis. He turned to his companion and forced a strained smile to his face. Their exertions, so soon after breakfast, had tired him more than he had thought they would. Adam was a fit man. He had been one of the first men at Cambridge to box under the new Queensberry rules for the sport and he had rowed on the river as one of the college eight. Since moving in to Doughty Street, he had been a regular patron of the German gymnasium in St Pancras where he had exercised with dumb-bells and weights. And yet the climb from the ancient agora to the Acropolis had taken its toll in the morning heat. Behind him, the white colonnade of the Parthenon gleamed in the sun. Adam took a handkerchief from his pocket. He removed his hat and mopped his brow. Now standing at his side, Rallis, just as elaborately attired as the Englishman, seemed not to feel the heat.

'It is a fine sight, is it not?' he said.

'The finest in the world,' Adam agreed. 'I saw it once before, in sixty-seven, and I have never forgotten it. The memory of it has warmed many a chilly day in London in the last few years.'

The two men continued to stand and admire the ancient temple to Athena. Adam, recovering swiftly from the rigours of the climb, was the first to move.

'It is a great pity that it was impossible to bring my camera to Athens,' he said, holding up his hands to frame the view he might have taken.

'It has been difficult enough to carry our own selves up to this point,' the Greek lawyer said, smiling. 'I am by no means certain that we could have carried your photographic equipment as well.'

'We could have hired men to bring it. It has been done often enough before. I have seen photographs of the buildings here while sitting in the library of the Marco Polo Club back in Pall Mall. A chap named Stillman showed them to me. An American who was staying in London.'

Adam began to pick his way across the rocks on the summit of the Acropolis. He gestured back towards the path where they had climbed up.

'What is that unsightly horror? I remember it from my visit with Fields. And it was in one of Stillman's photographs.'

Rallis looked over his shoulder at the tall stone building to which his companion was pointing.

'The Frankish Tower. It was built by the Florentines several centuries ago. The Turks, when they occupied the city, used it to store gunpowder.'

'It is a filthy excrescence,' Adam exclaimed. 'A blot on the landscape. It does its very best to spoil the approach to the sublime. Someone should use gunpowder to blow it up.'

'It would not be missed, would it?' the Greek agreed. 'But let us continue to turn our backs on it and feast our eyes on the temple to Athena. Or on the maidens of the Erechtheum.' He waved his hand towards the ruins of a smaller temple to their left, the columns of its porch shaped into female figures carrying the weight of the building on their heads.

'Ah, the caryatids!' Adam was filled with enthusiasm once more. 'I see these regularly in London.'

Rallis looked puzzled. 'In the photographs of Mr Stillman again?' he asked.

Adam shook his head. 'Copies of them stand guard over the crypt of the new church of St Pancras. In the Euston Road. But they look better here in the Greek sun than they do beneath the English rain.'

The two men seated themselves on one of the fallen stones that littered the surface of the Acropolis. It was still early in the morning and there were few other visitors to disturb the tranquillity.

'It is enjoyable to act the tourist,' the Greek said after a few moments. 'But I have also been busy in the days since we first met.'

Adam raised an eyebrow enquiringly. The meeting at the embassy party had been a huge success. Rallis had been intrigued by their plans. Adam, and more importantly Professor Fields, had been impressed by the Greek. It was now accepted that the lawyer would join them on any expedition out of Athens.

'I have asked questions of many people I know. Of scholars who know much about the ancient manuscripts that are still to be found in Greece. Not one of them knows anything of Euphorion.'

Adam looked crestfallen. 'It seems we *are* on a wild goose chase,' he said.

'Not necessarily, my friend.' The Greek was smiling to himself. 'I have spoken also to a fellow countryman who spends his days drinking coffee at the Oraia Ellas.'

'The café in town?' Adam knew the Oraia Ellas as a haunt of visitors to Athens. He had been there himself on two occasions. The tables had been filled with Frenchmen and Germans, Americans and English. Any Greek who spent long hours there, he thought to himself, was probably a government agent employed to eavesdrop on the conversation of foreigners.

'You know it, of course. My fellow countryman remembers an Englishman who came there several times. About a year ago.'

'Every Englishman who arrives in Athens visits the Oraia Ellas at least once, Rallis. What is the significance of one visitor out of hundreds? Thousands?'

'This Englishman was tall. And he had a scar near his right eye.' The lawyer waggled his finger above his own brow. 'Like a crescent moon, my fellow countryman said.'

'Creech. That must have been Creech.'

'Precisely, my friend, the man you described to me two days ago. And he was asking a lot of questions. Some of them were very peculiar questions. He wanted to travel out of the city. But not to the usual places Englishmen want to travel. Not to Marathon or to Missolonghi. This Englishman wanted to head north, out of the kingdom and into Turkey in Europe. He wanted to go to the monasteries at Meteora.'

'Meteora?'

'You do not know Meteora, Mr Carver?'

Adam again shook his head. 'Although Fields spoke the other day of Greek monasteries,' he said. 'Perhaps he meant these ones at Meteora.'

'They are on the plains of Thessaly. They are among the most surprising buildings that we Greeks have constructed.' Rallis smiled to himself at the thought of how surprising the monasteries were. 'This English gentleman with the strange scar, he wanted to go to one in particular. Agios Andreas.'

'And Agios Andreas is known to you? It is one of the monasteries?'

'Its fame is not as great as that of the Great Meteoron or the Holy Monastery of Varlaam. But, yes, I know of it. It has its own small renown.' The Greek continued to smile, as if at a private joke he might possibly be willing to share if the moment was right.

'What kind of small renown, Rallis? You must not keep me in suspense in this malicious way.'

'According to what I have been told, its library is said to contain many ancient manuscripts.'

'Endless works by the dullest of the church fathers, no doubt.'

'No, my informant believed that Agios Andreas held more than just religious works. It has manuscripts of the ancient pagans. Of Aristotle and Homer.'

'Aha! And of Euphorion, perhaps.'

The Greek lawyer inclined his head, as if to suggest that this was indeed possible.

'Did this man with the crescent moon scar who was so eager to visit Agios Andreas find the answers to the questions he was asking?'

'Alas, my fellow countryman does not know. The Englishman, he says, did not come again to Oraia Ellas after the summer months. But whether or not he succeeded in travelling to Meteora...' Rallis shrugged. 'Who can tell?'

Two days passed and Rallis invited Fields and Adam, accompanied by a grumbling Quint, to join him at his house overlooking Constitution Square. As noon approached on another hot and cloud-free day in the city, the professor climbed the three steps to the main entrance and stared at the large brass knocker on the door. It was fashioned into the face of an old man with flowing hair and untamed beard.

'It is intended to represent Poseidon, I believe,' he remarked, peering at the door knocker as if uncertain what purpose it might serve. 'It seems a curious choice of decoration. I cannot see what connection there can be between the god of the sea and admittance to a man's house.'

'Perhaps Hestia, as goddess of the hearth, might be more appropriate,' Adam said, 'but we are not here to debate Rallis's choice of household decoration, Professor. Do make use of Poseidon's head.'

'For gawdsake, knock on the bleedin' door, will you?' Quint muttered, although not loudly enough for the professor to hear him. 'It's 'ot enough to fry eggs on the pavement out 'ere.'

Fields lifted the hinged image of the god. He rapped it firmly against the door. The sound of brass on wood echoed and reverberated through the house and was then followed by silence. The professor was about to raise Poseidon once more when Adam rested a hand on his arm.

'There is no call to do so, sir. I can hear footsteps inside.'

It was Rallis himself who opened the door.

'I have allowed the servants to take the day off,' he said, spreading his arms in a gesture of welcome. 'All save one. We shall have the house to ourselves as we make our plans. No eyes or ears upon us. Come this way, gentlemen.'

The lawyer directed them towards the staircase across the hallway, its perimeter lined with statues of nymphs in loose drapery. With Quint loitering a moment to examine the marble maidens more closely, the three men followed their host up the stairs.

'My library,' Rallis said, throwing open a door on the first floor with a flourish. He stood to one side and allowed his guests to enter before him. There was another man already in the room. He was standing in the shadows by the window drapes. It was difficult to see anything of his face but it was impossible to miss his size. Quint whistled as he saw him.

'Jesus Christ,' he said under his breath. ' 'E's the size of St Bride's steeple.'

'Andros has spent much of the morning watching the traffic passing,' Rallis said. 'He is not accustomed to the city. It is only the second time he has been in Athens.'

The man, Adam thought, was like one of the Gigantes, giants of Greek legend. He towered over the other men in the room. Adam was more than six feet tall himself but Andros was at least a head higher.

'He was born on one of the farm estates my family owns in Attica,' the lawyer continued. 'He has lived and worked there, all his life.'

'Are they all 'is size in Attica?' Quint asked.

'No, Mr Quint. Andros is an exceptional man there as he would be everywhere else.'

The huge Greek moved out of the shadow but he continued to stand impassively at the window, looking down at the streets below. Adam could tell that he was aware the others were talking of him. The giant turned and spoke briefly to his master.

'He is curious about the carriages in the street. He had forgotten how many there were.' Rallis made a swift remark to his servant in Greek and then turned back to his guests. 'But let us go through to my study.'

The lawyer opened an oak door between the bookshelves and indicated that they should all walk into the next room. As they did so, Andros, bringing up the rear, was obliged to stoop in order to avoid knocking his head on the lintel of the door. Rallis's reference to his study had suggested some cramped retreat from the world, but the room they entered was almost as large as the library. Light streamed into it from a pair of long windows at its far end and fell onto

297

a baize-covered writing desk beneath them. Another escritoire, pens and paper spilling from its numerous drawers and compartments, was placed against the opposite wall. By its side was a large globe on an iron pedestal. Fields walked across to it and, reaching out his hand, set it spinning. More bookshelves ran along the walls at either side.

In the centre of the room stood a mahogany table and three chairs. They looked out of place, as if they belonged elsewhere in the house and had only recently been brought here for this conference. The Greek lawyer gestured towards them and Adam and the professor seated themselves at the table. Like two mismatched sentries guarding the entrance to a temple, Quint and the giant Greek took up positions standing either side of the door through which they had all just come.

Rallis walked to the bookshelves behind Adam. He reached up and took down something from one of them. He came to the table and placed it in front of the two Englishmen. It was a map. The lawyer carefully unrolled it.

'Please hold the ends of the chart, gentlemen,' he said. He crossed to the desk beneath the window and picked up first a glass paperweight and then a silver inkstand with a small figure of Hercules, club in hand, standing on it. Returning to the mahogany table, he positioned both on the map.

'Those will suffice, I think,' he said. 'And now we can look down, like eagles, on the land where we propose to travel.'

'Which road shall we be taking?' Adam asked, his eyes quickly scanning the chart.

'There are few roads in my country that are worthy of the name. I am embarrassed to admit it, but once we have travelled from Athens to Piraeus, there is no road to take. Certainly no road to match your English roads.'

'So we must find another means of transport.'

'Exactly. From Piraeus, we will sail up the coast as far as here.' Rallis pointed his finger. 'It is a good harbour and I can arrange for horses and mules to be awaiting us there.'

There was a noisy snort from behind them.

'Mules!' Quint said, putting as much disgust into one short word as Adam had ever heard. 'I 'ate mules.'

'Ah, but they love you, Quint. They see you as a kindred spirit.'

'I 'ate mules,' Quint repeated. 'Cussed beasts. No respect.'

'These will be mules of a most respectful nature, Mr Quint,' said Rallis, turning to smile soothingly at the manservant.

'Mules of a saintly disposition, I'm sure,' Adam said over his shoulder. 'You'll grow to love them, Quint, and they will grow to love you.'

Quint snorted again, as if to express his doubts and suspicions of all mules of whatever disposition.

'Them as I've come across are so cussed they won't even stand for saddling.'

'Then you will have to ride them bareback like Menken in *Mazeppa*.' Adam was gazing intently again at the map on the table. 'I doubt that your legs will show to the same advantage as those of the lovely Adah but you will be able to ride across Thessaly on one of the beasts, I am sure, saddle or no saddle. Do stop grousing and let us look where the mules and the horses will take us.'

Quint subsided into grumpy silence.

'From the harbour we will make our way inland,' Rallis continued, deciding that concerns about the mules could now be ignored. 'We will soon cross into European Turkey. We will keep away from villages and towns. We will also avoid the wayside khans and sleep instead under the stars.'

'That will be difficult, surely? To keep away from people?' Adam suggested. 'We will be passing through well-populated territory. We will not be in remote highlands or uninhabited wilderness.'

The professor had been hunched over the map and had said nothing during the discussion about the mules. Now he looked up.

'The papers I have obtained from the Ottoman consul here in Athens will allow us unhindered passage. We need not worry about that. But it will be easier to travel swiftly if we keep to ourselves as much as we can. We will also avoid the endless demands for baksheesh.'

'We will not be able to avoid people altogether.'

'No, that is true. But the journey will take little more than two days,' the professor said. 'The whole of Thessaly is little bigger than the county of Lincoln.'

'The journey may take us more days than two,' the lawyer said. 'We may have to go out of our path to avoid meeting thieves and robbers. There are many dangerous men in that country.'

'Brigands? We know the risks of brigands.' Fields waved his hand in irritated dismissal of these risks. 'We are not idle excursionists on a day's jaunt to Marathon. We have travelled extensively in the country before.'

'I am sure the professor is a man of wisdom and discretion.' Rallis was offended by the abruptness with which Fields habitually spoke. He now addressed his words to Adam alone. He spoke as if the professor was already in some far-flung corner of the country rather than sitting at the table beside him. 'I am certain that his knowledge of our country is such that it would put to shame that of one such as myself who has rarely ventured far beyond the boundaries of Attica. Nevertheless, I feel obliged to warn him of the dangers of the journey we are proposing.'

Fields, infuriated in his turn by the Greek's sudden indifference to his presence, was puffing out his chest in preparation for a lengthy riposte, but Rallis ignored him and continued to speak to Adam.

'The English gentlemen who lost their lives at Dilessi recently? Mr Vyner and Mr Herbert? They were idle excursionists on their way back from Marathon. They were less than a day's journey from Athens. Yet they were taken. And eventually they were killed. A party of travellers, however experienced, heading to the north would expose themselves to considerable risk.'

Fields could clearly contain himself no longer and now spoke loudly.

'I will not have our plans affected by worrying about a pack of damned rogues who ought to be rounded up and flogged.'

'It is a complicated question, this question, Professor.' The Greek lawyer made a determined effort to recover his good temper. He turned now to speak directly to Fields. 'You English are famously virtuous. You have won a great empire through your virtue. And so you look at our bandits and you see only thieves and vagabonds and murderers. But we Greeks are not so thoroughly virtuous. We look at the klephts from the mountains and we remember how they fought in our War of Independence. And so we see a little of the hero in the brigand chieftain as well as a little of the villain.'

For a moment it seemed as if the professor might continue the argument, but he was mollified by the conciliatory note in Rallis's voice. He examined the unfurled map on the table.

'I can only repeat, Rallis, that we know the risks.' He pushed back the inkstand slightly to reveal a little more of the map. 'We will not allow them to interfere with our plans but we will acknowledge that they exist and we will act accordingly. We must not travel in a large group. Only the five of us in this room will go. I assume that you are intending to bring along the giant who stands behind me?'

'Andros will be worth, as you say, a weight in gold.'

'Five will be enough. There will be safety in numbers but, paradoxically, the safety will lie in small numbers.'

'And what shall we carry with us?' Adam asked, relieved that the discussion had returned to practical matters.

'Our baggage must be light. Each of us must have no more than can be strapped to the back of a horse or mule.'

'The professor is right,' Rallis said. 'We must not overload ourselves.'

'We will have our bags in which to sleep. We will carry what food we can. Cheeses and bread. Smoked meats. We will need little else. A book or two, perhaps.'

'Bottles of wine?' Adam suggested.

'We can live a few days without the pleasures of the grape. It will be more important to have medicines. Quinine, for example. We must have quinine or we run the risk of being racked with fever.'

'I ain't spent a week without a drink since I was a nipper.' Quint, still standing guard next to the door, was again moved to contribute to the discussion. 'It ain't natural. Or healthy.'

'Many things that are wholesome in one country, my dear

Quintus, are deleterious in another.' The professor had entirely recovered his good humour.

'Not liquor,' Quint said, disbelievingly.

'You will recall from our days in Salonika that the spirits to be found there were not always beneficial to your constitution.'

'If you mean, they give me some stinkin' 'angovers, I ain't goin' to argue. But a week without a drink is more than a man can stand.'

'You will have to learn the arts of abstinence, Quint,' Adam said. 'It will not be beyond the capacity of a resourceful man.'

The manservant retired once more into sulky silence.

'We need someone to gather together the equipment we shall be taking,' his master continued.

'I think we can leave that to the man who knows the city better than we do.' Fields waved a hand amiably at Rallis, who bowed in response. He had now, it seemed, become the very man on whom the proposed expedition could depend.

'And what of a guide to the land beyond the border?' Adam asked. 'Shall we not require a dragoman?'

'Rallis can be our dragoman,' Fields said. 'We shall need no other.'

'I shall be honoured to undertake the tasks you have entrusted to me.' The lawyer bowed again. 'Let us all meet again tomorrow and I will let you know what success I have had. Let us join together again at the Oraia Ellas. "Beautiful Greece". What better name for a café in which to drink a toast to the success of our expedition?'

* * * * *

Constitution Square was, as it seemed to be both night and day, a hive of activity. As he emerged from the hotel, Adam was immediately thrust into crowds of Greeks hurrying about their business. Crossing the square in the direction of the embassy building, he was accosted four times in the space of two dozen yards by beggars with hands outstretched for alms. It was one of the perils of looking so obviously English, he thought, as he waved them apologetically away. He made his way across town to the British embassy. He found a café, one that provided a clear view of the embassy entrance, and took a seat outside it.

He did not have to wait too long for what he had hoped to see. For an hour, a steady stream of visitors passed in and out of the embassy doors. At one point, he saw Samways walk up the stone steps to the main entrance, in animated conversation with another gentleman Adam recognised from the pews of St Paul's. Sitting on the uncomfortable chair the café provided and drinking two cups of its foul coffee, he watched as other men approached the embassy, on foot or by carriage, and entered its portals. He began to amuse himself by trying to guess the nationality of each visitor. The English, he decided, were easily distinguished, as were two men with identical imperial beards and expressive hands who were clearly French. Others were less readily identified. Adam was puzzling over a swarthy individual in European dress and red fez, who had marched confidently into the building, when he saw two women emerge into the square. One was dumpy and dressed in black; the other was Emily.

Looking carefully from right to left and back again, they made their way through the traffic and headed towards a tree-lined garden close to the square. Adam threw a silver half-drachma on the café table and hurried after them.

He caught up with the two women as, parasols raised to protect them from the morning sun, they approached a fountain amidst the trees and shrubbery. He raised his hat and bowed slightly to them.

'We meet again, Miss Maitland, I am delighted to say.'

The young woman did not look equally delighted by the encounter. She half turned away from Adam, as if searching for a means of escape from him. Finding none, she turned back and forced a smile to her face.

'You chance upon us taking the air, Mr Carver.' She waved her hand towards the sky. 'It is impossible to stay indoors on a day such as this, do you not think?'

'Some ladies I know would never venture out into the sun for fear of spoiling their complexions.'

'Oh, I have no anxiety on that count. I have my parasol.'

His hat in his hand, Adam could feel the sun beating down upon the top of his head.

'I am particularly delighted that we should meet in this way, Miss Maitland. I am eager to continue the discussions we have had in the past. Perhaps I could walk with you a while and we could speak. In private.' He glanced meaningfully at Emily's short, middle-aged companion. Was this perhaps her mother? The young woman had said that her mother was with her in Athens just as she had been in London, but Adam had never met her or seen her. This lady in black did not, however, look very motherly.

'Leave us, Jane,' the young woman said, after a moment's hesitation. 'I shall meet you by the statue over yonder in ten minutes' time.'

Jane gave Adam a hard stare. She made no attempt to move.

'Go, I tell you,' Emily said, more sharply. 'I shall be safe under this gentleman's protection.'

The woman in black turned, with a distinct flounce, and walked away from the fountain.

'Jane is my maid,' Emily explained. 'She has a peculiar care for my welfare.'

'Her diligence in her duties is to be admired.' Adam offered his arm. 'Shall we stroll beneath the trees?'

'There is a seat by the fountain. I would rather sit.'

Not waiting for any response, the young woman walked to the stone bench and sat primly on its edge. Adam followed and took a seat beside her. He had been rehearsing what he might say to her for much of the hour he had spent sitting outside the café, but now that the moment had come, all his fine words had left him.

'Well, sir,' Emily said, after the silence had grown awkward, 'what is it you wish to say to me?'

Her manner, so different to the warmth with which she had greeted him at St Paul's, was brusque. Could this be the same woman who had kissed him at Cremorne Gardens? Adam almost began to wonder if he had imagined the more intimate moments of their previous meetings. He felt himself even more at a loss for the right words.

'I am simply curious, Miss Maitland.'

'Curious, sir? Curious about what, pray?'

'I have never learned why you came to visit me that first day in Doughty Street. Why you wished to see me again at Cremorne Gardens. Why you left me so abruptly there. And now here you are in Athens. You are a woman of mysteries, Emily. May I call you Emily? And I long very much to solve some of those mysteries.'

The young woman said nothing. Her eyes gazed into the distance as if seeking out the mountains that surrounded the city on all sides.

'Will you not throw a little light on my darkness? Will you not tell me what you are doing here? Staying with Garland in the British Embassy?'

Emily remained silent for a moment. Then her head dropped into her hands and she began to cry.

'Oh, Adam,' she murmured through her tears, so quietly that the young man could scarcely make out what she said. 'You must not ask all these questions. I cannot answer them.'

'But do I not have a right to answers to them?'

'Perhaps you do, but I cannot give them.'

'Why, Emily? Why can you not give them?'

Her face still covered by her hands, the young woman shook her head. 'I cannot,' she said again. 'I cannot.'

'Your questions are upsetting the lady, Mr Carver.'

Adam looked up in surprise. Garland was standing over them. To his right, lurking several paces behind him, was the maid Jane. She had clearly seen fit, Adam realised, to go back to the embassy and summon Garland.

'I think your conversation with Miss Maitland is now at an end,' the MP continued. 'She must return immediately to her lodgings.'

'It is surely Miss Maitland's decision, sir, as to whether or not our conversation is over.' Adam stood and faced the older man. He was suddenly filled with what felt like righteous anger at his interruption.

He clenched and unclenched his hands like a boxer awaiting the fitting of his gloves.

Garland smiled grimly. 'I am the young lady's godfather and thus, in some sense, *in loco parentis*. I believe I am well within my rights to insist on an end to this questioning of her. But we will ask Emily herself.'

He looked down at his god-daughter, who was still sitting on the bench. She had pulled a white cambric handkerchief from her pocket and was dabbing at her eyes.

'Emily, my dear, do you wish to bring your conversation with Mr Carver to a conclusion?'

Without looking up at either Adam or her godfather, the young woman nodded. Garland held out his arm for her to take and she rose from the stone bench. The maid moved forward and picked up her parasol which had fallen to the ground. The three turned from the fountain and began to walk towards the embassy. Adam could do nothing but watch them go. At one point, Emily looked back at him, but at a distance of thirty yards, it was impossible to tell whether her expression was one of apology or outrage.

* * * * *

Adam returned to the Angleterre via the telegraph office. Since arriving in the Greek capital, he had found time to send two lengthy telegrams back to London. With the Dilessi murders still so recent, he felt certain that, although Sunman and his colleagues would have plenty of informants at work in Athens, one more might be welcome. This was confirmed by a telegram back from Whitehall encouraging him to stay in touch. So a third message, conveying what news and impressions he had gleaned from conversations with Rallis and others, was soon sent. When he returned to the hotel, it was to find it, or at least the floor on which he and his party were staying, in an uproar. Members of the staff were hurrying along the corridor, bumping into one another and shouting excitedly at no one in particular. Polly, the usually unflappable manager, was giving a good impression of a man tearing out his hair. In the centre of the hubbub was Professor Fields, standing outside the door to his room. He was stabbing his finger in the air and bellowing with anger.

'It's an outrage,' he yelled at the unfortunate Polly. 'I leave my room for no more than an hour. And it is invaded by thieves.'

Adam hurried to the professor's side.

'What has happened, sir? You must calm yourself.'

'Calm myself? Calm myself?' Fields was red with rage. 'I cannot calm myself when my sanctum has been defiled in this scandalous manner.'

'Defiled?' Adam was bewildered. 'What has been defiled?'

The professor, now rendered speechless by his fury, could only gesture towards his room. Adam pushed at the half-open door and went inside. The room had been ransacked. The bedding had been torn from the bed and thrown to the floor. The door to the vast mahogany wardrobe was open and the professor's clothing was strewn on the carpet in front of it. His leather travelling cases had been turned upside down. A writing desk by the window had been emptied of its drawers. So too had those of a bureau and a mirrored dressing table. The whole room looked as if a small tornado had recently swept through it, uprooting everything within and hurling it to the floor.

Polly had followed Adam through the door. The manager had recovered some of his customary sangfroid.

'It is terrible,' he said mournfully. 'In all my years here, we have not had such a terrible thing.'

'Has anything been stolen, Professor?'

Fields had now entered his room again. He marched over to the wardrobe and stooped to pick up one of his shirts from the floor. He threw it onto the dishevelled bed and grabbed at another.

'Has anything been stolen?' Adam repeated his question.

The professor waved the shirt in his hand like a flag of distress. His rage had dissipated. He now looked more forlorn than angry.

'I cannot be certain, Adam,' he said, 'but I think not.'

'They have taken no money? No papers?'

'There was little in the room worth the thieving.'

'The professor placed some items in the hotel safe,' Polly explained. 'It is, perhaps, a blessing that they were not here.'

'They are of little value,' Fields said, still awkwardly holding his shirt as if he could think of nowhere to put it. 'They would have been of no interest to anyone other than a fellow scholar.' He threw the second shirt to the bed and seemed to feel another burst of rage.

'It is not the loss of any object that is so infuriating,' he said. 'It is the thought of some wretch invading my privacy. I thought better of your establishment, Pikopoulos. Can any rascal off the streets of Athens simply march into the Angleterre and rifle through the possessions of your guests?'

Polly launched himself into a further round of abject apologies. Adam picked up one of the drawers from the writing desk, which had been left lying on the carpet, and slotted it back into place. He looked around in search of the other drawer.

'We could contact the gendarmerie, if you wish, Professor,' he said.

'A bootless exercise.' Fields waved the idea aside, much to the hotel manager's relief, Adam noticed. 'The *Chorophylaki* may be of use in chasing bandits through the Attic hills but they will prove of no value in a business like this.'

'I regret to say that the professor is right. They will show little interest in the matter.' Polly's anxiety at the thought of gendarmes trampling through his hotel and disturbing his guests was obvious. 'If nothing has been taken...' The hotel manager shrugged and left his sentence unfinished. Meanwhile, Adam had found the other drawer from the writing desk, hurled into a far corner of the room, and was now putting it back into position.

The professor was making short circuits of the room, occasionally picking up one of his scattered belongings and throwing it towards the bed. Some landed there, some fell back to the floor.

'I will send two of the maids to put your room once more into good order,' Polly said, making towards the door.

'There is no need,' Fields called after him. The manager stopped and turned towards the two Englishmen; he looked uncertain what he should do next to placate them. 'I prefer to do it myself.'

'As you wish, Professor.'

Polly bowed first to Fields and then to Adam before leaving the room.

* * * * *

Clouds of tobacco smoke and the sound of half a dozen languages greeted Adam as he pushed open the door to the Oraia Ellas. Quint and the professor followed him into the café. At a table to their left, a group of Italians shouted cheerfully, one to another. Further into the room, three young Frenchmen, students perhaps at the École Française d'Athènes, were engaged in heated political debate. As Adam passed, he heard one of them loudly expressing his disgust with the conduct of Napoleon III and his undying support for Gambetta. He looked about the large, rectangular room that was one of the great gathering places for visitors to the city. As always, the place was noisy and full. Slightly to his surprise, he could see none of his fellow countrymen amongst the crowd of the Oraia Ellas's customers. Equally surprising was the presence of so many Greeks. Usually, native Athenians left the café to the foreigners, but there was no mistaking the nationality of several knots of young men scattered about the room. A number of them were even dressed in the traditional embroidered jackets and white *fustanelles* that advertised old-fashioned Greek patriotism. Rather incongruously, two of the men so dressed were bent over a billiards table. Adam smiled to himself as he saw how clumsily the clothing forced them to play.

He gestured to one of the waiters behind the wooden counter and led the way towards the only unoccupied table in the place. Even in the short time it took for the Englishmen to make their way to it, Adam was aware of the unexpected hostility hanging in the air of the Oraia Ellas. The café was usually a haven for English visitors but the atmosphere today was significantly less welcoming than usual. He glanced towards his companions but neither Quint nor the professor seemed to have noticed anything different. A plump and extravagantly moustachioed waiter came over to their table, looking acutely uncomfortable, and then scuttled away with their order as quickly as he could. There was no doubt that something was amiss. One of the players at the billiards table had straightened up and was staring insolently at Adam, holding his cue as if it was a hoplite's spear. Across the noise and smoke, the young man stared back. Eventually, the Greek's eyes dropped and he returned to his game.

The door opened again and Rallis entered, accompanied by Andros, attracting the sort of half-admiring, half-astonished attention he got wherever he went. The professor waved and the lawyer, returning the greeting, began to push his way through the crowd.

'The Oraia Ellas is in its usual pandemonium, I see,' he said, as he took his seat. His giant servant, head almost brushing the ceiling, stood behind the chair.

'A better name for it would be Babel,' Fields said amiably. 'Because the language of all the earth is certainly here confounded. Everywhere I turn I hear a different tongue.'

'Not quite all languages today, however,' Adam commented. 'Do you notice we are the only English present?'

Rallis glanced around the room. Adam could see that the lawyer was also surprised by the absence of English faces.

'It is certainly unusual,' the Greek said thoughtfully. 'But it is not just *your* countrymen who are missing from the happy throng.' He nodded in the direction of the young Frenchmen. 'It is perhaps also lucky that the café has no German visitor today.'

'Ah, yes, the Gaul and the Prussian are currently at each other's throats, are they not?' The professor sounded delighted by the fact. 'The French, as I understand it from the newspapers at the Angleterre, have shown once again that, when it comes to martial affairs, their bark is worse than their bite.'

'The emperor has gone, I understand,' Adam said.

'He is no great loss to the stage of European affairs,' Fields said, seizing hold of the lapels of his jacket as if about to launch upon a lengthy disquisition on international politics.

'We've got company,' Quint said shortly, interrupting before the professor could begin.

The other three men looked up to find that one of the billiards players, the one who had glared so markedly at Adam, had left the game and was standing over them.

'I spit upon you English,' he said in English and then very nearly did so. Little yellow blobs of phlegm spattered across the wooden floor close to Adam's foot. The young man began to rise in outrage from his seat but Rallis stretched out his arm to hold him back.

'Do not rise to his bait, Adam. The man is drunk, I think.'

Certainly a strong smell of spirits had accompanied the Greek to the table. Rallis began to speak to him in his own language, very rapidly and very angrily.

The man responded with equal vehemence. Adam, still held back in his chair, could make out snatches of what he said. The names of Herbert and Vyner could be heard amidst the Greek. After a short burst of invective, the man turned on his heel and marched to the counter where the waiters tended the coffee urns. Only then did Rallis release his grip on Adam.

'I should have thrashed the impudent wretch, Rallis,' the young man said. He was enraged by the insult that had been offered him. Only in the distant days of his childhood, during an argument with the eight-year-old son of his father's housekeeper, had anyone ever spat at him before. 'Did you see what he did? Why did you hold me back?'

'I saw how he insulted you. But the Oraia Ellas is no place to fight.'

'Rallis is correct, Adam,' the professor said. 'We cannot indulge in brawling in public, no matter what the provocation.'

'Why was the man so exercised?' Adam turned and looked towards the counter where the Greek was laughing with two of his compatriots. Adam was tempted still to stride over to them and knock their wretched heads together. 'Did I hear something about this Dilessi business?'

The lawyer nodded. 'Since the killing of Mr Herbert and Mr Vyner, there has been much anger against the English.'

'Why the devil should that be?' The young man turned back to

Rallis. He had mastered his anger and was now more curious than enraged. 'It was the English who suffered. Herbert and Vyner were English. They were the ones who were kidnapped by bandits on a perfectly innocent journey to Marathon and then murdered by their captors.'

'Ah, but it is not as simple a story as you think, Adam. There is much resentment in Greece.'

'Resentment? Why should there be resentment?'

'The patriotic Greeks wish that their government should be strong and independent. They do not wish it to be – what do you say? – a puppet of other nations. And yet, as a consequence of the murders, the English say, "Jump!" and our government says, "Yes, sir," and jumps. The young firebrands – they do not like this.'

'We want only justice,' Fields said. 'Someone must pay for the deaths of Herbert and Vyner.'

'Yet, in pursuit of this justice, hundreds of Greeks are now harried or imprisoned in the countryside north towards Dilessi and here in Athens. Very nearly all of them are innocent. This man who insulted us, perhaps his father or his brother is one of those imprisoned.'

'I still cannot see that the English are anything other than victims in the whole sorry story' – Adam raised his hands in mock surrender – 'but I am prepared to drop the argument. Quint, go and find out what has happened to the coffee we ordered. The waiter has been gone long enough to prepare a banquet.'

Quint stood and made his way to the wooden bar where the waiters stood when they were not scurrying between tables with drinks. When Adam glanced over his shoulder a minute later, he saw that his servant had buttonholed the plump waiter who was gesticulating in either excuse or apology.

'The agitation will soon die away, Rallis,' he said. 'The men who actually killed poor Herbert and Vyner are under lock and key, are they not? All but they will be released, if they have not been so already, and the country will return to its usual state.'

'Perhaps.' The lawyer looked unconvinced. He seemed about to say more but there were sudden sounds of commotion from across the room. All over the café, faces turned towards their source. Quint was standing by the wooden counter, his fists raised. At his feet a figure in embroidered jacket and white *fustanelle* was doubled up and writhing on the ground. Fists still high, Quint backed slowly away from the coffee urns and towards the table where his friends were sitting. He kicked out at a chair in his path and it fell to the floor with a clatter. The sound was lost amidst the café's continuing uproar of voices. Most people had turned back to their drinks. Quint had now stepped backwards as far as the others. He lowered his fists.

'I had to knee him in the gooseberries,' he explained.

'So we gathered.'

'It was the same cove as gobbed at us. He'd been outside to relieve hisself. When he come back, he started on at me. He give me a shove in the chest, and he spoke 'arsh words about my mother.'

'You never knew your mother, Quint.'

'No,' the servant conceded, 'but as the monkey said when he pissed across the carpet, you've got to draw the line somewhere. So I give him something to bellyache about.'

'I'm not certain it's his belly of which he will be complaining,' Adam remarked. 'But I think perhaps we should forget our coffee.'

'I agree, my boy,' the professor said. 'I believe the time has come to beat a strategic retreat.'

The young Greek patriot, still clutching his groin, was being helped to his feet by his friends. From the four corners of the Oraia Ellas, other Greeks, slowly realising what had happened, began to converge on the injured man. Voices were raised in unmistakeable indignation. A dozen men started in the direction of the English party. Chairs were scattered as they moved purposefully forward. The first man to come within striking distance aimed a clumsy punch which Adam easily ducked. He returned the blow and had the satisfaction of seeing his opponent drop to the floor, holding the side of his face. But others were upon them. Adam glimpsed Quint, a stranger to the boxing code so recently introduced to England by the Marquess of Queensberry, kicking out at two assailants. Rallis and the professor were backing away from another half dozen, holding out their arms in placatory gestures. The lawyer was calling out to them in Greek. Some of the patriots had pulled apart two of the café chairs and were beating broken lengths of wood menacingly on the tables. One man swung a section wrenched from a backrest towards Adam's thigh, but he was able to dodge it and aim a swift jab at the man's nose. Another Greek leapt upon his back and began to pull at his ears and hair. Tugging furiously at the man's arms, Adam was able to roll him sideways and force himself free. He aimed a series of short blows at the man as he fell. He could hear Rallis, abandoning any attempt at peace-making, shouting to his towering servant to enter the fray. Adam was seized from behind and his arms held. Another Greek approached him from the front, grinning evilly. Bidding a reluctant farewell to fair fighting, Adam followed his manservant's example and kicked out. The man fell to the floor, clutching his knee. Adam pulled one arm free and elbowed the man behind in his stomach. With a whistling intake of breath, his assailant released Adam's other arm.

The young man heard the professor's voice calling out a warning and turned swiftly to his right but he was just too late. He was struck a glancing blow with half the broken leg of a chair and fell to the ground, momentarily stunned. Consciousness deserted him for the briefest of periods. For the span of little more than a minute he was adrift in a dream world of bright colours and enchanting music before a soothing voice, speaking accented but near-perfect English, brought him back to reality.

'There is a side entrance, sir.' It was the plump waiter, leaning over him. He smiled ingratiatingly. 'If you will follow me.'

'What of my friends?' Adam asked, pulling himself to his feet.

'They are already outside.'

The young man looked over towards the table where they had been sitting. Only Andros was there, standing amidst a chaos of broken furniture. He was in the act of throwing one of the few Greeks still upright in the direction of the Frenchmen. Most of the other patriots were lying on the floor. None showed any inclination to rise again in the near future.

'Just the tall one remains,' the waiter said.

'He does not appear to require my assistance.' Adam wiped his hand, bloodied from one of the punches he had delivered, across his brow. He staggered after the waiter, who made his way to a low green door hidden behind a curtain in the corner of the Oraia Ellas. It opened onto the busy street outside where his three friends gathered breath after the fray. None seemed harmed save Quint, whose knuckles were bleeding.

'Ah, you have been able to join us, Adam,' the professor said, running his hand through what little remained of his hair. 'We were just beginning to feel a little anxiety for your welfare.'

'Andros will have dealt with our attackers, I assume,' Rallis said, with perfect confidence in the ability of his servant to have done so.

'Achilles killing the Paionians by the Scamander River could not have presented a more terrifying spectacle than your giant, Rallis.'

'He is a gentle man for the most part but he is a dangerous one to annoy.'

As the lawyer spoke, there were sounds behind him. Crouching to use a door that seemed designed for men half his size, Andros emerged onto the street. He smiled and nodded his great head at his master.

'Shall we make our way to the Angleterre,' Rallis asked, 'now that our little party is complete again? I have yet to partake of my mid-morning coffee and I doubt that any of us will be welcome again in the Oraia Ellas in the near future.'

PART THREE

THESSALY AND BEYOND

CHAPTER THIRTY-TWO

Quint stared morosely at the mule. The mule stared back. Quint had a wealth of bitter and unhappy memories of mules from his first journey through Macedonia. He had an unpleasant feeling that one more was about to be added to them. In the early morning sunshine, the mule had uncomplainingly allowed him to load it with an assortment of packs and panniers but, once loaded, it had refused point blank to move forward. No kind of cajolement or threat could make it budge an inch. Now, as Quint watched, a long jet of yellow liquid hissed into the ground between the mule's back legs. It trickled down the slight slope on which the beast was standing and formed two neat pools around Quint's boots. He swore beneath his breath and looked across to where another mule was tethered. Beyond that equally obstinate animal, he could see the three horses on which the gentlemen of the party rode.

A dozen yards away, Adam emerged from the blankets in which he had wrapped himself the previous night. He had spent the hours of darkness turning from side to side in the hope that he might chance upon the one posture in which sharp stones did not make their presence felt. He had failed to find it. He had ended by gazing up at the stars. He had wondered whether there were any other creatures up there somewhere in the heavens looking down on the earth and, if there were, whether they were as uncomfortable as he was. He had finally drifted into a fitful doze an hour before sunrise. Now, barely two hours later, a new day was upon him. He yawned and, rising to his feet, trudged towards the small stream beside which they had set up their encampment.

The giant Greek, Andros, as impassive as a cigar-store Indian, was already standing by the water. He was gazing to the north-east in the direction in which they would have to travel that day. He turned as Adam approached.

'*Kakos dromos*,' he said briefly and then walked away.

'A bad road, eh?' Adam said to himself. 'Well, we have little choice but to follow it.'

In the distance, about a quarter of a mile away, he could see Rallis and Fields, the other two members of their little party. The professor, as so often, appeared to be delivering a lecture. Adam could hear the sound of his voice but could not distinguish what he was saying. The lawyer was listening, his head politely inclined towards that of his companion. Adam crouched down by the stream and cupped his hands in it. He poured the water over his head and allowed it to course through his hair and down on to his chest. Refreshed, he stood up and made his way back towards the camp. Quint was still struggling to instil obedience in the mule.

'This bleedin' beast is aimin' to be the death of me,' he said as Adam approached.

'You must learn to have faith in the poor creature. It is behaving so wilfully because it is aware that you do not trust it.'

The animal lashed out a back leg and both men leapt sideways to avoid it.

'That mule has a sly look in its eye,' Quint said flatly. 'It ain't a mule a man *can* trust. And what's more, it's a mule as pisses pretty much where the 'ell it wants.'

'Mules are intended by nature to be intractable beasts,' Adam said complacently. 'The best one can do is cajole them in the direction you wish them to go. There is no point in trying to coerce them, Quint. And there is certainly no point in endeavouring to control their habits of urination.'

'That's what you say. But you ain't the one who's spent the last half-hour wading about in mule piss.'

'You have my sympathies, Quint.' Adam yawned and stretched

his arms. He did not seem unduly concerned by his servant's troubles. 'However, I cannot think seriously of anything until I have partaken of breakfast. Where is the bread? And the smoked meat?'

'On that mule's back,' the servant said, with noticeable satisfaction. 'The rest of us ate ours an 'our gone. While you was still snoring like an 'og.'

'Well, the victuals and viands must be unpacked. I shall have to breakfast alone.'

'Ain't no time. The professor wants to be on the move. That's why I'm lockin' 'orns with this bleedin' mule.'

Fields and Rallis had returned to the camp and were saddling their horses. The lawyer's servant, who had ambled with giant strides beside the horses the previous day, was awaiting his master's orders to set off once more. Adam looked to where he had left his tangled bedding in order to walk down to the stream. It was no longer there. While he was washing, Quint had folded the bag and blankets and strapped them to one of the mules. Both of these beasts, even the most troublesome of the pair, now appeared anxious to move.

'Come, Adam,' the professor shouted, already on horseback. 'We have many miles to go before noon.'

The young man sighed. There was no help for it. Breakfastless, he mounted his own horse and the expedition headed off towards the north-east.

They had left Athens a week earlier. On the first day, they had travelled by the newly finished railway line from the Greek capital to its port of Piraeus. There they had taken a boat. Sailing southwards, they had rounded the tip of Attica and turned north. With the island of Euboea rising mountainously to starboard, they had continued to sail towards Chalcis, the port on the narrow strait of Euripus. Negotiating the waters around the port, they had emerged into a huge bay with a distant view of Mount Pelion. 'Where Achilles was taught by Chiron,' the professor had been eager to tell the others. 'We are approaching the land of centaurs and lapiths.'

At the port of Volos, nestling beneath the slopes of Pelion, they had disembarked in the clear light of early morning. Turkish officials had hurried to intercept them, apparently intent on causing the maximum amount of inconvenience, but vigorous waving of the papers the professor possessed in front of the officials' noses, in conjunction with the judicious use of baksheesh, had limited the delay to a few hours. Just as he had promised back in Athens, Rallis had arranged for men to be waiting near Volos with mules and horses. Adam had briefly wondered how the lawyer's influence could make itself felt across the border with European Turkey, but the proof that it could was in front of his eyes. He had pushed the question to the back of his mind. Within a few hours more, they had climbed clear of the town. They could look back to the bay where they had landed and see its blue waters dotted here and there with the white sails of fishing boats. With the horses and baggage-laden mules, they had travelled nearly twenty miles on the first day before they had decided to make camp.

'We are well beyond the frontiers of liberated Greece,' Fields had said with great satisfaction.

Now, on the following morning, as Adam's empty stomach rumbled and Quint continued to mutter about mules beneath his breath, they made their way further into Thessaly.

Both Adam and Rallis were wearing English shooting jackets and broad-brimmed wide-awake hats. Quint had a shapeless canvas cap thrust onto his head. The professor had purchased in Athens a large white umbrella to shield him from the sun but he was finding it difficult to combine holding his reins in one hand and the umbrella in the other. He often rode bareheaded for an hour or more. Adam worried about the effects the heat might have upon him, but Fields showed no signs that he was troubled by it. As time passed, the younger man found himself marvelling anew at the stamina and endurance of the Cambridge scholar. At least twenty years older than any of his companions, the professor showed few signs that age was slowing him.

For more than an hour that morning they travelled through countryside where the roads were all but effaced. The fields had been left to return to an uncultivated state and the houses and villages were deserted. They saw no one.

'What has happened here?' Adam asked, but neither the professor nor the Greek lawyer could give him a conclusive answer.

'Perhaps the Turkish landlord has driven his peasantry from the land,' Rallis suggested.

'Why would he do that?'

'The Turks are often cruel masters. That is why we Greeks wish to be free.'

'I am not at all certain that that is the case, my dear Rallis,' Fields said, prepared as ever for argument. 'Not unnaturally, you believe that your fellow Greeks on this side of the border are all yearning to join your new nation, but I remain unconvinced. As long as they pay their taxes and commit no open crime, I suspect that the Greek subjects of the Porte are as happy with their government as those of their fellows who are ruled from Athens.'

For a moment, it seemed to Adam as if Rallis might dispute the professor's statement but he remained silent.

The party stopped for lunch under the shade of a group of plane trees. Horses and mules drank from the stream which ran past it. With the exception of Fields, who settled himself at the foot of one of the planes and opened a book, the men began to unload the saddlebags from the drinking beasts. After half a minute, Andros paused as he reached across the largest of the horses to unfasten its saddle. The huge Greek spoke briefly to Rallis and pointed towards the horizon. Rallis, shading his eyes against the sun, looked in the direction his manservant was indicating.

'We have visitors, gentlemen. There are men on horseback coming across the plain.'

Adam and Quint both turned from the saddlebags they had lifted to the ground and looked up across the sun-scorched landscape. The professor, either because he was oblivious to any danger the visitors might present or because he had not heard the Greek's words, continued to read his copy of Thucydides.

'Who are they?' Adam asked.

Rallis shrugged. 'Who can say? I think we are many miles from any village.'

Adam stood and watched the small group of riders. The sharp eyes of Andros had been able to pick them out from the landscape before anyone else, but now they were clear to all the travellers. Even Fields had lifted his eyes from his book and was following the horsemen as they approached in clouds of dust.

'Are they brigands?'

'I know no more than you, Adam,' Rallis said. 'We must hope not.'

'Should we make a run for it?'

'It would be pointless. We have only three horses for five men. And the mules could not move at a pace sufficient to escape. These men, whoever they are, will be with us in ten minutes.'

Rallis's judgement of time was a good one. Almost exactly ten minutes had passed when the riders, shouting and yelling to one another, pulled up their horses twenty yards from the trees. There were ten in the party, all of them looking like a cross between a pantomime villain and a scarecrow. Each man carried a miniature arsenal of small arms at his waist, a *yataghan* and a pair of pistols at the least thrust into his belt. All had long black hair which hung down to their shoulders in bedraggled tresses.

A man in a dirty white capote and breeches who appeared to be the leader spurred his horse forward and began to address Rallis in a loud and threatening voice. His followers crowded behind him, bellowing approval of his words and occasionally brandishing their guns in their air.

'What is the man saying?' Fields asked impatiently. He had hauled himself to his feet as their visitors clattered into the camp and thrust his volume of Thucydides unwillingly into his jacket pocket. 'He speaks such a barbarous dialect I can barely catch a word in three.'

The leader, urged on by his comrades, continued to roar his threats at the travellers.

'Oh, that the language of Homer and Pindar should descend to this!' the professor remarked to no one in particular. 'If I am not mistaken, he seems to be talking a great deal about blood and death and the valour of his ancestors.'

'He is certainly modelling his behaviour on that of a brigand chieftain in a Drury Lane melodrama,' Adam remarked. 'He could not have seen one in this desolate spot, could he? Surely no company has come this far on tour?'

The brigand chief was now pointing at the professor and was directing his words at him. Fields looked at the Greek as if he was an exceptionally dim student he was obliged to tutor.

'No, it is useless. I simply cannot understand enough of this ruffian's Greek to make sense of it,' Fields said. He seemed to imply that the ruffian was entirely to blame for this.

'He has been saying that his family have lived on this land for generations,' Rallis translated. 'He has also been saying that foreign dogs should not trespass on his lands. These things are probably not true. It is not his land, I think.'

'He certainly does not look like a farmer,' Adam remarked. 'What else does he say?'

'Now he says, "You foreign dogs are in our hands. Your money is ours. Your blood is ours."'

There was another impassioned burst of Greek from the man in the white capote.

'"I am the pasha here. I am a king to rule over English milords."'

'He knows we are English, then,' Adam remarked.

'If he knows we are Englishmen, he knows we are not men with whom to trifle.' Fields sounded exasperated that something as trivial as the arrival of ten heavily armed men should be holding them up. 'Tell him to be on his way. And to take his ragamuffin band with him.'

The leader of the band now made a gesture, first towards the mules and the horses and then towards the saddlebags.

'He wishes to inspect the baggage,' Rallis said.

'The impudence of the man!' Fields exclaimed. 'You will tell this rogue that—'

'Silence!' Rallis's sudden cry was the more surprising because of the studied politeness with which he usually spoke. 'I will tell him nothing. This is not a game that these men play. It is for us to listen, not to tell. And to obey.'

'He is right, Professor,' Adam said, placing a restraining hand on Fields's arm as the older man made to move towards the bandit chief. For a moment, it seemed as if Fields might continue to protest but he subsided into glowering silence.

The bandit chief shouted abrupt instructions and two of his men dismounted. They walked over to where the bags were lying on the ground and opened them. Within moments, all Quint's work that morning in packing the bags was undone. Meanwhile, another three men had also stepped down from their mounts and moved to where the horses and mules were tethered. They began to examine the beasts, prodding at legs and slapping flanks.

Rallis called out to the leader of the group. The man jumped down from his horse and strolled over to where the lawyer stood. He laughed and slapped him so heartily on the back that Adam could see Rallis stagger beneath the blow. The Athenian said something else and the man laughed again. Together the two of them walked away towards the shade of one of the plane trees. There they remained while the ransacking of the bags and the assessment of the horses continued. After five minutes, Rallis walked back to his companions, followed a few paces behind by the brigand.

'Put smiles upon your faces, gentlemen,' the Athenian said as he approached. 'I have told our friend here that we bear him nothing but goodwill.'

The travellers now stood, wreathed in smiles, as the brigand and two of his most ruffianly companions came closer. Even the professor twisted his face into a ghastly simulacrum of cheerfulness. The chief of the supposed bandits leered amiably as he approached.

'His name is Lascarides,' Rallis went on. 'He is at pains to assure me that he is an honest man. His colleagues are all honest men.'

'Damn grinning scoundrels, the lot of them,' Fields said, although, Adam noticed, he was careful to keep his mask of genial greeting in place.

'However, they require our horses. They apologise for the inconvenience but they insist that we hand over our mounts.'

'We appear to have little choice in the matter,' Adam remarked.

'None whatsoever,' Rallis said.

Lascarides, now beaming from ear to ear as if he had just chanced upon a long lost brother, approached Adam and chucked him under the chin. Adam instantly made as if to strike the man a blow but, recalling their situation, he restrained himself and merely widened his mirthless smile. The Greek laughed.

Beneath his fixed grin, Fields was almost beside himself with fury.

'Are we to allow this to happen?' he said, forcing out his words like a novice ventriloquist making his first appearance on stage. 'Are we going to stand by and do nothing while this ridiculous, tatterdemalion villain and his crew of scarecrows walk off with our horses?'

There was a burst of rapid chattering from Lascarides.

'The wretch really does speak a version of Greek no gentleman could possibly understand,' Fields dropped his pretence of grinning and spoke out loud. 'What does he say, Rallis? Something about trees and guns?'

'He says that he will tie the old man to the tree and get his men to use him for shooting practice unless he shuts up,' Rallis translated impassively. 'He is weary of hearing the old man's voice.'

'The impertinence!' Fields exclaimed and then fell silent.

Lascarides and his men now wasted no time in further threats or intimidation. Three of them hitched the horses they had commandeered to their own mounts and they all prepared to depart. Lascarides tipped his hat ironically at the professor. One of his followers yelled and shot his pistol in the air. The bandits wheeled their horses about and cantered away.

The travellers watched as they disappeared into the distance. Shouts and outbursts of raucous laughter drifted back to them as they turned their attention to the ruins of their campsite. No more than half an hour had passed since Andros had first drawn his master's attention to the riders approaching.

'At least they did not kill us or kidnap us,' Adam remarked.

'They thought we were madmen,' Rallis said. 'I told them we came from Athens to look for ancient writings. They decided we were insane. And who would kill lunatics?'

'Or pay a ransom for them?'

'Exactly.' Rallis smiled. 'They were particularly certain that the professor was one who had lost his mind.'

'Why did they not steal the mules as well as the horses?'

Rallis shrugged. 'Too much trouble to take them. Too little profit to sell them. Who knows?'

Andros and Quint repacked the saddlebags and loaded them on the mules. With the horses gone, the beasts that were left were doubly laden. There was no chance now for any of the party to ride. All five men would have to walk. Rallis looked up at the position of the sun and then stretched out his arm.

'That is the way we must go,' he said.

As they set off, they disturbed a covey of partridges which flew suddenly upwards with a noisy flapping of wings. Above them an eagle soared in the air currents, looking no doubt for the very prey the men had just put to flight.

Rallis strode out in front. Behind him Andros and Quint guided the mules. Adam followed them and the professor brought up the rear. Soon the group was stretched, Indian file, across the plain. For nearly thirty minutes they travelled in a silence broken only by an occasional bray from one of the mules. Then Fields increased his pace and caught up with Adam.

'What do you make of our Greek friend?' he asked, in a conspiratorial whisper.

'Of Rallis?'

'Who else? Should we trust him, do you think?'

Adam was taken aback by the question. Was it not the professor who had first argued that he was the ideal person to assist them in organising the expedition to Thessaly and beyond?

'I can see no reason why we should not.'

'You do not find the arrival of those thieving wretches today somewhat surprising?'

'We knew that we risked encountering bandits wherever we went in the countryside. Some of the regions in which we are travelling have an unpleasant celebrity for *klephti* and thieves and rogues of all kinds. But we made plans to evade them before we left Athens. *Rallis* made plans for us to evade them. Even so, we ran a risk. You are surely not suggesting that he deliberately arranged for those men to cross our path?'

'I merely suggest that our Greek friend should be watched. And what he says must be taken *cum grano salis.*'

'But you cannot think that he is conspiring against us?'

'I do not know what to think, Adam. I do know that those rogues appeared to have been informed that we were travelling from the bay of Volos towards Meteora. How else could they have come across us so conveniently in hundreds of square miles of terrain?'

'But what possible advantage could Rallis gain from the theft of our horses? Like us, he is now stranded miles from the nearest shelter. It makes no sense.'

'Little does make sense in this benighted country,' the professor said bitterly. 'Nothing has made sense in it for the best part of two millennia.'

'It is true that some of the most notable men of Athens have links with some of the greatest villains in the country. The Dilessi affair earlier this year proved that, if nothing else.'

'It's just as you say,' said Fields with sudden excitement. 'It's extraordinary. Politicians in the city are shamelessly and almost openly in league with brigands who roam the country looking for foreigners to kidnap and murder. It's as if Mr Gladstone were to be in charge of a gang of garrotters and send them out onto the streets of London to steal purses to add to the exchequer.'

'However,' Adam continued, striving to soothe the professor, 'there is not the slightest evidence that Rallis has any connection with brigandage. He is a lawyer and an amateur archaeologist – not a politician.'

Thirty yards ahead, the man of whom they spoke had stopped

and turned towards them. He waved his arm at the surrounding countryside.

'The beauties of Thessaly, gentlemen,' he shouted.

Adam returned his wave.

'You will notice,' the professor said, 'that our friend seems remarkably cheerful in the circumstances. Our loss does not appear to have hit him as hard as it has the rest of us.'

With this parting shot, Fields increased his walking speed again and caught up with Quint and the mules.

Left alone in the rear, Adam wondered if there could be any basis for the professor's sudden suspicions of the Greek lawyer. It was true that there had been times in the journey when Rallis had seemed uncertain of the path to take. There had been times when they seemed to be turning their faces in the direction of whichever point of the compass seemed momentarily appealing. There had been times, Adam was obliged to admit to himself, when he had thought that Rallis either did not know where he was leading them or, at the least, did not choose to tell them. And yet what purpose in travelling with them could the lawyer have other than the ones he had acknowledged? His love of his country's past. His desire to unearth more examples of its former glory. These provided him with his motivation, did they not? There was no evidence to support Fields's sudden distrust of Rallis.

CHAPTER THIRTY-THREE

or the next two days, they continued to make slow progress. Thessaly, Adam knew, was populous and prosperous. The plain was fertile agricultural land but the travellers came across little evidence of this. Rallis insisted that they keep off frequented roads and travel across rough country instead. They saw few people. On the first afternoon, they happened upon a wagon, with spokeless wheels of solid wood, which had been abandoned by the roadside. As they stood by it, they noticed a distant caravan of horses making its way along the road, laden with sacks and bags. Three tiny figures accompanied it, occasionally chivvying the beasts with sticks. Adam looked enquiringly at Rallis.

'Small traders carrying goods to the coast, perhaps,' the Greek said. 'We travel in a different direction. We will let them pass.'

That night they came near enough to a village to hear the furious barking of dogs in the distance and yet no one troubled them. They slept out under the stars once again.

On the second day, they came across the carcass of a horse with two black vultures circling above it.

'Those villains have left one of our beasts to die,' Fields exclaimed upon seeing it.

Rallis approached the dark shape on the ground, a kerchief in front of his face. Flies rose from the decomposing animal.

'It was dead long before we met Lascarides, Professor. It has been here a week at least.' The Greek lawyer looked up at the birds wheeling menacingly above their heads. 'Those are not the first to feast on the poor creature.'

'Why should it be lying out here?' Adam asked. 'We are surely many miles from the village where we heard the dogs last night. Who rode it and left it here to die?'

Rallis shrugged. 'Perhaps, like us, it had wandered far from home.'

Leaving the rotting beast behind, they moved on. The vultures, which had flown off as they examined the horse, returned. Another night in the open awaited the travellers, but as shadows lengthened and they began to think of stopping, Andros hailed his master. He pointed through the gloom to what seemed to Adam no more than a pile of stones in the distance. As they came nearer, the pile slowly transformed itself into a rude shed, its walls battered by the elements but its roof still intact. There was even a wooden door, hanging at a skewed angle on iron hinges. Rallis pushed it open and all but Andros made their way inside. Adam lit a candle and they watched as the flames flickered on the four walls.

'What is this place?' he asked.

'The hut of a shepherd, perhaps.' Rallis sounded uncertain. 'Or an outhouse from an old khan. A lodge for travellers.'

'There are no signs of any other buildings. The khan must have long gone.'

'Not only the khan,' Fields remarked. 'There is no indication that there is any road beside which it might have stood.'

'It may have been abandoned a hundred years ago,' the Greek said. 'Or more. A road may once have passed this way.'

'It is of no consequence to us now whether this was part of an old hostelry or the retreat of some lonely herdsman.' Adam held the candle high so it illuminated as much of the building as it could. Some of its stones had fallen to the ground but the walls were largely undamaged. 'The place is just about large enough to shelter us all.'

There was a silence, interrupted only by the sound of the mules moving restlessly outside. The men in the hut looked at one another in the dancing light of the candle.

'Quintus is unpleased by the idea, I see,' the professor said, after a moment. 'He is scowling like Stilicho when he looked upon the Goths.'

'I ain't a man to ask for much,' Quint said, sounding aggrieved. 'A comfy billet, a pint of pale ale and a twist of bird's eye baccy and I'm 'appy enough. But look at this bleedin' place.' He stretched out his arms as if to knock down the weathered walls of the hut. His shadow leapt against the stones. 'This ain't a bunk for a bleeding goat never mind a man.'

'You are too choosy, Quint,' Adam remarked. 'It is not as if you have much difficulty usually in entering the land of Nod. On previous nights, you have no sooner retired than you have been snoring loud enough to wake the Seven Sleepers of Ephesus.'

'I ain't going to get much chance of doing that if we bed down 'ere.'

'We have no choice, Mr Quint,' Rallis said, 'unless you would prefer to spend another night sleeping beneath the stars.'

Quint stared malevolently at the lawyer for a moment, as if the Greek was wholly responsible for dragging him from his urban comforts and out into this rural wilderness. Then he turned on his heel and marched out of the ruined building to join Andros and the mules outside. In the few short days they had been travelling, some kind of odd friendship had developed between the Londoner and the giant Attican. Andros spoke not a word of English. Indeed, he appeared to speak few words in his native tongue. Quint's Greek was limited to a small and ill-pronounced vocabulary connected to the supply of food, drink and sex. And yet the two men had discovered some common ground. Now they joined forces in unloading the mules and gathering together the materials for a campfire.

Later that evening, after they had eaten their frugal meal, all five men in the small expedition sat around the fire. The night was surprisingly full of the noises of animals. Snorts and screams and distant baying could be heard in the darkness on all sides.

'How are they off for wolves in this neighbourhood, do you suppose, Quint?' Adam asked teasingly. 'Will they venture into our poor shepherd's hut? Should we worry about being eaten as we sleep?'

'There ain't no wolves in this neck of the woods. Jackals, maybe.' Quint, reconciled by now to their accommodation, was not to be drawn. He tamped tobacco stolidly into his clay pipe. 'Anyways, it sounds more like wild hog than anything else. That ain't going to eat you. More like t'other way about.'

That night, despite the discomforts of their resting place and the sounds from the dark, Adam soon fell into a deep sleep. He dreamed more vividly than he had done for years. Strange, hallucinatory dreams in which he was back in Macedonia, digging up tombs long buried in the desolate hillsides. With his nails, he scrabbled at the soil to reveal cold stone coffins. When he pushed aside the lids of these coffins, faces from his past stared up at him from their depths. His mother, dead when he was a small boy, whom he could scarcely remember. His father, still apparently infuriated by the turns his life had taken. Charles Carver, the railway baron, had not been a happy man, his son now realised. His great successes as an entrepreneur had brought him little in the way of joy; the fraud and peculation which had ruined his company had also driven him to the point where he had believed self-destruction to be his only option. Adam was aware of how little he had known his father. Now, in the dream, Charles Carver's face was twisted with rage. He seemed to be shouting defiance at the fates which had propelled him first towards great success and wealth and had then plunged him into disgrace and despair.

Adam awoke with a start. He lay for a while, thinking of his father, and then turned his face towards the open door. It was still an hour or more to sunrise, but in the faint light of moon and stars that was drifting into the hut, he could see the shapes of his sleeping companions. Idly, he counted three and was about to fall asleep again when he realised that there should be one more. His eyes squinted in the semi-darkness as he strove to see who was in the hut. One of the party was definitely missing. He rolled out from under the blanket which covered him and began to make his way towards the door of the stone shelter. As he crawled past the other sleepers in the hut he could make out the giant form of Andros stretched beneath one wall. Next to him were Quint, snoring gently, and the professor. There was no sign of Rallis. It was only when he ventured outside that Adam located the missing man. The Greek lawyer was standing alone thirty yards from the hut. He was staring out into the darkness. Adam moved towards him.

'Rallis?' he hissed.

The Greek lawyer froze at the sound. Then he turned slowly in Adam's direction.

'It is a beautiful night, Mr Carver, is it not?' he said.

'What are you doing out here?'

'I could not sleep.' Both men were speaking in fierce whispers. 'I came outside to look at the stars.'

As Adam approached the Greek, he thought he saw, for the briefest moment, a light flicker far out in the night but no sooner did he look more intently in the direction from which it seemed to come than it disappeared.

'I have been picking out the shapes in the sky,' Rallis said. 'I have forgotten what you call them in English.'

'The constellations.'

'Con-stell-a-tions.' The Greek repeated the word, drawing out each syllable, as if this would help him now to remember it. 'It is from the Latin, of course. "Stars together", I think. But I have had enough of astronomy for the night and we will be disturbing our companions. Let us return to our beds. There is time yet to enjoy some more sleep.'

* * * * *

'Maybe he just went outside to water his nags,' Quint suggested the following morning when Adam told him of his encounter. Breakfast had been the swiftest of meals and the travellers were on their way less than forty minutes after rising. They had now left their resting place many miles behind them. Quint was leading the largest and most temperamental of the mules. His master was walking beside him.

'He claimed that he could not sleep,' Adam said. 'He was tempted outside by the beauty of the night.'

'Well, he ain't going to say, "Don't mind me, Mr Carver, I'm just 'aving a piss," now, is 'e? He ain't that kind of a bloke.'

'No, that is true. We do not all have the obsession with bodily functions that marks you out, Quint. But I did not get the impression that it was either the delights of nature or its demands that had driven him from our humble shelter. There was something else.'

'What was 'e doing then?'

'Looking out into the darkness.'

'What the 'ell for?'

'I do not know. A sign that someone else was out there?' The professor's suspicions about their travelling companion returned to Adam's thoughts. 'Do you suppose that our Greek friend has arranged for others to be following us?'

There was no opportunity for Quint to reply. As he opened his mouth, Adam reached out his hand to indicate that his manservant should be silent.

'Hush, Quint. What is that?'

A rhythmic drumming noise could be heard, echoing across the plain. At first, Adam thought the sound had only the one source but, as he continued to listen, it seemed as if it was travelling towards them from all the points on the compass. He found himself unable to guess what the drumming was or to judge exactly the direction from which it was coming. He turned and looked back at the professor but Fields, equally baffled, shrugged his shoulders.

'It is the *semandron*,' Rallis said, noticing their puzzlement.

'Ah, the *semandron*,' Fields said. 'Of course. I have read of it but I have never before heard it.'

'What is it?' Adam asked. 'I confess that I have never heard the word before.'

'The Greek Christians at these monasteries use it in place of bells, which were long forbidden to them by the Mahometans.' Fields dismounted from the mule he had been riding and stood by its side, listening to the echoing percussion of the *semandron*. 'It is a long wooden bar which they strike with hammers. It has something of a barbaric note, I feel.'

'It means that we are drawing close to the monasteries,' Rallis said. 'The sound of the *semandron* can travel many miles but I think, from its loudness, we must be near to them.'

Andros, pulling the last mule up a slight slope, joined them. All five men stood in the shade cast by a small grove of wild apple trees at its top and listened.

'Ain't a cheery sound, if you ask me,' Quint said. 'It fair puts the wind up you.'

'It is calling the faithful to prayer, Quintus.' Fields was standing almost on tiptoe, straining to locate the source of the drumming.

'Sounds more like it's calling 'em to the grave.'

As they spoke, the monk striking the *semandron* ceased to do so. The percussive noise came to an end and only the booming echoes of the final blow continued to reverberate in the air.

The men began to descend the slight rise. Emerging from the trees, they were thrust once more into the glare of the sun. Eyes dazzled, they could barely see the plains stretching ahead of them. Rallis was the first to recover his sight and his bearings.

'The monasteries of Meteora, gentlemen,' he said, throwing out his arm to point to the north-east. 'The monasteries that float in the air.'

Across the plain, perhaps two miles away, they could see some twenty or thirty outcrops of rock which arose, like giant stalagmites, from the ground and pointed towards the sky. Pyramids, obelisks, columns and monoliths of all shapes and sizes reared up from the ground. At this distance they looked like trees in some gigantic petrified forest. A village rested beneath the rocks, the roofs of its houses just visible amidst the shadows they cast.

'The monasteries are all in the village?' Adam was surprised. He raised his hand to his brow to shade his eyes, eager to make out more of their destination.

The Greek laughed.

'No, Adam. You must cast your eyes further up to heaven. That is just Kalambaka. The holy monasteries are much higher.'

Rallis pointed a finger at the shadowy buildings of the village and then raised it slowly to the sky, as if tracing the passage of a bird from one of the roofs to the pinnacle of one of the giant stalagmites.

'There,' he said. 'There is one of the monasteries we seek. I think it is Agios Stefanos although I cannot be certain from here. The other monasteries may be hidden from our view here.'

Adam stared in disbelief. At first, he could see nothing but the needle of rock itself. Only as his eyes grew accustomed to the distance and to the light could he make out what might have been a building perched precariously on its point. As he continued to look, he realised that there were others clinging to the sides or the summits of these strange stone obelisks.

' "Mountains that like giants stand/To sentinel enchanted land",' he quoted.

'Scott had not such prodigies of nature as these in mind,' said the professor. 'He was, as usual, singing the praises of his native land, was he not? And the Scotch, for all their boasting, have nothing to match this.'

'They're like bloody great skittles in a giant's bowling alley,' Quint said.

'More like the buttresses of some bizarre cathedral.' Adam continued to gaze in astonishment at the sight before him. How, he wondered, had he never before heard of this phenomenon of nature? 'Mr Ruskin himself would delight in their Gothic charms. But, surely, there is no mention of these extraordinary rocks in any ancient text.'

'The Greeks of Plato's day had little time for the wonders of the natural world, Adam,' Fields said. 'Who would know from their literature that in Athens the Lykabettos rises higher than the Acropolis?'

'The monks must be like the stylites of bygone centuries.' Adam was still lost in admiration of the rocks. 'Perched upon their pillars far above the temptations of the world.'

The professor was unimpressed. 'They are pious fools,' he said, 'wasting their lives in such isolation.'

'There are few of them left in Meteora,' Rallis said. 'Once there were hundreds of monks here. Now, I am told, most of the monasteries are deserted. And those that do still have inhabitants have but a handful. Even the Grand Meteoron, the holiest of them all, has only a score and most of them are old men.' He raised his hand to shield his eyes from the sun. 'But now we have seen our destination from afar, we must hasten to reach it.'

* * * * *

Hours passed before the travellers came near to the stone pillars, which from a distance had seemed to rise perpendicularly out of a sea of foliage. The sun was now high in the sky and beating down upon them. Closer up, it was clear that a labyrinth of smaller rocks and outcrops of stone had to be negotiated before the party could reach the foot of any of the main pinnacles. They began to clamber amongst the ruined architecture of the rocks, moving in and out of the shade the stone columns offered. Here and there, groves of mulberries and cypresses covered the ground between the pillars. Some small trees had even found a means of twisting their roots into crevices in the near-vertical rock and were growing green against the darker colours of the stone. Often the roots were invisible from the ground and it seemed as ifthe trees were suspended in the air, floating high above the travellers' heads.

After a short time, Adam stopped. Shading his eyes with one hand, he pointed with the other towards half a dozen black smudges up on the rock. 'There are caverns further up there,' he said. 'There is a ladder of some kind as well.'

Below one of the dark holes that peppered the cliff, a rickety wooden structure that could only be a ladder stretched down from the cave entrance to a ledge some sixty feet beneath it. It looked like the backbone of some strange creature that had died and rotted on the rock face.

'It is for a holy man,' Rallis said. 'He has turned his back on the world. He lives in the cave with only the eagles above him.'

'Good Lord, man.' Adam was shocked. 'Are you telling us that someone spends his life up there?'

'He prays there night and day. He beseeches the Lord to grant his soul eternal rest. Many have done so before him.'

'Much good it must have done them. Living like benighted troglodytes in holes in the rock.' Fields snorted with disgust, as if to suggest that this was only what he expected from those who adhered to the Greek version of Christianity. 'These monks are but a few steps away from pagan nature worship. Who knows by what process of reasoning they have persuaded not only themselves but others that they are leading holy lives?'

The travellers moved on, Adam looking back at the cavern entrance and wondering what could possibly drive a man to make his lonely home within it. They fought their way through tangled bushes and past fallen boulders. Eventually they emerged from the maze of rock and vegetation and stepped onto a square stone platform at the foot of what seemed a sheer cliff face.

'Up there. That is Agios Andreas,' said Rallis.

The others craned their necks upwards and could just catch a glimpse of a building perched on the top of the cliff.

'How the devil are we to reach it?' Fields asked.

The lawyer made no reply but nodded briefly to Andros. The giant Greek took several steps to the side, hauled out the ancient musket he kept strapped to his waist and fired a single shot into the air. The sudden sound of it, reverberating and echoing against the rock, made Adam start with surprise. For a moment, as the echo died away, there was no response. Then, from far above, like the cry of a bird circling in the air, came a voice. As they all strained their necks in peering up at the monastery, they could see what looked like a wooden shed projecting sideways from the rock. Adam could just glimpse a grey-bearded face staring down at them from some kind of door or window in it.

'He is asking who we are and what we require,' Rallis said, before shouting back at the monk in Greek. Adam could make out only the words for 'travellers' and 'friends'.

The monk disappeared briefly from view, but within a minute, he had returned and this time he was accompanied by two others, both similarly swathed in grey hair. All three were now calling down to the travellers and, as they did so, the door in the shed opened and a rope was flung out. Adam could see that the rope ran through a pulley, which was itself attached to the roof of the shed. Slowly the rope descended the cliff face until one end reached Adam and his companions below. Attached to it by an iron hook was a net. Rallis moved forward and unclasped the hook.

'They are fishers of men, these monks,' he said, spreading the net on the ground.

'Are we to be their fish?' Adam asked.

'It is our only way to the monastery. Each of us must sit in turn in the net. The net closes around. The hook is attached. The monks pull us up. It has been so for many hundreds of years.'

'Have they lost many fish in those hundreds of years?'

Rallis shrugged. 'Some, but not many.' He spoke briefly to Andros. The Greek shrugged off the white capote he wore around his huge shoulders and placed it in the net.

'Who will be the first to ascend the rock?' Rallis asked.

'Here is your chance to demonstrate your daring, Quint.' Adam gestured at the net. 'The monks await us.'

'I ain't going up in that contraption.'

'You have heard what Rallis has said. It is the only way we can get to the monastery.'

'I ain't being 'auled up in the air in a bleedin' net. It ain't natural.'

'Nor is descending into the bowels of the earth on the new underground railway from Paddington. But back in London I have known you to do it. Not once but several times.'

'Down in the ground ain't the same as up in the air.'

'Come, Quintus,' Fields said, 'one of us must be the pioneer in this venture. Why should the honour not be yours?'

Quint scowled at the professor, as if to suggest that the honour was one he would gladly relinquish, but at the same time he seemed to decide that further argument was fruitless. He moved to sit cross-legged on the capote, looking miserable but resigned to whatever fate might throw at him. Rallis took one of the corners and hung it over the large iron hook on the end of the rope. He did the same with each of the other corners until Quint was trussed like a turkey in the netting which dangled from the hook. He clung to the rope with his hands while both feet protruded through the holes. Rallis waved and shouted to the monks above and the net began its ascent. Almost immediately it began to spin and twist but slowly it moved further and further up the grey flank of the rock.

'Give our greetings to the abbot, Quint,' Adam called. 'Tell him we shall all join him for dinner.'

The distance from the ground to the monastery was more than 200 feet and, after only a short while, brief gusts of wind began to send man and net spinning around. There were shouts of alarm from below but Quint maintained a stoical silence. Looking up so far, Adam could not be certain but he thought that, at one point, he saw small plumes of smoke issuing from the tangled bundle. By some acrobatic feat, he decided, his servant had managed to light his pipe. After less than ten minutes, Quint's ascent was complete and he disappeared from sight.

The monks' net returned to the ground and Adam was the next to be hooked into it.

'You may wish to close your eyes,' Rallis said. 'It prevents the giddiness.'

'I think I shall keep them open. I have a fondness for seeing where I am going, even when I am curled up like a hedgehog.'

The monks above began to turn their windlass and Adam was tugged upwards. As he left the ground and was swiftly hauled a hundred feet into the air, he began to reflect on the ridiculousness of the position in which he found himself. There was little time, however, for such thoughts. He reached a point where, through the net, he could just catch a glimpse of his comrades below. At that moment the rope seemed to slip through monastic hands. Abruptly, he fell several feet before control was regained and he came to a halt with a stomach-turning jerk. He was still recovering from this shock when he heard the sound of a gun. His first assumption was that Andros had, for some reason, fired his musket again. It was only when a bullet ricocheted off the rock face that he realised someone was shooting at him. Twisting and spiralling in the monks' net, he was a more tempting target than a fish in a barrel. He heard the sound of another shot and flinched. The rock above his head shattered and splinters of stone cascaded into his hair and onto the shoulders of his jacket. Spinning in the trap the net had become, he strove to look first up at the monastery and then down to the ground below him. Shouts came from both directions. In his frantic efforts to see what was happening, Adam set the net spinning back and forth.

'Quickly, Quint,' he bellowed. 'Get them to pull me up more quickly.'

The face of the rock was suddenly upon him and he thrust his hands through the reticulations in the net in order to push himself from it. His knuckles grazed painfully against the cliff but he had no time to think anything of it. He spun out again into mid-air and braced himself for the awful possibility of another shot. He could almost feel the bullet hurtling into his soft flesh and the terrible pain it would inflict.

'Get me moving, Quint,' he yelled again and, to his intense relief, he felt the net jerk and begin to rise once more. He could hear more noise from the ground and thought he heard Rallis's voice shouting in Greek. Slowly, so slowly that it seemed to Adam as if the minutes were stretching into hours, he was pulled towards the monastery.

Trussed in the net and half-dazed from the buffeting he had received as he collided with the rockface, Adam was finally brought level with the entrance. Hands reached out to haul him in like a bale of goods at the West India docks and he was deposited on the wooden floor. He looked up. A man was peering down at him. The man was dressed in a long blue serge gown and had a straggling beard and moustache which merged in a wild hedgerow of white facial hair. Out of the hair stared two glinting eyes.

'I am Brother Demetrios,' said a voice from the hedgerow, in

Greek. 'Welcome to the monastery of Agios Andreas.'

The monk released the net in which Adam was held and he tumbled out of it. As he got to his feet he saw Quint, dishevelled and anxious, standing amidst a semi-circle of Brother Demetrios's fellow-monks, all bearded and clad in black. His manservant moved towards him and began to brush down his clothes.

'Told you travelling in a bleedin' net weren't natural,' he said. 'And why the 'ell was that lunk of a Greek shooting off 'is musket?'

'It wasn't Andros. Somebody was shooting at me. Somebody further down the path we ascended earlier in the day.'

Adam waved Quint away and turned to his hosts. They bowed politely to him, their hands laid upon their hearts. He returned their greeting, conscious that he was shaking with the shock of his journey up to their home.

CHAPTER THIRTY-FOUR

'ut who was taking potshots at me, Rallis?'

Another half-hour had passed and two other members of the party had been hauled up the rock-face and manhandled into the monastery. Andros had been left at the bottom with instructions to find a temporary resting place for the mules and much of the baggage in the village of Kalambaka.

'He will come up to Agios Andreas later,' Rallis had announced when he had arrived at the top. 'The monks will have time to recover from their exertions in bringing us to their home. They will need all their strength to fish Andros up from the foot of the rocks.'

The lawyer, now faced by Adam's question, shrugged as if the identity of any would-be murderer was of no great significance.

'One of the rogues who ambushed us, perhaps. Andros saw him and ran after him but the man was too quick. He had a horse waiting for him further down the rocks.'

'He might have killed me.' Adam was indignant as much as distressed.

'He fired his rifle from far away. Only the very best of shots could have hurt you.'

'That may be true, but two bullets at least struck the rocks not too far away from me.'

'Perhaps the man was from Kalambaka. He was trying to scare you. To scare *us*. They do not always like strangers in these villages of European Turkey.' Rallis waved his hand, his demeanour suggesting that Adam was making altogether too great a fuss about the incident. 'But he did not harm you. He did not shoot again. And now we are safely delivered to our destination. The monastery of Agios Andreas.'

Adam thought momentarily of pursuing the subject but there seemed little point. He could not very well ask the monks to winch him back to the ground so that he could chase some rifle-wielding will o' the wisp across the plains of Thessaly. The Greek lawyer, it seemed, did not take the shooting seriously. So why should he? Perhaps Rallis was correct. Perhaps it had been a villager with a dislike of foreigners. Perhaps the intention *had* only been to frighten him. Adam decided to put the incident from his mind. Instead, he looked around the place which had been the goal of their party since they had left Athens.

Covering just over an acre, the monastery of Agios Andreas stood on the very summit of the pillar of rock. It consisted of a church, side chapels, monks' cells and other buildings which surrounded a central, irregularly shaped courtyard. The whole monastery looked like a miniature village, its houses huddled around the church.

'How do the monks live up here, Rallis? How do they get their food? Their water?'

'The water is in cisterns cut deep in the rock. They fill with rain during the winter.' The lawyer motioned to a stone structure in the centre of the courtyard which Adam could now see was some kind of well. 'As for their food, it is hauled up on the ropes as we were hauled up.'

'And how in heaven's name did the first monks make their way up here?'

'The monks believe that Saint Athanasios – the holy man who built the first of the monasteries – did not climb the rock. He was carried to the top by an eagle.'

'That would be a more convenient means of transport than any other,' Adam admitted. He made his way across to the stone well and peered into its depths. He could see what might have been the faint glint of light on the water below.

'They tell another story about Athanasios,' Rallis went on. 'That he travelled at first only halfway up the rock. He lived in a cave there. But soon he saw demons flying about the entrance to his cave. So he went to the very top of the mountain, where the demons could not follow him.'

'They couldn't fly that high, eh?' Adam turned away from the well.

'It would seem not.'

'So whatever other perils we might face here, we need not worry about demons.'

Rallis laughed.

'It was another rock on which Athanasios built. Not this one of Agios Andreas. But the principle is probably the same.'

Adam nodded his head politely at the monks, who were still gathered round the winding equipment which had hauled him up the rockface. Bearded and bashful, the inhabitants of Agios Andreas were looking at their visitors as if they had never seen such strange and unaccountable men before. Perhaps, Adam reflected, they had not.

'We will meet the rest of the population at dinner, I suppose. Minus demons, of course.'

'This *is* the population, Adam. Except, I think, for the *hegumenos*. There are fewer than ten *caloyeri*, ten holy men, at Agios Andreas,' Rallis said.

'So few!' Although he remembered what Rallis had said about the depopulation of the monasteries, Adam was still surprised. 'How can they survive?'

'Perhaps they will not. I doubt there are more than fifty *caloyeri* in all of the monasteries together. Perhaps when they all die, there will be no more monks at Meteora.'

'But there are young novices, are there not? When I was bundled from the net I saw one lad standing behind the monks. He looked no more than twelve.'

'Some of the young boys from the village come up to the monastery to learn to read and write. They are the servants of the *caloyeri*. He must have been one of those.'

One of the monks had approached them and was trying shyly to attract their attention. He spoke to the lawyer, his words a jumble of half-familiar Greek words uttered so swiftly and in such a marked accent that Adam was unable to follow them. Rallis, it seemed, had no such problem.

'His name is Theophanes,' he interpreted for Adam. 'He will show you and Mr Quint and the professor to rooms where you can rest.'

Theophanes beckoned to Adam and his companions, who had both been engaged in peering over the monastery's perimeter wall at the plain beneath. Leaving the lawyer, the three men followed the monk through an arched opening into one of the buildings off the courtyard. A short flight of stone steps led upwards, which through the centuries had been worn away by the feet of generation after generation of long-departed monks. As they began to climb it, Fields gave a short cry and fell to his knees. Quint, following close behind, nearly tumbled over him. The professor peered downwards in the gloomy light of the stairwell.

'Most interesting, most interesting,' he said, removing his glasses and crouching even lower to examine one of the steps.

Brother Theophanes had stopped when Fields did and was looking down at him with polite puzzlement. Adam smiled at the monk as if to suggest that the professor's action was odd but not entirely unexpected.

Fields struggled to his feet. 'Fascinating, Adam, simply fascinating. It is a burial stele. I can make out the words "Attyla, daughter of Eurypothus".'

'How did it come to be here?'

'I have no idea. I can only presume that the monks in the Middle Ages, when they were building this place, brought it up from the plain. I must look at the other steps.'

Adam glanced at the monk, who was wearing the bemused expression of a courteous man faced by the inexplicable behaviour of foreigners.

'I think that task must be postponed a while, Professor. Our host is patient but we cannot keep him waiting for too long.'

'Ah, of course, you are right.' Fields was unmistakably disappointed but he waved his hand to Theophanes to indicate that he was ready to move on. 'Another time, perhaps, another time.'

* * * * *

As midnight passed, Quint and Adam prepared for a nocturnal excursion. Brother Theophanes had led the travellers to the sparely furnished stone cells which were the monastery's guest rooms. Adam had explained to their host that they were weary and wished to rest. They required no food. They needed only to sleep. The day was drawing to an end and darkness had already fallen. The monk, accustomed to retiring early to bed himself, had seemed to understand. Hand on his heart, he had bowed and left them. After a little conversation, the professor, Quint and Adam had gone their several ways to their own rooms. Some hours later, the manservant, obeying whispered instructions he had been given earlier, had tapped on his master's door. Now the two of them stood in Adam's room, ears cocked for the sounds of other people moving about, and prepared to reconnoitre the monastery.

'We must not spend too long in exploration,' Adam said. 'But I cannot resist the temptation to escape the eagle-eyed scrutiny of the monks and look at the place myself.'

'Ain't some of these bearded buggers going to be still awake?'

'They will all rise in the night at least once to perform their devotions. Probably several times. But they will be asleep now. I think we have an hour or two in which to investigate the monastery. Lead on, Quint.'

The manservant opened the door and peered out.

'What can you see?' Adam asked.

'Sod all. It's as black as Newgate's knocker out there.'

'There will be light in the courtyard. Light from the moon. Let us take candles for the corridors.'

Adam crossed the room and took the candles from the two iron sconces attached to the far wall. He handed one to Quint and the two men crept furtively into the passageway outside.

'Which way?' Quint hissed.

His master motioned to the left and they began to shuffle in that direction. They passed the doors to other rooms and then came to the top of the flight of stone steps they had ascended earlier in the day. Even with the light from the candles, they found it difficult to see where they were going and Quint, in the lead, nearly stumbled and fell before he realised where he was. He cursed briefly and began to edge down the stairs. At the bottom, the archway opened onto the courtyard, which as Adam had predicted was lit by the moon. Quint cupped his hand protectively round the flame of the candle but the night was so still that he had scarcely need to do so.

'Through the archway, Quint,' Adam whispered. 'Keep moving to the left. Let us see what other buildings face onto the court.'

The servant made his way through the next arched doorway, his master close behind him. They found themselves in what was clearly a chapel. It was tiny, only a few yards square, but its walls and roof were covered in paintings. In the flickering light of the candles, Adam could make out the figure of Christ in majesty, surrounded by what were, he guessed, images of the saints. Peering more closely, he could just see the Greek lettering that identified them all. Even in the poor light, the rich colours the painter had applied three centuries earlier still glowed. One saint had a model of a church in his hand and was holding it out as if inviting the viewer to admire its architecture. As Adam turned to the left, an image of the Virgin and Child swam into view, the pudgy infant grasping the middle finger of its mother's hand. She stared serenely into the middle distance. Fields would claim these paintings were nothing but primitive daubs, he thought, and yet there was something about them that held the attention. Numinous and otherworldly, they lodged themselves in the imagination.

A smell of incense percolated through the chapel. Adam moved his candle again to look at the next wall. Here the painting appeared to depict the martyrdom of two saints. On the left of the picture, a man hung upside down from a gallows while another, not much more than a boy, was stabbing him in the neck. Blood was dripping to the ground. To the right a gridiron stood over open flames and another saint, recognisable by his halo, was strapped to it. Given his circumstances, he seemed to be remarkably cheerful. There was even the slightest hint of a forgiving smile on his face, as if he pitied his tormentors and wished he could point out to them the uselessness of torturing one of God's elect.

The last of the paintings the candles revealed before the two men turned and left the chapel was the *pièce de résistance*. It was a depiction of the Last Judgement. At the bottom a huge and hideous devil was sitting in a pool of fire and gnawing upon the bodies of several unfortunates. Around him capered a troop of merry imps armed with tiny tridents who prodded the damned as they milled aimlessly around the flames of hell. Up above sat the souls of the blessed, appearing unsurprisingly smug.

'Look at them little bastards with the forks,' Quint whispered. 'They're 'appy as pigs in shit.'

'They do look as if they are enjoying their work, don't they?' Adam agreed. 'But we cannot stay to admire their devotion to duty. We must move on.'

They left the chapel and entered once again the small, paved courtyard which looked to be the centre of the monastery. In the dim light from the half-moon they could now make out two cypress trees in the far corner. Two more arched stone doorways opened off the courtyard. Quint looked briefly into the first one they approached.

'Nothing 'ere,' he said. 'It's just another door into the room where we come in. I can see the winding gear as fetched us up.'

The next building had the outward appearance of another chapel. The two men stood outside its door, which appeared to have been designed for exceptionally short monks. For a moment, Adam wondered whether or not it was even worth entering, but the temptation to look at whatever wall paintings it might hold was enough to persuade him to duck his head and go in. Quint followed him. The room they entered was like a prison cell. Once inside, neither man could stand upright without grazing his head on the rough stone that formed its ceiling. As the light from their candles illuminated the darkness, both of them started back in surprise.

'Sweet Jesus in 'eaven,' whispered Quint hoarsely. 'What in 'ell are these doing 'ere?'

At the back of the room, there was a recess in the wall. It was piled high with human skulls. More than a hundred stared sightlessly out of the shadows. Adam had now recovered his composure. He held his candle high and allowed it to throw its flickering light into the empty eye sockets.

'It is an ossuary, I believe,' he said. 'These are the skulls of monks from long ago.'

'Ain't they got no decency?' Quint said, in disgust. 'Why didn't they give 'em a proper burial like a Christian should?'

'They have different beliefs from ours in England. To them it is no disrespect to leave the bones thus.'

Quint shook his head as if in sorrowful acknowledgement that, beyond England's shores, the world was a bizarre and poorly governed place.

'Wouldn't take much to plant 'em in the ground,' he commented.

'You forget that we are a long way above it, Quint.'

There was a sudden sound from outside. Both men doused their candles and fell silent. They moved warily to the entrance of the ossuary and peered out. On the far side of the small courtyard, two figures were silhouetted against the dim moonlight. One was instantly recognisable from its enormous height.

'That's Andros,' Quint hissed.

'And, unless I'm much mistaken, the other is his master.'

Rallis had in his hand a dark lantern. As they watched, he slid back its shutter and its light shone out. Standing by the parapet overlooking the drop, the lawyer waved the lantern from side to side.

''E's signalling to someone,' Quint whispered, 'someone down on the plain.'

'So it would seem.'

'Where'd 'e get the light from?'

'The bags, I suppose. The monks hauled up two of our bags after we all made it to the top.'

The Greek continued to move his light from side to side. From where Adam and Quint crouched in the doorway to the ossuary, it was impossible to tell whether or not there was any answering signal from below. Several minutes passed and then Rallis closed the shutter on his lantern for the last time. He turned to his giant companion and spoke a few brief words which the watchers were unable to hear. The two Greeks left the courtyard. For a minute, the silence was broken only by the sound of some night bird cawing among the rocks beneath the monastery.

'What the 'ell was all that about?' Quint asked eventually, his voice still a whisper.

'I have absolutely no notion,' his master replied. Adam's mind was racing with possible explanations for the lawyer's behaviour. None that he could imagine cast Rallis in good light. It seemed as if the professor had been right to suspect the man of treacherous intent. And yet Adam could scarcely bring himself to think badly of the Athenian. Even in the short period of their acquaintance, he had grown to like and admire him. 'He was making contact with someone in the village below. Or someone camped on the plain. That much was evident. But, for what purpose, I cannot tell.'

'What would 'e want to be waving 'is bleeding lantern at anybody for?'

'As I say, Quint, I do not know.' Adam moved cautiously into the courtyard. He looked from left to right and then beckoned his servant to follow him. 'Presumably he was not relaying instructions to them about the feeding of the mules.'

'What we going to do about it? We going to ask 'im what 'e's been up to?'

'I cannot believe that he would necessarily tell us.'

'We got to do something,' Quint persisted.

'We will keep an eye on our Athenian friend. And we will not always assume that he *is* our friend. We will listen out for anything that might be said that will cast some light on his nocturnal prowling.'

'That won't do no good,' Quint said. 'Not for me. What with Rallis and the monks gobbling Greek all the time. Even if I do listen out, I ain't going to make much sense out of anything I 'ear.'

'Well, if your ears prove useless, keep your eyes open. But, for now, we shall retire. The monks will no doubt be stirring before too long. We would not want them to catch us creeping about their domain like thieves in search of booty.'

CHAPTER THIRTY-FIVE

I n the tiny cell he had been given, Adam awoke to the sounds of birds and to the muffled gong of the *semandron* summoning the monks to prayer. He had heard it once in the dark hours of the night but it had disturbed his rest only briefly. Now it proved impossible to ignore. He opened the shutters of the unglazed window to the room and allowed the sun to enter. After dressing, he ventured onto the wooden walkway that ran outside the guest chambers and skirted the eastern side of the monastery. A white goat, a bell around its neck, was wandering along the walkway. While Adam watched, the beast disappeared round the corner but he could still hear it jingling on the far side of the building. Looking across the flimsy railings of the walkway which were the only protection against a precipitous drop, Adam shaded his eyes against the rising sun. He could see where another of the pillars of rock thrust its way up from the plain. It too had a monastery on its summit. The building seemed almost like a natural outcrop of the rock. It was difficult to tell where geology ended and architecture began. Adam cast his eyes downwards. At the foot of the rock pillars, he could see the box-like houses of Kalambaka with their red roofs and he could just make out the tiny figures of some of the inhabitants as they emerged to begin their day. In the background, across the valley, the peaks of the Pindos Mountains soared into the sky, their slopes green with the trees that cloaked them.

He heard a sound behind him and turned to find that Fields had emerged from his cell and was standing on the walkway.

'Good morning, Professor. I trust that you slept well.'

'I did not, Adam.' Fields was flapping a hand in front of his face and looked to be in a cantankerous mood. 'Perhaps you recall the story of Domitian and the flies? Of how he spent days in seclusion doing nothing but catching flies and stabbing them with a sharpened stylus?'

'I believe I do remember it. From Suetonius, is it not?'

'I have often thought it a curious occupation for an emperor but, after a night amidst the insects of Agios Andreas, I can only wish that I possessed the same skills Domitian had. Do you suppose it is possible to stab fleas as well as flies?'

'It is probably an art that requires practice.'

'We shall undoubtedly have the opportunity for much practice before we leave this wretched abode of penury and superstition. I am bitten half to death and I am filthy. I could see no means of performing my toilet in that dingy stall they gave me.'

'Cleanliness seems to be a virtue not much admired in monastic circles,' Adam said.

'The old bastards stink is what you mean.' Quint had also left his cell and was standing by the wooden railings, scratching his stubbled chin and hitching up his trousers. 'I could smell 'em from yards off last night.'

'These are holy men, Quint,' Adam said. 'Their concern is with their souls not with their bodies. Anyway, if truth be told, neither you nor I nor even the professor can lay claim to great fragrance after traipsing the plains of Thessaly for several days.'

'I can accept the bodily odours of the monks,' Fields said. 'Anyone who has spent any time in the Senior Common Room of a Cambridge college has learned to accustom himself to the redolence of his fellow man. It is the insect life that I cannot abide.'

The same monk who had conducted them to their rooms the previous night now appeared to usher them towards their breakfasts. Beckoning the three of them to follow him, he set off along the walkway. He took them down a short flight of stairs and into a stone-flagged corridor which led to a massive wooden door. The monk pushed it open and entered a room larger than any other they had so far seen in Agios Andreas. Three long tables, with benches by them, stood within it. One crossed the room at its far end. The other two were set at right angles to it. In the far left-hand corner was a lectern.

'The refectory, I assume,' the professor said, as Theophanes indicated by smiles and gestures that the far table was to be theirs. 'And we are to be guests at their equivalent of high table. The similarity to colleges by the Cam grows. Although I suspect the food may not be as appetising.'

'But healthier, perhaps,' Adam suggested.

An elderly monk with a beard of particular luxuriance was standing by the top table, bowing repeatedly.

'This will be the hegumen.' Fields examined the old monk as if he were some curious animal of which no specimen had previously come to his attention. 'As ignorant as his fellows, I have no doubt.'

The monk, smiling beatifically, continued to bow and nod.

'The hegumen?' Adam sounded momentarily puzzled. 'Ah, the one in charge.'

'The abbot, in effect.'

'We must hope that he does not speak English, Professor. Or he might take offence at your words.'

'He will be a monoglot Greek, I have no doubt.' Fields, still staring at the hegumen like a visitor encountering one of the odder beasts in the Regent's Park zoo for the first time, was unabashed. 'And his Greek will be some barbarous dialect that is barely comprehensible.'

Adam responded to the monk's politeness with bows of his own and a greeting in Greek. The old man looked delighted to be addressed in his own language. He replied with a volley of swiftly delivered remarks, few of which Adam was able to catch. They all took their seats and watched as the door opened again and the other monks trooped in together. Behind the *caloyeri* were Rallis and his huge servant. Fields waved at the empty places on the bench and the two Greeks joined the Englishmen in their place of honour.

Andros, struggling to accommodate his vast legs beneath the table, made it rock gently on his knees before he was able to settle into his seat. Rallis, taking his place more gracefully, greeted his fellow travellers warmly. He bowed respectfully to the hegumen. There was no trace of embarrassment in his manner, Adam noted, no suggestion that he knew they had witnessed his midnight excursion and his mysterious signalling or that, if he did know, he cared greatly.

The young servant who had been present the previous day when the visitors were hauled up the rock now appeared, placing plates of dry bread and salt cheese in front of them. Another boy set glasses and a tankard of red wine on the table. Adam picked up the tumbler he had been given for the wine and examined it in the dim light. It looked very ancient and bore on it several unmonastic engravings of little cupids wrestling and shooting arrows. Was the tumbler Venetian, he wondered? It certainly looked to be. If it was, what roundabout journey had brought it to this remote spot? As he was pondering this, one of the monks moved away from his companions and stood by the lectern. Opening the large and ancient Bible on it, he began to read aloud. His fellow monks were silent but otherwise seemed to be paying little heed to him. Their attention looked to be more focused on the breakfast to come.

When, after a minute or two, the reader ceased speaking, closed the Bible and returned to his place, the others fell on the bread and cheese like men who had scarcely eaten that week. A slight hum of hushed conversation rose from the monks' table. From time to time, one of the younger *caloyeri* raised his head and looked at the visitors, but if Adam caught his eye, he looked down immediately at his plate. The others seemed remarkably uninterested in anything other than their food. The hegumen continued to chatter cheerfully to Adam in Greek which the young man found difficult to follow. The old man, he thought, was asking him about London. He wanted to know about the state of the monasteries there. Were they rich and well-populated? Adam laboured to provide the hegumen with adequate answers to his enquiries. Fields, meanwhile, was taking the opportunity to question Rallis.

'You have put forward our request to see the objects these monks possess?' he asked.

'I did so,' the Greek replied. 'But there was no need. The *hegumenos* assumed that the only reason we travelled so far was that we wished to pay our respects to the relics. He could imagine no other. He has agreed to show them to us later this morning.'

'And their library?'

'I believe that will also be included in the tour.'

* * * * *

Once breakfast was finished, the hegumen led his guests from the refectory. He beckoned them into a squat building that stood next to the chapel where Adam and Quint had admired the wall paintings the previous night. The two servants were left outside. The hegumen ushered Adam, Fields and Rallis into a rectangular stone cell where the treasures of the monastery had been laid out on a wooden desk for their inspection. From a cupboard in the corner, he took an embroidered stole and placed it round his neck. He waved his arm at the desk. The three visitors moved closer to examine what was on it.

'There are beautiful objects here,' Adam remarked, pointing to a jewel-encrusted box.

The hegumen made encouraging noises as he did so, like a schoolmaster trying to embolden a bright but bashful pupil.

'That is a very holy relic,' Rallis said. 'The monks believe it to be part of the body of Agios Andreas. Saint Andrew.' He reached his right hand behind his neck and tapped on his own back. 'I do not know the name of it in English but it is here.'

'The shoulder blade,' Adam said.

'Ah, the shoulder blade. Like the blade of the sword.' Rallis smiled at the curiosities of the English language. 'The monks believe they possess the shoulder blade of Agios Andreas in the jewelled box. It is their greatest treasure.'

Fields grunted with distaste. 'These Eastern Christians are worse than papists,' he said. 'All these saints' bones. What else do they claim to hold here? The right hand of St Thomas? Mary Magdalen's left foot?'

'They are not sophisticated, perhaps, Professor,' Rallis said soothingly, 'but their religious feelings are sincere.'

'They are mired in unreason. In thrall to absurd superstitions. Do they seriously expect us to believe that bits and pieces of the body of Saint Andrew, a man who died eighteen hundred years ago, are scattered about the monasteries of Greece and the Levant?'

'The relic is certainly many centuries old.' Rallis continued to speak to Fields in a placatory tone of voice. 'The monks say it belonged once to the emperor Constantine Porphyrogenitus. It was brought from Byzantium by the first abbot of the monastery.'

'Nonsense,' Fields barked. 'It is as likely to be my grandmother's shinbone as it is to be the shoulder blade of an apostle.'

If the hegumen realised, from the professor's voice, that the relic was not proving a success with one of his visitors at least, he gave no sign. Instead, he pointed to the wall behind the desk where an image of the Madonna, wide-eyed and solemn, looked down on them.

'Holy Mother,' he said in English, gesturing towards the icon. They all peered at it, the professor still tutting with irritation.

'The painting has been damaged, I see,' Adam remarked, indicating an area on the Virgin's gown which had clearly been repaired.

Seeing Adam's gesture, the hegumen launched himself on an excited speech in Greek which only Rallis could follow.

'It was a very bad man who did that, he is saying. A soldier, many years ago. He struck the icon with his sword. The Holy Mother began to bleed.'

Fields snorted in derision.

'She bled for many days. Only when the bad man repented and confessed his crimes did she stop. He became a very good man. He threw away his sword and became a monk himself. He died a saint.'

'Is there no limit to the fatuities these people will believe?' the professor asked of no one in particular.

'She does not bleed any more.'

'I should think not!'

'But she does weep.'

'Oh, I will hear no more of this!'

Fields was, by this time, in a paroxysm of exasperation. He turned his back on the icon and moved as far away from it as he could in the confined space of the room. The old monk, apparently baffled by the professor's behaviour, looked reproachfully at him.

'She wept in the wars forty years and more ago when the Greeks were defeated,' Rallis went on. 'And when the monasteries were obliged to remain within the lands of the Turks. The *hegumenos* is too young to remember this but the oldest monk, Brother Donatus, saw the lady weep. He can tell you about it.'

'He need not bother himself,' the professor said, from his position in the corner of the room. 'We have no interest in these preposterous superstitions.'

The hegumen had finished his short lecture. He picked up the icon and kissed it reverently before returning it to the table.

'Do they have no books or manuscripts to show us?' Fields had returned from his sulk but he was still beside himself with impatience and irritation. 'Do they think we have come all this way to look at ham-fisted daubs of the Virgin Mary and the scapulae of the long dead?'

'These monks are not learned men, Professor,' Rallis said. 'Mostly they are peasants and artisans. They are ignorant and uneducated. The relics and the icons they love but the books in their library often mean little to them. Some of them can barely read.'

'But they continue to look after them,' Adam interrupted.

'Not with any great efficacy, I would conjecture,' the professor said. 'Any volume that we get to see will doubtless be ruined by damp and neglect.'

'They tend their gardens because they relish the food that comes from them,' Rallis said. 'They do not so much relish the food of the mind. They tend their books only because the monks here have always done so. They respect them for their antiquity.'

'The books and manuscripts should be removed from the monasteries and from the hands of these ignorant men,' the professor said. 'Otherwise mice and mildew will destroy them.'

The hegumen, who had been waiting in polite silence, now spoke swiftly to Rallis. He had clearly understood at least something of what had been said.

'They do not keep their books here,' the lawyer interpreted. 'Their library is elsewhere. Perhaps, the *hegumenos* says, it will be possible to see it later. But now he must return the relics to their places of safe keeping.'

* * * * *

'The *hegumenos* was distressed by the lack of respect the professor showed to the relics and to the icon of the Holy Mother.' Rallis and Adam were talking together in the latter's room. Fields, still muttering to himself about the childish gullibility of the monks, had retired to read his Thucydides. The two servants, when Adam had last seen them, had been sitting on a stone wall above a precipitous drop, playing cards. Quint had been endeavouring, with little success, to teach Andros the rudiments of three-stake brag. 'He cannot bring himself to show more treasures to such a disrespectful man.'

'Aha, Fields has shot himself in the foot, has he?' Adam could not help but feel a little amusement that the professor's bad temper had rebounded upon him. 'With his inability to stay quiet?'

'So it would seem. But the *hegumenos* was impressed by the reverence you showed to the relics. He speaks a little English. He understood that you were asking about the books.'

'He will let us see them?'

'Only you and I are to see them. Not the professor. He will send Brother Demetrios to open the library for us.'

'Demetrios? The monk who helped me to my feet after that wretched journey up the rockface? I shall be almost as pleased to see him again as I was to see him the first time.'

At that very moment there was a tap upon Adam's door.

'Come,' the young man cried. The door opened and the wild-haired Demetrios, looking like a distraught prophet from one of the more obscure books of the Old Testament, bustled into the room.

He came to a stop when he saw the two men and bowed his head in greeting.

'Here is the very man of whom we were speaking,' Adam said, returning the monk's salute. 'And, like the earl in Tennyson's poem, his beard is a foot before him and his hair a yard behind.'

Demetrios spoke rapidly to the young Englishman, nodding his head up and down with great energy. Adam, able to follow only one word in three, smiled encouragingly.

'As you have probably surmised,' Rallis said, when the monk's brisk torrent of Greek came to an end, 'he is here to take us to the library.'

Beckoning the two men to follow him, Demetrios left the room and walked into the passage outside. He led them through an arched gateway at its end which took them into the main courtyard. Adam waved his hand in greeting to Quint and Andros, still sitting on the wall a dozen yards away and staring at cards. Both were too engrossed by their game to respond. Looking back to ensure that his visitors were still following him, Demetrios crossed the courtyard and approached a building which Adam had noticed earlier and assumed to be a storehouse for food. The monk stopped in front of its low wooden door and, delving into the inner recesses of his clothing, extracted a rusting key. He waved it in front of Adam's eyes for a moment or two, like a conductor using a baton to beat time with an orchestra. Then, with a final flourish, he thrust it into the keyhole. The key turned. Demetrios placed his shoulder against the door, shoved vigorously and disappeared into the interior of the building.

Adam and Rallis followed the monk through the door and found him struggling to light a candle. As the flame took hold, its light revealed the contents of the room. An ancient wooden cupboard stood against one wall. In one corner was a heap of rotting monastic robes. Opposite these were fragments of twisted metal that might once have been an iconostasis. The only other piece of furniture was largely hidden by curtaining. Demetrios twitched the fabric aside to display seven shelves of old and decaying books. The musty smell of neglect hung in the air above them. Leather bindings peeled away from cracked spines. Several volumes seemed to have disintegrated altogether and all that was left of them were handfuls of torn and stained pages thrust between their fellows.

'*Bibliotheka*,' the monk said, with a hint of pride in his voice. Silence followed as the two visitors stared in dismay at the shelves Demetrios had revealed. One of the books, disturbed by the monk thrusting aside the curtain, fell sideways on its shelf. Small clouds of dust rose upwards.

'This is the library we have come so far to see?' Adam asked eventually. He spoke to Rallis with a hint of reproach as if the Greek was solely responsible for the reputation the monastery had gained. The lawyer looked abashed.

'Many scholars I know in Athens tell me that Agios Andreas has very interesting books in its possession.'

'Your Athenian friends must have been misinformed.'

'Perhaps the books are more valuable than they seem.'

Adam reached out and took a volume at random from the middle shelf.

'*The Divine Liturgy of St John Chrysostom.*'

He put the book back in its place and extracted another.

'*St Basil on the workings of the Holy Spirit.* These are the sort of works we could find in many eastern monasteries, Rallis,' he said, deeply downcast. 'I doubt very much there is anything here for us.'

Demetrios had been standing by the library, beaming with pleasure and taking deep breaths, as if intending to inhale an aroma of scholarship that clung to the books. Now he sensed the disappointment of his visitors. He put a hand on Adam's arm and began to speak to him with great earnestness.

'Rallis, I cannot understand the Greek our friend here speaks. I would be most grateful if you would translate for me.'

'He is telling you that you are not the only Englishman to see the library. Another of your countrymen came here last year.'

'He must have been as disappointed as we have been, then.'

'No, the other Englishman liked very much what he saw in the library.'

'Did he, indeed? He is certain the visitor was English?' Adam asked, his interest now aroused. 'Perhaps he knew only that he came from the West.'

Rallis conferred with the monk once again.

'The man was most definitely English. He spoke English. And he behaved all the time as if the monastery belonged to him.'

The Greek's face was impassive as he translated.

'Brother Demetrios is also telling me that he was once English himself.'

'Was he, by Jove?' Adam said. He looked at the bearded and bedraggled monk who grinned at him, revealing a mouthful of blackened teeth. 'But he is no longer?'

The monk spoke rapidly to Rallis. Adam could make out only a handful of Greek words and could not connect them into any meaningful sentence.

'He was born in Cephalonia, he says. The English ruled there when he was born but they gave the island back to the Greeks. He likes to be Greek now but sometimes he wishes he still was English.'

The monk nodded as if in vigorous approval of the precision of Rallis's translation and then began to speak again.

'There is another library which the monks keep hidden,' Rallis said after Demetrios had finished. 'But for English travellers he opens it. Because he remembers being English himself. He opened it for the Englishman last year. He is asking if you also would like to see this hidden library.'

Adam could scarcely contain his delight at this information. 'I rather think I would,' he said. He bowed his head several times in Brother Demetrios's direction and was rewarded with another black-toothed grin. The monk moved to the large wooden cupboard in the corner of the room and opened its door. Inside, was a second door which he threw back to reveal a small chamber cut into the thick stone walls. Shelves had been fitted round the chamber and sitting on them were dozens of musty volumes.

'Holy books,' said Demetrios in English.

Adam began to examine them. Clouds of dust arose as he picked each book from the shelf. On first inspection, most seemed as commonplace as the ones in the outer room. Gospels and liturgies by the score. Works by long-dead Orthodox theologians. Editions of Greek classics that would have been welcome enough additions to college libraries back in Cambridge but hardly worth the trouble of travelling most of the way across Europe to consult. Adam continued to feel that only disappointment awaited them but he moved on into the dark recesses of the hidden chamber. Demetrios, who had left them briefly, returned with a lantern which lit up the furthest shelves. Beyond the last of the printed books were what looked to be the few bound manuscripts the monastery possessed. As Adam moved his hand to reach for them, the old monk spoke.

'Those are the ones the English always like,' Rallis translated. 'The other Englishman wanted to buy one of them.'

'Did they sell it to him?' Adam asked anxiously. The other Englishman, he felt certain, could only be Creech. The man with the crescent scar had been asking in Athens about travelling to the monasteries. He must have succeeded in doing so. He had found the manuscript he had been seeking. If he had been able to buy it, their own journey would be in vain.

Rallis spoke quickly to the monk, who sounded indignant as he replied.

'No, they did not sell to him. There is not enough gold in the whole of the country to buy any of the holy books.'

'This one is not very holy,' Adam said, examining one of the more ancient-looking manuscripts. 'Unless I am very much mistaken, it is a collection of poems by Anacreon. It is probably just as well that the monks choose not to read this.'

'Some of the *caloyeri* would not be able to read it, even should they wish to do so. They are very close to illiterate.'

'Well, that would save their blushes. Anacreon on drinking, they might like. But Anacreon on women might be rather strong meat for them.'

Adam continued to root through the volumes on the innermost shelves, picking up the occasional one and turning the pages swiftly. The smell of long-neglected literature hung in the air. Demetrios's hidden cubicle was not, he thought, so dissimilar to some of the darker corners of a college library back in Cambridge.

'Which was the manuscript the other Englishman wanted to buy?' he asked.

Rallis spoke again to the monk.

'It is the one by your left hand. The small one bound in black leather.'

Adam took hold of the volume indicated and carefully opened it.

'It is written on vellum,' he said.

'Are they not all written on vellum?'

'The majority will probably be paper. Vellum manuscripts will, I assume, be the oldest.'

'Is it the one which we seek?' The lawyer's voice was as hushed as if he was in the monastery's church.

Adam turned the leaves of the manuscript one by one. He blew gently on one of them and a small cloud of dust particles rose into the air.

'Adam, is it the book we have come for?' Rallis sounded as if he was struggling to maintain his usual calm.

In reply, Adam held out the manuscript, open at the page on which he had blown. He pointed to the Greek lettering inscribed on it hundreds of years earlier. The ink was fading but the letters were still clear and legible. He indicated one of the words at the top of the page.

'"Euphorion",' he said in a hushed voice. 'Unless my ability to decipher Greek has deserted me entirely, that word is Euphorion.'

'It is,' Rallis replied. 'And there beneath it is the word "*Periegesis*". There can be no doubt about it. This is the missing manuscript of Euphorion's travels.'

The two men looked at one another with poorly suppressed excitement. For a moment, neither man could think of anything further to say.

'You have come a long way to find this book,' Rallis said eventually. Adam was staring once again at the word 'Euphorion' on the leaf of vellum. He had indeed travelled far since he had first encountered the name written in the notebook belonging to poor Creech. And now here was the mysterious manuscript, the one in which, if Palavaccini, the editor of the first printed version was to be believed, the Greek writer spoke of "the golden treasure that lies hidden where the ancient kings buried it".

'We must show this to the professor,' he said. 'He will rejoice in this discovery as much as we do.'

CHAPTER THIRTY-SIX

think we must wait until the hegumen sees the logic in our proposal,' Adam said. 'To lose one manuscript from a library which they never use and gain in return enough money to feed his monks for months. He must see the sense in it.'

It was no more than an hour since he and Rallis had held the Euphorion manuscript in their hands. They had wished to remove it from the hidden library to show the professor. When they had proposed this, Demetrios had become very agitated. He had released a torrent of barely comprehensible Greek and had tugged at Adam's sleeve as if intent on hauling him bodily from the library. In the end, they had had to leave the manuscript where it was. The wild-haired monk had led them back across the courtyard to speak to the hegumen. Rallis, exerting all his charm and eloquence, had made the spiritual head of the monastery an offer. The manuscript, he had told him, was of great interest to the Englishmen. The Englishmen would pay the hegumen many piastres for it. The hegumen had listened politely to the lawyer's lengthy speech and then he had replied.

'*Ochi,*' he had said. The answer was no and always would be no. It was no to the other Englishman who had visited Agios Andreas. It was no to them. The treasures of the monastery were not for sale. Rallis and Adam had no choice but to retire to the professor's room and inform him of the morning's developments.

'If we are obliged to wait for these credulous dunces to learn logic,' Fields now remarked, 'we shall wait until the Greek Kalends. It will never happen.'

He was consumed by irritation with what he had been told. He could not keep still and strode about the room, tugging hard at his beard as if it were a false one and he were intent on pulling it off.

'We must force the abbot, *nolens volens*, to surrender the manuscript,' he said eventually.

'I do not think we can do that, sir,' Adam said. 'How do you propose that we dispossess him of it? At gunpoint?'

Fields stopped and stared intently at the younger man. For a moment, it seemed he was about to hail the suggestion as a brilliant means of breaking the deadlock. Then he shook his head.

'No. As much as we want the manuscript, we can scarcely point our rifles at men of religion. Even men of so debased and superstitious a religion as this Eastern Orthodoxy.'

The professor looked disappointed that his scruples prevented him from the action the situation demanded. He began to patrol the room again. The other two watched him and exchanged glances. Rallis raised his eyebrows. Adam lifted his shoulders in the smallest of shrugs.

'I shall go and speak to this hegumen myself,' Fields announced, bringing his restless pacing to an abrupt end. 'I shall see just how deaf he is to the voice of reason.'

The professor said no more but exited the room immediately. His boots could be heard clumping down the wooden walkway outside. His two companions looked at one another again.

'Will his intervention alter the hegumen's decision, do you suppose?' Adam asked.

'I doubt it very much.' Rallis looked as if he could not decide whether to be amused or irritated by Fields's sudden departure. 'The *hegumenos* does not like the professor. He knows very little English but he heard some of what he said at breakfast. And he knew later that his relics were being mocked. I fear that Professor Fields may make the task of acquiring the manuscript more difficult rather than less.'

'We had best hasten after him. Perhaps we can prevent him from insulting the old man's religion further.' Adam did not sound hopeful that they could. He and the Greek lawyer followed the professor from the room. They made their way back through the winding labyrinth of the monastery's ancient passageways and tiny courtyards to the small cell which its spiritual leader called his own. As they approached, they could hear voices in Greek. One was raised in anger, the other spoke gently but firmly. It was not difficult to guess which belonged to Fields. They entered the chamber, empty save for a ramshackle cot in one corner on which the hegumen slept. An icon of the Madonna and Child and one of Saint Andrew were the only decorations. They found the professor shouting about the significance to classical scholarship of the manuscript in the library while the old hegumen bent his head and examined the stone floor of his cell. He looked up as his new visitors arrived and immediately began to address Rallis. Fields continued to rant for a moment or two before falling sullenly silent. Rallis listened to the monk and then turned to the other two to translate.

'He says they are poor,' he began.

'Yes, yes, we know that already,' Fields interrupted impatiently. He was almost beside himself. 'Surely that means all the more reason for them to accept a gift in return for the manuscript.'

'They are poorer now than they have ever been,' the lawyer went on. 'They once had lands in the north. In Wallachia. Many farms and fields and vineyards. But the Prince of Romania confiscated their estates there. Now they are very poor indeed.'

'Damn him and his lost fields and vineyards!' Fields was clutching his head in both hands. He reminded Adam of the villain in a melodrama about to tear his hair following the frustration of his wicked plans. 'Why will he not sell us the manuscript?'

'But however poor they have been, they have never sold the holy treasures that have been entrusted to them.'

'Holy treasures!' the professor screeched. 'Does this old fool even know what we want? We have no interest in dispossessing him of his saintly shoulder blade. Or his lachrymose icon. We want a single manuscript from his library which probably no one has read since Suleiman the Magnificent was sitting on the Ottoman throne.'

'Pray, calm yourself, Professor.' Adam made soothing gestures towards the older man. 'This is no way to win the hegumen's agreement.'

'I am not certain that I can be calm, Adam.' Fields none the less made a mighty effort to recover his self-possession. 'When I am faced by this unthinking refusal to accept reasoned argument.'

For a moment, Adam entertained himself with the notion of what the professor might consider unreasoned argument when his reasoned variety seemed to consist of such frothing rage. But the hegumen was now speaking again. His Greek was very different to the classical language that Adam knew but there was no need for Rallis to translate. There was no mistaking the old monk's meaning. He was asking them, politely but firmly, to leave him alone in his stone cell.

CHAPTER THIRTY-SEVEN

A ll negotiations with the hegumen proved fruitless. Despite the offers of cash, despite the charm that Rallis deployed, despite the fury with which the professor raged against his intransigence, the old monk remained adamant. No manuscript was leaving Agios Andreas while it was in his care.

'Can we not read the manuscript *in situ?*' Adam asked. 'We could return with Demetrios to the hidden library and copy out the passages in Euphorion which are relevant.'

'I am not certain that we will necessarily know which passages *are* relevant,' the professor said gloomily. 'It may be that the importance of Euphorion's descriptions will become apparent only when the text and the ground it describes are closely compared. We will need the original when we travel north.'

'Your suggestion of reading the manuscript here is no longer feasible, Adam.' Rallis sounded in no doubt. 'The professor has offended the hegumen deeply. Mortally, is that the word you use? He is unwilling to let any of us enter the library again.'

'Wretched man that he is,' Fields said with venom. It was clear that the idea that he might bear any blame in the dispute had not occurred to him.

'We have only one option left open to us,' Adam said. 'We cannot use violence against the monks.' For a moment, Fields looked willing to dispute this but he contented himself with an angry shake of his head. 'We will have to go over their heads. The monasteries here at Meteora are under the jurisdiction of the Orthodox authorities at Larissa?'

Rallis nodded.

'Then we must go there and persuade the bishop to give us written permission to buy the manuscript. He is likely to be a more worldly man than our friend here. He will understand the logic of our arguments better.' Adam had no great desire to embark on the plan of action he was himself proposing, but he could see no other honourable way of taking possession of the Euphorion manuscript. 'When he approves our purchase, we can return to Agios Andreas and the hegumen will be obliged to bow before a higher authority.'

'Weeks will be wasted in this senseless rigmarole,' Fields protested.

'There is, alas, no alternative, Professor.' Rallis spoke with certainty. 'We will take advantage of the hospitality of the *caloyeri* for one further night and then we will journey to Larissa.'

And so, on the following morning, after they had breakfasted on bread and olives, the men sat once more in the monks' net and were lowered down the rockface. They collected the mules from Kalambaka where an amiable farmer, his palm crossed with the silver of several piastres, had stabled them, and took the road east towards Larissa.

For many miles, as they trudged on, they were able still to look behind them and see the strange pinnacles of Meteora on the horizon, like the unearthly architecture of a fevered dream.

They travelled for most of the day in silence. For Andros this seemed to be his natural state. The others were wrapped in their own thoughts. Quint was forced to struggle with the mule he was leading, and what little he said consisted largely of curses directed against its obstinacy. Adam and Rallis, relieved of any duty to guide the mules, had the leisure for conversation but found almost nothing to say to one another. The young Englishman spent his time running through the events of the last few days in his head. The delight he had felt at locating the Euphorion manuscript was fading a little but was still present. The obstinacy of the abbot in refusing to part with it, he thought, had been aggravating but understandable. Their enforced journey to Larissa was a nuisance. Nonetheless, they would soon return, almost certainly armed with the papers necessary to buy the manuscript. Despite what Fields's bad temper might suggest, the delay was endurable. And then they could read what perhaps only one other man since the old Venetian scholar Palavaccini had read. The very great secret of which Creech had spoken at the Speke dinner in London might be revealed.

And yet there was still so much of which Adam could make little sense. Where did Rallis fit into the equation? Whose side was he on? What had the Greek lawyer and his servant been doing in the monastery the night before last? To whom had they been signalling? Adam could think of few legitimate reasons to doubt the lawyer. Had Rallis not led them here to the manuscript as he had said he would? Had he not argued their case to the hegumen as eloquently as he could? However, the young man could think of equally few reasons to trust him. What, after all, did they know of him? Little more than what Samways had told them. Perhaps, as Fields had suggested before the party had even reached Agios Andreas, Rallis had some involvement with the brigands who had robbed them of their horses. Adam began to think he should have told the professor of the lantern-waving in the night. He had chosen not to do so because he still retained his belief in Rallis's essential goodwill towards them. Fields, if informed of what he and Quint had seen, would have had no such belief. Who knew what consequences would have followed?

Adam looked at the professor. Blessed with a more tractable beast than the one at which Quint was swearing, his old mentor was wandering ahead of the group. Earlier in the day, Adam had seen him take a book from his pocket and begin to read it. He was still holding it now. A volume of his beloved Thucydides, the young man assumed. The professor's mule was travelling towards Larissa with little need of any guidance. Fields had one arm looped through the animal's halter and his eyes half on the road in front of them and half on his book. Adam noted with surprise that the rage which had possessed the professor so thoroughly the night before seemed to have entirely dissipated. He was now a study in serenity.

That night, they camped once again beneath the stars. Andros took a hatchet from his bag and, hacking at branches of a tree only he could reach, swiftly gathered enough wood for a fire. The travellers sat round it in a circle to eat. They stared morosely at one another through the flames.

'We shall be in Larissa in little more than a day,' Adam said eventually, breaking the silence. 'Is that not so, Rallis?'

'Perhaps by tomorrow evening. Or the following morning.'

'With luck we shall quickly win an audience with the bishop. He will see reason in our proposal, Professor.' Adam was struggling to remain as optimistic as he had been in the morning. He was beginning to wonder whether the bishop might be no more willing to countenance their taking possession of what they wanted than the old hegumen. 'We will be back at Agios Andreas in no more than a week with permission to take the manuscript. They will not be able to deny us again. The manuscript will be ours.'

The professor was hunched by the fire, looking like a pile of old clothes awaiting a washerwoman. As he listened to what Adam said, his shoulders began to shake and strange sounds emerged from deep within him. For several terrible moments, the young man thought that Fields might be weeping. How, he wondered, was a gentleman supposed to behave in the wilds of a foreign land when a distinguished scholar broke down in tears in front of him? Should one ignore the outburst? Or attempt, however clumsily, to offer comfort? Adam was still pondering these unexpected questions of etiquette when it dawned on him that the professor was not crying, but laughing. The rocking of his body was not the result of sobs and lamentations but of great waves of laughter. Adam looked across the fire at Rallis. The Greek was clearly as puzzled as he was. He turned to Quint, whose face was split by a fiendish grin. The manservant began to make the unearthly wheezings that his master recognised as his own peculiar version of mirth.

'What is it, Quint? What is going on?'

The servant said nothing but continued to sound like an incompetent piper slowly filling his bag with air. The professor swayed back and forth in front of the fire and then let out one last shout of laughter.

'The manuscript is *already* ours, Adam,' he said. 'I sent Quintus out last night to take it from that damp hutch those benighted monks call a library.'

There was silence. Adam looked in astonishment from the professor to Quint and back again. Rallis, his face tight with anger, stood and moved away from the fire.

'You have stolen the Euphorion manuscript?' Adam was numb with disbelief.

'I would prefer not to use the verb "to steal" in any of its tenses or moods. I believe that what I have done is liberate Euphorion from the custody of those who did not understand what they possessed.'

'It remains theft, whatever words you choose to describe it.'

'Do not be so moralistic, Adam. It ill suits you.'

'We have taken shameful advantage of the hospitality the *caloyeri* offered us.' The young man turned to where the Greek lawyer was staring out into the night. 'I had no knowledge of this, Rallis, I assure you. I did not know what the professor planned.'

The lawyer, his back turned to the Englishmen huddled around the fire, made no comment.

'And, what of you, Quint? Damn you!' Adam rounded on his manservant in a sudden burst of fury. 'Did you not think to ask me whether or not you should be employed as a thief in the night?'

Quint, still wheezing slightly, was indignant.

'Don't get your trumpet out of tune. 'Ow was I to guess you didn't know all about it?'

'Do not blame poor Quintus, Adam.' Fields spoke in conciliatory tones. 'He was just the delivery boy, you know. What you might call an unlikely Hermes, with winged feet and *caduceus* in hand, who travelled between one part of the monastery and another, bearing a gift.'

'A fine choice of god with whom to compare him, Professor. As you know as well as I, Hermes was also the patron of thieves and liars.'

Fields shrugged, as if to acknowledge that Adam might have a point but it was now an irrelevant one.

'The professor asks me to do it so I done it.' The unlikely Hermes was now eager to defend himself. 'I thought you was as keen on getting 'old of the bleedin' book as 'e was. I wasn't about to say no now, was I?'

'Apparently not. Although refusing the requests of your superiors is scarcely an act with which you are unfamiliar.' Adam slapped his hand to the ground in exasperation. He leaned forward and, picking up a burning branch, thrust it further into the fire. Sparks flew upwards into the darkness.

'We must turn back tomorrow morning and return what we have taken to the hegumen,' he said decisively.

'That is out of the question,' Fields replied with equal firmness. 'I have not been lowered one morning from a precipitous height with an ancient manuscript strapped beneath my attire, only to return the next day and give it back. What am I to say to the monks? That I had not noticed it was there?'

'We will admit our crime and make our apologies.'

'I will not do so. It is ridiculous to suggest that I should.'

'What is ridiculous is that a gentleman and a scholar of your standing should stoop to such petty theft.' Adam had rarely, if ever, spoken to his mentor in such a way but he was almost beside himself with anger that Fields should have behaved in so dishonourable a way.

Rallis had walked back to the fire. He sat down once more.

'I am not certain that any good purpose will be served by going back to Agios Andreas, Adam,' he said. 'If the loss of the manuscript has been discovered, they may not wish to see us again. They will fear the theft of further treasures. They will not pull us up in their net.'

'And if it has not been discovered?'

The lawyer shrugged. 'Perhaps, for them – what is your English saying? – ignorance is bliss. We can show the manuscript to the bishop in Larissa. Tell him our story and let him be the Solomon who makes a judgement. Whether we should keep it or give it back to the *caloyeri*.'

'We shall not be going to Larissa.' Fields spoke with certainty. 'Or rather, we shall avoid entering the town. Instead, we shall journey through the mountains to the coast, through the pass at Tempe, and then up the coast towards Salonika.'

'And why the devil should we do that, sir?' Adam asked furiously.

'Ah, Tempe,' Fields sighed, smiling sweetly as if the young man had not spoken. 'The place where the peoples of Thessaly once gathered, Adam. For sacrifices, symposia and parties of pleasure. Aelian, you may recall, wrote that sometimes the whole air of the valley was perfumed with incense. I doubt that such aromas will greet us now but there will be much for us to see. And much perhaps for us to discover.'

Adam realised suddenly that it had not been the writings of Thucydides that had held the professor's attention earlier in the day.

'You have been reading the Euphorion manuscript as we rode,' he said.

In reply, the professor held up a small volume which Adam recognised from the hidden library at the monastery. 'Entirely correct. Here it is. Written some time in the thirteenth century, I believe. But undoubtedly copied from much earlier manuscripts. Who knows? Perhaps the line of transmission goes back another five hundred years. And now we have it – a little volume, bound in black leather by monastic craftsmen in the last century. So small, so simple to hide.' The professor laughed at the thought of how easy it had proved for him to carry it from the monastery.

'Your reading of it has suggested this change of plan, I assume.'

Fields ignored Adam's remark and asked instead, 'Did you not wonder why that man Creech was asking you about your visit to Koutles in sixty-seven? I assume he *did* ask you?'

'Of course I was puzzled by Creech's interest in that godforsaken spot,' Adam acknowledged, 'but what has Koutles to do with the Euphorion manuscript? Is it one of the sites that Euphorion visited?'

'Fifteen years ago, a French scholar named Heuzey travelled in the hills where you and Quint rode.' The professor once again took no apparent notice of Adam's questions. 'He saw what you no doubt saw – that the region is filled with tumuli. He realised the importance of these burial mounds. He returned to dig in them six years later, with money granted to him by that popinjay emperor who has just lost his throne.' Fields sniffed contemptuously. 'One of the few deeds of which *Napoléon le Petit* can be proud.'

Rallis, who had appeared lost in his own thoughts, suddenly spoke up. 'Did this Frenchman find anything when he dug in the mounds?'

'Very little. He abandoned his work because of the fear of malaria.' The professor's voice suggested that this was exactly the kind of cowardice to be expected from the French. 'But he was convinced that there was something there to be found.'

The Greek lawyer nodded as if this merely confirmed what he had already suspected.

'What was to be found?' Adam asked. 'Are you talking of the golden treasure of which the Aldine editor wrote? It truly exists?'

'Ah, those are questions I shall leave you to ponder yourself.' Fields stood and stretched. 'I am growing weary and there may be days of hectic activity ahead of us. I shall unpack my sleeping bag and retire for the night. I recommend that you should do the same. In the morning, you may feel differently. Unless, of course, like Achilles, you choose to remain sulking in your tent.'

As the professor walked towards the tree to which Quint had tethered the mules, Adam exchanged a glance with the Greek lawyer.

'I trust you understand that this is none of my doing, Rallis. I had no notion that Fields planned to steal the manuscript.'

The Greek made a dismissive gesture with his hand.

'The deed is done,' he said. He pointed out into the night. 'Let us walk for a while. Away from the fire. It will be easier to talk.'

The two men stood. Adam glared at Quint, still crouched by the flames, who stared defiantly back. For a moment, it seemed as if the young man might speak again to his manservant but he turned on his heel and strode into the darkness. Rallis followed him. When he had gone a hundred yards from the campfire, Adam stopped and allowed the Greek to draw level with him. In the moonlight, each of them waited for the other to speak.

'The time has come for us both to place our cards on the table, Rallis,' Adam said eventually. 'If we are to deal with this new turn of events, we should both be honest with one another.'

Although it had been his suggestion to talk, the Greek made no reply.

'I had no prior knowledge that the professor was planning to rob the monks of their manuscript. And I do not condone the taking of it.'

'So you have said.'

'And I was speaking the truth. But you have been hiding the truth from me. You have been signalling to someone following us. You have been doing so since we first crossed into European Turkey.'

The Greek continued to stare across the plain at the distant mountains. For the briefest of moments, Adam wondered if he had not heard him.

'You are right, Adam. I have not been honest with you,' Rallis said after a further pause, turning towards the young Englishman. 'I have been obliged to mislead you. The work I am doing has forced me into this – what is the word you English would use? – this subterfuge.'

'The work? What work? I was under the impression that Fields and I had invited you to join us on our travels in search of the Euphorion manuscript. That is the only "work" of which I know.'

'That is the impression I wished you to have,' the Greek said, with the smallest hint of complacency in his voice.

'What other work could there be?'

Rallis moved closer to Adam, so close the young Englishman could feel the lawyer's breath on his face when he spoke.

'Have you any idea how many antiquities, how many treasures of the past, leave my country each year?' the Greek asked in an almost menacing whisper. 'How many are lost to the country that produced them and end up in museums and the collections of rich men all across the rest of Europe?'

'Of course not.' Adam was surprised by the turn the conversation had taken. 'No one does. The number is incalculable.'

'Exactly. Every visitor takes away with him a part of our nation's past. I have no doubt that you yourself have transported objects to London. Coins, a vase, a small statue perhaps?' Rallis's voice had grown louder but was still little more than a hissing in the darkness. 'Trophies to adorn your rooms. To remind you of Greece and its former greatness.' The Greek made a gesture of obvious contempt for those who needed such spoils.

'I have a few mementoes of my travels, yes,' Adam said uncomfortably, thinking of a statuette of Artemis that was one of his most prized possessions. 'But, as you say, so does everyone who has ever visited Greece.'

'It cannot continue.' Rallis spoke with ferocity, suddenly and unexpectedly near to shouting. 'This looting of our past. Not so much the petty pocketing of objects that you describe' – he waved his hand to dismiss this – 'but the wholesale ransacking of sites. The despatching of hundreds and hundreds of objects from Athens to the four corners of Europe for financial gain. That must stop. Otherwise there will be nothing left that we can pass on to future generations of Greeks. Our history will be scattered to the winds.'

The cool and collected lawyer now spoke with an animation and a vehemence that Adam had never before heard in his voice. Silence fell between the two men when Rallis finished speaking. Adam could hear only the sound of bats flitting through the darkness above their heads. He was left with his own, far from gratifying reflections on what his companion had said.

'I agree with you,' he said, after a long pause. In truth, he had never given the matter a moment's thought, but faced by the Greek's passion, he was now certain that Rallis was correct. 'What happens is nothing but licensed piracy. But what has it to do with our own journey? Despite what Fields and Quint have done, we are not ransackers or looters. We have taken one old manuscript from a library where, until last year, no one had consulted it in decades. Centuries, possibly.'

'The manuscript is nothing.' The lawyer almost laughed. 'It is your precious Professor Fields. Have you really no notion of what the man has been doing?'

It was clear from the look of puzzlement on Adam's face that he had not.

'The professor and the man with the crescent moon scar, Samuel Creech. For many years they have been taking the treasures of my country and selling them. Creech lived in Athens until recently. He sent boxes and boxes of objects to Fields in Cambridge. And Fields sold them. To collectors around England.'

'Fields was working with Creech!' Adam could not contain his astonishment.

The lawyer nodded.

'But he has never spoken to me of knowing the man.' Adam was bewildered. 'He has not once suggested that he had even heard Creech's name before I mentioned it to him. Indeed, he denied knowing him.'

Rallis made a movement that was halfway between a shrug and a bow. Its implication was clear. Why, it said, would Fields do anything other than keep quiet?

'He needed you, Adam. Creech was dead. He needed a new partner to travel with him in search of the manuscript.'

'He knew about the Euphorion manuscript long before my visit to Cambridge.'

'Almost certainly. Creech would have told him of its existence. Although I think perhaps that the man with the scar had not said where it could be found.'

Adam thought for a minute. Was this Greek lawyer to be trusted? Could all of what he said be true? If it was, then most of what he believed about Fields's character would be wrong. Perhaps it was Rallis himself he should doubt. It was Rallis who had been signalling to unknown confederates from the monastery heights. It was

Rallis who had already fallen under suspicion during their journey. Why should Adam believe him now?

'Even assuming that what you tell me is true,' he said eventually, 'Creech and the professor were doing nothing illegal. You have no laws in Greece to prevent this.'

'For the present, no,' Rallis acknowledged. 'But that will change. That is my work. To gather the evidence to persuade my government that laws must be enacted. To prevent the trade in our past by people like Fields.'

Adam stood for a long time, struggling to assimilate all that the Greek lawyer had told him. It was painful to do so. From the very beginning, it would seem, he had been a dupe. The professor had apparently gulled Adam into believing that he knew nothing of Euphorion when, all along, he had been aware of the manuscript and what it might contain. Fields had wanted a companion to assist him in finding it and he had tricked his young friend into playing that role. Adam could now do nothing but contemplate his own foolishness. He was angry with Fields but even more with himself.

'The people to whom you have been signalling,' he said, after a minute or two had passed. 'They are in your employ?'

'In a manner of speaking. They are what you English would call brigands. But they have been following my instructions and I have been paying them.'

'You have been paying brigands to follow us?'

'You are shocked, Adam.' Rallis smiled. 'The thought of employing thieves and cut-throats offends your delicate sensibilities. But the reality of life here in Greece is more complicated than you English believe. The politicians in Athens say that brigandage no longer flourishes. Everyone knows that is a lie. Many of the greatest brigands are paid money by those very politicians. Are they paid money to give up their robberies and their murders? No – they are paid money to threaten and to scare the opponents of those politicians. I have merely chosen to pay some of those same men for more peaceful purposes.'

'But why the charade when we first arrived in Thessaly? Why

did that man Lascarides and his men search our baggage and leave us without horses?'

Rallis shrugged. 'I believed – I still believe – that Fields has records of his transactions with Creech. Of at least some of the antiquities they stole and transported from my country. If I had these records, they would assist me greatly in my campaign. I looked for them in Athens.'

'It was you who turned the professor's room at the Angleterre upside down?'

'While you were waiting for me at the Oraia Ellas.' Rallis nodded in acknowledgement of his responsibility. 'I found nothing.'

'So you decided that you would try again when our journey had begun.'

'Yes, but I could not very easily search his bags myself. And, if I found anything, I could not take it. Fields would have known immediately that I was the thief. I decided that the most convenient method was to use Lascarides. If he searched and found, he could take. What else would a brigand do? He was instructed to take the horses. I needed to persuade you that his ambush was a genuine one.'

'But he did not find the documents you wanted in the professor's belongings?'

'No, he did not. Either Fields has left them in Athens or they are on his person. Together with Euphorion.'

Adam was silent again as he thought through the lawyer's words. Rallis might be telling him the truth, but in the absence of the documents which the Athenian had sought, he could not prove it. Was Adam to believe him or to trust instead in the honesty of his old teacher? Once, the answer to the question would have been easy, but after the revelation about the theft of the Euphorion manuscript, he was no longer so certain of Fields's integrity.

'The rifle shots as I was being hauled up to the monastery in that confounded net,' he said at last. 'That was Lascarides as well, I presume.'

'I can only apologise once more, Adam. He was acting on his

own initiative. I instructed him to continue to follow us. He chose to fire on you. To scare you, I think, no more. It was probably his idea of a joke. I am assuming that you saw Andros and myself in the courtyard on the first night we stayed at the monastery?'

Adam nodded.

'I was ordering him to shoot no more. Under any circumstances.'

'By lantern?' the young Englishman asked sceptically. 'A difficult message to convey, surely?'

'Over the years, these brigand bands have developed a means of communicating across the hills by lights alone. You would be surprised by its sophistication.'

'Are Lascarides and his men still close by us?' Adam peered into the night, half expecting to see shadowy figures on horseback riding through the trees. The Greek shook his head.

'Alas, they are on their way back to their homes. Men such as they – they do not much respect the borders that politicians and diplomats impose, but they were growing nervous of travelling so far into European Turkey. They wished to return and I decided that I had no further use for them. I am now regretting that I did so.'

'What does all this mean, Rallis?' Adam sounded almost plaintive. 'Fields knows more than he has told me. You know more than you have told me. Sometimes, damn it, I believe that Quint and Andros know more than they have told me. What is this golden treasure of which Euphorion wrote?'

'Do you recall anything of the tombs of the ancient Macedonian kings, my friend?'

Adam looked at the Greek in surprise.

'The tomb of Alexander? It was in Alexandria. Destroyed by the Mahometans centuries ago, was it not?'

'Not Alexander's tomb. Those of his ancestors. Of his father Philip and of even earlier kings.'

'They are lost as well, surely? No one now can know where they lie buried. They went to their graves centuries before the birth of Christ.'

'But what if someone *did* know where those graves lie? Would that not be a secret worth having?' Rallis seized Adam by the arm. 'And would that not be a "golden treasure" worth possessing?'

'You are telling me that the manuscript contains information about the whereabouts of Philip of Macedon's tomb?'

'I believe so. The man Creech believed so. Your friend the professor believes so.'

Rallis released Adam's arm from his grasp and stepped back, satisfied with the effect of his words on the young man. His head whirling, Adam walked a few steps further into the night. Could Creech and Fields be right? Could the Macedonian kings be buried close to the villages he and Quint had visited three years ago? Could a manuscript lead them to the tombs? Philip of Macedon had died in the fourth century before Christ. Euphorion had visited the region nearly five hundred years later but perhaps some folk memory of the burial sites had survived the centuries for him to record. Adam turned to face the Greek again.

'And Fields plans to exacavate the tomb?' he asked.

'And ship its contents back to England. I cannot allow this to happen.'

'What are we to do? Does he suspect that you are watching him?' As soon as he spoke, Adam remembered the earlier conversation with Fields in which the professor had hinted at doubts about the lawyer. He wondered whether or not to report this to Rallis but decided against it.

'Perhaps, but I do not think so. Luckily, it was you who saw me in the monastery courtyard. And your man Quint. Can we trust Quint to say nothing to the professor?'

Adam paused a moment before replying.

'An hour ago, I would have vouched for Quint's silence immediately,' he said. 'But his part in the theft of the manuscript gives me reason to doubt him.'

'I do not think that you should do so. I think that he took the Euphorion because he thought it was what you wanted as well as the professor. But you must speak to him at the first opportunity. Insist to him that he says nothing of seeing me signalling to Lascarides.'

Adam wondered whether or not his insisting upon anything would significantly influence Quint's behaviour but he nodded in agreement.

'We have, I think, few options but to travel northwards with Fields,' Rallis said. 'It is what he is assuming we will do.'

'Can we not force him to go with us to Larissa? Or dispossess him of the manuscript? He is but one man against four. The Euphorion manuscript could be ours before we all retire to our beds tonight.' Even as he spoke, Adam wondered how circumstances could have so much changed that he was talking seriously of acting in such a way towards the professor.

'That is true but then what would we do? Retrace our steps to Meteora? Bury the secret of the treasure in Agios Andreas once more?' Rallis waved his hand dismissively at the thought. 'Euphorion is telling us where the tomb of Philip of Macedon is to be found. I believe that we should listen to him. If we do not, then others eventually will.'

Behind them came the sudden sound of voices and shouting. The professor had returned to the campfire and was calling to Adam.

'We should go back,' Rallis said. 'The professor has allowed us these moments of discussion, I think, but he is anxious to know what we propose to do. Shall we tell him that we travel with him?'

Adam needed little time to make a decision. As the Greek said, and as Fields had known, there were few alternatives.

'Onward to Macedonia then,' he said, and strode back towards the fire.

CHAPTER THIRTY-EIGHT

'Much more of this digging and they'll be measuring me up for a wooden suit,' Quint said bitterly, throwing aside his spade.

'Fear not, Quint. Those bones of yours will never be laid to rest so far from London.'

Adam's manservant was not listening to him. He had crouched to the ground and was scrabbling amidst the earth he had just upturned. He pulled something from the soil and held it up.

'What's this, do you reckon?' He sounded momentarily excited, as if he had chanced upon something new, but his voice soon fell. 'It's just another coin of some sort, ain't it?'

'We have found enough of those, have we not? And the villagers probably dig them up by the thousands when they plough.' Adam took the dirt-encrusted object out of Quint's hands and held it up to the light, angling it so that the sun would fall on its face. He brushed some of the soil from it. 'It has a figure on it. Heracles, I think.'

'He's 'itting something,' Quint said, standing and peering at the coin.

'Heracles spent much of his career hitting things. It was his special skill.'

'It's a lion. 'E's 'itting a lion.'

'The Nemean lion. The first of his labours. Heracles was forced to club the lion to death when his arrows failed to kill it. He stunned it and then strangled it.'

Quint whistled. ''E must 'ave been stronger than the Great Samsoni,' he said, with a note of respect in his voice.

'The Great Samsoni?'

'Cove I saw in a circus once down Lambeth way. 'E lifted an 'orse above his 'ead.'

'A horse? Are you sure, Quint?'

'A small 'orse,' Quint admitted.

'Well, there are no records of Heracles juggling horses above his head. At least none of which I am aware. But lions he could slaughter with ease. Once the Nemean lion was dead, he used its own claws to strip it of its pelt.'

Adam pocketed the coin. For a moment, it seemed as if Quint might protest as his master took possession of an object he had found but he decided against it. Instead, he picked up the spade from where he had thrown it. The two men began to dig again.

* * * * *

Two weeks had passed since the night by the campfire when Professor Fields had revealed the theft of the Euphorion manuscript. Adam still felt very angry over the deception Fields had practised upon him. Indeed, in his darker moments, he regarded the professor's behaviour as tantamount to a betrayal of their friendship. Yet he had reined in his feelings. He had deemed it politic not to take issue with Fields. He had not even informed him that he now knew of his apparent association with Creech. What, he told himself, were the choices before him? They were either going to find the treasure of which Euphorion had written or they were not. Either way, it would be best to wait upon developments. Fields clearly had some agenda of his own, and he would no doubt pursue it regardless of Adam's opinions on the ethics of doing so. And the young man was still unsure of Rallis. Were the Greek lawyer's revelations about Fields and Creech and their role in smuggling works of art out of the country entirely to be trusted? Adam remained unconvinced that his former tutor would involve himself in such basely mercantile transactions. The man was, first and foremost, a scholar. Although nothing, of course, was certain: the more he saw of Fields on this expedition, Adam had to admit, the more he felt that he did not really know the professor and never had done.

As for Quint's involvement in the theft of the manuscript, this matter was at least more straightforward. Adam's initial anger and outrage towards his manservant had soon dissipated. Quint had explained at great, even tedious, length that he had only done what he had done because he had thought it the best course of action. No servant, he had maintained with a look of injured innocence, had ever been more attentive to his master's needs than he and look at the thanks he got. Adam had taken his protestations of good faith with a pinch of salt but he had come to accept Quint's blunt arguments about the Euphorion manuscript: the theft of the book, however injurious to the monks of Agios Andreas and however ungrateful in the light of their hospitality, was a *fait accompli*.

They had made their way northwards by a circuitous route. In the first week, they had circled the city of Larissa, admiring from afar its minarets glittering in the noonday sun. They had moved on and, a day later, entered the Vale of Tempe. Cliffs had towered above them on either side of the ravine, surmounted by the ruins of two ancient fortresses which had once commanded the pass. For a further day they had journeyed through the valley. As they rode, Fields had explained what he had discovered in the pages of the volume he had stolen from Agios Andreas. On two occasions, he had even allowed Adam and Rallis to take the manuscript from him and read it themselves. The ancient Greek geographer had not only known that a treasure existed in the Macedonian hills. He had travelled in those same hills a few centuries after it had been buried there with the remains of the Macedonian kings. He had spoken to the peasants who lived there and listened to their legends of what lay beneath the tumuli in their native land. He had noted with remarkable precision the site which they claimed held the gold of the ancients.

'How can we know that he was writing the truth?' Adam had wanted to know, as the travellers had emerged from the Vale of Tempe and led the mules over a stone bridge across a meandering stream. 'How can we know that his informants had any real idea of what was buried? Perhaps the treasure was dug up long ago and long since disappeared? Although can we even be certain that Philip was able to get his hands on gold?'

Fields had handed the reins of his mule to Quint and crouched by the little bridge, peering closely at its stones.

'Probably a work of the ancient Macedonians,' he had said, making no immediate response to Adam's remarks. 'We have just ridden over stones that were in place when Alexander departed for Asia.'

He had then risen to his feet. 'There can be no doubt that the ancient rulers of this land had access to gold,' he had continued. 'There were rivers in Macedonia from which alluvial gold could be obtained. And Diodorus Siculus, for one, speaks about the mines Philip controlled. His mints were striking gold coins by the thousands, probably. The coins were even known as *philippeioi*.'

'So the Macedonians had gold in plenty,' Adam had acknowledged. 'But we cannot know that it is buried where Euphorion says it is. The villagers were reporting their myths to him, not what we would recognise as their history.'

'Perhaps,' the professor had conceded. 'As you say, we cannot know for certain. But it is a risk worth taking, is it not? To believe Euphorion? The worst that can happen is that we waste a few weeks of our life in fruitless digging. But, if the man was right, we will make the greatest discovery of the century. Layard and his exacavations at Nineveh will seem like little more than idle scrabblings in the dust of Mesopotamia.'

'When the villagers learn we are digging,' Rallis had said, 'they will assume we are looking for treasure.' The Athenian had seemed uncharacteristically anxious. 'They will either chase us from the land or they will rob us of what we find.'

'We have our papers,' Fields had said. 'I made certain of them before we left Athens. They will not dare touch us when we have a letter from a minister of the Porte.'

'Maybe so.' The Greek had looked unreassured. 'Maybe not so. This is a long way from Constantinople.'

But the professor had proved correct. A week later, they had arrived at a site near Koutles. The ground was uncultivated and was covered in tumuli for hundreds of yards in all direction. Fields had pointed with confidence towards the largest of these and announced that this was the spot that Euphorion had identified as the place to dig.

'His Greek is, for once, blessedly clear and correct on the point,' Fields had said. 'Many of the rest of his geographical descriptions are marred by the infelicities of his prose but of this one there can be no doubt. He writes quite unambiguously of the largest amongst a hundred mounds.'

The party had wasted no time before setting up their camp. The headman of the village, with whom Adam had been acquainted on his previous visit, had come to inspect the excavation the day they had begun digging, surrounded by a band of villainous-looking supporters. At first, they had shouted and raged at the travellers but they had regarded the *firman* Fields bore with an almost religious awe. Only the headman had proved literate but he had read the letter aloud to his comrades and all had been impressed. The document had been returned to the professor with much bowing of the head and the deputation had soon departed. From that first day, they had been little troubled by the villagers. Occasionally, small grubby boys had appeared on the crest of the hill overlooking the mound in which Fields had chosen to dig. They would stand and stare until their presence was noted. Then they would turn tail and disappear. Now the presence of the foreigners in the vicinity seemed scarcely to be acknowledged.

All the digging the foreigners had undertaken, however, had as yet unearthed little of interest. On the seventh morning, all of the party had stripped to their shirtsleeves and laboured in the earth with spade and pick. They had been standing in one of the deep trenches they had dug on the sloping bank of the largest tumulus for miles around. This, Fields had announced, was *undoubtedly* the one that Euphorion had singled out in his ancient text. Dig deep enough, he had said, and they would inevitably strike the vast stone slabs which made up the vaults of the Macedonian tombs. Inside these, indescribable treasures would lie. So far, they had come across little of any value at all. The digging had become a routine, a monotonous toil in the heat that all of them had grown to dislike.

This morning, however, the routine had been broken by the arrival of three visitors. They had not approached the trench but had stood close to where the travellers had pitched camp and shouted. They had sounded angry. Rallis, who had just climbed out of the diggings to fetch water, had been the only one who could see them.

'What is all the noise, Rallis?' Adam had asked, looking up from the earthwork. 'Whose voices can we hear?'

'It appears to be men from the village. The headman, I think.'

'What the devil do they want?'

'I do not know. They are waving their arms,' the lawyer had reported. 'They wave them towards the north.'

'Go talk to them, Rallis,' Fields had said. 'Point out to them that they cannot come here whenever they choose to do so. Tell them that our work is too important to be disturbed. Speak to them again of the *firman*, if necessary.'

The Athenian had looked down at Fields as if he was minded to disobey his instructions. Then he had turned and begun to walk back towards the camp. The others, scrambling out of the trench, had watched him as he neared the villagers. As he had come closer, the headman and his companions had increased the volume of their cries and the energy of their gestures. Rallis had made soothing movements with his hands as he approached. The men from the village had however refused to be soothed and an animated conversation ensued. After several minutes had passed, the lawyer had begun to make his way back to the group now standing awkwardly by the trench.

'What is it?' Adam had called when Rallis was still twenty yards from them.

'They have news that disturbs them,' the lawyer had replied, quickening his pace to join his fellow diggers. 'There is another party of strangers riding towards their village. From the north.'

'Are they so unused to outsiders that they panic at the very thought of more arriving?' Fields had asked, his voice thick with contempt for the Greek villagers. 'Perhaps they believe that the visitors are tax collectors come to squeeze more from them.'

'No, that is not what they fear, Professor.'

'I find it difficult to care greatly *what* they fear.' Fields had shrugged and made as if to turn back to the diggings. 'And I cannot believe that it is any of our concern. You have told them to depart and leave us in peace, I presume.'

'They will not do so. The riders, they say, are like you and Adam. They are Franks. They are your friends, they think.'

Fields sighed in exasperation.

'Do they believe that every European in the land is our friend? Who are these riders?'

'I do not know. But the headman has had word from his uncle who lives in a village further to the north. The party rested there last night. One of the Franks calls himself Garland.'

'Garland!' Adam was astonished. 'What on earth is Garland doing out here in the wilds?'

'That is not all, Adam. The headman says that one of the riders is a woman.'

'Emily!'

'Nonsense!' Fields had said sharply. 'That young woman will be safely home with her mother in Salonika. I cannot understand why Garland, if it is he, should be here. But, assuming that he is, he must be travelling with some doxy he picked up in Athens. He has a reputation, I believe.'

'We must make our way to meet them.'

'That is what the headman wishes,' Rallis had said. 'He will allow us the use of the only horses in the village. He wants us to confront the visitors. And tell them to turn back.'

'I will set out immediately,' Adam had said.

'Not you, Adam. The headman is of the opinion that only the old man, as he calls the professor, will have the authority to persuade Mr Garland to return to Salonika. Ever since he saw the writing from the minister in Constantinople, the headman has been of the opinion that the professor is a man of power and reputation.'

'One of that idle scoundrel's few opinions of any worth,' Fields had said complacently. 'But I cannot drop what I am doing here on a mere whim of his. Someone else must go to meet Garland and his party.'

'I tell you, Rallis,' Adam had declared, 'I shall set off northwards. Perhaps it *is* Emily.'

Adam had felt his heart leap at the prospect of seeing the young woman again. He had begun to make his way towards the camp where the three men from the village had still been standing. As he had moved past Rallis, the Greek lawyer had held out an arm to halt him.

'The villagers will not allow you to go, Adam, I can assure you. I have already spoken to them about it. They have two horses only. One is for the professor. On that point they are adamant.'

'I will take the other.' Adam had made as if to brush aside the Greek's arm but Rallis had still held him.

'No, I must go with the professor. That is what they wish. They know that I can understand both English and the Greek spoken here. That I will be able to assist Fields in conveying their message.'

'Garland will not listen to either of you,' Adam had said, wresting his arm from the lawyer's grasp. 'If he wishes to visit us here, he will do so.'

Rallis had shrugged. 'I suspect that you are right, Adam, but I think that we must do as the village headman asks. We must do all we can to remain on terms with him.'

Adam had looked towards the villagers and then back towards the trench. He had thought of continuing the argument. He had wanted very much to ride out of the camp, to see if it was, in truth, Emily who approached from the north. But he had known that Rallis was correct. They depended on the goodwill of the men of Koutles. He could not force the headman to provide him with a horse. He must contain his impatience and stay by the diggings.

'But if you meet Garland and he insists on coming back with you?' he had asked eventually.

The Greek had shrugged again. 'That is a bridge to cross only when we must.'

Rallis had then turned to his servant and spoken a few words. The giant Greek had nodded and strode towards the headman and his two companions. Rallis had turned back to the others.

'Come, Professor,' he had said. 'Andros will accompany us. He can move as fast on foot as a trotting horse.'

Fields had been staring unblinkingly into the middle distance during the debate between Adam and Rallis. Like a man emerging from a trance at the snap of a hypnotist's fingers, he had jolted into life.

'It is confoundedly inconvenient,' he had snapped, 'but I can see no viable course of action save to do what this wretched head man demands.'

He had begun to follow Andros. After he had gone a dozen yards, he had turned and called back to the others.

'I will speak to this man Garland. I will persuade him to leave us in peace. We cannot be disturbed by anyone at so crucial a moment in our digging.'

Adam had watched as the professor had made his way to join the Greek villagers. There had been a good deal of shouting and gesticulating as he did so. The young man had looked at Rallis.

'Well,' he had said, 'this is an unexpected turn of events. I do not think anyone, least of all the professor, will prevent Mr Garland joining us here if he decides to do so. He is a determined man.'

'Perhaps his arrival will benefit us, Adam.'

'You mean that Garland's presence will stand in the way of the professor's plans for any gold we might find?'

The Greek had nodded.

'Perhaps Garland is after the gold himself,' Adam had suggested. 'I cannot see how he could know about Euphorion and the lost manuscript, but it is possible.'

'These are all imponderables, my friend.' Rallis had taken off his hat and run his fingers through his thinning hair. 'But I must go and join the others.'

'Be on your guard, Rallis.'

'I will, Adam.'

The lawyer had shaken Adam's hand. He had turned and made his way towards the camp where Fields, his hand shading his eyes, had been gazing back at them.

Adam and Quint had then climbed down into the trench once more and continued to dig. Adam, perplexed by the turn events had taken, had been able to think of nothing but the riders from the north and the idea that Emily Maitland might soon arrive at the excavation.

* * * * *

A few minutes after examining the coin showing Heracles and the Nemean lion which Quint had unearthed, he nonetheless threw down his spade.

'You are right, Quint,' he said. 'We shall dig nothing here but our own graves. Into which, felled by heat and exhaustion, we shall soon tumble.'

Adam sat down on the floor of the trench, his back to his servant. There was silence apart from the sounds of the birds flying above them.

'Did you not hear what I said, Quint?' Adam took his hat from his head and wiped away the sweat that was trickling down his brow. 'It is rare enough that I agree with you. I would have thought you would seize upon such a moment of accord. Cast aside the spade and we shall rest a while.'

There was still no word from his servant. Adam turned to see what was keeping him silent. Quint was holding up an object he had found between his thumb and forefinger.

'I reckon this is gold,' he said, his voice little more than a whisper.

Adam took it from him and let it rest on the outstretched palm of his right hand. It was tiny, less than half an inch long and a quarter of an inch wide, but it was quite clearly in the form of a sculptured head. Beneath the soil with which it was coated, he could make out the eyes, the nose and the beard. And Quint was right. Also beneath its covering of dirt, the little head glinted with the unmistakeable shimmer of gold.

'What is it?' Quint asked, still speaking as quietly as a man in church might.

Adam tilted his hand slightly and admired the way the object glittered in the sunlight. He brushed some of the dirt from it.

'I'm not sure. It was probably part of some ornament. Is it the head of a god perhaps? Neptune?'

'We planning on telling the others we found it?'

Adam ignored Quint's remark and, crouching down close to the upturned soil, reached down to pick up another glinting object from the earth. He held it up for Quint to see.

'A ring,' he said. 'A gold ring that once circled the finger of some blueblood Macedonian lady long dead. Who knows what beauty used to own it? It must have fallen from her hand more than twenty-one hundred years ago.'

The young man stared at the two golden pieces in his hand. His mind drifted back into the Greek history his education had constructed for him. He lost his sense of the present, and the imagined past was briefly more vivid than anything around him. It was only for a moment and then he returned to reality.

'I think Fields and Rallis should be told of what we have found. As soon as possible. They should know before they get back here with Garland. Go after them, Quint. Take one of the mules. See if our friends have met these new visitors. Let them know of our discovery.'

His servant stared at him in disgust, as if he could scarcely believe what was being demanded of him.

'In this heat? You want me to go riding off into the hills on one of them bleeding mules? When it's fit to fry eggs in the shade?'

'Just go, Quint, will you?'

'They're on 'orses. 'Ow am I goin' to catch them when they're on 'orses?'

'You will not catch them. I do not expect you to catch them. You will meet them as they return from their rendezvous. I would have thought that it would be a pleasure to be the bearer of glad tidings.

For once in your life, why not do something without first listing all the reasons why you can't?'

Quint continued to gaze at his master with an air of truculence, but, after a few seconds, he turned and began to climb the short ladder propped against the trench wall. Adam watched him go. For several minutes the sounds of mumbled grousing drifted down to where he was standing. A mule brayed and Quint cursed. Then there was silence. Adam picked up his spade and began once more to dig.

CHAPTER THIRTY-NINE

An hour passed but there was no sign of Adam's companions returning. He continued to work in the trench. He came upon no more golden objects. Once again he laid down his spade. Quint had left a jacket at the far end of the trench. Adam spread it out on the compacted mud floor and sat on it. He leaned against the side of the deep ditch that they had dug. His eyes closed and within a few minutes he had fallen asleep. The sun rose higher and higher in the sky but Adam, still in the shade the trench offered, continued to sleep. He dreamed of Heracles in the Cremorne Gardens, startling the visitors with his lion skin and his club.

He awoke with a start. He could see the dark outline of a man standing on the lip of the trench. The man was holding a revolver, aiming it at his heart. As Adam, still half asleep and rubbing his eyes, began to struggle to his feet, the man silhouetted against the sun swivelled the revolver abruptly. He shot into the side of the trench and then swung the gun back towards Adam's body. The noise of the shot reverberated thunderously around the camp.

'Stay where you are!' the man shouted. Adam recognised the voice immediately. It was Fields.

'Professor?' Although the voice was so familiar, Adam could not yet quite believe that the person directing the gun at him was his old tutor and mentor. 'What is this? What are you doing? Where are Rallis and Quint?'

Fields shook his head in irritation as if Adam's questions were pointless distractions from the matter in hand.

'It is all over, Adam. I have thought through the possibilities most carefully. I have no other choice.' The professor sounded weary. He continued to point the gun at the young man. 'I regret very much that it should come to this. Rallis forced my hand at first with all his stupid ideas about stealing the legacy of the ancient Greeks. As if the wretched Greeks of today were capable of appreciating their past. The more of their treasures that pass into the hands of Englishmen, the better. At least we are civilised enough to look after them. And now the arrival of this man Garland puts paid to my alternative plans.'

He gestured with the gun.

'Climb out of the trench, Adam. But do so with the utmost care. If you make any movements that suggest you are planning to dispossess me of my weapon, I shall shoot you.'

Adam looked to his left to where Quint had cut primitive footholds into the side of the trench. He used them to haul himself out of the grave-like excavation. He pulled himself over the lip of the ditch and struggled to his feet. Fields still had the gun directed at him. Adam looked beyond the professor's shoulder. The older man noticed the movement of his eyes.

'There is little point lifting your eyes to the hills, Adam, for no help will come from that direction. Rallis is not on his way.'

'Where is he?' Adam was still confused, still uncertain of what was happening. 'Where is Quint?'

'The lawyer is out there lying under the Greek sun.' Without moving his revolver, which was still trained on Adam's midriff, Fields jerked his head in the direction the men had ridden no more than a few hours ago. 'It was necessary to shoot him. And his gargantuan servant.' The professor gave a short and mirthless laugh.

'The fools obliged me by travelling in the vanguard. It was easy enough to make use of the weapon I had hidden.' Fields shifted his weight from one foot to another. 'As for Quintus, I passed him an hour or more ago. Riding one of the mules and looking very sorry for himself. Luckily for him, he did not see me. If he had, he would have been even sorrier for I might have been forced to kill him as well. Which I would have regretted. I have always been fond of Quintus, rogue though he is.'

'I hope you are not planning to kill me, Professor?'

'Of course not, my boy. Whatever gave you that idea?' Fields laughed again, more amiably than before. He seemed to find Adam's question genuinely funny. 'Not unless you do something very foolish and I do not believe that you will.'

'I will do nothing foolish,' Adam promised. He had recovered from the surprise of the professor's arrival and was now struggling to make sense of the sudden revelations about Rallis's murder. Fields, it seemed, had lost his mind. What other explanation could there possibly be for the terrible deeds to which he was cheerfully admitting? 'But what is to happen next? We cannot stand here for ever like figures from Madame Tussauds.'

'It will be two hours, maybe even three, before Garland arrives.' The professor appeared curiously calm and rational. He might have been sitting down in his study in Cambridge to conduct a tutorial on pre-Socratic philosophy rather than standing by a half-dug trench in Thessaly, waving a gun at his favourite pupil. 'Before Rallis and I parted company with the village headman, he told us exactly where Garland and his companions were. However swiftly they travel, they cannot be here sooner. And they may well stumble across the bodies of Rallis and Andros, which will delay them further. There is time for us to talk.'

'Perhaps we should wait for Garland to arrive,' Adam said cautiously. 'We can travel back to Salonika with him.'

'Oh, I think not, my boy,' Fields replied amiably. 'You are assuming, of course, that I have gone mad. You are humouring me in the hope that rescue will arrive sooner than I expect.'

The professor shook his head from side to side. Adam had seen him do the same a hundred times in the past when confronted by the stupidity of the average undergraduate.

'I can assure you I am not mad. When the wind is southerly, I know a hawk from a handsaw, as the gloomy Prince of Denmark said.'

'I have no doubts about your sanity, sir,' Adam lied, 'but you have, by your own admission, killed two men. That cannot just be ignored or forgotten. We should wait for Garland. We will convince him that you shot Rallis and Andros in self-defence. That they attacked us when we discovered gold. Which Quint and I did only a short time after you left. We will tell Garland that—'

Fields did not wait to hear what they would tell Garland. With a sudden twist of his arm, he pointed the revolver upwards and shot into the air. The explosion of the gun sent birds squawking in terror from the nearby trees. Adam, silenced and half-deafened, watched the professor swing his gun back into a position where it was directed once more at him.

'That is enough,' Fields shouted. The sounds of the birds slowly died away and a strange quiet descended.

'Now, I shall tell you what will happen,' the professor said. 'You will submit to being tied and bundled into the trench. I will return to Volos. From there, I will be obliged to travel into exile. I do not think Cambridge will now welcome me back with open arms but I have always had a great fondness for Tuscany. I do not think that many questions will be asked of an Englishman who takes a villa in the hills outside Florence. Most probably I shall enjoy my exile. I have an income from my long-departed father's estate. I have the fruits of my association with Creech, of which I assume you know. I shall not be like poor Ovid in his banishment by the Black Sea.'

The professor paused as if to relish the prospect of an enforced sojourn in Florence. Adam could scarcely believe what he was hearing. Did Fields really believe that it was feasible for him not only to ecape from European Turkey but to make his way to Italy and settle in a Tuscan villa? Did he think that no consequences would follow his actions in shooting Rallis? If any further proof were needed that the ageing scholar had taken leave of his senses, here it was. Aware of the revolver pointing towards him, the young man was in no position to argue but he risked throwing a tentative remark into the silence.

'What of our excavations here?' he asked. 'The treasure may nearly be ours.'

Still holding the gun level in one hand, the professor swatted away the words like troublesome flies with the other.

'Thanks to the foolish interference of others, I must abandon our diggings,' he said. 'But I can return. Perhaps in a year, perhaps in two years. In five years, if necessary. I can wait. I have the Euphorion manuscript and the rest of the world does not.'

'Garland will know where to dig. He will see where we have been digging.'

Fields shook his head as if dismissing the idea but otherwise he ignored Adam's words. The young man wondered whether the professor was capable any longer of thinking clearly on such subjects. He seemed to have reached a point where he almost believed that his wishes alone could transform reality. The Macedonian gold was destined to be his so there could be no chance that Garland or anyone else would dig it up. It would sit here beneath the earth until Fields could return for it.

'Before I take horse for Volos,' he went on, 'I must explain myself. I wish you to know the precise reasons why I have acted as I have.'

Adam risked a glance to his left: perhaps Quint had turned back to the camp soon after Fields had seen him and was even now approaching. But he could discern nothing but one of the mules, tethered to a post and grazing on the grass at its feet.

'I wish you to understand what has been behind all this, my boy,' the professor said, speaking with sudden feeling. 'You must appreciate that I have been driven to these terrible but necessary deeds by the idiocy and avarice of others.'

Fields's head dropped. For a moment he looked like a man who had reached the end of his road. I can disarm him now, thought Adam, readying himself to rush towards the gun, but it was as if the professor overheard his inner voice. His head jerked up again and he waved the revolver at the young man.

'Move a yard or two back, Adam. You must not think of running at me. I am very fond of you but I will certainly shoot you. I have not come this far to fall victim to idle scruples about another death.'

The young man did as he was ordered, shuffling several paces backwards.

'That is far enough,' Fields said. 'I would not have you falling into the trench. Now, where were we?'

'You were about to explain to me why you have done this,' Adam said quietly.

'Ah, yes, so I was. I would not have you think entirely ill of me, Adam.'

For a moment, the eyes of the two men met. The young man was appalled by what he glimpsed in the red-rimmed and bloodshot gaze of his mentor. Here was someone who had stared at the abyss and then tumbled into it. Adam saw that there would be no return to reason for the professor.

* * * * *

Several miles further north, Quint and the mule were making slow progress. It would have been hard for any observer, had there been one close to hand, to decide whether man or beast was the more disgruntled. The mule had been aggravated by its removal from the area near the camp where it had been happily and idly grazing. It had retaliated by refusing to move at anything other than a snail's pace, no matter how hard its rider had dug his heels into its flanks and made encouraging noises. On a number of occasions, Quint had been obliged to dismount and pull the reluctant creature by its reins. The sound of its outraged braying echoed along the valley through which they were travelling so slowly.

Quint himself was sweating and cursing as he tugged and chivvied the mule into motion. He was a man who was rarely at a loss for a grievance and this unwanted journey, he felt, was an injustice that even the most saintly of individuals would have found difficult to bear without complaint. He grumbled incessantly beneath his breath as he remounted the mule yet again. One minute he had been happily digging in the trench. Well, maybe not happily, he admitted to himself. Digging was almost as much of a bleeding pain in the arse as dragging this mule halfway across Thessaly. But he'd been resigned to it. That was the word, resigned. And then Adam had got it into his head that a message had to be sent to the others. When they could have just given themselves a slap on the back for finding the gold ornament and settled down for a kip in the shade until the others got back.

'There's some as wouldn't reckernise a good thing if it came up and kicked 'em in the cods,' Quint said bitterly to himself. He sometimes wondered if his master wasn't as daft as a sheep before the shearers. How Adam had managed before he'd happened along to take him under his wing, he didn't know. 'Of course,' he acknowledged, struggling to be fair-minded, 'I got me a nice crib out of it.' But it was Adam, Quint felt, who had got the best of the bargain. And now here the young sprig was, sending him out into the heat of the day with a brute that wouldn't listen to a bleeding word you said.

'Giddyup, you long-eared bastard,' he shouted, digging his heels into the mule's sides once again.

To Quint's great surprise, the animal responded. It began to trot along the path they were following by the side of a meandering stream. As he clung to its reins, the beast increased its pace until it was travelling at a speed of which Quint had not imagined it capable. Bumping uncomfortably up and down on the saddle and watching the Greek countryside race past him, he began to wish that he had not given the mule any encouragement. This was worse – much worse – than pulling and wrenching at the beast to force it forwards a few yards.

'Whoa, you hee-hawing devil, or I'll see you in a bleedin' stewpan.' Quint had now abandoned his faith in the reins and stretched himself full-length along the mule's back, both his hands clasped around the creature's neck. 'This ain't Derby Day and you ain't Blue Gown.'

The mule took no notice of its rider. If anything, it upped its trot towards a gallop. Perhaps, Quint thought miserably, it did believe it was the famous thoroughbred that had won at Epsom two years earlier. He continued to wrap himself around the mule's neck and hope that it would soon tire of its exertions. For a minute, he closed his eyes, figuring that it might be better not to know exactly where they were going. After a hundred yards, he decided he was wrong and opened them again. The stream to the left, he noted, had widened considerably. He struggled to twist his head forward so that he could look ahead of him. All he could see was a blur of green and, far in the distance, the grey stones of the mountains. He felt the dry, hard skin of the mule's neck against his cheek. One of the hairs from its mane began to work its way up his nose, tickling him to the point where he wanted to sneeze. When he did so, his startled mount picked up pace even more.

'Christ in heaven,' Quint moaned. 'Ain't it jiggered yet?'

He risked raising his head slightly and was astonished by what he saw. A quarter of a mile ahead was a group of horses and riders. They had stopped by a small grove of trees and were all gazing towards Quint and his mule as the pair raced towards them. One of the riders was standing in his stirrups to get a better view.

Quint and his mount bore down on the group. At the speed they were travelling, the distance between them shortened rapidly. The man was yelling incoherently, the beast was braying at full volume. The horses and their riders scattered as the mule charged into their midst. It dug its hooves into the ground beneath it and came to a sudden stop. Quint did not. He hurtled over the mule's head and crashed to earth. Stunned and winded, he lay in the grass as confused thoughts drifted through his mind. Briefly, he was back in Doughty Street, ushering a young woman into the sitting room. She was looking at him in a strange way. He was, of course, used to people looking at him in a strange way. Usually he didn't mind but he felt a strong urge to explain himself to this young woman. He knew her name, he was sure of it, but he just couldn't recall it. She leaned forward and stared into his eyes.

'Mr Quint,' she said. 'Is that you? Are you all right?'

Emily, he thought, Emily something. Then he lost consciousness.

'It was that contemptible man Creech who began all this,' Fields said to Adam, his face screwing up with anger as he remembered the man with the crescent moon scar. 'He sought to cheat me. He sought to make use of my scholarship and knowledge for his own sordid ends. And yet, when our plans to travel to Koutles and unearth the treasure were already well advanced, he wanted to cast me aside. He approached you, one of the few other Englishmen who had travelled in the region recently. He sent his daughter to discover more about you.'

Adam started with surprise. 'His daughter?'

'Did you not realise the identity of your mysterious visitor in London, Adam? The chit of a girl who has followed us to Greece? Perhaps you believed that it was your charms that attracted Emily to your company?' The professor laughed. 'She was working on her father's behalf. At her father's behest. He assumed that you would be more forthcoming when questioned by a pretty girl than you would be if he came to you in person. He was correct, of course.'

Adam's face fell. He recalled the occasions on which he had met Emily Maitland. In Doughty Street. At Cremorne. Her questioning of him, he was forced to admit, had seemed odd. But not so odd that he had not wished to continue their conversations as long as possible. Not so odd that they had outweighed the power of her beauty and vivacity to stir him. He could not think what to say but that seemed to matter very little. Fields was in full flow. He wanted to talk.

'Emily is not English, of course,' the professor went on. 'Not in the sense that you and I are English. Or even in the sense that Quintus is English. Where the name of Maitland has come from, I do not know. Plucked from the air or borrowed from one of her mother's grubby cavaliers, I suppose. You must have noticed that although she speaks our language so well, she does not speak it as if it were her mother tongue. Her mother tongue – indeed, her mother – is Greek. She is the daughter Creech fathered on some

Peloponnesian trollop when he was in Athens twenty years ago.'

'But why has she not spent her life with her father?' The young man knew the answer to his own question as soon as he voiced it aloud.

'Do not be so naive, Adam. Why should Creech have acknowledged a child who was merely the unfortunate end result of an indiscretion? He proved surprisingly honourable in his own way. He paid a yearly allowance to her but no more. I doubt he saw her more than half a dozen times in twenty years.'

'So she lived with her mother.'

'The trollop has been mistress to a Jewish merchant for the last decade. She and Emily have trailed after him as he has moved from city to city. Constantinople to Salonika. Salonika to Aleppo. Aleppo to Athens. Athens back to Salonika.'

'But what was she doing in London?'

'The merchant – Margolis, I believe, is his name – had come to England on business. He was travelling in the north and he arranged for his supposed wife and supposed stepdaughter to stay at Brown's while he was gone. Under the name of Maitland. The good Lord alone knows why the people at the hotel allowed it. They must have been aware that all was not as it appeared. Their moral standards have clearly plunged in recent years.' Fields sniffed with disapproval. For a moment, he seemed genuinely concerned that Brown's was not maintaining its reputation. 'Emily had long wished to know more of her real father,' he continued. 'Somehow she had learned that he was also then in London and she contacted him. He saw a means of making use of her and she was happy to oblige him.'

'I cannot see that I could have told her anything that would have been of interest to him.'

'Perhaps not. But he learned enough to confirm what he already suspected: that you might also be of use to him. He went to visit that idle dauber Jardine and asked him a whole series of questions about you – and about myself and my whereabouts – which that young idiot answered. Then Creech contrived to meet you himself at the

Marco Polo. I found out about the dinner and I guessed that he had probably dropped hints about Philip's gold. But I did not know how much he had told you. I went to see him at Herne Hill Villa.'

'And murdered him,' Adam said, in little more than a whisper. Suddenly the young man could see the truth of what had happened and he was appalled by it. Somehow the killing of Creech in his own suburban London home seemed even worse than the shooting of Rallis and Andros here in Greece.

'I did not intend to kill him. Why should I? He and I had been partners in a very profitable venture for years, despatching antiquities from this benighted country to England for safe-keeping. Rallis has doubtless told you all this already, putting the worst possible interpretation on my actions, I have no doubt. No, I went to remonstrate with Creech.'

'With a pistol in your pocket.'

'Samuel Creech was a dangerous man, Adam. He was not only an importer of Greek statues and Attic vases. In London, you discovered much about his activities as a blackmailer. Do you suppose that a man can spend half a lifetime extorting money from the wealthy and the powerful and still thrive unless he is prepared to act ruthlessly? I knew Creech's temperament. I took the pistol with me for protection.'

Adam eyed the gun that the professor now had trained on him. He tried to judge the distance between them. Six yards, perhaps. Too far for him to run at Fields without being brought down. He could only hope that he could keep the professor talking until Quint returned and then, together, they might overpower him.

'So you were obliged to shoot him in self-defence?'

'He laughed at me, the wretch. He said he had no more need of me. That he was about to recruit another "assistant". Can you believe it? He referred to me as an "assistant". The arrogance of the man. But that was not the reason he had to die.'

The professor paused and shifted the revolver in his hands.

'He had been foolish as well as treacherous. In endeavouring to blackmail his old friend Garland, he had made a dangerous enemy.

The man was making enquiries of his own. Sooner or later my name would have emerged. I could not allow that to happen.'

'So you pointed your pistol at him and warned him that he must stop his attempts to extort money from Garland.'

'Yes. And the rogue laughed again. He refused to listen to reason. He said that his dealings with Garland were his affair only.'

'But I cannot understand why you felt obliged to kill the man.'

'For God's sake, Adam, he attacked me. He threw himself upon me and we struggled. The pistol fired as we fought.' Fields had raised his voice close to screaming pitch. He seemed on the verge of losing all self-control. 'Do you suppose I wanted to kill him? Do you suppose I want to kill you? Or Quintus? I did not even wish to kill that interfering Greek lawyer. I am a man of peace and scholarship. But events have conspired to drag me into blood and destruction. It sometimes feels as if I have faced a fate as inevitable as the doom of the House of Pelops.'

The professor looked to be on the verge of tears of self-pity. Adam wondered if the man's mind had collapsed completely. His account of Creech's killing could not be correct. There had been no signs of a struggle in his library. Fields had shot him quite cold-bloodedly as he sat at the table. The young man eyed once more the ground between him and the gun. Fields again guessed what he was thinking.

'Do not imagine for one moment that I will not shoot you if necessary, Adam,' he said. 'I am fond enough of you but nothing and no one must stand between me and the gold.'

A silence fell on the two men, frozen as they were like a stage tableau in the afternoon sun. To Adam, it seemed as if the professor could not decide what he should do next. Could he keep him talking for a while longer? Would Quint not be returning soon to camp? And what of Garland? His party might surely arrive at any moment.

* * * * *

'And you did not pass Professor Fields or Mr Rallis and his man as you made your way here? You saw no sign of them?'

Quint shook his head and then winced. Twenty minutes after his tumble from the runaway mule, it hurt still. He was sitting in the shade of a tree, a wet handkerchief across his brow. Lewis Garland stood over him.

'Ain't seen a soul,' the servant said. 'Not since a mile out of Koutles.'

'But you were travelling in their tracks?'

'So the Greek cove said. The one I met beyond the village. Least-ways I think he did.'

'You understand the language?'

'A few words. But 'e waved his hands around a lot as well. As clear as I could make out, 'e was saying that the professor and the others had passed 'im a bit before. So I keeps on going.'

'And then what happened?'

'And then that black devil of a mule took it into its 'ead to run away with me.'

'Never mind the wretched mule. Before it bolted with you, you saw nothing and no one on the trail. Is that correct?'

'Ain't I just said that? 'Ow many more times do you want me to say it? There was nobody between 'ere and Koutles save the Greek I told you about.'

Quint was getting very exasperated. When he had returned to consciousness after his fall, he had found himself to be the centre of attention. It was an unaccustomed position for him and he had begun to enjoy it. Emily Maitland had fussed over him, despatch-ing a servant to the stream to wet one of her handkerchiefs and place it on his forehead. She had ordered two of the other Greek servants in the group to pick him up from where the mule had deposited him and carry him to a grassy knoll beneath a tall tree. He had told his story to her and to Garland. He had described to them all that had happened since he and Adam and the others had left Athens. It had been a novel experience to find a beautiful young woman and a man of Garland's importance hanging on his every word and he had relished it. He had been eloquent and, he reckoned, comprehensive in his answers. He had said all that he wanted to say. Now Emily had retired to the shade of another tree further along the bank of the stream where a servant had set up a folding chair for her. Garland, however, was still leaning over him and badgering him with more questions. The enjoyment had disappeared. Quint just wanted to go to sleep.

'I give you the lowdown, didn't I? Can't you leave a man to get some shut-eye?'

He stretched back on the grass and half closed his eyes. Garland stared down at him for a moment before turning abruptly and walking away. Quint rolled over on his side and watched him go. The MP joined Emily and there was a brief but animated discussion between them. Quint could see the girl gesturing in the direction of the path along which the mule had so lately carried him. She seemed to want the party to take it immediately but her companion looked less enthusiastic about the idea. After two or three minutes, Garland began to walk back to where Quint was lying beneath the tree. The servant saw Emily start to follow him. He rolled hastily onto his back and shut his eyes again. He experimented with a few feigned snores as they approached.

'Wake up, Devlin.' The MP prodded Quint with his toe. 'If, indeed, you are asleep. We have one more question that needs to be answered.'

The servant made a great performance of yawning and stretching his arms.

'When you took the manuscript at Fields's promptings,' Garland went on, 'was your master pleased that you had obeyed the professor?'

Quint looked warily from the MP to the young woman and back again.

'Not exackly,' he said, after a brief pause. ''E give me a bit of a wigging, if truth be told.'

'So Adam is not implicated in this thievery, my dear.' Garland turned to Emily, who smiled at him. 'But I fear for the safety of our Greek friend.'

'He had his servant with him, had he not?'

'He could send Big Ben Caunt to grass with one 'and tied behind his back, that 'un,' Quint remarked encouragingly. ''E's the size of an 'ouse.'

'It matters little what size a man is,' Garland said. 'If he is not on his guard, he can be brought low. As I say, I grow anxious for Rallis.'

'That is why we must hurry on our way,' Emily said. 'We are wasting precious time here.'

'We may hasten into a trap, my dear.'

Quint was bewildered. 'Trap? What trap?' he asked.

Neither Garland nor the young woman answered him.

'We must be off immediately,' Emily said.

'What's up?' Quint looked at her and then swung his head round towards the MP. Both of them ignored him. ''Oo's going to set a bleedin' trap?'

'Be quiet, Devlin,' Garland snapped. 'And mind your language when ladies are present.'

The MP stared at the distant mountains, lost in thought.

'Very well, my dear,' he said, after a long minute had passed. 'After consideration, I believe that you are right. Let us be on our way. Devlin, you can ride with Giorgios. His horse will take two. You can leave the mule behind.'

* * * * *

'What of poor Jinkinson?' Adam asked, curious as to how much more the professor might tell him. 'Was it you in the darkness at Wapping? Did you kill him?'

'Do you recall that German braggart Schliemann we met once in Athens? In the summer of sixty-seven, I think it was.' Fields seemed not to hear Adam's questions. He made no attempt to deny responsibility for Jinkinson's death. He had set off on a digression of his own. 'I came across him again the following year. I was riding with two of the servants in the mountains south of Salonika when we saw a group of horsemen in the distance. At first, we feared they were brigands, but in the event it turned out to be Schliemann and a band of potential cut-throats who had taken his money to guide him

415

on a long and pointless tour of the region. I was obliged to join him in his encampment for dinner and to listen to his interminable rantings about Troy and the Homeric epics. About the discoveries he is destined to make. Of how his name will for ever be in the annals of archaeology. The man is impossible – a noisy megalomaniac who listens to no one but himself.'

'Why should anyone else listen to him? The plain of Troy has long been a battleground for scholars as well as for heroes. Schliemann will not be the first to fall upon it nor the last. Why should you concern yourself with him?'

'Because I fear that he may be correct. That he will unearth the secrets of Priam's city as he claims he will. It is so often the Schliemanns of this world who gain the glory.'

Suddenly the professor sounded so weary, like an ageing Atlas longing to take the weight of the world from his shoulders. His posture slumped and the barrel of his revolver began to point closer to the ground than to Adam's chest. The young man wondered yet again if he could make the six-yard dash to Fields that he had earlier dismissed. Before he could steel himself to do it, the professor seemed to gain a new energy. He jerked upright once more.

'The golden treasure hoard of the Macedonian kings! Can you imagine what it would be to unearth it, Adam?' Fields was excited now, and sweating profusely. 'It would be the archaeological sensation of the age! The discoveries of Layard and Rawlinson would pale into insignificance beside it. Even the discoveries Schliemann boasts he will make in Asia Minor. Would even the ruins of Troy match Philip of Macedon's gold?'

'Layard and Rawlinson did not murder men in pursuit of their discoveries. Nor, I assume, will Schliemann.'

'Do you think I wished lives to be sacrificed?' Fields sounded indignant. 'Of course I did not. But what choice did those fools leave me? That grasping devil Creech cared only for the money he thought he would make from Philip's gold. The history, the romance meant nothing to him. As for that sot of an investigator, he did not even realise what he had stumbled across.'

Adam could not yet see clearly in his mind the connection between Fields and Jinkinson. 'How did you know of the man's existence?' he asked.

'He approached me. He must have come across my name during his dealings with Creech. Perhaps Creech even confided in him, although I doubt that.'

'He came to visit you in Cambridge?'

'He arrived one evening just before dinner.' The professor laughed bitterly. 'The good Lord alone knows what my servant made of him. The man was half-drunk. He babbled to me of how we might work together to make our fortunes.'

'Jinkinson was aware of the treasure?'

'In some limited sense, I believe. He had succeeded in gathering little snippets of information from here and there. He knew of the Euphorion manuscript. He knew that it held the key to something of immense value.'

'But a London enquiry agent with a fondness for the bottle was unlikely to have the means to travel to Greece in search of the treasure, if you refused to help him. Why was it necessary to kill him?'

'He knew my name, Adam,' Fields said, as if explaining some elementary proposition in logic to a singularly dense student. 'He knew of the existence of the Euphorion manuscript and of my interest in it. And he was in contact with that man Garland. I feared that he would tell him of the gold.'

'His only interest in Garland was as a victim to be blackmailed. He had carried on with the extortion that Creech had begun.'

'Is that so?' The professor looked surprised. 'Ah, well, no matter. He knew enough that he could not live.'

'How did you trail him to that wretched tavern by the river?'

'It was not so difficult a task. You also found him, did you not? I had made an earlier attempt to dispose of him which had failed. He took fright and ran to his hiding-hole. I spoke to that ragged *hetaira* of his. What is her name?'

'Ada.'

'Ada was most forthcoming. I had taken it upon myself to offer money to the Polyphemus who guards the entrance to her place of work. Again, I have forgotten his name. If, indeed, I ever knew it.'

'Fadge, you must mean Fadge.'

'Well, whatever the one-eyed Cyclops is called, he proved very effective in persuading Ada that she should tell me where her ageing inamarato was lodged.'

'You did not allow Fadge to hurt the poor girl?'

'A little,' Fields acknowledged. 'She was surprisingly loyal to Jinkinson. But she was eventually persuaded that he was not worth the breaking of her arm.'

'You scoundrel!' Adam could contain his outrage no longer. How could he have been so mistaken in his judgement of the professor? Here was a man he had admired for his knowledge and his scholarship now revealed as little better than a common or garden brute.

'It was unfortunately necessary to employ such methods. I had to find Jinkinson.'

'So you went in search of him at the Cat and Salutation.'

'By happy chance, I travelled to Wapping on the very night that you went there yourself. I arrived an hour earlier than you and was in time to see the man leave that dismal alehouse for the first time. I followed him for some time but he walked along busy streets. I could not make use of the pistol in my pocket. Then he returned to the pub. I thought I had lost my opportunity. I had not reckoned on your presence in the place driving him out into the night once more. And onto the darkest path by the river.'

Fields ceased speaking, as if expecting Adam to make some contribution to the conversation. The young man was silent, contemplating the terrible truth that he had been indirectly responsible for the deaths of both Creech and Jinkinson. He had long realised that had Creech not sought him out, the man would have still been alive. Now it was clear that, in arriving at the Cat and Salutation in search of Jinkinson, he had inadvertently impelled the private investigator towards his nemesis.

'I thought that the figure in the shadows was familiar,' he said, after a pause. 'It was you.'

'For a while, I thought that you had recognised me,' Fields admitted. 'I returned to Cambridge on an early morning train, half-convinced that the police would soon be calling at the college to question me. When you wrote to me the following day, suggesting that you visit, I wondered whether it was part of a stratagem to unmask me. But, after your arrival in Cambridge, it was clear that you knew nothing. That you had not recognised me.'

'And so you decided to use me.'

'Creech had thought to recruit you. Why should not I? I knew from our travels in sixty-seven that you would make a good companion on any expedition to Greece. So I pretended to know nothing about Euphorion.'

Throughout the time he had been speaking, Fields had continued to keep the revolver trained on Adam's heart. The gun was still pointing there as he finished. Adam let out a long sigh of disillusion and disappointment.

'But what of the deaths, Professor? How could you bring yourself to murder in pursuit of your goal?'

'I have already explained,' Fields said, almost complacently. 'Creech and the sot were not worthy of the knowledge upon which they had stumbled.'

'And what of yourself?' Adam demanded. 'Have your motives for action been so pure?'

'I care for knowledge!' Fields screamed, his face suddenly contorted with fury. 'I care for scholarship! Why should my name not go down to posterity as one of the great archaeologists of the age? The chance had been offered to me. Why should I not take it? Why should a blackmailer and a drunk stand in my way?'

The professor had stepped forwards in his agitation, the gun shaking in his hands. His face had reddened and blue veins in his temple stood out like rivers on a map. He made a heroic effort to regain his self-control. His breathing came in short, sharp pants.

'You have nothing to fear from me, Adam,' he said eventually, his voice now eerily calm. 'I have long had your interests at heart. Since you were a schoolboy in Shrewsbury, I have seen you as, in some way, my successor. The son I have never had, perhaps. Is that too sentimental a thought? I would not harm you. Besides, I have not forgotten you saved my life that day in Athens. Had it not been for you, I would have been a mangled carcass beneath the wheels of that runaway cart.'

'An unfortunate accident.' Despite the professor's words, Adam had no confidence that he would not shoot him if necessary. Had he not said as much only minutes before? Fields seemed so deranged by recent events and by his own demonic urge to gain the Macedonian gold that he could not be trusted.

'I thought for a while it was no accident,' the professor continued. 'That some enemy in the city had attempted to kill me. Later, when my rooms at the Angleterre were rifled, I was sure of it. But I have since understood that the person responsible for upending my belongings was Rallis. And Rallis, whatever his other faults, was not a man to take another's life. No, you are right. The cart crashing into the café was no more than chance.'

* * * * *

'Which way should we travel, Devlin?' Lewis Garland, turning in his saddle, called back to Quint. Adam's manservant was perched behind Giorgios on the latter's bay horse as the party retraced the journey he had so recently made. The road before them divided. One fork of it continued to follow the bank of the small stream; the other headed into the hills. Quint waved an arm to indicate that the horses should begin to climb. Garland led the way as the small group of riders turned off the main path and made its way uphill. For an hour they climbed steadily if not steeply, the path rising ahead of them and the distant view of Mount Olympus permanently before them. The ground hereabouts was uncultivated and rough. On several occasions, the horses came close to stumbling on the rocks and loose stones that were strewn across the path. At one point, they heard the sounds of what might have been a shot coming from the countryside far ahead of them. They all turned to look at one another.

'That was a gunshot, Lewis, was it not?' Emily asked.

'I cannot tell,' Garland replied. 'It is difficult to be certain in this terrain. Sounds carry for many miles. And they can be distorted in their journey.'

'We must hasten on our way. Adam may be in danger.'

'The shot – if it was a shot – could be from the gun of a villager out hunting, my dear. We should not risk the horses by riding at too great a speed amongst these rocks.'

The MP had reined in his horse and dropped back to join Emily. Quint and Giorgios were immediately behind them. Bringing up the rear were half a dozen young men hired by Garland in Salonika, all now looking as if they wished they were back in that city. In the vanguard, fifty yards beyond his master, was another of the Englishman's servants. As he came to the top of a gentle rise in the land, the man cried out. Garland and Emily spurred their horses forward to join him. The young woman gasped and raised her hand to her mouth as she saw what had attracted the servant's attention. On the path ahead was a body. Sprawled in the dirt was the huge form of Andros. He looked like one of the giants felled by Zeus in his battle with them.

'Stay where you are, Emily,' Garland ordered. He dismounted and approached the vast figure, its back reddened with blood. He knelt by its side and held his fingers to the side of Andros's neck.

'He is dead,' he said, rising to his feet. 'He has been shot in the back.'

'The sound we heard?'

'No, he has been dead for some time. We shall have to carry him with us. We must give him a decent burial when we can.'

Garland shouted instructions to his hired men, who reluctantly climbed down from their mounts.

'Ain't the only one we might have to bury,' remarked Quint, who had slid down from behind Giorgios and was standing in the middle of the path, arms akimbo.

'What the blazes do you mean, Devlin?'

Quint pointed to a small knoll of earth a hundred yards away.

Beneath the inadequate shade of a stunted tree was another figure. It was clearly that of a man.

Garland began to walk rapidly towards it, followed at a more leisurely pace by Quint. As they did so, the figure suddenly raised itself on its arms.

'He is still alive,' Emily cried.

The two men broke into a trot. As they did so, the figure sank into the earth again and remained motionless.

'It's Rallis,' Garland called, as he neared the crumpled shape. He squatted on his haunches by the side of the Greek lawyer. 'He has been shot in the back as well, but he is breathing.'

* * * * *

The rock was lying inches from Adam's left foot. It was a tempting weapon if only he could reach down to pick it up. But how was he to do that with Fields's revolver trained upon him?

'Now I have told you all I wish to tell you, Adam,' the professor said. 'And I must leave you. Garland, I think, is within a few miles of us. Unlike Prometheus, you will not have to remain in your chains for long. Nor will an eagle devour your liver. Although it will be uncomfortable down there in the mud we have dug.'

Fields nodded in the direction of the trench. Still pointing the gun at his young protégé's heart, he motioned towards his horse.

'There is strong rope enough to bind you, I believe. It is looped around the pommel of the saddle on this beast behind me.'

'I can see it,' Adam acknowledged.

'I think it would be best if you took it off yourself. Then drop it at your feet.'

Fields began to back and wheel slowly to his left, allowing Adam a path to walk towards the horse. The young man was about to move forward when he saw that the professor was edging in the direction of two mounds of earth, upturned from the trench earlier in the day. He chose to wait for a moment.

'Come, Adam. We have not all day.' Fields gestured impatiently. As he did so, his foot caught on one of the piles of earth and he stumbled slightly. Involuntarily, he swung the gun away from the young man's body. Adam saw his chance. In one swift movement, he ducked to the ground, seized the rock and threw it at the professor. It struck the older man a glancing blow on the forehead and he stumbled still further. Adam, pushing up from his crouching position, hurled himself towards Fields and the gun. He collided with him just as the professor was recovering his balance and both men crashed to the ground. Winded, Adam still managed to seize the barrel of the revolver with one hand. Fields, spread-eagled beneath him, was clinging desperately to the gun as well. With a strength that belied his years, he succeeded in pushing Adam off him but the young man, realising that his life depended upon it, refused to let go of the gun barrel. The two of them rolled over one another, the weapon trapped between them. Both had their hands upon it but neither could claim possession of it.

As they continued to grapple near the edge of the trench, clouds of dust rose about them. Both men began to cough. The revolver was still caught between their bodies. Adam felt his head and shoulders being forced over the lip of the trench and fought back as best he could but his opponent seemed to possess the vigour of a man decades younger than he was. The young man could sense that Fields was gaining the upper hand. He himself was slipping further and further into the earthwork they had dug. He clung desperately to the barrel of the gun as his feet scrabbled to keep a purchase on the upturned soil. Fields continued to push his upper body over the edge. Adam could feel his balance slowly going but he would not let go of the revolver. That was the only thought that still possessed him. Keep hold of the gun. For what seemed like long minutes, the two men swayed on the rim, spluttering and struggling.

Then the professor, in his effort to hurl Adam into the pit, momentarily lost his own balance and involuntarily reached out a hand to steady himself. It was enough. The younger man was able to snatch the revolver wholly from the professor's grasp, but as he did so, the world gave way beneath him. He tumbled backwards into the trench. His fall was accompanied by a deafening roar as the gun went off. There was a scream from Fields. Adam, plummeting backwards into the earthwork, struck his head against its solid floor. A black pool appeared before him and he dove gratefully into its depths.

* * * * *

When he came round, Adam was still sprawled in the trench like an upturned beetle. He had no idea how long he had been unconscious. He stared up at the cloudless blue sky. He attempted gingerly to move his arms and legs and found, to his relief, that he could do so. He reached a hand around to the back of his head and winced as he felt an egg-shaped lump on his scalp. Hearing a voice, he froze. Could Fields still be up there on the surface? Surely he would have fled the camp by now? Unless Adam was dead, and this was a poor version of the afterlife, the professor had clearly shown him mercy after his fall into the pit. But he would not have lingered long before departing, would he? The voice could be heard again. Certainly it sounded familiar. What was it shouting? Adam sought to sit up in the trench but he found that many of his muscles refused to obey him. He was obliged to remain where he was. The voice echoed in his head, evoking memories which he could not quite place. He knew the rhythms and timbre of it so well. It must be Fields. As he strove to gather his scattered wits, a dark figure appeared over the edge of the trench and looked down at him. Silhouetted against the light, it spoke.

'You planning on being down there all day?' the figure asked.

It was Quint.

Adam found that he could now move. He hauled himself to his feet and reached up his hand to his manservant.

'Get me out of here, Quint. I feel like Hades in the Underworld.'

Quint seized hold of him and, with his assistance, Adam was able to hoist himself out of the earthwork. Once again on the surface, he brushed as much of the soil from his clothing as he could and shook his hair free of the earth lodged in it.

'We been shouting for the last five minutes,' Quint said, in a tone of voice that suggested Adam had been deliberately concealing himself, like a child playing hide-and-seek.

'We?'

Quint nodded in the direction of the camp. Adam could see horses tethered to posts. Two figures were making their way towards them. Blinking in the fierce sunlight, he could just recognise Garland and Emily.

'Where's the professor?' he asked. 'Was he still here when you returned?'

'You could say that,' his servant said.

'Well, where is he now? He must be apprehended. His mind is overthrown. He is a danger to us all.'

By way of reply, Quint inclined his head again, this time towards a pile of earth they had upturned when they had all first arrived at Koutles. Lying across it was what Adam at first thought was a pile of old clothes. He moved a step towards it and realised that it was Fields. His body lolled back across the ground as if it had been dropped from on high. The whole of his front was stained red with blood and innards. Adam could imagine only too well what had happened. In falling into the trench, while still clinging to the gun, he had inadvertently pulled the trigger. The full force of the shot had taken Fields in the midriff, virtually eviscerating him. He had staggered backwards to collapse and die on a mound of newly turned Greek earth.

'He tried to kill me,' Adam said, still scarcely believing the truth.

'Tried to kill Rallis as well,' Quint replied. ''E *did* kill the tall bugger. Poor old Andros.'

'Where is Rallis?'

'On the road back to Salonika. Garland told two of his men to get him to the Catholic sisters there. Fast as possible.'

'Will he live?'

Quint shrugged.

''E's got an 'ole in him 'alf the size of an Essex Pippin. But 'e probably will. The professor here didn't catch him full on like the tall cove.'

Adam walked away from the sorry sight of Fields's body. His manservant followed him, a pace behind.

''E 'ad you fooled as much as me,' he said, managing to sound both truculent and plaintive at the same time.

Adam made no reply.

''E'd 'ave got 'old of that Euphorion book with or without me.'

'I have no doubt that he would.'

'I don't do what any old swaggering Bob tells me to do. But I thought 'e was the boss.'

It was as near to an apology as Quint was ever likely to offer.

'I do not blame you, Quint,' Adam said. 'The responsibility for all this lies with Fields. Let us bury all that has happened with him.'

* * * * *

'I cannot say how happy I am to see you unharmed, Mr Carver. Such terrible pictures filled my imagination as we approached the camp. Of you wounded. Or dead.'

Emily, who had left Garland to supervise the care of the horses, approached Adam as if unsure of the greeting she might receive. Quint, showing unwonted tact, immediately retired.

'As you can see, Miss Maitland, I have survived my ordeal.' Adam looked to catch Emily's eye but she turned away.

'I rejoice to know that we arrived in good time and that you are unhurt.'

A silence fell between the two.

'Oh, Emily,' Adam said, after a long pause, 'how long ago it seems since you came to Doughty Street for the first time. When Quint broke the plates.'

'That was not my first visit. I came to your rooms several days earlier. When neither you nor Mr Quint were present.'

'Of course,' Adam said, smiling wrily. 'I had forgotten. My land-lady – a formidable termagant named Gaffery – saw you as you left. I am surprised that she did not attempt to detain you. Or have you arrested.'

'I was convinced that she would.' Emily laughed. 'She watched me descend the stairs with the door to her own rooms ajar. But she did not show herself any further.'

'I think perhaps she must have feared that the respectability of her house would have been compromised had she confronted you. But she spoke to me. She berated me fiercely.'

'I am sorry to cause you such trouble.'

'It was nothing. Her bark is worse than her bite. But how did you breach the Gaffery fortress in the first place?'

'There is another lodger on the floors above you.'

'Dupont? The Frenchman?'

'Is he French? I knew only that he was not English. I approached him as he was leaving the house. I told him that I was your lady friend and that I needed to leave you a message.'

'And he believed you.' Adam could easily envisage the delight with which Dupont, an engaging and chatty salesman for a French furrier in Mayfair, would have responded to Emily's approach. He would have been only too pleased to assist a beautiful woman in any scheme he thought might further a romantic dalliance.

'He let me in. I thought perhaps you would not have locked your doors. But I could find no way to enter your rooms.'

'So you returned a few days later.'

'On the Tuesday, yes.'

'But why did you leave us so abruptly? Was Quint's clumsiness with the plates so terrifying?'

Emily paused. For a moment it seemed as if she might not reply.

'You were so kind to me. Such a gentleman. I grew ashamed of what my father had asked me to do. When Mr Quint provided the distraction, I decided to leave.'

'Ah, your father. I had not realised that Creech *was* your father until Fields informed me of the fact. I am sorry that he met his death so cruelly.'

Emily bowed her head.

'We should not have plotted to deceive you. But my father was eager to learn as much of you as he could. That is why he wished me to make your acquaintance.'

'And Garland? When did you meet Garland?'

'As you must surely be aware, my father and Lewis Garland were boys together at school. We have known one another for a long time.'

'Of course, he is your godfather.'

There was another pause as Emily turned her head towards Garland, thirty yards away, who was pointing to the horses and delivering instructions to two of the servants.

'Mr Garland is not my godfather.'

Adam waited for her to say more.

'He is my fiancé.'

'That cannot be,' the young man blurted out and would have spoken further, but Emily held up her hand to stop him.

'There is no more to be said, Adam. I am engaged to Lewis Garland and that is all that you need to know.'

'But the difference in your ages.'

'Many a happy marriage has been contracted between a man of mature years and a younger woman.' Emily spoke with a confidence that Adam was certain she did not feel. He stared miserably at the distant mountains. The highest peak of Mount Olympus, where the gods of the ancient Greeks held court, glittered in the afternoon sunshine. They would be looking down and laughing at this latest unexpected twist of fate, he thought.

'I can think little of a man who would place the woman he loved in such danger,' he said eventually. 'Garland should never have allowed you to leave Salonika with him.'

'It was at my insistence, Adam.'

'She was really most persuasive, Mr Carver.' Unseen by either of the young couple, Lewis Garland had left the horses by the camp. He was now standing six feet from them. Adam noticed once again the deep black of his hair and beard, so dark that it must be dyed. He felt he should hate this older man, engaged to marry the woman he now recognised he loved himself, but he found that he could not. 'I defy any man to resist the arguments she used to carry her case.'

'I am still uncertain why you travelled out here from Salonika in the first place. Although I am glad, of course, that you did.'

Garland took two paces closer to them and rested his hand on his fiancée's arm. Was it Adam's imagination, or did Emily move ever so slightly away from him as he did so?

'I was curious as to why my old and – forgive me, my dear – wicked friend Sam Creech was interested in this place Koutles. He had told Emily that he was. Although he had told her little else. We were spending time in Salonika anyway. As you know, Emily and her mother live here. I thought it would be easy enough to satisfy my curiosity by an excursion out here.'

'He was blackmailing you, was he not?' Adam could see no reason now to beat about the bush or indulge in the evasions of polite conversation. Garland looked startled at first by his directness but he rapidly recovered what little composure he had lost.

'Yes – the ties of old friendship meant little to Sam where money was involved. And then, after he was killed, the canary man came calling. Also intent on extorting money from me.'

'Jinkinson was also killed.'

'I am sorry to hear that. In a strange way, I rather liked the man, garrulous and greedy as he was. But I hope you now understand that I was not responsible for his death.'

'No. It was the professor who killed him. He killed Creech as well. And Andros. He thought he had killed Rallis. He was planning, I think, to kill me, although he denied it. Once he had unburdened himself to me as much as he did, I do not think he could have allowed me to stay alive.'

'You must tell us all that Professor Fields confessed,' Emily said.

'It will be a long story.'

'We have the time,' Garland said, gesturing towards the camp. 'My men have prepared the horses for departure, I believe. It will take us several days to return to Salonika.'

'What of the professor's body?' Adam asked.

'We shall bury it here. Where his dreams turned to ashes.'

CHAPTER FORTY

ike distilled mud, the fog swirled in filthy and foul-smelling clouds around Adam's head as he stepped out into Doughty Street. Although it was still the afternoon, the city was given over to the gaslights as he made his way to the Marco Polo. The smoking room was empty save for Mr Moorhouse, sitting in his favourite chair, lost in thought. Adam joined him.

It was nearly two months since his struggle with Fields on the edge of the pit in Macedonia. Together with Emily and Garland and Quint, he had left the camp near Koutles and ridden back towards Salonika. On the way, they had overtaken Rallis and the two men deputed to look after him. Perhaps it was as well for his own comfort that the Greek lawyer had remained more or less unconscious for most of their journey. Once in Salonika, in the care of Roman Catholic nuns there, he had made a surprisingly swift recovery from his wounds. When it came to the time to make their farewells, Rallis was once again on his feet.

'Goodbye, Alexander,' Adam said as he stood by the dock, awaiting the moment to step on board Garland's private yacht. 'If you ever visit London again, I shall insist that you see the sights in my company.'

'I shall accompany you to the British Museum, my friend,' Rallis replied with a smile, holding out his hand. 'And I shall point out all the treasures there that one day will be returned to Greece.'

Adam laughed and took the lawyer's hand. 'I might even help you to smuggle some of them out of the museum,' he said.

430

The journey back from Salonika to Athens had proved uneventful. After a few restorative days enjoying Polly's hospitality at the Angleterre, Adam and Quint had taken ship for Malta. From there, another steamer had transported them to Marseille. The French railways had taken them to the Channel coast and the end of October had seen the pair settled once again in Doughty Street.

To Adam's misery, Athens had been the scene of a parting from Emily and her husband-to-be. Looking, in Quint's words, 'as sad as a sick monkey', the young man had been a poor companion on the journey back to London. Once back in his rooms, he had been unable to find the enthusiasm to return to any of his former pursuits. His photographic equipment had remained untouched. His friends had seen nothing of him. He had spent his days locked away in the sitting room in Doughty Street, idly reading novels and brooding over the events of the summer. There had been times when he had thought that he would never be able to reconcile himself either to Fields's treachery or to Emily's preference for Garland. Quint, his spirits oppressed by the atmosphere in the rooms, had spent long periods away from them. On many occasions, Adam had called for his manservant only to find that he was alone in the flat. He had been too melancholy to complain when Quint, often smelling strongly of brown ale, had returned to Doughty Street long after night had fallen.

One afternoon, more than a fortnight after they had arrived back in England, Quint had strode into the sitting room from his own reeking little den at the rear of the flat. Adam had looked up from his copy of Wilkie Collins's *Man and Wife*, the latest book to fail to hold his attention. His manservant had thrown down a newspaper on the table.

'Thought you might want to cast your peepers on that,' he had said.

'What is it, Quint?' Adam had asked irritably. 'I am busy.'

'*Reynolds's News* from last Sunday.'

'Since when did you become a follower of the press?'

'I likes to keep myself informed,' Quint had said indignantly. 'Anyways, there's word in it of someone we know.' He had opened the newspaper and pressed a grubby finger on the centre of one of its pages. 'Here.'

Curious, Adam had stood and walked across to the table. He had looked to where Quint had been pointing. It had been an item in what seemed to be a kind of gossip column.

'Word has reached your correspondent,' it had read, 'of the return of a distinguished parliamentarian from a long sojourn abroad…'

After months spent travelling in Greece, Mr L-w-s G-rl-nd is once more a resident of our noble city. Rumours of his impending marriage to a beautiful maiden from fair Hellas have proved to be unfounded. Your correspondent understands that the lady in question, a Miss Em-l- M--tl-nd, has brought the engagement to an end and that the heartbroken Mr G-rl-nd is, and is likely to remain for the foreseeable future, one of the city's most eligible bachelors.

Adam had read it through and read it through again. He had looked at Quint, who was visibly smirking.

'But this is splendid news,' the young man had said.

'Reckoned you might see it that way.'

'Emily is free.'

''Alfway across bleedin' Europe, of course.'

'But she is free. She is no longer engaged to that man.'

''Ard to bill and coo between 'ere and Salonika, mind.'

'This calls for a celebration.' Adam had ignored his servant's remarks. 'I shall go to the Marco Polo. I have not been there since we returned home.'

And so Adam now found himself in the smoking room of his club, puffing cheerfully on a cigar from Philip Morris's shop in New Bond Street and gazing companionably at Mr Moorhouse.

'Bit of a fog out there, I gather,' the old man said.

'A London pea-souper, Mr Moorhouse. The strangest atmospheric compound known to science.'

'Quite like the fog myself. Damned inconvenient, of course, if you're a man of business. But the city always looks rather beautiful in it, I think. Shapes looming out of the dark and all that.'

The two men fell silent. The smoke from their cigars drifted towards the ceiling.

'I do like a play with a good murder in it, don't you?' Mr Moorhouse said suddenly. He had a faraway look in his eye, as if he was recalling happy theatrical experiences from his youth. 'Blood and gore. *Murder in the Red Barn*. That kind of thing.'

'With the murderer brought to book at the end, of course,' Adam suggested. Did Mr Moorhouse, he wondered, know something of the dramatic events that had overtaken Adam while he had been abroad? Perhaps the old man was not quite the innocent he usually appeared. He looked across at his companion but Mr Moorhouse's face revealed nothing more than bland contentment.

'Absolutely,' the old man agreed. 'All topped off with repentance in the condemned cell. And a speech warning younger members of the audience not to follow his example. Educational *and* moral. Not enough plays like that any more.'

Silence descended again on the room. All that Adam could hear were the distant sounds of voices in another part of the building. Probably the Marco Polo's servants, he thought, preparing for the influx of members in the evening.

'Haven't seen you around for a while, Carver,' Mr Moorhouse said. 'Been up to anything interesting?'

Adam thought for a moment or two, then decided there could be no harm in satisfying Mr Moorhouse's curiosity, regardless of how much, or how little, the old clubman already knew. His decision was vindicated, since Mr Moorhouse proved a good listener as Adam related the salient points of his adventures in European Turkey. He said little himself but he made the right noises of encouragement at the right points in the narrative. When all was told, he sank back in his chair and stared upwards at the stucco decoration on the ceiling.

'So this Euphorion chap was wrong, then, was he?' he said, after thinking the matter over for a while. 'No gold to be found?'

'On the contrary, Mr Moorhouse. Euphorion was entirely correct, I think. We were the ones who went astray. We failed to find the right place in which to dig. Garland arranged further excavations but nothing was found. As a consequence, all we have are a few beautiful objects like this.'

Adam held up the gold ring to the gas lamp and, for a minute, both he and Moorhouse admired its twinkling in the light. Then the young man folded his hand round it and slipped it back into his pocket.

'But the tomb of Philip is out there somewhere in those hills,' he said. 'Someday it will be found. And when it is, the treasures it holds will make that poor ring look like a trifle indeed.'

The young man drew deeply on his cigar and allowed himself a brief reverie of future triumphs. One day, he would return to the Macedonian hills himself. He would follow the trail to Philip's tomb and he would unearth its hidden riches. It would, as Fields had predicted, be the archaeological sensation of the era. He would be a famous man. And – who knew? – perhaps Emily would be there to share his success. Despite what Quint said, Salonika was not so distant.

Adam Carver blew out the smoke of his cigar and watched it spiral and disperse into the already fuggy air of the room. It was now early evening and other members of the Marco Polo were conversing in the corridor outside. He felt himself called back to the present and so turned to speak once more to Mr Moorhouse. But there was little point. The old clubman had fallen fast asleep.

HISTORICAL NOTES

Although, as Professor Fields rightly points out, there are several Ancient Greek writers with the name of Euphorion, there is no record of any Euphorion of Thrace, nor is there any trace of a work similar to Pausanias's *Ellados Periegesis* that could have contained clues to the whereabouts of Macedonian gold. However, Creech and Fields were right to suspect that the hills in central Macedonia did contain a treasure worth discovering. In 1977, the Greek archaeologist Manolis Andronikos undertook an excavation near the small town of Vergina and unearthed what he claimed was the tomb of Philip II, father of Alexander the Great. The exact identity of the tomb's inhabitant is still the subject of scholarly debate but there is no doubt about the significance of the objects that Andronikos found there, and in other tombs, in what was clearly an important burial site for the ancient Macedonians. Many of the objects, including delicate golden crowns and a beautiful golden *larnax*, the box used to contain human remains, can be seen in the museum at Vergina.

The monasteries at Meteora, now a UNESCO World Heritage site, provide one of the most extraordinary tourist attractions in Greece, but there is not and, to the best of my knowledge, there never has been one called Agios Andreas. They were visited on a number of occasions in the nineteenth century by English travellers who left accounts of the hair-raising methods employed by the monks to haul their guests up to their lofty retreats. The watercolour painter and writer of nonsense verse Edward Lear visited Meteora and painted some memorable views of the rock formations, although, unlike the characters in my story, he chose not to be winched to the monasteries on their pinnacles.

The Marco Polo Club does not exist outside the pages of my novel but I have imagined it to be somewhere close to the other gentlemen's clubs in Pall Mall and to share some of the characteristics of the Travellers' Club. Poulter's Court, home to Jinkinson, is an imaginary London address. So, too, are the lane near Holywell Street containing the brothel in which Adam and Quint find Ada and the Wapping backstreet in which the Cat and Salutation is open for business. With the exception of a few individuals (Sir Richard Burton, W.S. Gilbert, Effie Millais and others) who flit peripherally across its pages, all the characters in *Carver's Quest* are my own invention. Any historical errors in the novel are similarly my responsibility.

ACKNOWLEDGEMENTS

My first thanks must go to Angus MacKinnon and Toby Mundy at Atlantic Books who originally suggested that I might be able to write fiction and were extremely patient when, for some time, it seemed only too likely that they were mistaken. Angus has been an inspirational editor and his thoughts and advice have made *Carver's Quest* a much better novel than it would otherwise have been. Thanks also to Sara O'Keeffe, Maddie West and Lauren Finger at Atlantic. Melissa Marshall copy-edited the book with great skill and insight and I am grateful for her help and suggestions. Friends, including Susan Osborne, Hugh Pemberton, Gordon Kerr, Andrew Holgate, Travis Elborough, Kevin Chappell and Dave Lawrence have lent a sympathetic ear and/or given practical support over the years. My family proved a great source of love and encouragement throughout its long gestation. Particular thanks go to my wife Eve and to my sister Cindy Rennison, who read earlier drafts and provided invaluable feedback.